The Vacant Chair

Chair

KAYLEA CROSS

ISBN: 0991905016
ISBN-13: 978-0-9919050-1-0

DEDICATION

I dedicate this book to my husband, Todd. Thank you for letting me drag you to all those Virginia battlefields, and for being so tolerant of my obsession with the Civil War. And most of all, thank you for getting down on one knee in the middle of that cemetery at Fredericksburg and popping the question. Hands down the most romantic gesture of ALL TIME, and all these years later I'm still glad I said yes. Thank you for all your support and encouragement. Love you.

ACKNOWLEDGMENTS

Despite the ridiculous amount of research I did for this book, I could never have made the story shine without the advice and talent of two very awesome people.

Katie Reus, you have no idea how wonderful it feels to know that I have you in my corner. You mean the world to me, and I feel so blessed to have such a talented and loyal friend.

And to my long-suffering editor, Rhonda Helms, thanks for helping me whip this WIP into shape!

AUTHOR'S NOTE

You know that saying, "Truth is stranger than fiction"? That's very true for The Vacant Chair. I've done my best to be as historically accurate as possible, from the weather on a particular day to the precise movements of the Fifth Michigan Cavalry, and their unfortunate deployment to the plains after the war. It's my hope that you'll learn something new and fascinating about the Civil War as you read the story.

Happy reading!

Kaylea Cross

CHAPTER ONE

Near White House Landing, Virginia
May 22, 1864

Brianna Taylor toyed with the wedding band hidden beneath her glove and tried to keep up with what her companion was saying next to her on the wagon's hard seat. The uncomfortable vehicle rocked and swayed over the ruts in the road, caught in the stream of supplies and soldiers heading toward the Union base at White House Landing.

Ella-May chattered on excitedly about a soldier she'd met the week before when she'd visited an elderly aunt at Harper's Ferry. She was a cheerful little thing, with plump cheeks and glossy brown curls that bounced with her animated recounting of the event. "He's promised to write to me and wants to see me again at the first opportunity," she added, her face flushed and her powder-blue eyes sparkling. "Isn't that wonderful?"

"It is wonderful. I'm glad for you." Ella-May was

three years younger than Brianna and had lost her own husband at the battle of Fredericksburg a year-and-a-half ago. If there was a chance for Ella-May to find happiness again with this new beau, Brianna wanted her friend to have it.

Ella-May's smile faded and she set a hand on her arm. "I'm sorry, I'm being insensitive. Should I not speak of it? I didn't mean to make you sad."

"Don't be silly." Brianna reached for her hand, squeezed it. "The sun is shining, the birds are singing, and I have you to keep me company. Why on earth would I be sad?"

Her friend's gaze flicked to Brianna's left hand and the ring concealed beneath her glove. "I know you still miss him."

She did. "I expect I always will. He was a wonderful friend and husband, though he was only mine for a short while."

Almost three years since Caleb had passed, yet she couldn't bear the thought of taking her ring off. It felt like an act of betrayal to do so. At least the pain wasn't as sharp anymore, faded instead to a dull ache that never quite went away. Sometimes she found the loneliness difficult, though since it was self-inflicted, she had no grounds for complaint. She squeezed her friend's hand again. "Tell me more about this handsome corporal your aunt introduced you to."

With a delighted smile, Ella-May obliged her. Brianna responded or nodded when she was required to, part of her attention remaining on the leather-bound books in her lap. She had to return them to Dr. Healy tomorrow. Now that the roads were clear, the spring campaign was already in full swing. She and Ella-May had been kept busy at the hospital recently, inundated by a flood of new patients wounded in the latest battles.

Turning her thoughts from the shattered men she tended every day, Brianna gave Ella-May her full attention and enjoyed her friend's enthusiasm.

"When do you suppose we'll be granted leave next?" Ella-May asked, curls swaying beneath her bonnet in rhythm with the wagon's movements. "Corporal Riley thinks he'll be stationed in Harper's Ferry for a few more months yet."

Brianna noticed the rhythm of the wagon change as she answered. "Not for quite a while, if we continue to see the numbers of casualties we have been." If possible, the war seemed to be even bloodier this year. A terrible realization to make.

The wagon gave a sudden, hard jolt, and they both threw out an arm to steady themselves against the wooden sides. Ella-May shot her free hand up to hold onto her bonnet, while Brianna gathered her books closer. Gracious. She was going to have bruises after this ride.

"Perhaps Corporal Riley can get leave and come to see me instead, then," Ella-May mused.

"I look forward to meeting him."

Her friend studied her with a wistful expression. "Tell me the truth. Don't you ever get lonely?"

Brianna hesitated before answering. "Sometimes. But not as much as I used to." It wasn't that she objected to the idea of having a relationship again; it was simply that she'd had no interest in one yet. Perhaps that part of her had died with Caleb.

She and Ella-May gasped when their vehicle suddenly lurched to one side, bringing them out of their seats by a few inches. They both grunted at the impact of the wheel slamming back into the ground. Brianna clutched the edge of the seat, the books sliding off her lap to land on the wooden floor with a thud. Up front, the driver cursed and pulled back on the reins to slow them. One of the horses, a dappled gray, protested the sudden yank on its bit and lashed out with its hind legs. Its hooves struck the damaged wheel and knocked it askew. The right front corner of the wagon bed listed at a sharp angle and hit the ground, bouncing the driver from his seat. He managed to leap free and roll away from the broken vehicle, the horses still dragging them forward.

Ella-May cried out in alarm, and Brianna lunged over the seat back to grab the reins before the animals could bolt. The wagon jolted and scraped across the corduroy road, rattling her teeth in her head. Bracing one foot on the front board of the wagon, she leaned back and used her body weight to bring the team to a plunging halt. When they stood still at last, she climbed down from her perch to stand beside the nervous horses, their flanks quivering in the braces. "Whoa now," she told them, keeping a firm hold on the reins.

Ella-May sat up from her crouch and gingerly exited the wagon, lying broken in the middle of the road. The huge line of traffic behind them ground to a sudden halt. "Are you all right?" Her eyes were wide as she stared at Brianna holding the agitated horses, as though she expected them to trample Brianna into the dirt at any moment.

"Just fine." The same couldn't be said for the wagon's other contents, including Dr. Healey's books. They were dumped a few yards from the wagon, some of the pages having come loose from their bindings to lay scattered in the dirt. "You?"

"I shall tell you in a few minutes once my heart climbs down from my throat," Ella-May replied, pressing a hand to her chest. "What do we do now?"

"Wait until someone clears the mess and find a new ride." The driver limped toward them while carrying on a heated argument with another man, waving his arms at the mess. Food and other supplies were strewn across the road, the number of broken crates, boxes and barrels littering the area making it impassible. With what seemed like the entire Army of the Potomac lined up behind them, it would be some time before the road was cleared enough to allow the rest of the column by.

So far, no one was doing anything but argue about what to do. A group of civilians were engaged in a discussion with several soldiers, who appeared none too happy about the delay. Rather than clear away the debris and drag the wagon to one side, they all seemed more interested in fighting about it. Really, did it matter whose fault the mess was at this point? If she hadn't taken hold of the horses, they'd likely still be racing down the road, wreaking havoc.

Quelling her irritation, Brianna turned her attention back to the animals, since she couldn't hold them and help clean up the road at the same time. For the moment she contented herself with soothing them while she waited for someone to step up and take charge of the situation.

"I thought the Reb cavalry would let up for a while after we killed J.E.B. Stuart."

Captain Justin Thompson grunted at Lieutenant Williams's statement and shifted in the saddle to stretch his stiff back. "Wishful thinking, I'm afraid." Ten days had passed since Stuart was mortally wounded, yet through all the battles and skirmishes, the Union cavalry had yet to gain the upper hand in spite of the ground they'd won.

Riding in the warm May sunshine, the Michigan Brigade filed toward the army's supply base at White House Landing on the Pamunkey River. The men were weary of marching but alert, the horses plodding along at an easy pace down the tree-lined road. Justin took another sip from his canteen and replaced it behind the saddle, sparing a smile when Williams told a bawdy joke and burst into a peal of raucous laughter.

"Do you kiss your wife with that mouth, Lieutenant?" Justin asked.

Williams's chocolate brown eyes twinkled, his mouth twitching beneath the mustache of his neatly trimmed brown goatee. "Yessir, as often as she'll let me. And I'm here to tell you, no one kisses like my Charlotte."

"I'll take your word for it," Justin replied blandly.

The column began to slow, and within a few minutes it had ground to a complete halt. Distant shouts and the whicker of horses from up ahead reached his ears, but he couldn't tell what was happening farther up due to the screen of leafy trees obscuring his view. However, one of the advantages of being in the cavalry was the added mobility it afforded.

"Let's go see what the commotion is all about, shall we?" he said to Williams, nudging his trusty mount Boy-o out of formation and into a trot.

Around the bend in the road, he saw the problem. A broken wagon lay in disarray in the middle of the road, its wreckage strewn all over the place. In front of it, two hitched horses shied and danced in their braces, their legs tangled in the leather straps. Both animals had their ears back, tossing their heads as if they might bolt at any moment. Groups of men stood around gesturing and arguing, but not doing anything to rectify the situation.

Williams let out a low whistle. "That's one hell of a mess."

It was. "Well, none of us are getting through until it's cleared, that's for sure." He thinned his lips in irritation. Since it appeared he was the ranking officer on scene at the moment, he dismounted behind the wagon with the intent to grab the nearest horse himself, and realized someone was already holding the team. He ordered some men to begin the cleanup, and his steps slowed when he noticed the hem of a skirt moving in front of the horses. A woman? He frowned. Why wasn't anyone helping her? She could be trampled, for God's sake.

"Looks like someone's got everything under control up there, sir," Williams said, coming abreast of him.

An odd stillness overcame him, his focus sharpening on her trim silhouette. "Yes, she does, doesn't she?"

Ignoring Williams's blank look, Justin stepped closer. The woman turned her head and when she saw him her expression tightened for a split second before she put on a polite smile. Her deep brown hair flashed hints of red in the sunshine and a pair of darkly lashed gray eyes peered out from beneath the brim of her wide-brimmed bonnet.

Justin doffed his hat as he approached, careful to move slowly so he wouldn't startle the horses. "Good afternoon, ma'am."

"Hello," she replied, dropping her free hand from

7

the nearest horse's coat.

"Here, let me take these two fellows from you," he offered, meeting her eyes as he gathered the reins in his gloved fist. The impact of her gaze hit him in the gut like a punch. She blushed under his intense stare but didn't glance away, and something about her reaction told him he wasn't the only one affected.

"Thank you, Captain," she replied, a hint of the South in her clear voice. "But if you could manage to untangle the reins instead, I'll hold these two steady for you."

Not beautiful in the traditional sense perhaps, yet there was still something arresting about her. Her bearing was confident and calm, her gaze intelligent. It was obvious she knew her way around horses. Though she didn't seem strong enough to hold the team steady, the animals stood still as she stroked each muzzle and spoke to them in a soothing tone that would give him pleasant dreams for many nights to come.

Before he could protest, Williams skirted past Boy-o to take the reins from her and engaged her in conversation, leaving Justin to deal with untangling the team. Since she was safe enough at the moment, he bent to untangle the twisted leather around the horses' legs, watching for any signs of nervousness from them. Wouldn't do for him to be trampled in front of an attractive woman he wanted to impress.

As he worked, he listened to her talk with Williams while men scrambled to clear away the debris in the road. When he finished with the last snare, Justin eased the straps into position and turned the horses over to a passing trooper.

The lady smiled her thanks to both him and Williams then excused herself. She crossed to the side of the road where another woman waited for her, gathering scattered books and pieces of paper. Intrigued by her, Justin tucked his gauntlets into his belt and strode over to offer a hand.

"Is this all of them, Ella-May? There were four books altogether." She completed a slow circle, searching for any stray pages, and stopped when she noticed him standing nearby with a fistful of them.

"Some light reading?" he asked with a smile, handing over the pages of medical textbooks he had gathered. Why on earth would she be reading that?

"Thank you." Her thick lashes lowered as she accepted them. "I nurse at the depot hospital in Fredericksburg. My friend and I are taking a steamer there this morning."

Up close he noticed the light dusting of freckles across the tops of her cheeks and the bridge of her nose. She gave an impression of elegance and strength that belied her delicate appearance. Justin found he didn't like the thought of her amidst the horrors of the army hospitals. Checking behind him, he called for Williams. "Find another wagon to take these ladies to the landing—"

"Oh, no, thank you, Captain," the lady cut in. "My friend and I will walk."

Justin eyed her in surprise. White House Landing was another few miles away yet. He didn't want her covering the remaining distance on foot. "I insist." He staved off her protest with an upheld hand and ordered Williams to find a vehicle to carry them.

While they waited, he helped her gather the last of the scattered pages. She eyed his uniform, her attention lingering on the red neckerchief around his throat. "I see you're one of Custer's Wolverines," she said with a

9

smile.

"Yes, ma'am. Born and raised just outside of Detroit."

"I understand the Michigan Brigade is a force to be reckoned with."

"That we are. It's a reputation we're proud of."

She tucked the pages back into the books and cradled them to her breast, drawing his gaze there in spite of his best intentions. "Is it a long march for you today?"

"Always," he said with a grin. Whenever they weren't skirmishing or in outright combat, they had reconnaissance and other duties to carry out.

Williams arrived with a commandeered buckboard and climbed out of it to assist the other nurse up, while Justin helped the auburn-haired woman into it.

Her gloved fingers closed around his as she set her foot on the running board. She flashed an almost shy smile at him when he handed her up into the back of it beside her friend. The spices of Christmas morning filled his nose as she passed him, hints of cinnamon and cloves. He caught himself taking another deep breath of her and sent a warning glare at a group of soldiers staring in her direction, who quickly got back to work clearing the mess. Once she was settled, Justin released her hand and returned to his horse, busy eating tender shoots of new grass at the side of the road. Setting his left foot in the stirrup, he mounted Boy-o and rode beside the buckboard as escort, his every sense attuned to the auburn-haired woman.

"He's a beautiful animal," she commented a moment later, studying him. "A Morgan?"

Her knowledge of horses took him by surprise. "Yes, ma'am. You've a good eye."

She shrugged. "My father bred many different kinds of horses. And my brother's name is Morgan as well." There was a note of wistfulness in her voice.

"This is Boy-o," he told her, giving his mount's coal black neck a solid pat.

He was vividly aware of her gaze on him, direct and unflinching, and how it stirred his blood. Cocking her head, she picked up the thread of conversation. "Did you name him?"

"I did."

"You're Irish, then?"

"Through and through. I hope that doesn't lessen your opinion of me in any way." He lifted a teasing eyebrow.

She laughed softly. "Not at all, since I'm half Irish myself."

"Yes, and her temper is completely Irish," her friend—Ella-May?—put in with a cheeky grin.

The woman gave her a playful smack on the arm. "Hush, or you'll ruin the captain's impression of me. My temper's much better than it used to be," she assured him. "It only flares up occasionally now."

"Yes, and mostly because of a surgeon or orderly being negligent in their duties," Ella-May said in her defense. "Then Brianna's a force to be reckoned with."

Brianna shrugged, her expression set and unapologetic. "I won't tolerate having a patient's wellbeing or comfort jeopardized because of neglect or ignorance."

He eyed her in curiosity, wondering why the devil a woman like her was toiling amid the horrors of a military hospital. She seemed too elegant, too refined for that sort of work. "I hope you'll pardon me for saying so, but you don't look like a nurse."

11

She raised her eyebrows in surprise. "Oh? And what, pray tell, does a nurse look like?"

Nothing like her, that was for certain. "In my experience? Old. Stern. Ugly."

She burst out laughing and he smiled, enjoying the happy sound. "Well, I am one, though believe me, it took me a long time to secure my position."

"Did you nurse before the war?" he asked, curious as to what had made her choose such a bloody vocation.

Her smile dimmed a fraction. "No." She dropped her gaze to her hands where she smoothed them over her dark gray muslin skirt. "I lost someone important to me at the start of the war and made up my mind I had to do something to stop others from losing loved ones if I could. And so, here I am."

A noble enough cause, to be sure. Had she lost a husband? With her gloves on, he couldn't tell if she wore a wedding band or not.

She tilted her head, those cool gray eyes taking him in. "What about you? Did you enlist when the war broke out?"

"No, only last year." His reasons for waiting were complicated, and the most important one was riding behind him somewhere in the column. "My younger brother signed up with me." He had no idea why he was telling her this, but she made him feel completely at ease and he wanted to keep her talking.

She nodded. "Family is one of the most precious gifts of all, one we take for granted far too often."

"That's true." But family responsibility also weighed on his shoulders like a yoke.

Her observant gaze settled on his shoulders and slid down his arms, taking in the tiny holes burned into his uniform. "It looks like you got too close to a fire recently."

"I did. Only a few hot cinders got me though," he answered. It could have been much worse. Almost had been.

Brianna studied him more closely. "Was it at the Wilderness?"

"Yes," he said, again impressed by her perception. Perhaps she knew about the fires because she'd taken care of patients from that battle. God knew there'd been enough of them.

"Got it into his head to save a wounded Reb trapped by the fires," Williams said from the other side of the buckboard. "He and his brother barely escaped the flames and came out half roasted themselves. Blacker than soot by the time I saw them come back out of the woods."

"He exaggerates," Justin said, remembering the horror of the wounded men's screams as the voracious flames consumed them. Their terrified and agonized cries had made his skin crawl, so much worse than any he'd heard before. "We got out before the fire could trap us, with only our lungs the worse for wear." He and Mitch had coughed for days afterward from inhaling all that thick black smoke.

Brianna's face softened with admiration. "That was very gallant of you, especially since he was a Rebel. I'm sure he was grateful."

"He was, though I didn't know he was a Rebel when we went in after him."

She tilted her head with a frown. "Would you have left him there had you known?"

"No," he answered immediately. No man deserved to die that way. "So many wounded were trapped that night. The soldier we pulled out just happened to be close enough for us to reach in time and get him to a field hospital." Justin had been about to hand the wounded man off to the orderlies when the Confederate had suddenly shot out a hand and gripped his forearm with surprising strength. *Thank you, Captain,* he'd whispered, the gratitude in his glistening brown eyes dispelling Justin's weariness. He'd been in terrible pain, weak from blood loss, and still he'd found the strength to speak. *I will never forget you...or what you've done for me.*

"Then perhaps you saved his life a second time, as well," Brianna added with a soft smile. "First from the fire, and then by taking him to the hospital where he could receive treatment."

"I don't know about that. His wounds were likely mortal." Cahill, the man's name was. Doubtful that he'd survived, considering the nature of the bullet wound in his bowels and how much blood he'd lost. Still, dying in a field hospital drugged with morphine was a far better fate than burning to death.

They passed the remainder of the ride in an easy silence and all too soon reached McClellan's old supply base at White House Landing. Convalescing men in varying degrees of disability waited to board the white steamer berthed there, its funnel spewing a thick column of charcoal smoke. From arms in slings and heads in bandages to men on crutches and many missing limbs, Justin saw every conceivable kind of wound represented. Some men, too weak or injured to stand, lay on the ground on litters.

"War is a terrible thing, isn't it, Captain?" Brianna asked from beside him, seeing the direction of his gaze.

"Yes, it is." But sometimes, there was no other

14

way.

He dismounted to help her alight from the wagon. He closed his hands about her trim waist and she tensed, a pretty blush rising in her cheeks as she avoided his gaze. Justin smiled and set her on her feet in front of him, enjoying her response to his nearness. She was taller than average, the top of her head coming up to his shoulders. It fascinated him that an elegant woman like her could blush at such innocent contact. When she tugged off her gloves, he snuck a peek at her left hand and was surprised at the stab of disappointment he felt when he saw the wedding band on her finger.

Whoever he was, her husband was a lucky man.

Justin looked back up at her face and caught her staring at him. Flushing darker, she quickly averted her gaze and settled it on Boy-o. "May I say hello?"

"Of course." Anything to delay her departure for another few minutes.

He held the bridle while his horse sniffed the palm she extended, the animal's ears pricking forward as he blew a breath out of his flared nostrils. Her long, delicate fingers stroked his coal black forehead and nose while she crooned to him. Boy-o snuffled at her palm for a moment then butted her shoulder with his nose. She laughed, the clear, bright sound hitting Justin in the chest and making him smile.

"Oh, you're just a big sweetheart, aren't you?" She scratched the center of his forehead with one hand and ran the other along his sleek neck.

Justin was becoming jealous of his own damn horse for being petted and fawned over by this fascinating, self-assured woman.

After a minute Brianna stepped away and

smoothed her skirts, meeting Justin's gaze briefly as she tugged her gloves back on. He could see the feminine awareness in her eyes, mixed with curiosity. Interest and arousal flared to life inside him.

She gave his horse's neck a final pat. "Goodbye, Boy-o. Take care of yourself and your owner." That cool elegance was back firmly in place as she faced Justin once more. "Thank you for seeing us here safely, Captain."

He tipped his hat. "Not at all, ma'am. I hope I will have the pleasure again someday."

She stilled at his words, searching his eyes so intently that he swore she was looking *into* him. Then, with a sad smile and a pointed glance at all the wounded men spread out before them she said, "For your sake, Captain, I hope you *never* see me again."

Justin stared after her retreating figure, fighting the urge to deny her words. As though she felt the way his gaze lingered, she turned back once to offer a smile and wave from the dock, then left him watching her until she disappeared into the crowd.

Someone slapped a pair of reins into his hand. He blinked.

His brother Mitch released Boy-o's bridle with a knowing smirk and sat up taller atop his chestnut mare. Four years younger than Justin, Mitch never passed up a chance to needle him. "Quite an interesting day so far. Never seen you rendered speechless by a woman before."

Well, it wasn't every day a man got hit by lightning, was it? That's what it had felt like the first time he'd looked into her clear gray eyes. And that voice...smooth and soft, with a hint of a southern accent. What was she doing up here in the middle of Union country, nursing

16

Yankees?

Mitch chuckled and reached down to slap him on the back, all military protocol between officer and NCO forgotten. Or to be more precise, ignored. "She's gone, Romeo, so pull yourself together before I decide to write a letter and rat you out to Laurel."

"Who's Laurel?" Lieutenant Williams asked as he rode up and stopped his horse beside Mitch's.

"Nobody," Justin muttered, shooting Mitch a dark look.

Mitch grinned like the devil he was, deep blue eyes identical to Justin's gleaming with a wicked light. "She's his sweetheart."

"She's not my sweetheart," he growled. Laurel Stevens was as immature as she was annoying, and the last woman on earth he wanted to be saddled with, which he'd made abundantly clear. He looked back at the dock to search for Brianna, who seemed to be Laurel's polar opposite in almost every way. That alone made her ten times more appealing.

Following his gaze, Williams laughed. "I don't blame you, sir, even though I'm a married man. She was something, wasn't she?"

She sure was, Justin thought, casting one final glance at her trim figure on the steamer's upper deck as he led Boy-o away. Damn shame he'd never see her again.

CHAPTER TWO

Cold Harbor, Virginia
June 1, 1864

Canteens and scabbards made hollow clanking sounds against each other as the regiment rode through the relentless heat. The sweat-stained horses kicked up clouds of dust thick enough to choke on in the stagnant air. Justin drew his dusty sleeve across his damp forehead and took a moment to fan his burning face with his hat. This entire campaign had been a series of bloodbaths. So many thousands had been maimed, butchered or killed already since the start of the spring campaign, and there was plenty of fighting left to be done. How much longer could his or Mitch's luck hold through this sort of continuous slaughter?

The northern papers called Grant a butcher because of all the casualties. They could say what they wanted, because whatever conscience Grant lacked about losing men he made up for with sheer tenacity. Under any other general, the Army of the Potomac would have been retreating to Washington to lick its wounds right now. Instead, they were moving southward toward Richmond in a relentless series of flanking maneuvers. It boosted morale, but Wade Hampton and his cavalry were nearby, and another hard fight waited for them in the coming days.

Hoof beats drummed against the hard earth as a staff officer galloped up to him. His horse was lathered, its nostrils flaring as it sucked in air, sides heaving. "Captain!" the man shouted. "General Custer has received orders to form a line of battle. Bring your company up at once." Without waiting for a reply, he tore down the dusty road to the next company officer.

Justin's pulse kicked hard in his throat. Forcing an air of calmness, he ordered his men to the front of the column. In a clearing up ahead, they dismounted and took cover in the copse of trees lining the field. In the distance he saw nothing but dust and the outline of low hills to the south and west. Where were the Rebs? He pulled out his field glasses.

Officers galloped up and down the battle line, shouting orders and forming ranks. Their only reinforcements were the remaining cavalry in the rear. God knew how far behind them the infantry was. Could be hours, even days. For now Justin and the others were on their own, and being dismounted meant they were at three-quarter strength, with every fourth man behind the lines holding the horses. Taking into account the casualties they'd suffered, their fighting strength was well below what it should have been. Not a comforting thought.

A sudden boom shook the air, reverberating in his chest. A shell streaked through the sky toward them, fell short of their position and exploded, sending up a spray of earth and rock. "Get down!" he yelled to his men.

As the Confederate artillery opened up, the men scrambled to lie flat beneath the trees. Shells burst amongst the leafy branches, showering them with deadly splinters of wood and metal. Justin shouted at them to keep down and still, but the roar and the screaming shells drowned out his voice. He lay on his stomach with his troopers, covering his head with his arms to protect himself from the pelting dirt and debris. His heart hammered, instinct screaming at him to run. Training overrode it.

Keep still. One place is as safe as the next during a barrage.

It seemed a long time before the cannon fire stopped. His ears rang in the sudden silence. Raising his head, he caught a flash of movement and watched as his brother fell into position near the end of their line. Where the hell had he been? The choking dust kicked up by the barrage dissipated, replaced with an eerie stillness as they awaited the enemy attack they all knew was coming. Behind their line the horses pranced, as if they too sensed the imminent assault. His men crouched in the suffocating tension, weapons at the ready, their company positioned left of the main line. His muscles tightened as the interminable seconds ticked by.

When a scramble of hooves arose from the far right, he swiveled his head and held his breath. A squadron from the First Michigan burst from their position in a mounted charge, a galloping wall of sinew, muscle and bone hurling itself upon the enemy. A flash of brilliance gleamed as they drew sabers from scabbards, and a thunderous roar went up from the charging men.

Goose bumps erupted over his skin. Then a sheet of flame exploded from the distant enemy lines. The intense volley tore men and horses to pieces. Caps, weapons and body parts tossed up into the clear spring sky like leaves in a windstorm. Men fell to the ground, armless, legless, headless, twitching, heaving. Men screamed and choked on their own blood, clutching at their wounds with frantic hands. An injured horse dragged itself back to their lines by its forelegs, whinnying shrilly, its entrails trailing behind it.

Clenching his jaw, Justin drew a steadying breath and lowered his field glasses. He glanced over at his brother then farther down the line at the rest of his boys, many of them frightened green recruits rushed from the base at Culpeper to replace the wounded and dead lost early in the campaign.

At a movement in the distant screen of trees, his head snapped up. A line of Rebel troops materialized on the ridge. Sporadic shots whizzed overhead from the advance pickets, alerting him that the main body was ready to advance. The high-pitched whine of Minié balls pierced the air as the Confederates marched out. The heavy bullets slapped into the ground around him with audible thuds. Justin's heart clattered against his ribs. Those damned rounds were getting closer with each volley.

"Get ready, boys," he called. They raised their Spencer carbines.

Moments later, he glimpsed the first lines of gray filtering out of the trees. He tensed. With their tubular magazines, the Spencers gave them the advantage of superior firepower, but the shorter barrels meant they sacrificed distance. It seemed to take forever for the

Rebels to come near enough for Justin and his men to do real damage.

"Aim."

The rattle of hammers cocking filled the air.

The Reb's advance line cleared the brow of the ridge and moved steadily toward them. Time slowed down with each step they took forward. Justin counted the paces, gauged the distance.

"Fire!"

The men opened up with their Spencers, the combined firepower deafening. Justin's vision tunneled to his field of fire. He waited, focusing on his own targets amidst the rifle shots and smoke, the acrid bite of gunpowder strong in the air. More shots whizzed past him, some so close he heard the sizzling sound they made. When the enemy came within killing range of his own weapon, he aimed his revolver at the closest man to him and pulled the trigger. A red splotch bloomed on his chest as he fell. Justin pulled back the hammer for the next shot and chose another target.

Behind him, another officer snapped orders as he made his way down the line. "Keep your boys where they are, captain! They're coming up full force at us."

Justin risked a glance behind him. "How many?" he shouted, ducking instinctively as a bullet zipped by his shoulder.

Atop his horse, the officer threw him an exasperated look and set down his field glasses. "Plenty. Give 'em the hot lead, boys! That's it, that's the ticket!" He waved his hat above his head, spurring on the troops. In the midst of his encouragement, his horse reared, unseating him as a bullet tore into its chest. It stumbled to its knees, thrashing and screaming while frothy blood poured from the wound. The officer scrambled to his feet, pulled out his revolver and put a bullet in its head. The horse slumped to the ground, but the man was already waving his saber around. "Give it to 'em boys! Pour it into 'em!"

The firing continued, growing thicker as they fought off the waves of infantry facing them. The lines seemed to melt on the distant slope. One dissolved in a hail of bullets, only to have another march up and immediately take its place. Justin's men couldn't keep up this volume of fire for long. Jesus, how many more were there? He pushed to his feet and ran in a crouch along his company line.

"Hold your positions!" They'd been ordered to hold the line until the reserve cavalry or infantry could relieve them, and there was no telling how long that would be. Worse, limited ammunition made shooting accuracy and reloading speed essential, and the raw recruits would be a liability. He glanced over and caught Mitch's grim expression as he fired his carbine. Facing the enemy once more, Justin drew a deep breath and shouted, "Fire on my command! Ready!" The rhythmic clicking of hammers followed.

"Aim, low!" New recruits always overshot their targets, especially under the stress of battle.

Gaining momentum as they advanced down the slope, the Rebels started up their eerie howl. A young recruit in front of him went pale, his hands shaking so badly one slipped off his rifle.

"Steady, boys," Justin ordered, resting a solid hand on the youngster's shoulder. The muscles under his hand vibrated, and he understood the trooper's fear exactly.

The enemy drew closer with each breath, that damned Rebel yell raking over his skin like icy talons. His gut tightened.

Wait. Steady, wait...

Closer. Almost there. Almost...

Now. "Fire!"

The combined explosion from the company's Spencers rocked the line. The cloud of smoke worsened the visibility, and for a few agonizing moments Justin couldn't see what they were shooting at or the effect their fire had.

He barely caught the whine of the bullet before a flash of pain seared his temple. The impact spun him around, and he crashed to his knees in the dust. Blood trickled down his face, warm and sticky, distorting his vision. He shook his head to clear it, his ears ringing. *You're still alive. Get up.*

The flesh wound burned like a swarm of hornets had stung him. Struggling to his feet, he swung his head around to see what was happening, wiping at the blood that dripped into his blurry eyes. Gray bodies littered the field, the remaining ranks battered but not destroyed. Justin's company had managed to help repulse another wave of the attack, but more would come. He groped around for his revolver, found it next to his foot. His fingers curled around the grip, oddly clumsy.

"Here they come again."

He jerked his gaze up at the muttered words. *Already?*

Shrieking their spine-chilling yell, the southerners suddenly charged across the field straight toward them. One of his new men panicked and ran, only to take a bullet in his spine and sprawl face down in the dirt, twitching in his death throes.

"Steady, boys," Justin yelled again. He swayed

dizzily on his feet, gritted his teeth to stay upright. "Hold that line!" he warned his junior officers, who scrambled to keep the formation.

Oh, Jesus. They were so outnumbered. Had no reinforcements to help them. He couldn't let the Rebs overrun their position. If he did, all was lost.

He cocked his weapon and shot a Rebel who was about to bayonet a wounded youngster's chest, hitting him between the eyes. The back of his enemy's head exploded like a melon.

Justin's gaze swiveled to find his brother, mounted at the rear, grappling to hold onto a group of shying horses. As he wheeled to drag them away, Mitch jerked backward in the saddle and fell. He didn't move.

He didn't *move*.

"Miiiiitch!" The scream tore out of Justin as he sprinted to his brother.

Mitch was struggling onto his side, sheets of smoke closing around him, hiding him from view. Justin wanted to howl in relief. *Still alive—*

Something slammed into his ribs. A shockwave of pain exploded through him and hurtled him backward to the ground, knocking the breath out of him.

When he opened his eyes, he was lying on his back, staring up at the swirling treetops. The battle continued to rage around him but it was strangely muted, sounding far away. A strangled cry escaped through his clenched teeth. When he pressed a hand to his side, it came away slippery, blood dripping through his fingers. *How bad is it?* He tried to roll over, couldn't move.

Pain's so bad...can't breathe. It blotted out his vision and hearing. Blackness closed in on him. *Mitch! Have to find him. He was hit. Have to help him.*

Fire tore through his ribcage, sucking the air from

his lungs.

Dear God, they got both of us.

A horrible weakness seeped through him, making his eyelids heavy as lead. He fought to turn over, to get up.

Mitch. Can't see him. Have to get to him.

The edges of the world folded in, and a bolt of anguish ripped through him.

Didn't reach him in time...

The spinning trees faded into nothingness.

CHAPTER THREE

Depot Hospital, White House Landing, Virginia
June 2, 1864

Fanning herself in a patch of shade she'd found under a Virginia pine, Brianna looked away from the opposite riverbank back toward the hospital. The blistering sun beat down on her head through the thin branches, making the air so thick and humid she could hardly breathe. A bare breeze stirred, teasing her with the promise of relief.

She fanned faster, the slight movement of air across her flushed face helping a fraction. Only a few minutes' more rest. That was all she needed. A short break from nursing the steady flow of wounded who'd been arriving nonstop for the last two days. She hadn't had time to eat, had slept only in snatches in a cramped supply tent, where she and Ella-May had set cots up while they were so busy. The breeze picked up again, and her empty stomach clenched at the stench of decomposing flesh from the amputation piles awaiting burial.

Dropping the fan in her lap, she toyed absently with her wedding band. Almost three years had passed since Caleb had died in that dingy hospital across the river from Washington, and around a year since she'd left home to work as a nurse. It seemed a lifetime ago instead.

During her first few months as a widow, she'd applied to the Union Army depot hospital in Fredericksburg, but they'd rejected her because she was too young. Eventually the hospital staff had become so overwhelmed that by the summer of '63 they had approved her application. Since then, her days were filled with laundry, cleaning wounds, changing dressings, cooking, washing and reading to or writing for the grateful men in her care. Sometimes, when Dr. Healey asked, she assisted him in surgery. He was the only one to acknowledge her medical skill and allow her to use it under his supervision. Brianna adored him for that.

This year's fighting was the most intense she'd seen yet. Ambulance trains arrived continually, the casualties so numerous that General Grant had ordered the depot hospital moved from Fredericksburg to White House Landing to shorten the distance between the lines and supply depot.

Brianna scanned the hospital grounds. A sea of three hundred wall tents filled the property near the docks where wounded men went north by steamboat to Washington, and when they were well enough to travel, to other convalescent hospitals in their home states. Far too many of them made the journey in coffins instead.

Blowing out a weary breath, she turned her head

and noticed a cloud of red dust rising from the road in the distance. A knot formed in the pit of her stomach. Another ambulance procession. An endless line of human misery stretching as far as the eye could see. Wagon loads of wounded and dying men crying for death's release from pain and exhaustion, sweltering heat, and the swarms of flies that hovered over their shattered bodies like vultures waiting to pick their bones clean.

Brianna pushed to her aching feet, gathered her skirts and hurried up the pathway, bracing herself against the reek of death as she burst into the main surgical tent. "More wounded coming!" She gathered bandages, morphine granules, carbolic acid solution and a pair of scissors to put into a basket.

Beside her, one of the surgeons stopped work on a patient to wipe a stream of sweat off his face with the back of a blood-smeared hand. Lines of strain and mauve shadows ringed his eyes. He looked twenty years older than when she'd first met him last summer.

When she reached the far end of the grounds, nothing could have prepared Brianna for the sight that met her eyes. So many ambulance wagons were lined up that she couldn't tell where they ended. There was no way the hospital could accommodate all these men.

Don't think about it. Get to work.

Moving fast, she instructed the stretcher-bearers where to take each patient: either directly to the operating room, or to be left aside until the more seriously wounded had been taken care of. If they were too far gone already, the attendants set them away from the others and administered morphine to ease their pain before they died.

It took until after sunset to see to the most critical

cases. Butchered blue bodies littered the grassy slopes, staining the soil red with blood. Most had been treated at a field hospital before being transported here, but any pain medication they'd received had long since worn off. Everywhere she looked, men writhed in agony and delirium.

She was acutely aware of the minutes slipping past, knowing they might make the difference between life and death for some of these men.

Setting aside her exhaustion, Brianna brushed a lock of hair from her eyes and set to work on another soldier. Even though she'd learned early on to develop a kind of emotional distance, sometimes she still found it hard to stay detached from it all. She kneeled beside a young blond enlisted man and swept her gaze over his ashen face. He gazed up at her stoically, his skin waxen.

Doubting he was older than eighteen, she smoothed the hair from his sweat-soaked forehead and cut away the filthy blue woolen sleeve of his tunic to expose a hopelessly shattered arm. A Minié ball had splintered the humerus down to his elbow. The jagged ends of the bone jutted out at a sickening angle, most of the flesh and muscle ripped away, while the lower half of his arm dangled uselessly. It had to come off, but he was too deep in shock and had lost too much blood to survive an amputation.

His fever-bright eyes met Brianna's imploringly, and she touched his hot cheek in an offer of comfort. He twitched and closed his lids. When she placed a flask of whiskey to his lips, he submitted without opening his eyes. She pushed away the stark sadness that filled her. He was going fast, but she forced enough of the tepid liquor down him to at least help lessen the pain. After instructing the hospital steward to administer some morphine granules to the wound, there was little else she could do for him. He wouldn't make it through the night.

She stood to wipe her hands on her bloody apron and caught sight of another patient out of the corner of her eye. He lay near the pine tree she'd rested beneath earlier, his bandaged head propped on a bedroll. He wore black boots and the telltale yellow trim on his uniform. A cavalryman. He appeared to be unconscious. A blood-stained dressing covered the left side of his ribs.

"Leave that one," one of the surgeons snapped behind her as she started toward the wounded trooper. "Don't waste your time on him."

The curt dismissal in the physician's voice only made her more determined to help. She ignored the command and hurried toward the wounded man. As she approached, something about him tugged at her. He seemed familiar somehow. Did she know him? Not that it mattered. Every man deserved a chance, and she was going to make sure this trooper got his.

Kneeling beside him, Brianna studied his face. A gasp tore out of her when she finally realized who he was, and a strange twisting sensation curled in her chest. The kind captain from White House Landing. He'd not only come to her aid, in the short time she'd spent with him he'd managed to stir a feminine interest within her that Brianna had thought long dead. Her entire body had reacted to his presence, something she hadn't experienced in years. Lord, he was so still and pale now. The hope that he would never see her under these circumstances had proved futile after all.

Unwrapping the bandage around his head, Brianna studied the shallow wound. There was no way to tell if his skull had been fractured by the impact, and she wouldn't know for certain what damage it had done unless he regained consciousness. Leaving it for the moment, she cut off his ruined shirt and checked the more serious wound in his side. He was breathing well enough, and he was pale but not gray. Someone had sewn the skin closed with a few hasty stitches, enough to keep him from bleeding to death on his journey here. She bent to get a better look.

The bullet had entered through his ribcage, where the external abdominal oblique and serratus anterior muscles interdigitated. She slipped a hand beneath him but didn't find an exit wound on his back, assuring her the bullet had not passed through his body. Removing the crude sutures in front, she called an assistant to help her position him. A scissor blade served as a probe as she checked for any cloth or other debris trapped beneath the skin. Thankfully, whoever had sewn him up had managed to pull the bullet out first.

It took her a while to find and remove the bits of bone and uniform from the entry wound, and her tired eyes didn't help matters. But as long as the bullet was out and she cleaned the wound well enough before infection set in, he had a chance. Provided his blood volume was sufficient and his skull was still in one piece.

Almost an hour passed before she could return to him with her favorite doctor to check his internal organs. By some miracle, they were all intact. None of the rib splinters seemed to have caused any significant damage, and that gave her hope. Because Dr. Healey trusted her ability, he left her to properly stitch, dress and bind the wounds tightly to minimize the risk of hemorrhage. Whatever his name was, the Wolverine had lost a lot of blood, but at least now he had a chance to recover. It was all Brianna could give him.

She washed the blood and grime from his face, noting his sooty lashes, the coal-black brows and stubble on his jaw. He was tall, at least a head taller than her, she remembered. About six feet, with a muscular build. His ebony hair had blue highlights, like a raven's wing. He'd been so handsome atop his horse that morning at the landing, almost this same exact spot. And she also remembered the frank male interest in his deep blue eyes when he'd looked at her.

Pushing the thought from her mind, she said a silent prayer for him and moved to her next patient.

****

The next morning, as the sun drenched the countryside with liquid gold, staff buried the stiffened bodies in graves scraped out overnight by civilian volunteers. By noon only a handful of dead lay out in the open. At least a third of the wounded brought in yesterday had died, and many more would die yet.

The Wolverine Brianna had treated was in her section. She made her rounds with the other nurses, male and female alike, stopping to visit with those who were well enough to talk of their homes, families and sweethearts. She was on her feet all day. She fetched food and medicine, spooned broth and water down dry throats, changed linens and bandages, dressed wounds and held the hands that reached for her, noting which men liked to be fussed over and which wanted to be left alone. Most were friendly and grateful for her ministrations, but occasionally one would snap and snarl at her, whether out of pain or plain bad temper. She didn't let it discourage her.

33

Toward the end of the day, Dr. Healey caught her rubbing her tired eyes and told her to go home and sleep. Brianna refused. There was far too much work that still needed to be done, and there were only so many hands to do it.

After eating, she went to check on the Wolverine. Since she'd met him and he'd been so kind to her, she felt compelled to watch over him. Slipping inside the canvas tent flap, she found him still unresponsive and decided to give his wounds a thorough cleansing and change the bandages while he couldn't feel it. He hadn't woken yet, but that wasn't uncommon after losing so much blood, and she still held out hope he didn't have a skull fracture or any damage to his brain. His pupils responded to the lantern light when she lifted his eyelids, and that eased her.

She used a wet sponge to remove the blood-soaked gauze from his head. Still no signs of infection, and the injury appeared to be healing. His respiration rate was slow and even, with no rattling sounds. His chest wound was oozing and no scabbing had started, but at least there were no new fragments of lead or cloth in the wound. All she could do was keep it clean and hope for the best. After she finished, Brianna returned to the tent she slept in when she worked late, crawled into her narrow cot and went out like a snuffed candle.

Her eyes snapped open when someone shook her. She blinked up at Ella-May's uncharacteristically somber face.

"You'd best come quickly, Bree. Your Wolverine has developed a serious fever."

Damn.

Fumbling in the darkness, she lit a lantern and

followed her friend to the captain's tent. Dread curled in her chest when she saw him writhing in the bed. Her hand on his forehead verified dry, fire-like heat. At her touch he moaned in delirium, twisting, the ropes in the cot's frame creaking.

Brianna flinched at the sudden stab in her chest. His suffering hurt her. She hated seeing anyone in pain, but his anguish was especially painful. "We have to cool him down." She snatched a sponge and dipped it in a solution of vinegar and water. Ella-May helped her strip him and wash him down over and over.

A few minutes into their efforts, he began to shiver so violently that his teeth chattered. While Brianna tried to comfort him, Ella-May threw a heavy blanket over him, and both of them gasped as his hands closed around Brianna's wrists and hauled her nearly on top of him.

She held her breath, staring down into the impossibly deep blue eyes. They were glazed, almost feral with desperation. He clenched her wrists as though someone would drag her away from him, his grip like iron bands.

Her heart hammered. Paralyzed by the wild look in his eyes, she ached to soothe him. The feeling was so foreign and powerful it frightened her, because it meant her defenses were already down around him. She didn't want to feel that acutely anymore.

"Wait..." he croaked, his gaze far away and bright with fever.

She pulled her wrists free and held his burning fingers, clenched tight around hers. He couldn't recognize her. He was too incoherent. His touch jarred her deep inside, echoing through her.

"I'm sorry," he rasped, "I tried..." His face filled

with grief, making her stomach knot. "Tried to help him... Couldn't get to him in time. So sorry..."

Helpless to ease his pain, Brianna spoke to him in a low voice, aware that most of the conscious men in the tent were awake, riveted to the scene before them. She touched his scalding cheek. "It's all right." He gripped her other hand and she let him. "No one is angry with you. You were brave and you did your duty. Lie still now. You need to sleep so your body can heal." She kept her voice quiet, sure.

The words must have reached him through the hallucinations because his eyes lost their panic and the hold on her fingers loosened. But he didn't let go, and a tiny part of her was glad that her touch seemed to comfort him.

Brianna stayed beside him until he fell asleep, though dread formed in her gut as she recalled the wildness in his eyes. It might have been the high temperature, but maybe he did have a brain injury. She bathed his flushed face with cool water, haunted by his tortured gaze. They'd know by morning if he would survive or not.

Covering him up tight, she left him and blew out the lamp, saying a quick prayer for him. If he could make it through the night, the odds of him pulling through were good. There was still a chance he could survive the shock and the loss of blood, but only if the fever didn't claim him first.

CHAPTER FOUR

The healing hands were on him again. Gentle, soothing hands he'd felt before, so different from all the others that touched him. Hers. Justin recognized them because they were soft and comforting and brought the scent of Christmas baking.

The hands stroked a cool cloth over his face and throat, down his chest. Heaven. Another swept across his cheek and up to smooth the hair back from his forehead.

He sighed, floating somewhere between dream and consciousness, savoring the feel of those magical hands. Then pain began to register, radiating throughout his body until he was afraid to breathe.

Justin surfaced slowly. A searing throb persisted in left his side and a relentless ache pounded in his head. He couldn't seem to open his eyes so he lay there, listening. The tormented cries were gone, the rumbling of cannon silenced. Only the occasional cough broke the quiet.

He noticed a new smell, a fresh scent like

disinfectant and air touched with pine. Clean, crisp sheets met his fingers as he groped around and forced his heavy eyelids to lift. White light blinded him. He squinted against the sudden stab of pain in his eyes, blinking while his vision adjusted.

A swish of cool air hit his face, and he glanced up at the woman at his bedside. The light streaming in from behind her gave her the look of an angel, and he wondered if he had died and wound up in heaven.

But if you were in heaven, you wouldn't still be in pain.

Yes, there was that.

The angel was smiling at him, fanning his hot skin. Her deliciously cool hand lay upon his brow as she spoke. "Well, hello there. You had me worried."

He stared back at her, gathering his thoughts. She seemed familiar somehow, but he didn't know why. Her eyes were a pretty, clear gray.

"I'm Mrs. Taylor, one of your nurses. You're in the hospital at White House Landing."

A hospital. God, he'd been shot, hadn't he? He struggled to remember what had happened, slid a hand down his chest and found the bandages over the ribs on his left side. He covered a wince as the wound seared beneath the light pressure of his fingers.

"Are you thirsty?"

He tried to speak, but his voice failed him. His mouth and throat were so dry he felt like a parched desert, desperate for a drop of rain.

In answer to his silent plea, the angel nurse raised his head in the crook of her arm and placed the cold, hard rim of a glass to his lips. His dehydrated body cried out for the wet, sweet liquid that covered his burning tongue. It felt so good he wanted to moan, but that would hurt even more.

Her touch was light as she ministered to him. Calming. She patiently refilled the glass and let him drink in slow sips. Her manner was steady, unhurried, incredibly soothing. But even that small amount of water seemed to gurgle in his gut, wanting to come back up. The muscles in his jaw tightened, his mouth pooling with saliva. He broke out in a clammy sweat as a bolt of panic hit him. *Oh, God, don't let me throw up—*

"More?"

Justin swallowed and shook his head slightly, and the movement proved too much for his stomach. Damn thing violently emptied its meager contents, oblivious that it did so in front of a beautiful woman.

Oh, dear God in heaven, it hurt. The heaving continued without mercy, even when there was nothing left to come up and tears were leaking from his eyes. His left side felt like it might tear open, burning as though someone had plunged a white-hot branding iron between his ribs.

Agony engulfed him with each convulsion, leaving him breathless and afraid to move when he finally collapsed against the pillow. Gasping, mortified, he recovered to see his nurse calmly placing a pan full of watery vomit on the bedside table. She wiped his face, gave him a little more water to rinse his mouth and brushed back his hair. A humiliated flush heated his cheeks. He'd never felt more miserable in all his life.

"Please, Captain, don't be embarrassed. You've been terribly ill." Her smoke-gray eyes rested on his face like a caress. "I'll go get you some clean bedding and something light to eat to settle your stomach." She had the most beautiful eyes he'd ever seen. A dimple appeared in her right cheek at the hint of a smile. "Try and rest while I'm gone. You need to build up your strength." She put a hand beneath his shoulder and one on his hip then carefully turned him onto his uninjured side, whisked the soiled bedding off the cot and covered him with a warm blanket before making her way into the bright daylight.

The pain seemed to worsen when she left.

Justin closed his eyes. His insides were on fire and he had to fight back the residual waves of nausea that washed over him. He tried to focus on his breathing to numb some of the pain, letting exhaustion overtake him. When he began to drift into a troubled doze, the memories came flooding back.

The screams of wounded men and horses, whining bullets...and his brother's body lying in the dirt.

Mitch.

He jerked awake, hissed at the pain shooting in his side.

Christ, was Mitch dead? A film of sweat settled over him. His heart throbbed so hard he thought he might be sick again. The fear snaked through him, twisted his gut.

"Captain?"

He opened his eyes. The pretty nurse stood at the foot of his bed, holding an armful of linens.

"Are you all right?"

He couldn't answer, couldn't seem to catch his breath, dragging shallow gulps of air into his aching lungs, every motion of his ribs painful.

"Are you all right?" she repeated, a frown creasing her brow.

No. My brother was hit. He glanced away and cleared his throat, his voice hoarse when he spoke. "Yes."

Shutting out the image of his brother hitting the ground, Justin concentrated on his nurse. God, those eyes. He'd seen them before.

Her smile was full of concern. "I hope Boy-o escaped the same fate as his master."

The breath froze in his lungs as he finally realized who she was, and the flames lit off in his side again. "Yes." He couldn't believe he hadn't recognized her sooner. Maybe she'd know about Mitch.

"What's your name?"

He cleared his throat. "Justin. Thompson." He felt as weak as a newborn colt.

"Hello again, Captain Thompson. I'm only sorry we had to meet again under these circumstances."

He swallowed, aware of how close he'd come to dying. Unless he still might? The pain in his side he could deal with. What he didn't know how to cope with was the agony of losing his only brother.

"I'm going to put some clean sheets on your bed. Just lie still and let me turn you." Her strength surprised him as she slowly maneuvered him once more, using her hip to keep him from shifting. Within minutes she had him comfortably settled on his back in fresh bedding and a clean pillow tucked beneath his head. Her hand smoothed his hair, something she seemed to do often, and he had to stop himself from resting his cheek into her palm for comfort.

"I bet you'd like something to eat?"

He attempted to shake his head, but the movement made him long to retch again.

"Once you get something in your stomach, you won't be as nauseated." She sat in a chair beside his bed and brought a spoon filled with broth to his lips.

He took it reluctantly but found if he sipped slowly,

his stomach could tolerate the tepid liquid. After a few spoonfuls, he paused to rest.

"More?" She lifted her eyebrows in invitation.

"Please." He finished it all and turned his attention to her.

"I promise we'll take good care of you here, but for now I should leave you to sleep." She wiped his face with a cool cloth. It felt wonderful. "I'll come back to check on you later." She gathered up the dishes and stepped away.

"Wait." He lifted his right hand in protest, hating how weak he was. "Have you seen my brother?"

She frowned and tilted her head. "What's his name?"

"Mitchell. He's a corporal...Fifth Michigan Cavalry. He was with me at Cold Harbor. We look alike." He gasped as a fresh wave of pain sliced through his side. He put a hand to his ribs, took a moment to gather his strength. "I don't know what happened to him."

Her clear eyes held his. "I haven't seen him, Captain, but I'll find out if anyone else here has."

"He was shot."

"You sure?"

"Yes." God, he'd never forget the sight of his brother lying on the ground.

"He could be here. There are so many. And even if he's not, it doesn't mean anything bad has... I'll find out," she promised.

"Thank you." He prayed someone had news of Mitch.

"He's doing extremely well. Much better than I anticipated." Dr. Healey's voice was low as he re-bandaged the wound in Captain Thompson's side and stepped away from the bed.

The tension in Brianna's stomach eased enough to allow her a full breath of air. Her first since the doctor had begun his examination a few minutes ago. "I'm glad to hear that."

"If things continue to improve at this rate, he could be up and about in a few days."

Careful to hide her smile, Brianna bent to adjust the pillow that propped the captain's arm up and away from the bandages on his ribs. He'd slept most of the afternoon and through their whispered conversation, but the instant she touched him, he opened startled, sleepy blue eyes and focused on her.

"Sorry I woke you," she murmured, fighting the growing heat and awareness in her body under the power of that gaze. Her breasts tightened and tingled, a completely inappropriate reaction that embarrassed her.

A slow smile curved his lips. "I'm not. Means I'm still alive."

"How is your pain?" Congratulating herself on her professional demeanor despite the havoc transpiring in her body, Brianna straightened.

"Bearable. Just tired."

Her fingers itched to smooth a lock of hair back from his forehead.

"Go back to sleep, then," Dr. Healey told him. "You need the rest."

The captain nodded, his eyes sliding closed as though his lids were too heavy to keep open. Brianna stared down at him for a few moments, watching him sleep before following the surgeon to the next bed. Somewhere in his thirties, the new patient was a powerfully built man with a kind face and friendly green eyes.

A tight smile appeared beneath his heavy beard. "Hello, doc." His voice was raspy and weak.

"Hello, Tim. How are you feeling today?"

Tim shifted under the blanket, his restricted movements telling her he was in a great deal of pain. "I believe I'm better than yesterday."

Without thinking, Brianna leaned down to straighten the blankets over him and barely concealed the gasp that rose in her throat. Beneath a thin covering of linen bandages, two large bullet holes bled through from his chest. They must have punctured his lungs, explaining the wheezing quality of his breath.

She cast a glance at Healey, then met Tim's steady gaze. The wounds were mortal, promising a horrific, suffocating death. Did he know? He had to be in unspeakable agony, fighting for every breath.

With unsteady fingers, she tugged the blanket up over the wounds, shaken by the sad green eyes that watched her. "It's bad, isn't it, ma'am?" The sagging of his body told her he had accepted his fate.

What could she say? Brianna bit down on the inside of her cheek. She searched for the right words but found none, and pressed her lips together to keep from blurting something silly. Or choking up. Something she hadn't done since she'd first started nursing.

As though sensing her distress, Tim gave a tired smile. "Don't do that, ma'am, please. I'm strong as an ox. Isn't that right, doc?"

"He's right, Brianna."

It was unusual for Healey to drop formality and address her by her given name, let alone in front of anyone. Her attempt at a smile was futile at best. She was thoroughly sick of this damned war and the

44

senseless butchering of these brave, stoic men.

Tim's face held a wistful expression. "Brianna," he murmured, as though testing the sound of her name on his lips.

Ten minutes later when he was fast asleep, she turned helpless eyes to her favorite doctor. "What can we do?"

Healey shook his head. "War is so cruel."

Cruel wasn't near strong enough. War was suffering, agony and death. Her only comfort at the hospital was that her work offered something good to the mutilated and the dying. With every pass of a damp sponge over fevered skin, she offered kindness, compassion. Every murmured word, every touch she hoped brought some measure of peace. Maybe even hope.

Dr. Healey smiled at her, trying to buoy her spirits. "You have a miraculous effect on the men. It wouldn't surprise me if Tim recovers as nicely as Captain Thompson has."

She stole a quick glance over her shoulder at the patient in question. The memory of those deep blue eyes and melting smile made her heart flutter, and she was careful to hide it. She was already much too aware of him as a man, rather than a patient. It baffled and annoyed her, because she had no business thinking about him as anything *but* a patient. She'd been so certain she'd never be interested in a man again. Now, despite her barely knowing him, this officer was somehow slipping through the wall she'd erected.

Disturbed by her reaction, Brianna sternly reminded herself she had a job to do. He was a patient, and she was his nurse. Nothing more. And he no doubt already had a wife or a flock of worried women waiting for him back in Michigan.

****

When Brianna—he didn't want to think of her as Mrs. Taylor—returned that evening, Justin felt well enough to give her a wan smile of greeting. A spark of hope burned in his chest. Had she heard anything about Mitch? She set a palm to his forehead and he had to withhold a sigh at the blessed coolness of her skin against his.

He waited until she turned from the bed before speaking, careful to take shallow breaths to spare the wound in his side. "Did you find out anything about my brother?"

"Not yet, but I'll keep checking." She bent to pick up a washbasin and stopped dead, her gaze fixed on his bandages. "Captain, have you any idea when your wound began bleeding again?"

"No. Is it?" Shifting gingerly, he tried to look down at the bandages, but the movement made him break into a cold sweat.

He lay still while she pulled the blankets down to his hips and removed the stained bandages from his side. Her brow knitted in concentration, the sweep of her dark lashes casting shadows on her ivory skin. She lifted her eyes to his, presumably watching for signs of pain as she tested the wound with a fingertip. Despite his resolve not to flinch, he tensed and bit back a wince.

She frowned. "It looks fine, but I'm going to put some carbolic acid on it to keep it from festering. I'll clean your head wound too." With a cloth dipped in some liquid from a bottle in her basket of supplies, her hand folded around his. It seemed so delicate in his grasp. "Hold on and breathe out slowly." When he did, she dabbed it onto the raw flesh. The hot burst of pain sucked the remaining breath out of his lungs. He clenched his jaw, tightening his grip on her hand. She spoke to him in soothing tones until she had thoroughly cleansed both wounds and sprinkled a few grains of what he sincerely hoped was morphine into them.

Fighting for breath though the effort hurt his ribs, he pried open his blurry eyes, skin slick with sweat.

"All finished, Captain."

He expelled a long sigh and met her gaze, relaxing without removing his hand from hers. He liked her touch too much to let go.

Her expression turned serious. She didn't pull from his grasp and he was glad. "I didn't find anyone who'd seen your brother yet, but that doesn't mean something's happened to him." She kept her voice low so as not to awaken the other patients. "There are so many wounded coming in... I'll keep looking. Someone will know something about him."

"Thank you," he murmured, concentrating on the way her thumb caressed his hand, offering sympathy and hope at the same time. It was impossible to believe that his devil-may-care brother might be dead. The shock of it numbed him. He was too exhausted to even contemplate the full implication of it.

When a doctor came by a moment later, Brianna pulled her hand away and cleared her throat. "I'm leaving for the night and won't be back until morning. Other staff members will help you if you need anything. Please rest as much as you can, and I'll come check on you as soon as I'm able." She rose. "Perhaps then I can help you write a few letters for back home. In the meantime I'll keep trying to find your brother."

"Thank you." He hated to see her go.

Her smile was gentle, a little sad. "Try not to worry about him too much. He hasn't been brought here, so that's a good sign."

Or it meant he'd been killed, and they'd buried him somewhere close to the battlefield he'd fallen on.

Fighting back the dread in his gut, Justin forced a nod.

Rather than leave, Brianna studied him for a moment then gave a little shake of her head. "You're very lucky, you know. Men die here every day from wounds much less serious than yours, so there must be a reason why the bullet and the fever didn't kill you. Try to remember that." Her gaze mirrored his sorrow, as though she too understood the guilt he felt for surviving.

The war must have done that to her. She hid the hurt well beneath her composed exterior, but he could see it now in the depths of her eyes. Lying motionless, he savored the brush of her fingers over his forehead as she smoothed his hair back. Even though he'd noticed she did it to all her patients, Justin wasn't immune to the warmth her touch left in its wake.

"Good night, Captain."

Trying to hide his disappointment when she withdrew her hand and walked away, he followed her with his gaze. When he closed his eyes, Justin called her face to memory to blot out the possibility that Mitch might be dead. With each of her retreating footsteps, he felt increasingly hollow inside.

CHAPTER FIVE

In the middle of writing a soldier's letter the next afternoon, Brianna glanced up and noticed a man with his arm in a sling standing inside the open tent flap. She excused herself from her patient's bedside and strode toward the newcomer, and her breath caught when she got a good look at his profile.

Before he even turned his head toward her, she knew exactly what shade of blue his eyes would be. When he noticed her, he removed his hat with a polite smile. Deep shadows lay beneath his eyes and lines of strain bracketed his mouth. He inclined his head. "Ma'am."

She couldn't help but smile. "Are you by chance looking for your brother?"

Those familiar indigo eyes widened in surprise. "Yes, ma'am. He's Captain—"

"Captain Justin Thompson, Fifth Michigan Cavalry," she finished for him. "I know. There's a strong family resemblance."

He stiffened. "Is he here? He's alive?"

"Yes, and recovering well so far."

The brother—Mitchell, she remembered—gave her a brilliant smile and let out a short laugh. His free hand came up over his heart and he sagged a bit. "I thought he'd died. I came to find out where he'd been buried. You don't know how happy you've made me."

Her heart raced with excitement. "Believe me, I'm glad I could help. He'll be thrilled to see you, since he thought *you* were the one dead and buried." They were both lucky to have survived the carnage at Cold Harbor. The casualty numbers had been horrific. "Come with me."

Barely able to contain herself, she asked Justin's brother to wait outside the tent then went to the captain's bedside and laid a hand on his shoulder to wake him. Sleepy blue eyes focused on her and a slow smile of recognition touched his lips. Her heart tripped at the sight of it.

"Don't tell me you've come to clean my wound again," he said in a groggy voice.

She laughed and wrapped her arms about her waist. "No. I have a surprise for you instead."

His gaze sharpened. "Surprise?"

"Yes, a wonderful one." Brianna tightened her arms around herself to keep from bursting. "You have a visitor."

Brianna's eager smile made his heart thud as he gingerly eased up into a sitting position, moving inch by painful inch with her help. "Who is it?" he croaked, hardly daring to hope.

In answer, she glanced over her shoulder and motioned for the visitor to enter. When Mitch appeared in the open flap wearing a sling, Justin sagged against the pillows, eyes squeezing shut in relief, and when he opened them they stung with unshed tears.

Laughing, Mitch came over and bent to embrace him around the shoulders with his good arm, tousling Justin's hair. "You look like hell," he announced.

Justin grinned up at him. "You don't look so good either." His chest felt like it was going to split wide open from a mixture of pain and relief. "I didn't know what happened to you. The last I saw of you was sailing off your horse and hitting the ground. I thought you were dead."

Mitch snorted. "You don't give me much credit, do you? It takes more than a busted collarbone to do me in."

He fought back the lump in his throat so the little bastard wouldn't know how emotional he was. His voice was rough. "It's damned good to see you."

Brianna snuck out of the tent before he could ask her to stay.

Mitch slid into a chair beside the bed, propped his bound arm on his stomach, and shook his head. "You have to be the luckiest son-of-a-bitch I know. Not only did you avoid the pearly gates, but here you are, doted on by the most beautiful nurse in Virginia, a born-and-bred southerner who just happens to have a soft spot for Yankees."

"I know."

Mitch's eyes twinkled. "Is she spoken for?"

"Don't even finish that thought," he warned.

"Like her all that much, do you." Mitch's expression filled with mock horror. "What will Laurel say?"

The remark made Justin realize just how much he had missed the bastard. His glare brought a hearty gust of laughter from Mitch and a teasing poke in the chest.

Justin growled in agony and when he was able to get his breath back, refocused on his brother with a glower.

Mitch's devilish grin evaporated. "Sorry." He leaned over to peer more intently at Justin's side. "Is it bad?"

"Bad enough." He lifted the covers and revealed the bandages on his side. His brother made a face, paling as he saw how easily the bullet could have pierced Justin's heart or lung.

Mitch gave a low whistle. "You were damned lucky."

"I know it. I have Mrs. Taylor to thank. One of the doctors told me everyone else had written me off, but she had me personally moved into her ward, wouldn't give up on me. If it weren't for her, I would have died a few days ago."

Besides being kind and gentle, she was skilled at her work. She did everything in a competent, self-assured manner, examining her patients as thoroughly as the doctors did. She rarely had to call on them for help, and when she did, it seemed to be the same surgeon, a younger man with a neatly trimmed, coppery beard. He always listened to her, appeared to treat her more like a colleague than a subordinate. From what Justin could tell, none of the other nurses received that kind of respect from the surgeons.

When the young doctor had come in earlier to check another patient's progress with her, Justin had overheard them discussing complex medical terms that made him remember the texts she'd carried at White House Landing. She must have studied them from cover to cover to attain so much knowledge. Not only a skilled nurse, then, but a rare and highly educated one as well. Intelligence was one of the things he found most attractive in a woman. Combined with the attraction between them, it was no wonder his pulse quickened whenever she came near.

And that wasn't all that quickened. He must already be on the mend, because his body reacted the instant she touched him. Twice now he'd had to bend a knee to tent the sheet over a pounding erection because of her hands on his bare skin. Hers and hers alone. Lucky for him she either hadn't noticed or pretended not to, and a dose of carbolic acid in his wounds made short work of his aching arousal.

Justin couldn't explain it, but in the short time he'd been here he'd already developed a strong attachment to her, and the attraction wasn't merely physical. He sensed she was interested in him as well, though she remained completely professional in her dealings with him. He wasn't sure how he knew. Something in her eyes perhaps, or in her touch.

Or maybe it's wishful thinking.

As if hearing his thoughts, her voice rang out from the tent entrance. "Excuse me, gentlemen. I hope I'm not interrupting the happy reunion." Her gaze fell on Mitch, who cocked his head and ran an appreciative eye over her. "I'd like to change your brother's bandages so he can be more comfortable while he rests." She handed Mitch her supplies, leaving him to juggle them awkwardly with his one good arm.

Bringing his knee up to hide his body's inevitable reaction to her, Justin spared a glance at his brother. "I have the cleanest wound in the entire Eastern theatre."

Brianna smiled in reply and set her dressing kit on the edge of the bed. He watched her face as she cut away the bandage and peeled it back without tearing the sutures. They were dark against his red, swollen skin. "I kept the stitches as close together as I could, but you're still going to have quite a scar."

His brows rose. "You stitched me up?" It was damn hard to ignore the trails of heat licking over his skin wherever she touched him.

"I did." She reached for the bottle of carbolic acid and arched a sardonic brow. "Afraid you'll burst open?"

"No, not at all."

The hint of a dimple appeared in her right cheek as she turned her attention back to his wound. "I'm sorry I have to do this again."

Well, at least his erection would go away now. Justin withheld a sigh and clenched his jaw, vowing to take the pain stoically in front of his brother. He didn't make a sound when the now-familiar burn tore through the wound, but he was sweating and breathing fast as she finished, his side on fire. He lowered his knee, any threat of an erection long dead. Damn, he hated that stuff.

With efficient hands, Brianna re-covered the wound with moist lint, bound it tight and collected her supplies from Mitch, whose face was blanched of color. "Are you all right?" she asked him, a teasing note in her voice. "Is your arm bothering you? Perhaps I should have a surgeon look at it."

"No," Mitch blurted, unconsciously shifting to hold it away from her. "No, thank you, I'm fine. Tired is all."

"Ah. Perhaps I'll go find you something to eat, then." She spared Justin a wink before leaving.

Justin let out a slow sigh when she disappeared through the flap, though it pulled at his stitches. "She's something, isn't she?" He hadn't realized she'd sewn him together with her own hands. He'd bet most nurses weren't granted that kind of latitude from the doctors.

Regaining some color, Mitch nodded. "Yeah. Something."

Soon Brianna returned with bowls of beef stew and cornmeal cakes. Justin's mouth watered at the scent. "Is your stomach up to trying something a little more hearty than broth?" she asked him.

"It's willing to try."

Mitch stood and offered her his chair. "Will you join us, ma'am?"

She seemed startled by the invitation and glanced between them. "Oh. Well yes, I will join you for a moment. Thank you." She passed them their meals and took her seat, folding her hands demurely in her lap. "Eat up before it gets cold."

His empty stomach growling, Justin took a small spoonful and swallowed, relieved when it stayed down. He took another, keeping an eye on his nurse. There were so many things he wanted to know about her. As usual, his nosy brother wasn't shy about asking questions.

"So, Mrs. Taylor, where are you from?" Mitch asked her, balancing the bowl on one knee while he ate.

"Lexington, Kentucky."

Prime horse farm country. Of course. Her knowledge about horses made perfect sense now.

Mitch's brows went up. "You're a long way from home."

"I am, yes."

"And—pardon my curiosity, but how is it that you are a Union sympathizer, ma'am?"

Justin fought back a groan at his brother's bluntness.

She shifted in her chair, for the first time looking the slightest bit uncomfortable. Justin would have told

Mitch to mind his own business, but he was curious about her too and stayed silent while she answered. "Kentucky is a border state, so there are plenty of Unionists. I'm proud to say my brother, Morgan, is a Union cavalryman too."

Mitch didn't know when to leave well enough alone. "So then you have family fighting for the South as well?"

The barest tension pinched her expression. "Yes. My father."

It wasn't an uncommon story, yet Justin couldn't imagine what it would be like to have his family divided by the war. From her closed expression and body language, he sensed she was uneasy with the turn in conversation. He aimed a warning glare at Mitch, who didn't seem to notice her distress.

"And your husband?" he pressed, apparently having noticed her wedding ring. "Did he enlist as well?"

Brianna's expression froze, something like grief flashing in her eyes.

"Mitch," Justin warned, longing to smack him.

"No, it's all right," she answered. She lowered her eyes, paying a lot of attention to a pleat in her skirt. "I'm a widow. Three years this summer. But yes, he served in the army. The Union army," she clarified.

Justin's gaze automatically went to the gold band on her finger. The significance wasn't lost on him. She might have lost her husband at the start of the war, but she hadn't let him go yet. The realization was damned discouraging.

"Oh, sorry," Mitch mumbled then cleared his throat. "Any other family?"

She shook her head, this time with a delicate blush staining her cheeks. Mitch frowned and exchanged a puzzled glance with him.

Still fussing with her skirt, Brianna responded. "My mother died before the start of the war and I haven't seen my father since it started, so other than my brother, I don't really have any family left."

The flash of sadness on her face made Justin long to stuff his brother's booted foot into his flapping mouth. He aimed a withering glare at him instead, silently commanding him to stop talking.

"I'm sorry," Mitch said, rubbing a hand over the back of his neck. "I wouldn't have asked you had I known—"

She waved his concern away, the sadness evaporating into a calm, almost remote expression. "That's all right. It's all in the past now. What about you two? Do you have any family?"

"Our mother lives at home in Detroit," Mitch answered.

She looked at Justin. "And your father?"

"Was killed in the Mexican War," he said.

There it was again, that spark of understanding in her eyes. "Oh, I'm sorry."

He shrugged, but before he could say anything else, Mitch broke in.

"That's partly why we didn't enlist right away when the war broke out. After what happened to him, our mother was beside herself at the idea of us going to the front."

She looked pointedly at Justin's chest wound, then Mitch's injured arm. "I wonder why?"

Mitch barked out a laugh. "You sound just like her. We'd be getting an earful right now if she were here."

"I would be happy to perform the honors in her absence," Brianna offered, a teasing glint in her eyes.

Justin declined with an upraised hand. "I'll be hearing it soon enough, I fear." He envisioned the scene when their mother laid eyes on her wounded boys. The wails, the hysterics... He grimaced.

"She sounds like a very wise woman." With a quiet sigh, Brianna pushed to her feet. For a moment she looked weary, and Justin wished he could do something to lighten her burden. She worked hard. Too hard, from what he'd seen. And from the sounds of it, she had no one to take care of her when her long day nursing was over.

"I have to get back to my duties now, but thank you for the visit." She shook a warning finger at Mitch. "And I'm holding you personally responsible for his welfare, so try not to keep him up for long. It's imperative that he gets adequate sleep."

Mitch bobbed his head up and down in an earnest nod, probably would have sat up and begged if she'd asked him to. "Yes, ma'am." After she was out of earshot, he rounded on Justin with a wide grin. "I think your nurse likes you. And you've never once looked at a woman that way in your whole life." He narrowed his eyes in suspicion. "Were you shot by a Minié ball, or one of Cupid's arrows?"

Justin bit back a grin and set his spoon down. Mitch always insisted on sticking his nose where it wasn't welcome. Growing up, he'd been like a sliver buried under Justin's skin, a constant irritant, plaguing him with questions, chattering his ears off, pouting and throwing temper tantrums when things didn't go his way.

He wouldn't have traded the brat for anything.

His lids grew heavy as the medication pulled at him, languor stealing throughout his limbs. He would sleep soon, rescued from Mitch's incessant prattle, even though he was damn glad to be hearing it again.

"—Wouldn't Laurel turn green if she saw your nurse! I bet—" Mitch stopped short when he noticed Justin staring at him. "What?" he demanded.

Justin studied him a moment longer, thankful his brother had finally shut up. "As far as nurses go, you're the ugliest I've ever seen. And you talk too damn much."

"Well, that's a fine thing to say, since I look almost exactly like you." Mitch batted his lashes. "Get some sleep. Maybe your vision will improve the next time you open your eyes."

Justin snorted and closed his heavy lids. As much as he loved his brother and was glad to see him, he hoped it was Brianna's pretty face he saw when he awoke.

CHAPTER SIX

Brianna corked a bottle of laudanum she'd just dosed her patient with and pulled the bodice of her brown muslin dress away from her sweaty skin. The canvas tent was stifling, even with the flap open and the sides pulled up to let in the breeze. She dropped into a chair and wiped the back of her arm across her damp forehead as she fanned the man's pale face. She'd laid a wet sheet over his torso to cool him, but it wouldn't stay damp for long in this heat. Some of the air swished against her and brought a measure of relief. Her muscles ached a little. Her skin hurt, too. She frowned at the thought. Maybe she was getting sick.

You don't have time to get sick.

The man sighed at the cool air moving over his face and closed his eyes. His chest rose and fell in a shallow but steady rhythm that belied the worsening rattle in his lungs. Glad she could ease him somewhat, she let her mind drift and found herself daydreaming about Captain Thompson.

Over the past week she'd gotten to know him

better, learning many things about him, his brother, and the lumber mills their family owned that Justin had run until his enlistment. His eyes were the most beautiful shade of blue. She'd never seen anything like them. And he was always so calm and polite, regardless of how much discomfort he was in. So self-assured. In spite of her resolve to see him as just another patient, she enjoyed his company and the low tones of his voice—

She *had* to stop thinking about him.

With a mental kick, she collected her things and walked outside. The sulfate of iron used to treat the latrines wasn't doing much good these days. The air hung around her like a damp towel, stifling and foul with human waste. Brianna wrinkled her nose at the stench and wiped a sleeve over her forehead to mop up the moisture. When she'd last checked on Captain Thompson early that morning, he'd been fast asleep, utterly relaxed in his slumber. His brother had been propped in a chair beside him and glanced up to spare her a wink before burying his nose back in his newspaper.

Several officers and enlisted men from their regiment had come by in the last few days to give their regards to her favorite patient before riding out with the rest of the Michigan Brigade. That they made the effort to come and see him spoke volumes about the high regard they held him in. More than a few of the men had raved to her about what an excellent officer he was and that his character was beyond reproach.

Hearing it from others who knew him made him even more attractive to her. Yes, he was handsome, but he was also kind, and she enjoyed their conversations. She'd already spent more time with him than necessary, though she'd taken pains to ensure she hid her growing attraction. It was easy to see why he'd been elected as an officer. Even laid low by his wounds, he exuded an unmistakable aura of authority that told her he was comfortable being in command. Whenever she drew near, she sensed the quiet, controlled power of him. His gaze was direct, magnetic.

She'd also have to be blind not to notice the desire in his eyes when she caught him looking at her. Brianna liked it far too much for her own comfort.

You'd best stop thinking about him if you know what's good for you.

With a frustrated sigh, she returned to work and went to check on Tim.

For the first time in a week, the hospital seemed to be in some semblance of order. Given the recent pandemonium, it was a relief to know the men were finally all sheltered inside tents under the best care possible. A trickle of perspiration slid between her breasts and she once again pulled the muslin away from her hot skin.

She found Tim sitting up in bed in his new tent, his forearms resting on his bent knees as a doctor checked the exit wounds in his back. Poor, stoic man suffered with every breath, yet he'd asked to be moved to a less crowded tent so his constant coughing wouldn't keep everyone awake.

The elderly surgeon tapped here and there, probing into the swollen bullet holes with his fingers. Tim coughed and gave a sad, helpless sigh, his even expression belying the agony he must be in. She stepped closer, about to offer the doctor assistance in cleaning the wounds when something dripped from Tim's face onto the sheets.

Oh dear God, he was crying.

Pain twisted in her chest, like someone had taken red-hot pincers to her heart. Brianna rushed over to him and rested a hand on his sandy hair. "Ah, Tim, you poor, stubborn man," she murmured. It was more than she could bear to watch him suffer like this and she knew his pride was taking a beating for crying in front of anyone. To shield him she kneeled before him on the bed and placed herself between him and any curious eyes.

Without a word he leaned gratefully into her, his wet, bearded face resting on her shoulder. She stroked his dirty hair helplessly, wishing she could take some of his pain into herself and let this wonderful man heal again. "No one can see you now," she whispered.

His big arms came around her back and held tight, his grip still gentle, even with his immense power. "Oh, thank you, ma'am," he whispered.

The gratitude in his voice made her want to cry. She braced him while the doctor finished his examination, and all three breathed a sigh of relief when he was done.

The surgeon rested a hand on Tim's shoulder. "I'm sorry I hurt you, son."

Tim coughed once and smiled against her shoulder. "That's all right, doc. My guardian angel came to comfort me." His voice remained weak and raspy.

The elderly man's eyes swept over her, his expression thankful. "She certainly did."

Tim waited until the doctor left then slowly straightened, avoiding her gaze. "Do you suppose you could find me more of that custard for lunch today?"

"Certainly." If a man could endure what Tim was suffering, he deserved whatever comforts she could give him.

He let her settle him against the pillows and wipe his face and neck with a damp cloth, a smile playing about his lips. "You're so gentle with me."

Her fingers tightened around the cloth. "You deserve gentleness, Tim." He deserved much more than that. His stoic suffering tugged at her heart, made her want to fuss over him like a child, even though he was a giant of a man nearly six and a half feet tall and strong as a draft horse. God knew she'd spare him this slow, terrible death if she had the power.

When he was as comfortable as she could make him, Brianna fixed him with a hard stare and pointed a warning finger at him. "Next time someone comes to examine your wounds, send an orderly to find me first." If he wanted to be brave and refuse medication, that was one thing, but there was no reason for him to suffer as he did. It took a lot for her to lose her composure, yet this man managed to slip past her emotional shields every time. Didn't he know how hard it was for her to watch him endure that kind of pain?

Tim gazed up at her with tired eyes and put on an endearing smile. "Yes, ma'am. I'll do just that."

On her way to the kitchen to arrange for that custard she had promised, she passed the neat rows of tents. Other nurses—mostly convalescent men—walked about with armfuls of bedding and clothes that needed washing, others with stacks of newspapers and assorted reading materials. Shoving a wisp of hair back into its tight chignon, Brianna wondered what she would do with Tim. That man would endure less torment if he wasn't so damned stubborn.

On impulse, she stopped to poke her head into Captain Thompson's tent and found him awake. He greeted her with a friendly smile, his appreciative gaze triggering that now-familiar flutter in her belly.

"Bree?"

She glanced to the side to find Ella-May near the wall of the tent, rinsing out a cloth. "Hi. Need any help in here?"

"Actually, yes." Ella-May took her by the arm and led her a judicious distance away from the men. She seemed to search for the right words before finally blurting, "Your patient needs to be washed. And shaved."

Her patient? "Who? You mean Captain Thompson?"

"Captain Thompson," Ella-May agreed dryly.

"Oh." If even her friend thought of him as *her* patient, she wasn't being very discreet, was she? Brianna had washed hundreds of men in her tenure as a nurse, but in light of the growing attraction she felt toward him, the last thing she wanted was to have to touch him so intimately while he was awake and there were witnesses around. "Could you do it for me? I've promised to get something special for one of my other patients. I'll come back and give you a hand once I'm done." By then Ella-May would be long since finished with Captain Thompson.

"Me?" Her friend gave a short laugh. "Why on earth would I? You can do it yourself as soon as you've changed his bandages." She cocked her head and narrowed her eyes, scrutinizing her. "Can't you?"

Brianna fought the urge to fidget. This was far different than tending to his wounds. Washing and shaving him now meant intimate contact while he was fully alert, with an audience. No. She couldn't possibly. Not now, with the way her stomach fluttered around him. Not when she shouldn't be feeling anything for him but empathy. Anything more was unprofessional, and if anyone suspected she had more than a clinical interest in him, she'd be sent packing. Brianna had worked too hard to secure her position here to let that happen.

"I would, but I promised another patient a special dessert, so could you please do it?" Her fingers played with the pocket on her apron.

Ella-May turned incredulous pale blue eyes on her. "What has gotten into you? You're acting like a ninny," she finished in a whisper. "I've got my hands full already. Now go shave that poor man before he itches his skin off."

When she brushed past her, Brianna shot out an arm and grabbed her friend's elbow. "Would you do it this once as a favor to me?"

Ella-May stared at her in consternation for a moment. Then a shocked smile stretched across her lips. "Why, Brianna Taylor," she drawled, too low for anyone else to hear. "If I didn't know better, I'd think that Wolverine makes you nervous."

Oh, lord, Ella-May knew. She *knew*.

"I wonder why that would be?" her friend mused with a look of mock confusion on her face. "After all, he's handsome, and every *inch* the gentleman." She chuckled and glanced over her shoulder at him before facing Brianna once more. Her dark brows rose, a sparkle in her eyes. "Now what were you saying about that special dessert?"

Brianna's cheeks had to be flaming red by now. "I promised Tim some custard," she muttered.

"I'll take care of it. Now get back to work." Ella-May shoved the damp cloth into her hand.

Mind scrambling, Brianna gave her a bland smile

and darted a glance at *her* patient. His indigo gaze settled on her with welcoming warmth, making the butterflies in her stomach flutter even harder. She wanted to sneak out of the tent and hide when Ella-May left with a conspiratorial wink. As if she'd just done Brianna a huge favor.

Ooh, just you wait, Ella-May Davison. Just you wait until I get my hands on you!

Well. She was going to have to do it, and that was all there was to it. It was only a wash and a shave, after all. He couldn't do it himself, as he was still too weak. He could slit his own throat if he slipped with the razor. She was being ridiculous.

You have a backbone. Use it.

Fine. He was just a man, no need to be nervous.

Drawing a deep breath, she gathered her professional demeanor around her like armor and approached his cot, careful to avoid his gaze while she collected the necessary items.

"Are you going to shave me?" His deep voice held a hopeful note.

"Yes, Captain. I would imagine your face is rather itchy."

"A little, yes." He rubbed one hand over his bristly cheek. His color was marginally better today, a sign he was feeling at least a bit improved.

She kept her expression blank even though her stomach did somersaults at the thought of what she was going to do. Her lack of control over her body's reaction was vexing, to say the least. Deciding it was safer not to talk any more, Brianna mixed the lather and steeled herself before sitting in a chair beside his bed.

She could feel his eyes on her, the heated interest in them. Since becoming a nurse, men had looked at her like that plenty of times, but none of them had ever affected her like this. She'd never *let* them affect her, until now. Around him it seemed hard to inhale a full breath of air.

Brianna might not want to do this, but since retreat wasn't in her nature, she spread the lather on his whiskers and tried to ignore the sparks that danced in her fingertips whenever she touched him, hoping he didn't notice the fine tremor in her hands. When he bent his knee to bring the sheet up a few moments later, she flushed and avoided his gaze. She knew exactly what he was trying to hide. Her breasts tightened, her nipples going tight against the fabric of her shift, and she was thankful that he was unaware of her response.

At least he was gentleman enough to make the attempt at covering his erection. But it should absolutely not please her to know her touch aroused him to that extent. What was *wrong* with her? The carefully built walls she'd barricaded herself behind were crumbling.

Her insides shivered at the thought. From out of nowhere, a forbidden image of her hands sliding over his naked body flashed through her mind. Her palms were flat against him, following the contours of hard muscle over his chest and shoulders, lower, down to his taut belly...

What are you doing? her conscience demanded in outrage. She fumbled with the shaving brush.

"You have done this before, I hope," he murmured.

She frowned in annoyance. "Yes, of course. Many times."

"You seem nervous, is all. You won't cut me, will you? I have enough holes in me at the moment."

She shot him a glare, expecting to find a smile on his face, but found only mild concern instead.

"No, Captain, I will not cut you. Not on purpose, anyway," she added under her breath. She scraped at his whiskers with the razor, wiped it on the towel she kept handy. The intense way he watched her was completely unnerving, and after only a few minutes she dropped her hands to her lap with a sigh. "Will you please close your eyes?"

His raven brows went up. "Why?" At her aggravated expression he obediently shut them. After all, she was holding a very sharp weapon in her hand, wasn't she? "All right."

"Thank you," she bit out. "And stop talking before I nick you." She was willing to bet her entire wage he knew exactly what he was doing to her and was enjoying every second of it. Awful man.

No sooner had she uttered the words than his eyes popped opened and he stared right at her. "Does it bother you to have to touch me like this?" He pitched his voice low so the other men wouldn't overhear him.

Her spine snapped straight, indignation flooding her. "Of course it doesn't. What a question. How many times have I changed your bandages? I am a widow and a nurse, Captain, not some flighty schoolgirl. Now close your eyes and stop speaking, if you please."

He studied her for a moment longer before shutting them as she had requested.

Her fingers shook as she raised the razor once more. "Bother me, indeed," she muttered to herself, fighting scandalous thoughts of his strong hands caressing her naked body, pushing her thighs apart to settle between them and press what was currently hidden beneath the sheet against her aching center.

Think of something else! Anything else.

She began mentally reciting the muscles of the upper limb.

In the tense silence that followed, Brianna kept on with her task, turning his face for a better angle with the blade. He helped her along by tucking his tongue into his cheek so she could shave the hollows, then under his lower lip. He had nice lips, she couldn't help but notice again, the lower one a little fuller than the upper. He shifted, bringing that knee up higher, and she started thinking about what was under that sheet, the size and shape of it, how it would feel sinking inside her—

Stop it!

Composing herself once more, she focused on the movement of her hand. Then she caught the slight quivering in his cheek. Oh, he found her discomfort amusing, did he? Indignant, she tossed the razor into the basin with a plop, spraying droplets of water across his face and neck. "Captain, I'll thank you to not make fun of me," she whispered, her composure slipping into ragged shreds.

Rather than apologize, he reached for her wrist and wound his long fingers around it, caressing it subtly. Her body tightened under a whiplash of pleasure at the care in his touch and the heat in his eyes. "I'm not making fun of you," he said, "but there's no reason to be nervous. I won't bite." His eyes strayed to her mouth as if he wanted to kiss her.

Her belly flipped. She tugged her wrist away, irritated at her lack of control over her reaction to him. "I already told you, I'm not nervous." Her face was so hot she feared it might burst into flame. "Please, just be quiet and let me finish."

His slow smile made her hands tremble even more. "You're beautiful when you blush."

She sent an anxious glance about the tent, but to her relief everyone else was either sleeping or oblivious to her plight. She set her jaw. "Be still." Hesitating for only a heartbeat, she picked up the razor and completed the task with as much efficiency as she could, thankful he kept his eyes closed for the duration.

The end result was worse, somehow. Uncovered by the thick growth of black beard, he was absolutely heart-stopping. How had she ever forgotten that face? The mutual longing between them was so intense that when he opened his eyes and smiled at her, she tore her gaze away and shoved to her feet to pull a breath of air into her lungs. The tent suddenly felt too small for the both of them, and she swore he must have been able to hear the pounding of her heart.

When she spun away, he caught her hand in his. His touch seared her as he tugged her back toward the side of the bed. Her pulse beat frantically in her throat as she resisted.

"Don't go yet," he said.

She flashed him a frown. She'd be an idiot to stay. Her feet, however, refused to move.

A slight frown creased his brow. "Why didn't you tell me before that you were a widow?"

The question surprised her so much that she went still. He was only touching her hand, yet it brought her dormant body to tingling wakefulness no matter how she fought to curb the reaction. She raised her chin. "I didn't realize it would be of any importance to you."

"It wasn't."

A stab of disappointment dulled her annoyance, confusing and irritating her even more. "Good." Why wasn't she yanking her hand away and leaving?

"But it is now," he added. "You've never talked about him."

This time she tugged at his hand and his grip didn't lessen. She huffed out a breath. "I don't make it a habit to talk about my personal life with my patients."

"I've noticed that. But I don't want to be just another patient to you."

Unexpected warmth bloomed in her abdomen, spreading up to her breasts and down between her legs. His eyes were so intent on her face, making her believe there was more than simple physical attraction between them and that he really cared about her. Impossible. He'd only been here a week.

"Did he die in the war?"

Her lips thinned. "Not that it's any of your business, but yes."

He threw her off balance again by continuing. "How old were you when you got married?"

The blood rushed to her face as her temper lit. "Old enough," she blurted at his rudeness. She didn't want to discuss this.

"Did you love him?"

"I *still* love him," she corrected. "Very much." She managed to wrench free of his grasp and bent to scoop up the soiled bedding, her face flaming from a mixture of anger and confusion. "I have to get back to work." She rose, brushed the front of her skirts, and barely made it a step before he called out.

"Wait—"

"What?" she snapped, casting a hard look at him over her shoulder. Everyone in the tent had heard him. She felt their gazes keenly.

He maintained eye contact and beckoned her

closer with one hand, which she refused to do. "Why are you avoiding me?"

Her hands stiffened around the bedding. How could he know that? She covered the distance between them quickly and lowered her voice so the other men wouldn't overhear the rest of this wretched conversation. "I'm not *avoiding* you."

"Yes, you are. Have I done something to offend you?"

Other than just now? "No."

"Then why are you suddenly so uncomfortable around me?"

You know why. She would rather suffer torture than admit her attraction to him. "I'm not anything but exasperated at the moment, Captain."

He kept studying her with that maddeningly knowing expression on his face. "No?"

"No, and I wish you would stop trying to imply otherwise."

He lowered his voice to a murmur. "Because it makes you uncomfortable."

"Yes." And he damn well knew it.

"Because you feel something more for me than professional interest, and you don't want to. Right?"

Her mouth fell open, but no sound left her throat. How *dare* he? How dare he speak to her that way? His truthful words cut her, and the hungry, knowing expression in his eyes was too much to bear. As if he had *any* inkling of how she felt, how confusing and unsettling all this was.

In her haste to blast him, she'd dropped the bedding. She had to get out of there. Now. As she stooped to retrieve the sheets, his fingertips grazed her cheek. Brianna froze, something making her look up at him. A sudden, suffocating pressure gripped her chest. His touch was light and, to her shame, it ricocheted throughout her whole body. Her nipples throbbed and a traitorous dampness gathered between her thighs.

"Don't be afraid of me," he whispered, gaze lingering on her parted lips. "I would never do anything to hurt you."

Oh, but she was afraid. Afraid to move, afraid of the strange yearning she felt for him. Brianna jerked her head back and shot to her feet, intent on escaping.

She was almost outside when he called to her, his tone a strange mixture of amusement and exasperation. "You can run away now, but when I'm well enough to get up I intend to finish this conversation."

Was that so? Eyes blazing, Brianna faced him, her stupid heart tripping at the sight of his handsome face before she steeled herself. *Damn it!* "I haven't the faintest idea what you think you stand to gain from this, Captain. And as for running, the only place I'll be going is home to my boardinghouse. I'm almost finished for the day and won't be back until morning." She added the last with a good measure of satisfaction, certain it would put him in his place.

To her chagrin, he merely smiled as though she'd just issued a challenge he couldn't resist. "I suppose I'll wait here for you then." He had the unmitigated gall to wink at her.

In his condition he didn't have the strength to crawl to the tent flap, and he must have known it. "Good day, Captain. I wish you a recovery of the *utmos*t haste." With that, she marched out, the weight of his gaze following her into the midday heat. Her angry strides lengthened as she made her way through the rows of tents, her mind churning. Imagine the nerve of the man, implying that she had feelings for him, and right in front of the other patients or anyone else who cared to listen! She was a widow, had loved her husband with her whole heart, and no one had ever dared question her decision not to engage in another romantic relationship—

Brianna drew up short.

No one had ever questioned her decision to remain unattached and uninterested, except Ella-May. Though her friend meant well, she had voiced her opinion several times about Brianna finding a husband since in her opinion Brianna had grieved for Caleb long enough. And it appeared she wasn't above trying to play matchmaker now that she saw how attracted Brianna was to Captain Thompson.

Brianna clenched her jaw so hard her back teeth ached. If Ella-May knew what was good for her, she would find another hospital to nurse at before their next shift together.

CHAPTER SEVEN

Justin was feeling well enough the next afternoon to lift his head a few inches off the pillow when he heard voices outside his tent. He recognized his brother, and there was a woman with him. His heartbeat sped up. Was it Brianna? She had to be back by now. All morning he'd lain staring at the tent ceiling, wanting to kick himself for pushing her so hard yesterday. He'd meant to reassure her that the attraction was mutual, not scare her away or insult her.

Booted feet hit the wooden steps leading into the tent, and then Mitch burst through the flap, wearing an irritated expression. Wincing, Justin pushed up onto one elbow. "What's the matter?"

"Wait for it."

He had only a second to wonder at his brother's annoyed tone before Laurel Stevens appeared in the opening. Justin's heart sank. The instant she saw him, an elated smile spread across her face and her dark eyes turned liquid with tears.

Stifling a groan, Justin dropped back onto the

pillow, the apology he'd prepared for his nurse dying on his tongue. Damn, hadn't he suffered enough the past week without this?

"Justin." Laurel pressed a lacy hanky to her nose and sniffed back tears as she moved to his bedside, completely ignoring the way Mitch blocked her path. She plowed right past him like a color bearer intent on leading a regiment in a charge. Her gloved hand came up to cradle his cheek, and the obvious tenderness in her gaze made him want to fling it away. Only there was no escape. "Oh, look at you..." At least she was genuinely distressed to see him like this.

Justin withstood the contact for another moment to be polite then pushed her hand aside. "Laurel, what are you doing here?"

"I was in Washington with Daddy when we got a telegram from your mother," she answered, fishing in her reticule for a fresh handkerchief. After dabbing away her tears, she sniffed and looked down at him with worried brown eyes. "I was just sick when I heard the news."

Not as sick as he felt now.

"I insisted that I come see you."

"I appreciate your concern," he said, choosing his words with care so he wouldn't encourage her infatuation with him. "But I'm on the mend."

"You're so pale," she whispered, putting a hand to her mouth.

"Of course he's pale," Mitch said in an exasperated tone. "He was shot through the ribs not too long ago."

Laurel swallowed visibly and sank into the chair beside the bed. Oblivious of the way her presence discomfited him, she reached up to stroke his hair. It took all his self-control not to bat her hand away. He shot a do-something look at his brother.

Mitch cleared his throat. "Laurel, he really should be sleeping. Let's go."

She shook her head, dark curls swinging around her face. A beautiful woman, but so damned cloying and annoying that Justin all but broke out in hives after five minutes of her company. "I can't leave him like this when he needs me."

"I don't need—" He clenched his jaw and stopped the "you" just in time. There was no point in telling her again that he had no romantic interest in her. Being brusque never kept her away, and it made him feel bad for hurting her. "Mitch is right, I just need to rest. I'm sorry you came all this way when I'm not up to visiting." There was only one woman he wanted to see right now, and she'd been conspicuously absent all day. It made him resent not being able to get out of bed and go find her.

Laurel kept stroking his hair, her expression full of the kind of affection he could never give her in return. "That's all right. Father and I have reserved a room in a nearby hotel for the next week, but we can always stay longer. I'll stay as long as you need me to."

Oh, God. He wanted to scrub a hand over his face in frustration. "That's not necessary." He turned his head to evade her touch, but she merely took his hand instead and stroked her thumb over the back of his knuckles. Fighting the urge to shake it off, he shifted on the bed, and winced as a bolt of pain jolted through his side.

"What's wrong?" she gasped.

"Nothing," he said between gritted teeth. If the woman didn't stop touching him, he'd get out of the damn bed just to escape her and to hell with ripping his stitches open.

Mitch set a hand on her shoulder. "Leave him alone, Laurel. Let's go."

She shrugged off his hold. "No." Before Justin knew what she was doing, she pulled the blanket down to expose his naked chest. Shocked, he grabbed for the blanket before it reached his waist, but her eyes were already riveted to the bandages covering his ribs. Her cool palm covered his left pectoral muscle. She swallowed, a sudden flush tinting her cheeks. "Your skin is hot. Maybe a cool cloth would make you feel better."

Taken aback by her audacity—not to mention the impropriety of her actions—Justin cast a disbelieving glance at her, then Mitch. His brother's eyebrows were up near his hairline.

Justin had never realized she could be so bold. If she thought he would let her give him a sponge bath, she was about to be sorely disappointed. "No, thank you."

Her eyes met his, a hint of censure in her expression. "I'm perfectly capable of nursing you."

"I don't—"

"You lie still, and I'll make you more comfortable," she insisted, grabbing for his pillow. His head hit the mattress as she fluffed the thing, and Justin grabbed her wrist, holding it in a firm grip until she looked at him.

"This is no place for you," he said in a low voice.

"You can come over here and make me more comfortable, miss," a man in the far bed called out.

Laurel's gaze jerked to the other soldier, her cheeks now bright pink. Then she turned her gaze on Justin as if waiting for him to reprimand the man for speaking to her in such a rude manner. He merely stared back at her, brows lowered.

A muscle in her jaw moved. "I want to help you. I came all this way."

Justin shook his head. "I appreciate that, but you should go, Laurel."

"Yes, you should."

All three of them turned their heads toward the tent flap at the sound of that voice. Justin's heart kicked hard when he saw Brianna standing there, her gaze locked on Laurel. She walked over with a quick stride that spoke of complete confidence, her arms full of bandages and nursing supplies.

"Who are you?" Laurel asked.

"His nurse," she answered, nodding at Justin, the flash of irritation in her eyes letting him know she hadn't yet forgiven him for yesterday. "And you are?"

"Laurel Stevens, a very close family friend. I'm here to help him," she answered evenly.

Brianna gave her a tight smile. "Pleasure to meet you. And while I'm sure Captain Thompson appreciates your visit, it's time he got some rest."

Laurel's face fell. "I only arrived ten minutes ago."

Brianna took out her scissors and some bandages. "I'm sorry about that, but I need to change his dressings and check the wounds before he can sleep."

"I'll help," Laurel offered.

Justin watched, fascinated, as his nurse's eyes frosted. "Thank you, but no."

Laurel blinked, as though stunned that anyone would refuse her help. "I think Justin would be more comfortable with me tending him than you."

"I disagree."

Laurel made a shocked sound and turned to confront her with hands on hips. "I've known him since I was a girl."

Ignoring Laurel's growing anger, Brianna continued preparing her supplies. "That may be, but you have no nursing experience, and it's my job to ensure my patients have all they require to recover quickly. In this case, Captain Thompson needs fresh bandages and a lot of sleep. Visiting will have to wait."

Laurel lifted her chin. "Then I'll sit with him while he sleeps."

"No, you won't."

Laurel looked nonplussed for a moment before she found her voice again. "You can't order me to leave—"

"Laurel, stop," Justin commanded, annoyed beyond words at her behavior.

Mitch grabbed her by the arm and towed her back from the bed, holding on in case she tried to shake him off.

With a gasp of outrage, Laurel whirled and stared at Justin. But if she was looking for support, she was about to be disappointed yet again.

"I appreciate your concern, Laurel," he said, struggling to remain tactful, "but I'd prefer it if you and your father went home. You can tell my mother in person that I'm on the mend."

She swallowed, and for a moment he thought she might cry. Thankfully, she regained her composure, though the hurt lingered in her eyes. "Perhaps you'll feel better in a few days and I can come back then."

Before he could answer, Brianna came to his rescue. "Perhaps you'd best honor his wishes and wait to see him when he goes home on furlough."

At Laurel's incredulous expression, Justin bit back a grin and prayed she wasn't about to explode at Brianna.

The younger woman's eyes flared with anger, and for a

moment Brianna wondered if the interloper was going to have a fit. She barely refrained from raising a taunting brow to see what would happen but corralled her annoyance with a firm tug on the reins. Her temper was something she'd struggled with since she was a child. Though she'd learned to control it for the most part, sometimes it was difficult to hem it in. This new development with Miss Stevens was sorely testing her limits.

It was the sight of the other woman reaching for Justin's bandages that had bothered her, she told herself. Not because Miss Stevens had her hands on his naked chest when Brianna walked into the tent.

One look at his irritated face had convinced her he wanted nothing to do with the woman. Knowing that, Brianna had no qualms about kicking her out.

Miss Stevens sucked in a deep breath, all but quivering with outrage. "You have no right to speak to me like that."

Brianna held her ground, not the least bit intimidated by the woman's anger. "I tried being polite, but now you've forced me to use less subtle language."

Mitch made a strangled sound. She glanced up to see him biting the inside of his cheek, his eyes dancing with laughter.

"Laurel," Justin began, "I'm tired and not up to visiting anyway."

"Mitch isn't a visitor?" she demanded.

"He's family."

She stared at him, a glimmer of hurt showing through her embarrassment. "I thought I was too."

"Corporal Thompson," Brianna interrupted, now feeling sorry for the woman and not wanting any more of a scene, "perhaps you could help Miss Stevens find a wagon to take her back into town."

"Yes, ma'am." He ushered the woman away from the bed, and Brianna ignored the look she aimed first at Justin, then at her.

When she was gone, Brianna went back to work. With a fresh bandage and her scissors ready, she stepped to the bedside and began removing the old dressing as the tent flap closed behind them. She exposed the stitches without looking at him. "That's a very determined suitor you have, Captain."

"I'm beginning to realize that." His tone was dry, but weary.

"She came all the way from Michigan to see you?" Much as it annoyed her, she couldn't deny the twinge of jealousy at the thought of that woman being his sweetheart.

"No, she was in Washington with her father when they heard I'd been wounded. They've been friends of my family as long as I can remember."

Well, evidently the girl didn't want to be merely his *friend* any longer.

Back in control and in her domain now, Brianna checked the stitches. No bleeding, no foul odor. The bruising was already fading to yellow around the bullet wound. "Starting to feel better?"

"I was."

She raised a caustic brow. "Really. That one visit from Miss Stevens set your recovery back?"

"Well, that too. But no, I meant because I've made you angry with me."

Though she wasn't looking at him, she could feel his gaze on her face. "I'm not angry with you."

"Then why won't you look at me?"

To placate him, she glanced up into his face for a

moment and was hit by the instant bolt of heat that flashed in her lower belly when she met his eyes. "There, I've looked at you." She went back to bandaging his side.

He laid a hand over hers, the warmth and quiet strength in it wreaking havoc on her nervous system. "I'm sorry if I offended you yesterday. That wasn't my intention."

Brushing away his hand, she kept at her task. "Apology accepted. Can you turn over a bit?"

He hesitated a moment, but when she didn't look at him he shifted gingerly onto his uninjured side. He had to be sore, and any movement would still cause him great pain. The bruising had spread right across his ribs to his back.

"I wasn't trying to offend you," he said again.

Why wouldn't he let this go? "I've already accepted your apology."

"But you're still angry."

"I'm not."

"Yes, you are. I can feel it in your hands."

That made her stop and look up into his face. "What?" Had she hurt him without realizing it?

His deep blue eyes regarded her steadily as he nodded. "You're not being as gentle as you usually are."

Instantly contrite, she snatched her hands away from him. "I'm sorry." She couldn't believe she'd let this situation affect her to the point that she'd inadvertently been rough with him.

"Apology accepted. Though I admit, I rather like the feel of your hands on me." His eyes held a wicked gleam.

Her lips quirked in response. "You might not be in fighting form yet, but there's nothing wrong with your sense of humor."

"That's good news. I'm going to need it when I go home to face my mother and adoring suitor," he said wryly.

Brianna quickly finished her task and tucked the blankets back around him, unprepared to face the thought of him leaving yet.

CHAPTER EIGHT

Whatever she'd been fighting off for the past few days had finally caught up with her. By Monday morning, Brianna was feverish and achy. She hadn't slept well last night, both from the fever and because she'd twisted on a rack of guilt that made her alternately blink back tears and stare at the ceiling.

When she'd received word three years ago that Caleb had been wounded in battle and lost an arm, she'd been terrified he would die before she found him. She remembered the night she arrived at the hospital so vividly.

The old courthouse sheltered the wounded and the dying, its lawns strewn with bandages, crammed with rows of haphazardly parked wagons. The reek hit her the moment she set foot on the lawn, blood and unwashed bodies combined with the foul mud that sucked at her shoes.

She quelled the urge to cover her nose and mouth with a handkerchief to blot out the stench of the horrible place, hardly able to believe they called it a hospital.

Oil lamps cast swaying shadows across the mournful ward. The conditions appalled her. How could anyone survive here, let alone recover? Her anxious eyes scanned each bed for Caleb. All around, men were missing arms and legs. One soldier had lost his eye and another's jaw was gone, leaving a gaping mass of mangled flesh, his upper teeth and soft palate yawning wide open. She stared; she couldn't help it. How was he still alive? Tear marks tracked his filthy face and she looked away, her heart squeezing. He couldn't possibly survive that wound.

"Brianna?"

She whirled about at the sound of his voice, weak as it was. His green eyes gave him away through the filth covering him. Mindless with relief, she rushed over and wrapped her arms around him, trying not to stare at the bloody bandages covering the stump at his shoulder where a muscular arm had been. She whispered his name like a prayer, covering his dirty face with desperate kisses.

He hugged her close with his one arm, and her throat tightened. "You're really here."

She squeezed him, burying her face against his neck. He was filthy, but she could still smell his special scent beneath the stale sweat. "Of course I am."

"They took my arm," he rasped weakly.

He was feverish and thirsty, had been lying there for God only knew how long without anyone washing him or seeing to his comfort. In that moment she'd made up her mind to nurse him back to health on her own.

She washed his face and throat and paused, faltering at the idea of seeing the amputation for the first time.

"You don't have to, Bree. I can do it."

She saw the embarrassment in his face and realized she was making things worse by hesitating. "Don't be silly. I'm not about to faint on you, I promise." She helped him remove his nightshirt, revealing for the first time the bandages covering the stump. She glanced up at him. "Does it hurt?" she whispered, aching at the sheen of tears in his beautiful green eyes. Didn't he know she'd love him even without all his limbs?

"Not so much anymore."

She studied the shoulder for another moment. "Should I clean it?"

He took a breath that seemed a little labored then let it out slowly. "You can, but it makes my arm itch something awful."

"It makes your arm itch?" she repeated, frowning at his one whole arm. How could washing the right shoulder make the left one itch?

"Not that one. This one." He nodded toward the stump, and when he spoke again his voice was unsteady. "Sometimes I can feel the arm as if it's still there. The doctors tell me it's normal."

She'd had a lot to learn back then. She'd observed the nurses at work, pestered them with questions, and sometimes followed the doctors during their rounds. One of the surgeons became intrigued by her interest and loaned her his medical texts. In every spare moment, she devoured the books, reading everything she could find about the anatomy of the arm and shoulder, what exactly had been involved in the amputation, how to care for the amputation site and which complications could develop. Including pneumonia.

Caleb had begun to fade, the telltale rattling cough filling her with terror. One night a doctor confirmed her worst fear—her husband had pneumonia and was not expected to recover. Brianna did everything in her power to pull him back from the brink.

You will not die. I will not let you.

The night before he died, he'd been lucid enough to hold her hand and speak to her, though the effort cost him what little strength he had left. "Bree...have to...let me go." His overly hot fingers squeezed hers for emphasis. "Promise me..."

He asked the impossible. She'd clung to him, willing him to absorb the strength from her body, begging God to take her instead.

Caleb palmed the back of her head, and she turned into the unnatural heat of his fevered body. Memorizing the imprint of his flesh and bones against her.

She stayed like that into the night, whispering her love for him whenever he opened his eyes, fighting death's pull to be near her. Yet hour by hour, he slipped further away.

Just before dawn, his lids flickered open and he stared up at her through glassy eyes.

"I love you, Caleb," she whispered, caressing his face while the wheezing shuddered through him. His mouth twitched in his attempt at a smile and he clasped her hand, the movement feeble. *I love you too*, it said, as clearly as if he had spoken. Then his green eyes closed for the last time. As the final, terrible gasps rattled through him, she felt like she was suffocating with him. *Please stop his suffering,* she prayed. *Please, I beg you.*

She gathered him close and cradled his ravaged body, pressing her wet cheek against his. "I love you."

Brianna knew he was only holding on because she wasn't ready to release him. She drew all her strength inward. The pain burned like a hot coal beneath her sternum. She forced the words out, silently choking on each one. "It's all right to let go now. I'm here, and I won't leave you."

And as if he'd been waiting for her permission, he'd slipped away from his earthly suffering, secure in the comfort of her arms.

Surfacing from the painful memory with a ragged breath, Brianna dragged herself out of bed to wash and dress. Her skin ached, the delicate cotton of her chemise seeming rough against her body. Her muscles felt stiff and sore. She stepped outside to find the sky was still a rich indigo, the mysterious color of those hours between deepest night and the first hint of dawn as she left her boardinghouse.

All night she'd thought about Caleb's quiet, solid presence, always near should she need him. Holding her so tightly she couldn't breathe after she'd fallen out of the tree he'd dared her to climb when she was a love-struck girl of twelve and broken her arm, the concern on his face worth every second of the pain. Caleb smiling at her in the moonlight that filtered through the trees above her parents' veranda before he'd kissed her for the first time on her sixteenth birthday. Their wedding night and the awkwardness they had banished with laughter; the way her heart had turned over in her chest when she'd woken beside him the next morning as dawn gilded his body with brushstrokes of gold.

But most of all she remembered that haunted expression in his eyes, terrified but mustering a brave front for her, holding her with his remaining strength.

Promise me...

Part of her was terrified of fulfilling that promise, because it meant she was moving on. She'd been frozen and numb for so long, until Justin had come into her life and thawed the ice encasing her heart. Now that he had, she felt everything more acutely than she had in a long time and it hurt so much she didn't want to face it.

Where the footpath met the main road, fresh wheel ruts and hoof prints indicated the hospital must have received more wounded overnight. She quickened her pace, her aches and pains subsiding under a rush of adrenaline. A rumbling groan reached her ears at last, only audible from this distance if made by a large group of men. She hurried the rest of the way, and the sight awaiting her when she arrived tore a gasp from her throat.

Men were strewn everywhere around the hospital, on the grass, in wagons. The angel of death had been at work again, and the harvest he had reaped spread across the grounds in a writhing blue carpet.

Brianna rushed through the mass of tents, shocked by the level of chaos. So many soldiers packed the grounds that the wards were indistinguishable. Doctors worked in groups, performing amputations in the open in front of their horrified audience.

Heart clattering against her ribs, she raced to gather supplies and went to work even though she ached all over, her body chilled one moment and burning the next. Climbing to her feet beside her first patient, the world spun and she had to steady herself. She raised a shaky hand to her forehead, took a few breaths.

Definitely ill, but it didn't matter. The men were suffering much more than she was and they needed help.

She worked with the wounded until late evening. When she'd done all she could for the men placed in her care, she went to check on Tim and found him sitting up in his bed reading, most comfortable in that position since the blood and mucus didn't clog his lungs as much. His breathing had worsened some since the last time she'd seen him, but his smile was as cheery as ever.

Outside in the enveloping twilight, exhaustion crept in with its heavy cloak, pulling her down like a weight. She shivered and placed a hand to her cheek, knew it must be raging hot. Just the fever then, she reasoned. The fever was making her weak.

This was no time to get sick. The staff had enough patients to look after. If she worsened to the point where she couldn't do her work, she'd go home.

Walking across the grounds, a hollow emptiness filled her. Maybe her illness and intensifying feelings for Captain Thompson were to blame, but it had been a long, long time since she'd felt this alone.

Overhead, stars winked in the purpling sky. Tendrils of mist swirled on the grass and spilled into the hollows, pooling in puddles. Crickets sang, their chirps blending with the bass notes of male voices and coughs. She strode past wagons filled with severed limbs and dead bodies, a burial detail as it passed by on its way to the cemetery.

Tonight her ability to stay detached was gone. It was so hard to watch men she had nursed slip away before her eyes, though she'd learned long ago how to remove herself emotionally from it. It was the only way she could do this sort of work. Now it felt as if a giant fist was closing around her heart, squeezing, its grip ever tightening. Obviously her protective shell wasn't as thick as it needed to be, and her emotional distance from her patients wasn't great enough.

Especially when it came to one man in particular. She sighed, fighting an overwhelming urge to see him in spite of the inappropriate things he'd said to her. Despite her growing feelings for him.

But oh, how she would have loved for him to gather her up in his strong arms and hold her right now. Something twisted in her chest at the thought.

Without conscious thought she began walking to his tent. Standing outside it, she hesitated. What was she *doing?* The last thing she needed was to encourage whatever attraction existed between them. Nothing good could ever come from it. He'd be going home soon. She'd already had her heart broken when Caleb died. Did she want more pain when Captain Thompson left?

Standing outside in the dew-dampened grass, she had to admit he was worth the pain. She shivered, longing to go to him. Her heart slowed, throbbing hard in her chest. God help her, but -she needed him. Craved him with a power that frightened her.

Go to him.

The thought was so clear and commanding that she obeyed.

On the top step, she peered in. He was propped up, watching the flap like he'd been expecting her. The other beds were empty.

She swallowed. They might never have this kind of privacy again.

Brianna wrapped her arms around her ribs and took a step forward.

His gaze tracked her, filled with warmth and the same longing she felt. "Hello," he said in that deep voice that made her belly curl.

"Hello." She retreated into her nursing role. "How are you feeling? Any new bleeding?"

"No, and the pain's a bit better today. I can even sit up and turn over without help now."

She reached out and eased the placket of his nightshirt open to check the bandages on his ribs, relieved to find them clean. "Are you hungry at all?"

"No, I ate earlier." A heartbeat passed before he spoke again. His gaze probed hers, intimate enough to send a bolt of heat through her. "I was afraid you weren't coming back because of all the new wounded. And because of what I said the other day."

She averted her eyes. "Not at all."

"To think I waited around here all day for the chance to see you," he said with an exaggerated sigh. When she didn't so much as smile in response, he frowned and tilted his head, regarding her with growing concern. His gaze narrowed on her cheeks, then flicked up to meet her eyes. "Are you all right?"

Oh, his voice. Low and smooth as velvet. She shook herself. "I'm a little tired, is all." The fatigue pulled at her, more shivers passing over her chilled skin. She glanced at the stool beside the bed and gathered her nerve. "May I sit with you for a while?"

His expression softened with pleasure. "Of course."

She sat, wanting instead to curl up in his lap like a child and absorb his easy strength. His right arm pillowed his head, the gap in his shirt giving her an eyeful of his powerful biceps and sculpted chest. The lamplight played over his jaw and formed glowing blue highlights in his hair. She shouldn't be here. Not given how weak and vulnerable she felt. Not with this pull between them. Definitely not when they were alone.

As though he sensed her uncertainty, Justin reached out and took her hand, and let go when she winced. His sharp eyes found the angry marks coloring her skin, though the fever made her whole body felt bruised. He rubbed his thumb over them as if to soothe them away and met her eyes with another frown.

He raised a hand to her cheek, sucked in a breath the instant he touched her. "Brianna, you're burning up."

Brianna, he'd said. Not Mrs. Taylor. He sounded so concerned, his voice at once comforting and protective. Why did that make her want to cry? "I thought so."

"You need to see a doctor—"

"We ran out of ether and chloroform earlier," she said softly instead, taking solace in his presence. One patient had nearly bent the bones in her hands, he'd squeezed so hard in his agony. "That's how many men came in."

His frown deepened. "We need to get you some medicine."

She shook her head, not wanting to cause a fuss. Besides, the best medicine for her right now was being with him. He'd been right about her not wanting to admit her feelings, but it was a difficult thing to confess.

It hurt to feel this much again and know she was about to lose him. Of their own volition, her fingers slipped up to his cheek and swept a lock of hair from his temple, her need to touch him overpowering everything else.

He stilled at the contact, concern and growing heat battling in his eyes.

Something about the quiet way he watched her allowed her to keep talking. "I'm so tired of this war," she admitted in a whisper. "I hate all the butchering and the suffering and the death...I'm so tired of it all." He was a soldier. He must understand what she meant.

He hesitated a moment then lifted his hand and stroked a thumb across her cheek. The tenderness of the gesture zinged through her like lightning, speared her heart. In a different time and place, she might have leaned forward into that touch and kissed him.

Instead she stared at their joined hands resting on his chest. "I became a nurse to care for our soldiers, but instead I help patch them up so they can charge right back into battle." *Like you will when you recover.* Regardless of her efforts to stay calm, her eyes stung. "So they can go and get shot to pieces all over again. I *hate* it..." Her voice caught, throat too tight to continue. The prospect of him returning to the battlefield terrified her, even more than watching him leave here when he was strong enough.

"Brianna."

"What?" She drew a steadying breath.

He cupped her cheek in one large hand, eyes intent on hers. "I wish I could get out of this bed and hold you, but I can't, so you'll have to come here."

The air whooshed out of her lungs. She wanted that so badly she almost whimpered. Yet she didn't dare give in.

Those deep blue eyes never wavered from hers as he eased his hand around to cradle her nape and tugged gently. "Come here," he repeated in a low voice.

She sat paralyzed, fighting the compassion in his eyes, the longing his touch stirred within her. Her skin tingled all over. She held her breath as he cupped her jaw and trailed a thumb over her lips. His touch burned her.

Before she could protest, he made the decision for

her and pulled her close with the hand on the back of her neck. She sucked in a breath and made a last-ditch effort to resist, but it was futile. She could hear his soft breathing and feel the heat of his skin, the rapid thrum of her blood as it rushed through her body.

Undeterred by her hesitation, he determinedly brought her closer and angled his face until his cheek grazed hers. His breath fanned her temple. Goose bumps raced over her body. Patient fingers moved through the back of her hair and around her neck to her jaw, up the sides of her face. With agonizing slowness he caressed her skin with his fingertips, nuzzled her hairline.

Hunger roared through her in a blast of need. Her lashes fluttered against his cheek like the beat of a trapped butterfly's wings. Pressing her closer, he touched his lips to her eyelid, light as a sigh. She grabbed his hard shoulders and stiffened, but he didn't release her. Her entire body hummed with awareness as his gossamer kisses moved across her cheek, slowly enough to make her tremble.

Brianna grasped fistfuls of his shirt to keep from taking his face in her hands. She wanted to turn her head and kiss him back. Wanted it until her heart slammed against her ribs.

"Closer," he urged in a whisper. "Lay your head on me."

She trembled, part fever, part longing. "I can't. If someone sees—"

His grip on her nape tightened a fraction. The coolness of his hand felt so good against her hot skin. "I won't let that happen."

The protective tone melted her. She was aching for him. Weak.

That gentle grip turned firm, commanding. "Angel, don't fight me. Let me hold you." His voice was a velvet whisper at her ear.

Angel. His tenderness broke her heart. She didn't want to fight it anymore. This time when he guided her head down to his shoulder, she went willingly, careful to stay away from his bandaged side so she wouldn't hurt him. A soft groan of relief came from his throat, as though he'd wanted this as much as she had. His heavy arms encircled her, cradled her against the warmth of his body. He was strong and solid, even better than she'd imagined. The scent of soap and musk filled her nose, wrapping around her in another layer of comfort. She closed her eyes as he began to stroke a hand through her hair and a shudder rippled through her. Sweet God, she'd needed this.

His breath whispered against her temple, stirring more shivers. "I hate seeing you sick like this. And so sad. "

She laid a shaky hand over his heart. The steady beat of it beneath her palm soothed her. It was so wrong of her to want their bodies pressed flush together.

He shifted and brought her closer still, one broad palm gliding over the length of her back. She snuggled her cheek into him, craving so much more.

"I know you feel disheartened. I wish you'd never seen the things you have. And even though I would do anything to take it all away, you have to know you're a *wonderful* nurse." His other hand settled on the back of her head, caressing her nape beneath the thick knot of her chignon.

She shook her head, battling tears. A good nurse wouldn't be crossing a boundary that would surely get her dismissed.

I need him. Eyes still closed, she absorbed every sensory detail of the forbidden embrace. If this was all she'd ever have with him, she intended to remember all of it.

He continued the soothing motion on her back. "And you have magical hands."

Her throat closed up. "I wish that were true."

Justin stroked the crown of her head. So comforting. She yearned to crawl up and wrap around him, experience the full imprint of his body against her. Just for a minute.

"It is true," he insisted. "I would know you anywhere by your touch. When I was first brought in and couldn't even open my eyes, I knew instantly when you touched me. Your hands are gentle and soothing."

Brianna smiled against his shoulder. "That may be the nicest thing anyone has ever said to me." Did he feel this longing as strongly as she did? Or was he offering comfort because he considered himself indebted to her? She was on the verge of falling in love with a man she hardly knew. Maybe she was already falling. She wasn't sure anymore. "I have to go." Hating to do it, she pulled away from his embrace and forced her shaking legs under her.

He caught her fingers, moved them up to encircle her wrist so he wasn't touching the marks on the back of her hand. "Stay."

She shook her head. "I want to, but I can't."

His eyes searched her flushed face. They were shadowed with concern and something else she couldn't identify. "Promise me you'll see one of the doctors." He sounded so frustrated, she knew if he'd been well enough he would have been out of that bed in a heartbeat and coming after her.

"It's nothing serious."

His grip tightened. "Promise me."

Promise me...

Caleb's dying wish. She never thought she'd see the day where she might consider granting it.

"I'll see someone in a while if I don't improve." Maybe after she'd finished her next rounds she'd find Dr. Healey. If it was serious, she'd better do what she could before she became too ill to function.

He didn't look like he believed her. "Promise?"

"Yes." God help her, she wanted to lie back down beside him and burrow into his arms for the night. They'd felt like heaven around her. "Sleep well, Captain."

"Justin." The forcefulness of his tone jolted her. His gaze bored into her, demanding she acknowledge the irrevocable shift in their relationship. "Call me Justin."

She inclined her head, realizing there was no going back now. "All right. I'll see you in the morning, Justin." It felt so strange and forbidden to say his name aloud. Another boundary crossed. One of so many.

Wrapping her arms around her body, she walked out into the damp night air and shivered at the sudden chill pervading her.

CHAPTER NINE

Early the next morning, Dr. Healey burst into the tent Brianna was working in, carrying a pile of mail. Knowing he'd see the fever in her face, she ducked her head to avoid his sharp gaze. She pulled her shawl tighter around her shoulders and tried to stem the shivers wracking her so he wouldn't notice.

"Two letters for you today." He handed her the thin, yellowed envelopes with a smile and walked away. She left after him for some privacy, and walked to Justin's tent to stand outside it.

She shook her head at herself, the motion pulling at her cramped, stiff muscles. Her head throbbed. *You are pathetic and shameless. And you need to go home to bed.*

Turning her attention to her letters, she tore one of them open. Morgan's scrawling hand covered the page and she closed her eyes in relief. It was dated almost six weeks ago, but at least at that time he'd still been uninjured, in Georgia. They'd promoted him to lieutenant, since the others had been either wounded or killed.

She folded it to tuck it into her apron pocket and glanced up to find Justin watching her from his bed. He gave her a welcoming smile. "Good morning," he called out. "Feeling any better?"

"A little," she lied. The sight of him made her heart swell. His color was better and he seemed to be moving with much less difficulty. She entered the tent and bade the other men good morning, still embarrassed by her bold behavior the previous night.

Justin frowned as she reached his bedside. "You're still flushed. Did you see a doctor?"

"It's just the flu."

"Then shouldn't you be resting?" He arched a condemning brow at her, making her feel like she was one of his troopers facing his disapproval.

"I'll be fine."

He sighed but let it go and gestured to her hand, where the marks had faded a little on her skin. "News from home?"

She was glad for the change of subject. "Yes, from my brother, and thankfully he's doing well."

"I'm glad to hear it. Don't let me keep you from your reading." He eyed her with mock wariness. "I'll be a willing accomplice in any activity that spares me from having my wounds doused in carbolic acid."

Smiling, she tore open the remaining letter and read the unfamiliar handwriting.

Dear Madam:

We regret to inform you that on the evening of May 19, 1864, Major John Douglas succumbed to the effects of pneumonia after battling it for several days…

Her smile vanished. The words blurred on the page. All the blood drained from her face, making her feel even colder.

No.

She couldn't take this. Not now.

Brianna slipped the letter into her apron pocket, aware of an aching hole in her chest. Her father, dead? She swallowed, catching Justin's concerned expression.

He started to sit up, then winced and placed a hand against his bandaged side. "What's wrong?" he demanded.

"Please excuse me," she blurted. Without a backward glance, she hurried off to her temporary tent and sank down on the bed, staring numbly at the letter. *I should be crying.* She touched her cheek, found it dry and hot. There should be tears. What was wrong with her? Was she that callous?

Without warning, a memory came flooding back in a suffocating rush.

"What the hell are you doing here?" a male voice roared.

There was no mistaking the harsh tone, the fearful volume. She closed her eyes and squeezed her hands into fists to stop their trembling. *Do* something. She had to get Morgan away from the house before a fistfight broke out.

The housekeeper's voice carried up the stairs, shrill with panic. "For God's sake, Mistah John, let him go!"

Something smashed against the wall. A body?

She sucked in a breath and ran for the stairs.

Morgan's voice, cold and angry. "I won't fight you, Father."

"You'll be fighting me soon enough, you traitorous bastard! Might as well get this over with right here."

Her father stood in front of her brother, fists raised. Morgan's nose was bleeding. They faced off like prizefighters, unwilling to back down.

They locked gazes until Morgan strode past their father toward the front door. A deadly click halted him mid-stride. Brianna gasped, a hand flying to her mouth. Her gaze fastened on the revolver clutched in her father's hand.

Morgan stared impassively down the barrel of the weapon.

"Father, no! What are you doing?" The words tore out of her as she flew down the stairs and launched herself at him, trying to pry the revolver from his grasp. Drawing a gun on his flesh and blood? Was he insane?

His face was a mask of rage as he peeled her hand free. "Goddammit, Bree," he shouted, trying to push past her without hurting her and dodging Morgan as he came forward to protect her. "Get out of the way." He shoved her, sent her skidding into the wall at the same instant as a shot exploded.

Everything stilled.

The bitter tang of gunpowder hung in the air. Everyone was staring at her in horror. Or, rather, just above her. Slumped against the wall, eyes wide, she followed their gazes up to the single bullet hole marring the plaster, inches above her head. The blood drained from her face. She stared at it for a long moment, then back into her father's shocked face.

He'd nearly killed her.

Ashen, he cursed and stuffed the pistol into his waistband, then reached down to help her up.

"Don't you dare touch her," Morgan spat. He pulled her off the floor himself and brought her behind him, protecting her with his body.

From their own father.

A hysterical laugh bubbled up her throat. She

choked it down and lifted blank eyes to his as cold swept through her. He looked at her, then Morgan, pain marking every feature. He reached for her, expression full of apology, but she shrank back and pressed close to her brother.

His eyes dulled. He swallowed a couple of times, as if he might throw up. "I wouldn't have shot you," he said gruffly to Morgan. "I only meant to make you leave the house."

"Just get out of our way before someone does get shot." No one could have missed the threat underlying Morgan's words.

Her father's eyes pleaded with her for forgiveness, but she was too numb to say anything. She was cracking apart, screaming inside. Without a word, she turned and ran out of the house.

Brianna sucked in a shuddering breath and pulled herself out of the past.

That horrible day was the last time she'd ever seen her father. Now there would never be a chance for reconciliation, a hope she'd held on to all this time. Her stomach balled up hard beneath her ribs, nausea roiling through her. Oh God, she was going to be sick.

With effort, she jerked her mind back from the nightmare of her past and forced a few slow breaths to quell her uneasy stomach. She was still staring at the letter when Ella-May poked her head in.

"Bree, come quickly. Mr. Cunningham insists on seeing you—he's arguing with the surgeon about his leg and causing quite a scene." When Brianna didn't move, she gave her an odd look and came closer. "Bree? What on earth is the matter with you?" She laid a motherly hand on her shoulder. "You don't look well. Are you sick?"

Brianna looked up at her friend, wanting to cry. How could she bear this? "I...this letter..." She trailed off, unable to continue.

"Mr. Cunningham asked for you specifically."

Who? Oh, the cranky Texan she'd been looking after. "Is it serious?" She shivered, her body burning, hands and feet like ice. Just like the lump where her heart was supposed to be.

Her friend arched a dark eyebrow. "Would I have come for you if it wasn't?"

She sighed and pressed her hands against her throbbing temples. She was a moment away from cracking in two. *Focus. Don't think about it right now.* "All right." She got to her feet and navigated her way through the avenues of tents to find her distressed patient.

Turned out she could have found him blindfolded from all the yelling and cursing. By the time doctor Healey arrived and dismissed the other enraged—and clearly intoxicated—surgeon, a flood of weakness threatened to lay her out on the floor. At least they'd saved Zach's leg from a premature amputation. For now, anyway.

Facing her, Dr. Healey narrowed his eyes and stalked over to lay a practiced hand on her forehead, strong and comforting against her hot skin. She closed her eyes and leaned into it for a moment, her trust in him overriding decorum.

He pulled his hand away and shook his head at her. "I told you before you needed rest. Now go and lie down before you fall." His words were clipped.

"All right." She said goodbye to Zach, heartened by his grateful expression.

"Good day, soldier." Healey took Brianna by the

elbow.

"Good day, Mrs. Taylor," the Texan called, the lone Confederate in this part of the hospital. He waved at her, his silhouette outlined by the sunlight against the walls of the tent. "I can't wait to tell the folks back home how a brave little spitfire stood toe to toe with a man twice her size—drunk at that—and whupped him. Whupped him, by God! Are you sure that's not Rebel blood running through your veins? I'll never forget this, I surely won't. I'll tell my family about a nurse who had eyes the color of thunderclouds—"

Healey's lips thinned as he propelled her away from the delirious patient. "Let's get out of here before he starts writing sonnets about you," he grumbled. Outside, he took her by surprise by catching her chin in his hand and tilting her face up, his sherry-brown eyes delving into hers. "Your fever is high. I bet you hurt all over, don't you?"

She dropped her gaze and didn't bother to deny it.

He sighed. "Vomiting or diarrhea?"

Leave it to Dr. Healey to be blunt. "No."

"Abdominal cramps?"

She shook her head. If she'd had those symptoms or feared she was contagious, she would have gone home so as not to risk spreading them to the patients.

He grunted. "I want you to go to bed and stay there until you're better, do you understand? I'm going to send Ella-May in with some hot tea and broth, and then I'll be back to check on you when I can." He didn't release her, though his grip gentled and the hand on her elbow moved in a tender stroke over her skin.

Jerking her head up, Brianna caught the tenderness and quiet yearning burning in his eyes. It stunned her. How had she never noticed it before? He was her friend; she didn't want to hurt him.

He stepped back, cleared his throat and said a perfunctory goodbye. Brianna went straight to her temporary tent and crawled beneath the covers on her cot, too numb to know what to feel anymore.

When Ella-May woke her a few hours later, Brianna took in her friend's pinched expression and knew something awful had happened.

"I'm so sorry to wake you, but... It's Tim," she told her softly.

No. Not Tim.

Shivering, Brianna dragged herself out of her bed, stiff and achy, legs rubbery beneath her. The second she entered Tim's tent, she knew why Ella-May had come to her.

Tim lay on his back, wheezing. His face was an ungodly shade of gray and shiny from perspiration. She dropped her basket of medicine and moved to his side, pressing a hand to his forehead. Clammy and cool.

Her brain refused to believe it. *Don't quit, Tim!* She fought the sting of tears, struggled to raise his upper body from the mattress with desperate hands to help ease the strain on his lungs. The room swung for a moment before she could right herself and find her voice. "Someone help me!" she cried, bringing two more nurses rushing into the tent. They lifted him, propped pillows behind him, and he managed to open his eyes. Hope swelled, tight and painful in her chest.

"You're all right now, Tim. You can breathe easier." He was suffocating before her eyes and there was nothing she could do to help him. Tears clogged her throat.

Tim gave her a shadow of the smile that was so

dear to her. "Don't you...cry for me, ma'am," he rasped. "No...crying. I'll be—" He gasped and jerked upward, choking, his eyes growing wild with a moment's panic. Her heart twisted. After a few moments he seemed to calm again. "Heaven...soon."

He closed his eyes and relaxed, as if he was still aware that she was with him and would not leave him alone for even a moment. Brianna fought for every breath with him, dying a little each time he choked on the fluid in his lungs, hating the gurgling noises that told her he didn't have much longer, loving him even more for the way he tried to die as bravely as he had done everything else.

Pneumonia had eventually taken Caleb from her. And her father...his death must have been much the same as this.

Time dragged on while Tim labored for each rattling breath, the rhythm becoming slower, fading before her eyes. Brianna stayed beside him.

When that huge chest that had been full of nothing but heart finally stopped moving, she closed her eyes and a tear flashed down her cheek. The wheezing noises ceased and the tent filled with an eerie silence. Tim's eyes were closed, a faint smile on his lips even in death.

She barely noticed the other nurses leaving. She wanted to howl in agony.

Suddenly she couldn't hold back the tears any more. Resting her head atop her folded arms, Brianna split wide open, rocking herself with the pain. She tried to control it, but the grief crashing down on her was too overwhelming. It was too much. Everyone she loved was gone, taken from her by this damned war, and Justin would be leaving soon too.

As the torrent finished, she let out a painful sigh

and wrapped her arms around herself. She couldn't do this anymore. Couldn't deal with the constant suffering and loss.

Finally she stumbled back to her tent, only her stubborn will forcing her feet to keep moving. She was dizzy and numb. The fever had sucked the remaining strength out of her, had her trembling so hard she wobbled with each step. Someone asked her if she was all right, but she couldn't answer. Words formed in her brain and died on her lips. She wove, wanting nothing more than to fall down and sleep.

Her head swam. She was breathing too fast and her legs were about to give out. She'd never make it back to her tent on her own. The pain in her heart eclipsed all of it.

Her weary body carried her to Justin's tent. She dragged herself up the steps, knowing instinctively that he would take care of her. When he glanced up and saw her, his expression transformed to instant alarm. A loud hum filled her ears. Bright lights exploded in front of her eyes.

"Justin—" she mumbled. Her knees gave way and crashed to the wooden boards, but she barely felt the impact. She managed to crawl toward his cot. He reached for her, pulled her up, saying something to her in an urgent tone.

She struggled to get closer to him. He held her to his chest with one arm and murmured to her. She clung to him as the world tilted and swirled, his voice receding.

Then a pair of strong hands pulled her from him. She tried to shrug them off, refusing to be dragged from her only source of comfort. Dr. Healey's voice finally registered and she glanced away from Justin's worried blue eyes into the doctor's face, blinking as he grew fuzzy. Waves of darkness engulfed her. The graying world shrank to a pinpoint of light before she fainted in his arms.

CHAPTER TEN

His brother's urgent voice woke Justin from a deep and dreamless sleep. He blinked up at Mitch in confusion, struggling to see him in the dark.

"Get up, quick," Mitch ground out, shoving a boot at him. "Mrs. Taylor just collapsed."

What? Shaken from his sleepy stupor, Justin's hands felt clumsy as he struggled with his clothing and boots. Movement still took supreme effort, each tiny shift sending shards of pain through his side. Mitch helped him to his feet and supported him the best he could, ignoring his grunts of discomfort.

"What do you mean, collapsed? How bad is she?" Justin demanded.

"Bad enough that she thought I was you," Mitch said. "She stumbled into your tent looking for you and hit the floor before I could get to her. She was burning up, crying. And she kept saying your name—your *Christian* name. A doctor heard me yelling and carried her out. Now come on, move your ass."

He was already moving as fast as he could, and it

was too damn slow.

Justin knew he shouldn't be on his feet so soon after his earlier attempt had nearly landed him on his face. He'd received word he was being discharged and sent home in two days, so he'd figured he'd better get out of bed and try a short walk. If he hadn't made it into this tent and managed to climb into the empty bed he'd found, he'd be lying out on the ground somewhere right now instead.

With his right arm draped over Mitch's sturdy shoulders, his brother dragged him along in his wake, heedless of the pain it caused Justin. He clenched his jaw and fought through it. His legs were so weak he wasn't sure if he had the strength to make it to the surgeon's tent, but if Brianna needed him he'd get there, even if he had to crawl.

"Slow down, dammit," he finally rasped when he couldn't take it anymore, doubled over and hating that he couldn't keep up. It felt like there was a knife between his ribs.

"Sorry," Mitch muttered, easing his pace and shortening his strides. "It's only a little farther."

Justin grunted in reply and pressed on, his skin covered in sweat from the effort the walk cost him.

When he entered the tent and saw her lying on the cot, he stopped dead, heart clenching. *Oh, sweetheart.*

She was so still, so pale except for the fever spots burning on her cheeks. Jesus, how sick was she? Mitch hung back at the tent's entrance.

The young surgeon with the coppery beard hovered over her, applying cool compresses to her face and neck. "She asked for you," he said in a hard tone, clearly not happy about it. "I need someone to stay with her, and I have more surgeries to do. I'm willing to forgo rules and protocol for her sake and allow you to take over, but only because she wants you here. Are you up to it?"

"Yes." She'd asked for him. Even in her delirium, she'd asked for him. His chest tightened. He would do anything to protect her from harm, yet there was nothing he could do but sit here and watch her suffer.

The doctor grunted in reply and wrung out a cloth drenched in cold water. "Better make yourself comfortable."

Justin pressed his hand to his left side and sank into the chair with a wince. Another wave of clammy sweat broke out as his rib wound pulled, but all he cared about was Brianna. Taking her limp hand in his, he gave the doctor a questioning glance, and his guts clenched at the concern in the other man's eyes.

"She's damn sick," the surgeon said angrily, "and I don't like the sound of her breathing. I warned her again and again to rest, but she didn't listen. She needs about a week of sleep to put her right, if we can keep the fever down. If all goes well, she should be fine. Should be, that is, but Brianna will undoubtedly throw herself right back into her duties—"

"Unless you order her to take convalescent leave," Justin pointed out.

Healey faced him, something close to bitterness burning in his eyes. "If that's what I feel she needs, that's exactly what I'll do." He slapped the cool cloth into Justin's hand, none too gently.

Ignoring the other man, Justin placed it against her forehead, alarmed at the heat radiating from her skin. She didn't stir as he bathed her burning face, and he'd have given anything for her to open her eyes and look at him so she knew he was there. *Please be all right.* He brushed the damp tendrils away from her fevered brow, battling the helplessness.

Healey expelled a breath and watched him. "I'll be back to check on her as soon as I can. Stay with her while I find Ms. Davison to relieve you. If anyone questions your presence here, tell them they can take it up with me. Send for me immediately if anything changes." His gazed down at Brianna with an intense expression, and Justin read the anger and longing in the other man's eyes.

The surgeon cared deeply for Brianna and wasn't at all pleased she had called for another man in her distress. Well, that was just too damn bad, Justin thought with a surge of protectiveness. He was here and he would stay with her as long as he could, even if he ended up collapsing beside her.

Healey stalked out, and Mitch spoke up from the entry. "Want me to stay with you?"

Justin shook his head. "Go get some sleep. It's going to be a long night, and I'm not going anywhere."

The hours dragged on in an exhausted blur. Several times, Brianna's friend Ella-May came in to relieve him, and every time Justin refused her help. When the sky outside began to lighten, he started losing the fight to stay awake. The next time Ella-May came in, he finally acquiesced and allowed her to help him onto the cot next to Brianna's. Contenting himself that he was still beside her, he fell headlong into sleep and woke in the early afternoon. Brianna's condition hadn't changed much, but the fever was down a little. Dr. Healey had come to see her while Justin was asleep. After eating the bread and soup Ella-May forced on him, Justin resumed his turn with the nursing duties. Time dissolved in a repeat of the same routine.

At midmorning the next day, he rolled his head from side to side to ease the tension in his neck and shoulders, damning the sapping weakness that had him all but sprawled out beside Brianna. He didn't want to leave her until the fever broke. She'd been like this for almost two days now, in and out of delirium, and he'd stayed with her as often as he could. Whenever she opened her eyes and mumbled his name, something twisted in his chest to know she realized he was there.

I'm here, angel. I'm right beside you.

He wished they'd been alone so he could say it out loud, but instead he stroked her hair and murmured words of comfort until she settled. If he'd been able to, he'd have gathered her in his arms and cradled her against him. Seeing her so ill and fragile scared the hell out of him.

Shifting in his seat, he glanced up when Mitch entered the tent.

"How is she?" his brother asked.

Justin lifted his shoulders. "I don't know. A while ago she thought I was her brother." He blew a breath out. Surely hallucinations were not a good sign.

As though disturbed by their voices, Brianna opened her fever-bright eyes and squirmed. She tried to sit up, and he pressed her back against the damp sheets with a firm but gentle hand. "Shhh, lie still," he whispered, keeping his tone soft. "Just sleep for now. It's all right." She quieted and closed her eyes, turning her hot cheek into his palm with a sigh.

The implicit trust in the action set off a fresh ache in his chest. He wasn't sure when it had happened, but somewhere between the first time he'd opened his eyes to find her at his bedside and when she'd come to him last night, she'd managed to steal his heart.

She was kind and strong, yet he'd seen the startling vulnerability in her at times as well. The war had torn her family and world apart and she'd come here as a nurse, trying to help the men while earning enough of a living to support herself.

Justin had spent his entire adult life avoiding the prospect of marriage, and now that he'd met and gotten to know Brianna, the idea held a wealth of appeal. Though the knowledge shook him, it was the truth. He just had no idea what to do about it. The timing was all wrong.

It ate at him to know how alone she was in the world, with no one to turn to and no one to protect her. He wanted to offer all of that to her, and more. If she were his, there was nothing he wouldn't do to protect and take care of her.

But she *wasn't* his. And when he left this place in two days' time, he'd be leaving his heart behind with her.

****

Something cool touched her face. Brianna opened her eyes to find Justin in a chair next to her bed. He was holding her hand, his expression full of relief and tenderness. She blinked and tried to speak.

"Shh, save your strength," he murmured.

"You—you're up," she managed weakly, saying the first thing that came to mind. What was he doing out of bed? How long had she been lying here?

His lips curved. "Someone had to look after you."

What? She turned her attention to the doorway as Dr. Healey entered.

"Mrs. Taylor, you gave us all quite a scare." He took

her pulse then nodded in satisfaction. "Ella-May and one of your patients took it upon themselves to watch you in between my visits."

She blushed. "Oh, no…" Justin had been looking after her? While he was recovering from a bullet wound that had almost killed him? "I'm terribly sorry for the trouble." Her gaze darted to his side, visualizing the damaged flesh beneath his uniform. Had it started bleeding again because of her?

He opened his mouth to say something, but the surgeon beat him to it. "Captain Thompson's wound is healing nicely—thanks to you, I'm sure—and he has been up and about since your illness. Quite miraculous, really." He scratched his beard and exchanged knowing smiles with Ella-May, then turned his attention to Justin. "Captain, it appears you are quite a capable nurse. Keep her comfortable and let her rest. I'll leave you to it."

When he and Ella-May were gone, Justin squeezed her hand. "How do you feel, angel?"

The endearment made her heart swell, despite the embarrassment of him seeing her this way. Why had he stayed with her when he was still recovering from such a serious wound? "You look much better," she told him with a smile.

"Thank you. I feel much better now that I know you're going to be all right." He rubbed a thumb over her knuckles. "Because of your care, I'm starting to feel like my old self again. I'm still too damn weak, but I'm on my feet and ready for a visit home for convalescent leave."

Her eyes widened in denial, her heart stuttering. "You're leaving?" So soon? She'd already lost two precious days with him because of her illness.

He nodded, eyes full of regret. "Day after tomorrow."

You can't. "And you'll go back to the war, after you recover?"

His expression tightened at the accusation in her voice. "I have to."

A knot of dread formed in her belly. She closed her eyes to hide the pain that had to be written on her face.

Mistaking it for exhaustion, Justin drew the covers around her and stood, placing a hand on his injured side as he straightened. "You need some water and more rest." A moment later he pressed a cup in her hand and waited while she drained it. The cool liquid felt wonderful in her dry mouth. His white teeth flashed as he smiled. "Get some sleep and thank your lucky stars I didn't need to pour carbolic acid all over you."

"I'm grateful for that," she said with a weak grin.

His expression turned serious. Taking one of her hands, Justin raised it and placed it over his heart. His body heat warmed her palm, and the affection in his gaze tore at her. "You saved my life, Mrs. Taylor. I'll never forget that."

"I didn't—"

"Yes, you did."

A lump formed in her throat. "You're my favorite patient, you know. I don't know what I'll do when you leave." She felt a splitting pain as her heart cracked a little more.

His eyes glowed with tenderness, his expression inscrutable. "You probably say that to all your patients."

Only you. She held her breath as he leaned over the bed to touch his lips to her temple. When she felt strong enough to open her eyes, he was gone.

What a cruel whim of fate to bring him into her life

and then take him away before she had the chance to make anything come of it. War was a brutal teacher. The most important lesson it had taught her was that life was as short as it was precious. Closing her eyes, Brianna turned onto her side and nestled her cheek into her pillow. She'd lost so much already, she wasn't sure she could withstand this final blow to her heart.

CHAPTER ELEVEN

During her light duties the next day, Brianna felt much improved except for the lingering fatigue, and was grateful to be on the mend. Her father's death and Justin's announcement that he was leaving weighed heavy on her heart. She resisted the temptation to go to him, driven by self-preservation to start shoring up the defenses that lay in ruin around her heart, some part of her hoping it might hurt less that way when he left. Back in her tent that evening, she caught sight of her drawn face in the mirror and stared at her reflection. She looked awful. Pale skin, dark circles beneath her eyes.

She washed up, placed her towel back on its peg and escaped into the cool evening air. Breathing deep, she headed toward the copse of oaks along the riverbank to think about what she was going to do.

The hospital was no place for her right now. She wanted to go home.

It seemed strange to think of returning there after being away so long. Maybe rather than merely visit, she should take a leave of absence to see to her father's affairs. Perhaps she could get everything in order before Morgan came back when the war ended. The depot hospital was moving to Grant's base at City Point in a few days anyway, and she needed a reprieve from nursing. She was in no condition to look after anyone and refused to burden the staff by not doing her share. No matter how much it would hurt to enter the empty house or to visit Caleb's grave again, she had to go home.

Brianna pressed her lips together and fought back the pressure of tears. Crying was pointless. She needed to take back control of her life, start moving forward again.

She'd just reached the riverbank when hushed footfalls approached behind her. She whirled around.

Justin was walking toward her, his strides stiff and measured due to his wounded side. He wore his freshly laundered uniform trousers and shirtsleeves, the collar of his shirt open. Although her heart tripped at the sight of him, she glanced away. There was no way she could maintain an emotional distance from him.

"Brianna?" His low voice almost undid what was left of her composure. "Are you all right?" When she didn't answer, he set his hands on her shoulders and gently turned her around.

She squeezed her eyes shut at the contact and bit her lip.

"Ella-May saw you come down here and came to get me. Tell me what's wrong," he urged.

She looked up at him, eyes stinging, no matter how hard she fought the tears. Where to start? "My fath—" She pressed her lips together to choke back a sob. *Hold on. One breath at a time.* She paused and took a shaky inhalation, then another, until she had control once more.

"Your father?" he finished for her, searching her face. He dwarfed her with his size, made her long to hide in his arms.

Instead she nodded, exhaled. "He died of pneumonia a few weeks ago. I found out the day I got sick." Her voice caught. She swallowed and cleared her throat. "First my mother, then Caleb, now my father. The last letter I received from Morgan was dated almost six weeks ago—he could be gone too." The pain gouged her but she forced the words out. "He and my father had a falling out. Hadn't seen or spoken to each other since the day Morgan left for the front. My father threatened to shoot him." *He nearly shot me instead.* The shock on Justin's face made her close her eyes against the weight of it all. "If my brother's gone, there's no one left."

And now you're leaving me, too. She would never say it aloud. The last thing she wanted was his pity.

Justin made a low sound and slipped his arms around her back to draw her to him. She pushed against his shoulders, afraid she would cry. He didn't relent. "Angel, I'm so sorry. I had no idea."

She shook her head and held herself rigid. The pain worsened when he touched her, reminding her of all she couldn't have. It tore her apart.

The muscles beneath her hands flexed as he eased her nearer, his strong arms closing about her. "Stop fighting it."

"No." Struggling to hold in the sobs, she twisted away, but he wouldn't let go. She didn't want to risk pulling his wounds so she stilled when he kept insisting, her muscles so tight they trembled. "Let me go."

He didn't. "I can't."

Oh, *God.*

With a choked sound, she gave way to the unstoppable tide of grief and leaned against him, her face pressed into his chest. Justin sighed and held her tight, cradling her against his body. Sheltering and protecting her. Ragged sobs tore from her no matter how hard she fought to contain them, sharp and painful.

"Let it go," he murmured into her hair. "I've got you."

His stubbled cheek rested on the top of her head while his body absorbed her shudders. He held her in silence, not trying to placate her, and stroked her hair until she quieted and sagged against him. His quiet acceptance of her grief allowed her to remain burrowed against him during the last quivering gasps. The warmth of his body surrounded her, seeping into her cold skin. It had been so long since she'd had someone to lean on, and he was so big and solid.

Then she felt a sudden tension in him, the subtlest shift in his muscles.

She stiffened when Dr. Healey's voice called out from behind them. "She all right?"

Justin shielded her from view with his body. "She's fine."

Her stomach dropped. What would Healy do? He could have her dismissed for this. The silence stretched out, thickening by the second. Unable to stand it a moment longer, she peeked around Justin's shoulder.

Healey was staring at them, his expression a combination of concern and barely leashed jealousy. "I'm sure you are aware that Mrs. Taylor has her reputation to consider," he said in a flat voice. "Certain kinds of gossip could ruin her career, not to mention her good name."

She sucked in a breath, but Justin merely nodded, his arms steady about her. "I'm aware of that."

Healey smiled thinly. "Yes, well, just be sure to have her back to her quarters before anyone else stumbles upon you. You seem to have everything under control. As usual," he added under his breath as he trudged away.

As soon as his footsteps faded, Brianna let out a breath she hadn't realized she'd been holding. "Thank you," she said with a sniff and pulled out of Justin's embrace to wipe her face with her sleeve.

"Here," he offered, brushing tears away with his hands. Then he gingerly sank down to sit on the riverbank and drew her down beside him. He draped his right arm across her shoulders and gazed out at the water.

Night was closing in. Visible beyond the treetops, the three-quarter moon touched the river with its pale rays as the water flowed past them, each ripple sparkling like diamonds. The cicadas sang their evening serenade, creating a lullaby with the breeze whispering through the canopy of oak leaves above them. The damp scent of the river drifted up to blend with the green of the grass. What was Justin thinking? She waited for him to speak.

"The letter about your father," he finally said. "You read it while you were in my tent, didn't you?"

She nodded.

"Why didn't you tell me?" He leaned back enough to meet her eyes. "About any of this?"

"I didn't want to burden you with my personal problems."

He shook his head at her as though disappointed. "You're anything but a burden to me." Tucking her in close to his uninjured side, he rested his chin on the top of her head. "Leaning on someone once in a while doesn't make you weak."

Well, it made *her* feel weak. These past few years had forged her into a stronger, less vulnerable version of her former self. She'd had to learn to face everything alone. Brianna stayed nestled against him, allowing the peace of the evening and Justin's company to wash over her like a healing balm.

"What will you do now?" he asked after a long pause.

Being pressed up against him made her tingle from head to toe, but she did her best to ignore it. "Go home to Lexington. It would be the least I could do in my father's memory—get everything in order before Morgan returns."

A sudden tension crept into his body. "How will you get there?"

She smoothed her skirts, tried to lighten the mood with a bad attempt at a joke. "By train."

His stare weighed on her like a stone. "You plan to travel all the way to Lexington alone?"

She kept her gaze on the quiet river. "I've become quite accustomed to traveling on my own since Caleb died." It surprised her that it didn't hurt to say his name in front of Justin.

He made a frustrated sound. "How am I supposed to go home and recuperate when I know you're out there somewhere all alone?"

"I've made the trip before. I'll be fine."

A muscle in his jaw flexed. "I wish this damned war would end."

"We all do." How could she still breathe with this pain in her chest? He was leaving, and she would probably never see him again. If she didn't tell him how she felt about him now, she never would. Still, she cringed at the thought of baring herself to him that way. "By the way, thank you for staying with me. For taking care of me."

"You don't need to thank me for that."

She swallowed. "I also...owe you an apology."

He looked down at her. "For what?"

"For snapping at you the other day when you asked me about Caleb. I'm sorry."

One corner of his mouth turned up. "I'm the one who should apologize. I shouldn't have baited you. Actually, I admired the way you defended him. He was lucky to have you." He tipped his head back to stare up at the stars. "So you're sorry and I'm sorry. That makes us a sorry pair, doesn't it?"

Brianna rested her head against his shoulder and gave a sad smile. Digging deep for her courage, she forced the words she needed to say past the lump in her throat. "I was doing just fine until you came along. No one has made me feel anything in three years, and then you showed up."

He smothered a chuckle. "I hope you don't expect an apology for that, because you won't get one."

Her cheeks flushed. "I don't understand how it happened, but..." *Just say it. Say it and get it over with.* "I have very strong feelings for you." She almost strangled on the admission.

"Is that right?" His fingertips stroked over her sensitive nape, spreading the growing heat inside her. "How strong?"

She risked a glance at him, swallowed at the

longing she saw in his eyes. "I... Strong."

"Strong enough that you would wait for me?"

Her breath caught. She gaped at him, sure she must have misunderstood. "Was that some sort of a proposal?"

He gave a rueful laugh. "Not a very romantic one, but...after a fashion, yes. I want to be with you and take care of you." His gaze locked with hers as he cupped her cheek in his palm. "I'm falling in love with you."

Her eyes widened. It was the last thing she'd ever expected him to say.

"In light of all that, I want to be sure you'll wait for me until the war is over."

Her throat tightened. This was more than she'd ever dared hope to find again, but a promise to wait for him? They couldn't be together until the war ended, and there was no guarantee he would still feel the same when it did. It didn't make sense that she would even contemplate the idea of marrying him, let alone allow herself to imagine having a family with him someday. But she did anyway, the flare of hope too strong to deny.

When he opened his mouth to say something else, she stopped him by placing her fingers over his lips. "Wait, just... Tell me again."

Justin's gaze darkened with longing. He gathered her hands in his and squeezed them, staring straight into her eyes. "I'm falling in love with you."

Her heart drummed in her ears. Brianna's feelings for him were so intense she hadn't dared trust them. Was that possible? For her to fall in love so quickly? She couldn't speak, simply drank him in and knew that no matter what happened, she'd remember this moment for the rest of her life.

"I think you care about me too," he continued, his hands warm around hers. "But are you willing to wait for me?"

A nervous jitter started in her belly. "Yes, I absolutely will." Her heart pounded like she'd jumped off a cliff.

Justin laughed at her astonished expression. "I realize we haven't known each other very long, and there's always a chance I won't live to see the end of the war—"

She put a hand over his mouth to stop the awful words and shook her head. "Don't even *think* like that."

He pressed a kiss to her sensitized palm before pulling her hand away. "With you waiting for me, how could I not come back?"

Fear bubbled up, thick enough to choke on. She buried her cheek into the hollow of his shoulder, afraid of losing him as she had everyone else. "I don't want you to go."

Justin cupped her face between his hands and tipped her head back to settle his gaze on her mouth. Her heart skipped a beat when his lashes dipped down and he lowered his head toward her. Brianna met him half way.

A rush of sensual heat swept through her when his lips settled over hers, firm and warm. She made a soft sound of relief and gripped his shoulders as long-buried desire exploded inside her.

Justin angled his head and took her mouth in a velvet caress of lips and tongue. His clean scent wrapped around her, citrus and soap, and he tasted of the lemon tarts she'd seen in the kitchens earlier. Her body tightened, pulsed, and her thoughts scattered. Even wounded he was much stronger than her, yet so gentle as he held her head still. He slid his tongue over her lower lip, turning her liquid with the hunger she sensed raging beneath his controlled exterior.

It only intensified the ache inside her.

Raw need ignited in her blood. Her breasts tingled as a wave of heat engulfed her, making her breathless. This kiss wasn't enough. She wanted his hands on her, all over her bare skin. Wanted to hold him inside her body as deeply as she could. She craved the release her body clamored for. Brianna shifted to her knees and twisted closer to him. A frustrated whimper slipped out of her and she arched her back to press her breasts against him to find some relief.

Justin held her firmly in place, teasing her with his tongue. Impatient, Brianna touched her tongue to his. He tangled both hands in her hair and groaned as he fused their mouths together.

More. She buried her hands in his hair and kissed him with all the longing burning in her heart. He stroked his tongue against hers and trailed a hand down the side of her neck to her shoulder, then lower to graze the side of her breast. She pushed into his palm with a ragged moan as her nipples hardened, aching for his touch. Still kissing her senseless, he obliged her and rubbed his thumb over one distended peak through the bodice of her dress. The sudden jolt of sensation set off a desperate throb between her legs, made worse by the hard length of the erection she could feel pressed against her belly. She pressed her hips against him and arched into his hand, begging for more, crying out into his mouth when he gently tweaked her nipple.

"Sweetheart," he rasped against her lips and repeated the caress, making the pleasure burn hotter. God, she wanted him, his weight on top of her and his naked skin against hers. She wanted to feel him inside her body, filling and stretching her while the waves of pleasure took her higher.

Before she could get enough of him, Justin broke away and stared back at her with smoldering blue eyes. "Brianna..." His voice was strangled. He dragged a hand through his hair, scrubbed it over his face. When he met her gaze, the naked hunger in his expression made her breath catch. "If we had more privacy, I'd—" He stopped whatever he was about to say and shook his head. The muscles in his jaw bunched, and as quickly as it had appeared, the flame in his eyes was extinguished behind an unreadable mask. "I'd better get you back to your tent before someone else comes looking for you."

Disappointment filled her. Her body ached and throbbed with unfulfilled need and there was no relief in sight, but she knew he was right to stop. "I... All right."

For a long moment Justin didn't move, searching her eyes. Then, as though he couldn't help himself, he leaned down and pressed a slow, lingering kiss to her lips. When he eased back he pulled in a breath and covered a wince, one hand pressed to his wound.

"Careful," she warned, coming to her knees on the grass to lay a protective hand over his bandaged side. She hated that she might have hurt him.

Justin caught her wrist and pressed her palm against his prickly cheek. Banked heat glowed in his stare, and this time as he leaned in and kissed her his embrace was fierce, possessive. The slow glide of his tongue against hers made her whimper. He tore his mouth away and sucked in a breath. "God help me, Brianna, stop tempting me."

"Am I tempting you?" she whispered, glad he was

as frustrated as her.

"Enough to make me lose my head." He hugged her to his chest with one arm, his low chuckle muffled against her neck. His lips trailed soft kisses there, the stroke of his tongue causing her to shiver and close her eyes. "The instant the war is over, I'm coming to find you," he vowed, pulling back to stare down at her. "I swear I'll find you." Rising stiffly to his feet, he offered his hand and helped her up.

Joy bubbled inside her, a bit alarming, since the happiness she'd known with Caleb had been bittersweet and fleeting. Just for a moment, Brianna allowed herself to hope for a future with Justin.

He escorted her back to her tent in the moonlight with his arm tucked through hers. She was hyperaware of him, every sense heightened by the feel of the muscles shifting beneath her hand and the clean, musky smell rising from him.

He stopped in the shadows to kiss her once more, held her tight to him and let her feel the length of his erection pressed against her belly. If he was leaving tomorrow, she wanted to be able to sear his scent and taste into her memory. Kissing him slow and deep, she made a soft sound into his mouth and twined her hands in his thick hair. With a raw groan, Justin swept his hands to her hips and pulled her flush to his body, rubbing his hardness against her. But all too soon he stepped back, breathing hard.

His eyes seemed to glow in the darkness. If they'd been somewhere with enough privacy, Brianna knew without a doubt that he would have stripped her naked and given her everything she was begging for, his healing wounds be damned.

And she would have loved every moment of it.

Instead, Justin pressed his forehead to hers a moment, then cupped her cheek and brushed a thumb over her kiss-swollen lips. "Will you see me off in the morning?"

Unable to speak past the sudden lump in her throat, she forced a smile and nodded.

He seemed to relax at that. "Sleep well, angel."

With how tightly wound her body was, she wasn't going to sleep at all, but she had to let him go. "Goodnight." With a final longing glance at his tall frame as he strode away, she closed the tent flap and crawled into her cot beside Ella-May's. Turning her face toward the canvas roof, she stared into the darkness and let the bittersweet tears trickle into her pillow.

CHAPTER TWELVE

The sky above the distant ridge of trees was touched with rays of coral and tangerine the next morning, heralding the arrival of dawn. Wrapping her shawl tighter around her to ward off the early morning chill, Brianna scanned the landing for him. Beyond the growing crowd at the dock, the river flowed past on its journey to the sea, its surface cloaked in a silvery mist.

She'd hardly slept last night, trying to process everything that had happened. Had she really agreed to wait for Justin? It was madness, practically guaranteed another broken heart.

Caleb had known her for years before courting her, and their relationship had been based on long-lasting friendship. She and Justin had known each other less than two weeks. If he was serious about coming for her when the war ended, what did they have to build on besides admiration and explosive physical attraction?

People get married every day based on less.

Hugging herself to chase away the chill in the air,

Brianna hurried along the bank toward the dock with her heart full of dread. After today, she might never see him again. The thought made her hands shake.

At last she neared the wharf. Soldiers scurried about their morning routines, wagons creaked as they passed. The hospital was a flurry of activity as it readied patients for transport to Washington aboard steamships sailing down the Pamunkey River to the James. Justin and his brother would be among its passengers, making their way back to Michigan via Washington. She took solace in knowing they'd be traveling together.

The landing came into view at last, shrouded in mist. Men loaded coal onto the ship's deck to be stored below. Others ported luggage and stretchers. She'd dreaded this moment. Another painful goodbye.

When the wounded began boarding and she still couldn't find Justin, her heart lurched. It was too *soon*. They wouldn't have much time to say goodbye. She drew a shaky breath and scanned the length of the dock for him. He wasn't there.

Had he already boarded? She searched the crowds of men. Her stomach drew tighter. Had she missed him? Would he have left without saying goodbye?

When she turned back toward the hospital, a man appeared out of the mist. He stood in profile to her, outlined in the morning light as he made his way toward the landing, pausing to glance around. Looking for someone.

"Justin!" She flew across the dewy ground toward him.

He whirled around, a smile of relief crossing his face. He waited for her, watched her run across the damp grass in a flurry of skirts. She reached him at last, breathless in her haste, and wrapped her arms around his neck, careful of his healing wound. He gathered her tight to him anyway.

"Hi, angel."

She held on as tight as she could. "Hi."

After a minute, he raised his head to gaze into her eyes. "Thought maybe you'd changed your mind."

"Never."

He looked down at her for a long moment, as though he didn't know what to say. Finally, he reached into his pocket. "I have something for you." He handed her a package wrapped in cloth.

She unwrapped the gift, gasping when the fabric fell away to reveal a solid gold pocket watch. She tilted her head questioningly, knowing it must be precious to him.

"It was my father's. I wish I had something else to give you instead."

"It's beautiful. But I really can't—"

His hand closed around hers, pressing the watch into her palm. Infusing it with his warmth. "Take it. It'll make me feel better knowing you have it." His voice was low, shaded with regret. "Now at least you'll carry a piece of me with you wherever you go, and maybe you'll feel less alone." His fingers caressed the back of her hand. "Every time you look at it, you'll know I'm with you."

The words touched her much more than the gesture. She blinked back a sheen of tears. "Thank you."

The tenderness in his answering smile turned her heart over. In that moment, any doubts about her promise to him vanished. She would wait, and he would find her once the war ended. That was all she needed to know for now. All she would let herself believe.

Justin's thumb stole out to brush across the side of

her jaw, and she slid her hands up to rest against the solid wall of his chest, his heart thudding strong beneath her palms. She couldn't tear her gaze from his.

Someone cleared his throat. She jumped back to find Mitch grinning at them and smiled, trying to hide a guilty blush. "Good morning."

"I wanted to say goodbye myself, and thank you for the excellent care you've given my brother." He shot a knowing glance at Justin. "He's come along famously, hasn't he?"

"Thankfully, yes. I hope you heal just as quickly."

"I will." He took her right hand with his good one and pressed a kiss to the back of it. Then he turned to his brother, eyes twinkling. "I'll meet you on board, provided you don't get too distracted and miss the boat." He jerked his head over his shoulder. "It's that big white floating thing at the end of the dock."

"You'll have to excuse him," Justin apologized as Mitch strolled away. "He lives to annoy me."

"I think he's sweet." *And full of the devil.* How could they be having this inane conversation when he was about to board that ship and sail away?

Justin made a rough sound and shook his head. "I *hate* having to leave you here to face everything alone."

The churning in her stomach worsened. "I'll be fine. Let's both just hope the war ends soon."

"It'd better."

Glancing around, he tugged on her arm and led her behind one of the warehouses where the shadows gave them some privacy, then took her face in his hands and kissed her. One last kiss, she told herself, bracing for the moment when she had to let him go. There was a chance they might never see each other again, and she wanted a final memory of him to carry with her during this endless war.

She melted against him and closed her eyes, lost in the feel of him, warm and strong. He took her mouth hard this time, sending a bolt of heat into her belly and between her legs. More. She wanted more. Parting her lips, she stroked her tongue over his and pressed her breasts flush to his chest to stem the ache there. He explored her mouth with a raw groan that left her throbbing.

With one last fierce kiss to her lips, Justin buried his face in her hair with a low growl. "I don't want to leave you."

"Just stay safe and come back to me." She fought back the stinging rush of tears, blinking hard. "Please be careful," she blurted into his shirt, still clinging, not caring who saw them or what conclusions they would draw. She would be gone soon enough, oblivious to the gossip mill. The thought of something happening to Justin made her feel sick.

"I will be." He set her away from him to cup the back of her neck with one hand, his expression full of torment. "Promise me you'll look after yourself. No more making yourself sick by working too hard."

The ship's whistle blasted. Her heart squeezed in misery.

As the sound faded away, Justin's eyes brimmed with regret. "I have to go, angel."

With their last seconds together slipping away from them, Brianna hugged him tight, memorizing everything about the way he felt, the way he smelled. The strength of him wrapped around her. A sob worked its way up her throat. His arms tightened protectively.

"Don't cry," he whispered fervently against her temple. "I'd rather be shot again than make you cry."

"I'm not crying," she choked.

He kissed her temple, her eyelid to catch a teardrop before it could fall, and pulled away. *Don't go!* her heart cried in agony. *Don't leave me.*

"I'll write as often as I can, but there might be stretches when you won't hear from me." His smile was impossibly tender, so sad she thought her heart might break. "I'm coming back to you. Just swear you won't give up on me, Bree."

"I won't." Not while she was still breathing.

He pressed one last lingering kiss to her lips, then let his eyes sweep over her face. "Bye, Brianna. Never doubt or forget my feelings for you."

How could she ever forget? She smiled, though it felt like her face would shatter like glass.

Tell him you're falling in love with him too.

The words stuck in her throat.

Tell him.

God help her, she couldn't get the words out. They were too terrifying. "Bye." Holding her arms around her middle, she watched him walk away and bit the inside of her cheek to keep from calling him back. He glanced back at her from the dock and raised an arm to wave once.

She lifted a hand in reply, fighting back the hideous pain ripping through her chest. Why hadn't she told him?

You might never see him again.

Her heart pounded, urgency clawing at her.

You have to tell him.

She stood on tiptoe to catch sight of him. Too late. He was already boarding the ship.

Tell him.

Her breathing was shaky, her whole body

trembling at the pressure in her ribcage.

Justin was halfway up the gangway.

Tell him!

She took a stumbling step forward. *"Justin!"*

He whipped around at her cry and, when he saw her running toward him, pushed his way back through the throng as she raced over.

Tears clogging her throat, Brianna caught him around the waist and buried her face in his wide chest.

His hard arms closed around her in a protective embrace, one hand cradling the back of her head to press her cheek against his solid chest. "What? What's wrong?"

She lifted her head. *I can't let you go.* With a hard swallow, she gazed deep into his eyes. "I'm falling in love with you, too." The moment she said it, the painful pressure in her chest eased.

His eyes darkened, and a slow smile spread across his face. "I knew it."

Rather than laugh, she kissed him, dizzy with relief, not caring if she was making a spectacle. The ship blew its whistle again, sharp and grating on her nerves.

"Damn," he muttered against her lips. "I really have to go."

"I know. I *know.*" It was so hard to step back.

He bent to kiss her one last time, gave her a heart-stopping smile that warmed her insides. "I'm glad you told me."

"Me too. Now go." She stepped back and tucked her arms around her waist, tried to stay strong so he wouldn't see how devastated she was. Her teary gaze followed him back up the gangplank. Blowing out a deep breath, she lifted her hand in farewell, and at last he disappeared from view.

Alone on the dock, Brianna wiped her wet cheeks and tipped her head to gaze up at the vivid blue sky overhead, praying for strength. She'd never expected to find love again. *Did you do this, Caleb?*

Maybe she had a guardian angel watching over her after all.

Knowing better than to prolong the inevitable, Justin didn't dare look back at the shore until he was at the upper deck railing with Mitch. Brianna still stood where he'd left her, putting on a brave face when he knew she was hurting as much as he was. Maybe more. At least he had family to go home to, had Mitch with him now. She was going home to an empty house and her late husband's grave. It damn near killed him to know she had to face all that she'd lost alone.

He drank in the blaze of her mahogany hair as it moved in the breeze, her proud, graceful figure lit by the early morning sun, and knew that if he were close enough he'd find tears in her eyes. She was so compassionate and brave and beautiful it made him ache.

The ship's whistle let out a final blast. His heart seemed to stop beating.

I'm falling in love with you, too.

God, he'd live on those words the rest of his life.

As they pulled away from the dock, Mitch stood beside him, watching Brianna. She waved, and Justin nearly reeled from the pain in his chest, as bad as the bullet that had almost killed him. Wearing a brave smile, she blew him a kiss. He leaned over the rail to catch it with a fist, placing it first over his lips and then over his heart. Her laughing reply seemed to light up the entire horizon. He stared after her until she faded

141

into a speck in the distance and then rested his chin against his forearms with a groan.

A hand landed on his shoulder, and he glanced up into Mitch's face. He'd forgotten his brother was still standing there.

"You all right?"

Did he *look* all right? "Fine."

"Don't worry, old boy. You'll be with her again one day." Mitch's lips curved in a devilish smile. "You're lucky I'm letting you have her, though. You wouldn't have had a prayer if I'd decided to use my considerable charm on her. She likes me better." When Justin arched a brow, he added, "I didn't see her blowing you a kiss just now, did I, Romeo?"

Brat. He appreciated his brother's efforts in lifting his spirits, though. Since he was in no shape to give Mitch the beating he was begging for, he chuckled, drawing a startled look from his brother. "Guess I haven't told you, but I asked her to wait for me."

Mitch looked surprised. "And she said yes?"

"She did."

Mitch frowned. "But she seemed so intelligent."

He slapped his brother's uninjured shoulder. "So how about you do your older brother a favor and distract him from his misery with a game of cards? We could even make a friendly wager."

Mitch's eyes narrowed in suspicion. "What kind of wager?"

"Poker. Winner gets pick of the stable when we get home."

"And the loser?"

"The loser—that'll be you, of course—gets Miss Stevens."

Justin pressed a hand against his healing wound at

the horrified look in Mitch's face. The idea of his headstrong brother saddled with Laurel made him laugh, despite how much it hurt his ribs.

Mitch snorted in disdain. "Forget it. I'll play for a different wager. Loser has to explain to Mother what happened to us."

Both of them grimaced at the thought.

"You realize this means you'll have to stop encouraging Laurel," Mitch added as they strolled inside. "It wouldn't do to string her along anymore."

Justin shoved him toward the staircase with a chuckle and a growled, "Go to hell."

CHAPTER THIRTEEN

June 13, 1864

Brianna gazed out the boxcar window at the emerald hills they passed, not really seeing anything. Her thumb toyed absently with Caleb's wedding band, now in its new location. Though she'd felt guilty doing it, she'd removed it from her left hand and placed it on her right because it didn't seem appropriate to keep it on her ring finger after she'd promised to wait for another man.

Justin would be almost in Washington by now. Was he all right aboard the ship? His wounds had seemed to be healing well enough, but infection or bleeding was still possible. At least they'd be home with their mother to look after them in a few days. Brianna had already sent a letter ahead to her with instructions about their conditions and special care Justin's wound might require once they arrived.

Stepping off the train in Lexington, she took a deep breath. Confederate soldiers moved to and fro, and women towed small children about by the hand. Men in civilian clothing stood in groups smoking, discussing politics and the war. She hurried past them all and hired a carriage to take her into town. On the way through the familiar streets, memories flooded her as she passed various buildings—shops and restaurants she'd frequented, the boutique where she and her mother used to have their dresses made, the livery stables her father and brother had visited so often. Before the war had ripped everything apart.

The driver helped her out of the carriage in front of Magruder and Son, attorneys at law, and she brushed at her wrinkled skirts. How would Gavin and his father react to her visit? The last time she'd seen them had been almost three years ago, standing over Caleb's freshly dug grave.

Squaring her shoulders, Brianna loped up the steps and opened the wooden door, the bell tinkling softly overhead. Gavin appeared in the foyer a moment later, his brown eyes widening in shock behind his wire-rimmed spectacles.

"Bree?" He rushed over to hug her, sweeping her off the floor. She was laughing breathlessly when he set her down.

"Hello, Gavin. How have you been?"

His clean-shaven face split into a wide grin, revealing the crooked front tooth she'd always found so endearing. "Fine. Been out east somewhere all this time, have you?"

"Yes, in Virginia, near Richmond." Close enough, anyway.

"Richmond?" He shook his head, brown eyes filled with wonder. "You look wonderful," he gushed, taking her arm and leading her to the offices at the rear of the building. "Dad," he called out, "you'll never guess who just showed up!"

Phillip Magruder came around the corner, his eyes rounding when he saw her. "My God!" he whooped, swinging her off the ground as well. "The very image of her lovely mother." A portly man somewhere in his fifties, he had graying hair and a neatly trimmed moustache and beard. His black eyes danced with humor. "Where have you been all this time, young lady?"

"In Richmond, nursing." She didn't care to elaborate and admit she'd been tending Yankees, knowing what staunch secessionists they were.

Phillip made a face at that and seated her in an overstuffed chair, settling behind his massive walnut desk to beam at her. "Can I help you with anything, my dear, or is this a social call?"

Brianna glanced down at her hands in her lap. What she was about to say would hurt him. "Actually, this is a business call." He waited expectantly for her to continue. "I recently received word that my father died of pneumonia."

Phillip's face grew ashen.

"I've come to see about his personal affairs."

He lowered his gaze to the papers spread on his desktop. "When did he pass?"

"In May."

He rubbed his fingers over his eyes. "My condolences, sweetheart. I know things were left unsettled—Gavin, get me a brandy, will you?" He swiveled to the file cabinet behind him, rifled through one of its drawers and set the appropriate documents in front of her as Gavin placed a brandy on the desk. "He had these drawn up before he left for the front,"

Phillip told her. "I'm afraid the changes he made might upset you."

She met his dark eyes without flinching, prepared for the worst.

"In effect, he cut Morgan out of his will and left everything to you."

Her stomach dropped. She stared at the papers in shock. "Everything?" she croaked. He had cut his only son entirely out of his life, just like that, after the incident at the house. She supposed she should have expected it.

Gavin laid a comforting hand on her shoulder. "He was angry. Felt he'd been betrayed."

She could easily imagine her father storming into this office after the shooting incident in the foyer, demanding Morgan be cut off for good. She cleared her throat to remove the catch of tears before she dared to speak. "Did he say anything else?"

"Yes." Phillip met her gaze, his own eyes moist. "He asked me to make sure you were well looked after, because he wasn't coming back. He said to tell you goodbye."

A chill raced down her spine as the meaning behind the words sank in.

Her father had left Lexington with every intention of dying to escape what had happened. He'd been grief-stricken, overwhelmed by guilt. She bit down on her lip, but the tears managed to slip down her cheeks nonetheless. Gavin hunkered down beside her, laying a hand over hers. She blinked fast and stared up at the ceiling in an effort to staunch the flow.

No more crying. No more tears. It doesn't help anything.

When she was back in control, Phillip laid the

papers in front of her, and she dipped a pen into the inkwell to sign her name at the required intervals. Expelling a deep breath, she raised her eyes to his. "You should know I intend to change all this. I'm going to sign everything over to Morgan when he gets back."

"I expected as much. Do you need someone to drive you home?"

She nodded. *Home.* The mention of it made her stomach knot. It would never feel like home again.

Gavin grasped her hand. "I'll take you, Bree. I think you'll be pleasantly surprised at what you'll find there."

A pleasant surprise would be welcome right about now.

He drove them through town in his carriage and turned onto the road that led to Greenbriar. Giant oaks lined the road, and freshly painted white fences enclosed lush green pastures. Horses grazed in the hot sun, their graceful necks bowed as they nibbled at the Kentucky bluegrass. Here it was like the war had never touched the land. She reveled in the sweet scent of clover and the fresh breeze blowing over her face.

"Almost there," Gavin said, squeezing her hand.

Her heart beat fast as the slope marking the driveway to Greenbriar appeared. Then she glimpsed the white-columned portico of the federal-style house she'd grown up in and bit her lip.

At the foot of the front steps she didn't wait for Gavin to help her from the wagon, but jumped down and hurried up to the wide front verandah. The house was still in amazingly good condition. Her fingers fumbled in her bag for the key to the front door. She turned it with shaky fingers and entered, holding her breath.

Everything was just as she'd remembered it. The

floorboards in the foyer still gleamed and smelled of wax, and the parlor still echoed with the tick of the antique grandfather clock she loved. Her eyes strayed to the upper wall, but the bullet hole was gone. Someone had patched and wallpapered the plaster in an attempt to erase that terrible event.

"Welcome home," Gavin said.

"It looks wonderful."

"It should. Someone's been waiting for you to come home."

"Well, I'll be!"

Brianna whirled around at the familiar voice. Teela, Greenbriar's housekeeper since Brianna was a girl, stood by the upper floor railing with her gnarled black hands on her lean hips, her thick gray curls pulled into a tidy bun at her nape. Her deep brown eyes glowed with joy.

Brianna squealed and launched herself up the stairs and into the aging woman's open arms. Teela held her tight and Brianna squeezed back, smiling past her at her husband, Ray, who stood in the hallway.

They had stayed. After all that had happened, Ray and Teela had chosen to stay at Greenbriar. "It's so good to see you," she breathed. "I thought you would leave after—"

"Now, girl, you know I'd never leave this place. Not while there's breath in this body."

"I'm so glad."

Teela's dark eyes sparkled. "How are you, chile?"

"No worse for wear."

"You look terrible thin to me."

"I was sick not long ago, but I'm fine now. Just glad to be home again." Her stomach growled at the thought of Teela's cooking.

The old woman frowned hard at her middle. "Your belly's talking. You come with me right now. And you too, Mr. Gavin."

They followed her swaying, bony form into the kitchen that smelled of cinnamon and molasses. Trays of freshly baked cookies cooled on the windowsill, half a row already gone.

Teela's lips compressed into an irritated line. "I hope them cookies done burned his thievin' fingers," she muttered, and stalked off to find her errant husband.

Gavin's eyes twinkled at Brianna as he cocked his head to one side and chewed a bite of cookie.

"What?"

He shrugged. "You've been gone for a long time and we haven't heard much from you. Just wondered if you have anyone special in your life now. Maybe someone you met in Virginia?"

She certainly wasn't going to tell him she'd promised herself to another Yankee. Gavin had accepted Caleb's choice to join the Union army only because they'd been friends since childhood.

"Ah, I see. There is, but you don't want to tell me who, is that it? Well, that's fine, because a little mystery is welcome in this dreary town. I wonder who he might be. Hmm...a young Confederate officer, perhaps? I'll bet he's handsome. And charming. Am I close?"

Not at all. "I don't know if I'll ever see him again."

Gavin barked out a laugh. "If that man has any sense in his head at all, he'll come back for you. And if he doesn't, it means he's either dead or stupid, and so in either case, not an acceptable suitor for you. Morgan and I would both kill him if he did anything to hurt you, and you know it."

"I do." She smiled and dusted the crumbs off her hands, feeling better already. "Well, I suppose I should take a look around, shouldn't I? See where we're at if I'm going to get this place up and running again."

He cast her a skeptical glance. "You're really going to do this? Run the farm, I mean?"

"I want to have something for Morgan to build on when he comes home."

"Bree, nobody's got stock around here anymore— whatever's left belongs to the armies. And you being a woman..." When she arched a brow, he folded his arms across his chest. "You sure you can do it?"

A fierce smile firmed her lips. After all she'd been through? "Watch me."

CHAPTER FOURTEEN

Near Belle Grove in the Shenandoah Valley, VA
August 19, 1864

Dearest Justin,

The property at Greenbriar is in much better condition than I could ever have hoped for, and there is little to be done for now except to secure some of my father's finances and purchase breeding stock. I know none will match Boy-o's exquisite beauty, but I shall have to make do with the animals I can find and afford.

Riding at the head of his men, Justin smiled at that and reached down to pat his mount's sturdy neck. This particular letter from Brianna was weeks old but one of his favorites because he knew he'd shocked her with his bold question in the previous note he'd sent her. He imagined her cheeks flushing wild-rose pink as she read it and wrote her reply.

In response to the question at the end of your most

recent letter, yes, I have always dreamed of having children someday. I was happy to learn that you want them as well.

In truth Justin had never put much thought into it until recently, though he couldn't deny that the thought of Brianna carrying his unborn child stirred a primal reaction in him. She was a passionate woman. Imagining being able to partake of the pleasures of the marriage bed with her left him hard and aching in his tent night after night. He could still recall the exact feel of her in his arms, the way she'd tasted and the hungry sounds she'd made as he kissed her.

This was neither the time nor place to be thinking about such things, however. With a mental shake, he refolded the letter and tucked it back into the left breast pocket of his frock coat, then pulled out the one he'd received from her that morning.

Dearest Justin,

I rec'd your letter of July 8th with much anticipation, and was relieved to hear that both you and your brother have been pronounced fit once again. I expect by the time you receive this note you will be back with your regiment. I pray that God will keep you both safe in His care. I think of you constantly, and fervently hope that we will be together again soon...

Lord, he prayed for that every day as well.

Justin skimmed down to re-read the way she'd closed the letter, and his heart squeezed.

Since becoming a widow I never expected to be able to give my heart to anyone again, until you. As terrible as those initial circumstances were, I thank God for bringing us together. I anxiously await your reply and pray that the war will come to a swift end. Until then, know that every night I dream of holding you in my arms again.

Ever yours,
Brianna

Boy-o snorted and tossed his head with a jingle of the bridle. Justin expelled a sigh and tucked the missive safely away. The tin of homemade cookies Brianna had sent along with it lay in his saddlebags, already half empty. Oatmeal with raisins and cinnamon were his favorites, and she'd remembered. Her thoughtfulness never ceased to amaze him. The words she wrote left him aching and anxious to see her again.

Justin focused on the terrain ahead. The steady beat of hooves on the dirt road mixed with the breeze sighing in the leafy branches above them. The column stretched in front of him as far as the eye could see, right up to where the lead element disappeared behind another hill. Receiving mail call before they'd moved out this morning had greatly boosted the men's spirits.

Since he'd left White House Landing he and Brianna exchanged dozens of letters, and he kept hers bundled in his saddlebags so he could pull them out whenever he had a moment to himself. He'd learned so much about her through her writing, things little and small that added so much to his understanding of her. She hated snakes yet loved lightning storms. Adored lemonade and baked ham dinner, and loathed lamb. He'd laughed at the amusing stories she'd told him about her childhood, the practical jokes Morgan had played on her and how she'd managed to get even with him. He'd shared the same with her in turn, telling her of the infamous exploits he and Mitch had gotten into as boys.

War made the future uncertain, and Justin was more conscious of that than ever. Not knowing what the next battle would bring or if he'd live to see her again made it far easier to be forthright with her about his feelings, and he put his heart onto the page in each letter he wrote her.

God, he missed her. The whole time he'd been recuperating at home, he'd thought of little else but her. Much to Laurel's bitter disappointment, he remembered with a shake of his head. She'd been just short of icy to him after she'd found out about Brianna, except for the day he and Mitch had left for the front. Then she'd cried and clung to him until her father had been forced to peel her off him.

It felt good to be on the move again. He stretched his spine and exhaled to loosen some of the lingering tightness in his chest. The healed wound in his side still ached when he was in the saddle for more than a couple of hours, but at least he was back with his regiment. The lush Virginia countryside they were traveling through was stunning. Rolling hills and hollows in every shade of green were crisscrossed with sparkling creeks flowing down from the Blue Ridge Mountains. If it hadn't been for their orders, moving through the Shenandoah would have been an idyllic assignment.

Since the cavalry had undergone another reorganization during his convalescence, the Michigan Brigade was now under Brigadier General Wesley Merritt's command. General "Little Phil" Sheridan had ordered the cavalry to follow Jubal Early and his forces to the death while stripping the Shenandoah of everything that might be useful to the Confederates. For the past four days, Justin and his men had seized and burned countless mills, barns, haystacks and warehouses, leaving plume after plume of black smoke hovering on the horizon.

Pushing the grim thought away, he recalled how Brianna had ended this latest letter and a smile curved his lips. She might dream of holding him in her arms again, but from other things she'd hinted at in her letters, he knew she also dreamed of more intimate things as well. Damn, he was a lucky bastard.

"You're in a fine mood," Williams said, riding beside him. "Got another letter from your sweetheart this morning, did you?"

"I did." He couldn't hold back a grin. Mail call was something they all looked forward to, and now he did more than ever.

Justin still worried about her being home, looking after her family's property alone except for her two servants. If the damn war would end, he'd go straight there and help, but there was no end in sight yet. This campaign was supposed to hasten the Confederate's surrender, and Justin fervently hoped it would prove true.

Raising his free hand, he wiped a sleeve over his sweaty brow. The late summer sun beat full strength on their heads and lathered the horses. The men were tired but in good spirits, always active on scouting missions, foraging or skirmishing with the enemy. Namely Mosby's Rangers, a partisan group from this part of the valley that was proving to be a thorn in the side of the Army of the Potomac's cavalry corps. Sheridan wanted the guerrillas dealt with at the first opportunity, but they were hard as hell to pin down.

The whole division had orders to confiscate supplies and destroy probable hideouts of the partisan troops, including the houses of five local families thought to be connected to Mosby's command.

As the column neared the farm of Benjamin

Morgan, Justin could hear Mitch chattering away behind him to another trooper. Ahead, the advance guard had reached the farm, and some sort of commotion had broken out. They kept their horses to a walk until shouts reached Justin's ears. Senses on alert, he palmed the butt of his Colt revolver and cantered ahead with Williams. His guts clenched when he saw the spectacle awaiting them.

Major Hastings and a group of officers stood staring at eighteen blue-clad corpses, all from the Fifth Michigan. Justin recognized several of the men. The grass was saturated with blood from their bullet-riddled bodies and two of them had had their throats slashed wide open. The cloying, iron-tinged smell of it hung in the air, thick enough to choke him. Clenching his revolver, he dismounted and peered at Hastings for an explanation. The major's clean-shaven, boyish face was a mottled red.

"Goddamn them to hell!" he spat, hands fisted at his sides.

Staring at his dead comrades, Justin understood his commander's rage. Those men had been slaughtered without any regard for the rules of war, as if they were livestock instead of human beings. Had Mosby done this?

"Captain?"

Justin shook his head at Williams, unable to speak as he swept his gaze over the carnage. One survivor, shot in the face, held a cloth to the wound in an attempt to stop the bleeding as a surgeon attended him. At least they had a witness to tell them what had happened here.

Hastings followed his gaze and grunted. "He says Mosby's men came through here disguised in Union uniforms. Shot them all in cold blood while they were on a burning detail."

Justin clenched his jaw until it ached. Every man in the Fifth, including him, would want Mosby hunted down like a dog for this. Once it reached headquarters, news of the heinous crime would make Custer fly into a rage and demand satisfaction. Justin imagined sparks of fury flashing in those bright blue eyes as the general ordered everything in the vicinity burned to the ground.

And so be it.

Brianna's letter pressed against his pounding heart like a weight. He could never tell her about this. Didn't want her knowing his part of the war had turned so ugly, or to find out what he would have to do in the coming days. Because reprisal for these murders would be swift and terrible.

Oh yes, he thought as he looked at the bodies of the fallen troopers. Someone was going to pay for this. In blood.

****

September 19, 1864
Lexington, KY

My darling Brianna,

I rec'd your letters of August 15th and 19th with great eagerness. Having word from you regularly is a great comfort to me, and as always I find myself looking forward to mail call each day in the hopes that another of your letters has arrived.

You might have heard that we are under Sheridan now, and that we are conducting a difficult and unfortunate campaign in the Shenandoah Valley. The work is terrible, but the men are in fair spirits. My hope is that our effort, while hard on the civilians, will expedite the end of the war and my return to you. I loathe the thought of you shouldering all the responsibilities you have undertaken on your brother's behalf, and regret that I cannot be there to help relieve you of the burden.

I miss you so very much and also pray that we will be together again soon. Until then, stay safe and warm, angel.

Affectionately yours,

Justin

Brianna's eyes stung as she folded the letter and placed it in her apron pocket. *She* was safe and warm, while he was deep in enemy territory, sleeping out in the field every night while conducting a miserable task. She'd read about the atrocities committed in the Shenandoah in the papers, though this was the first time Justin had mentioned it in his letters. She missed him so much she ached, and the time apart hadn't dulled the pain at all. Nearly every night she dreamed of him, sometimes erotic dreams that woke her with her heart pounding and her body aching for fulfillment. Other times she dreamed of death and carnage and woke with tears on her cheeks.

Rising from her chair, she stirred the fire, anticipating the moment when she could finish up for the day and soak in a hot tub. If she had the energy to haul all that water to the tub once the ledgers were finished. The return trip from her disappointing venture in Louisville had sapped whatever reserves of optimism she'd left with.

She'd known from the outset it wouldn't be easy to replenish Greenbriar's stock, but she'd hoped to have more success than this by now. So far, none of her father's old sources had helped much. She'd managed to buy a couple of mares and one stallion, but they wouldn't arrive for weeks and it was a pitiful number of animals to try and restart the business with. She braced her hands against her lower back and stretched the sore muscles with a sigh. Without Morgan's guidance, she'd have to do the best she could. She hadn't heard a word from or about him since leaving White House, so for now she was on her own.

As for Justin, she had a stack of letters tied with blue ribbon and many trinkets from him in the desk next to her bed. Every day she tracked his progress through the Shenandoah via the papers. What an odd courtship they had, she mused, rubbing the back of her neck. Without being able to see one another, they were forced to rely on correspondence to grow closer. And somehow, even though they were hundreds of miles apart, learning what he was thinking and feeling through his own words made her feel especially connected to him. She admired his principals and his courage, and that he was willing to lead men in the fight he believed in. With every letter she fell a little more in love with him.

She still worried about him, though, and not just about his safety. He never said it outright in his letters, but she could tell he hated what they were doing in the Shenandoah.

As far as Brianna was concerned, the end of the war couldn't come soon enough, though she felt badly for the civilians the burning affected. She hated the thought of families and children being hungry and cold in the coming winter if the war continued. Why was it always the non-combatants who ended up suffering the most in war?

The rattle of a buggy pulling up in front of the house broke her from her thoughts. Her heartbeat quickened. Could it be Morgan?

Brianna pushed the drapes aside to peer out into the darkness. She didn't recognize the vehicle. Someone knocked on the door a moment later, and an internal voice warned her not to answer it.

She opened it anyhow. "Mr. Ramseur," she said, surprised her father's former business partner would come calling so late at night. Over the past few weeks he'd developed the disagreeable habit of showing up unannounced, but never this late, and never when she was alone. Teela and Ray had already retired to their small house beyond the back pasture.

The intense way Ramseur watched her never failed to make her uneasy, even with his offer to help her obtain stock for the farm and locate her brother. Last she'd heard, Morgan had been somewhere outside of Atlanta, though the city had fallen on September first and there hadn't been a word from him since.

"Hello, Brianna." Ramseur's amber eyes glimmered in the low light. "May I come in?"

She resisted the urge to case a glace over her shoulder. He really shouldn't come in when no one else was here, but he walked right past without an invitation, apparently mistaking her silence for permission. Biting back a sigh, she pushed the door shut and followed him into the parlor, where she stood next to the fire.

"I don't bite," he teased. "Come and sit down. I have something to discuss with you."

She sank stiffly into the chair. "May I offer you some lemonade and cookies? I have some fresh—"

"No, thank you, dear."

She hated it when he used endearments, something he couldn't have failed to notice.

He leaned back in that deceptively casual way of his and stretched his legs out. "I think you'll find what I have to tell you of great interest."

She waited, annoyed that he kept her waiting. "And that is?"

He met her gaze. "I know where your brother is."

Her heart seemed to stop beating. "Where is he?"

"Libby prison. Richmond."

"What?" She shot forward in her seat with a hand on her throat, the painful thud of her heart loud in her ears. Libby was notorious for its awful conditions.

"It's quite true, I assure you."

She couldn't believe it. "How long has he been there?"

"A few months now. But he's alive."

Yes. For now. "Will he be exchanged?"

Ramseur shook his head. "Not likely, things being as they are after the Fort Pillow incident. You can be thankful he's an officer. He's living in much better conditions than most of his men, who were sent to worse places."

She stood and paced in front of the fire, mind working furiously. "How can I help him?"

"Well, now, that all depends on you, dear, and exactly what you are willing to do."

His tone sent a warning prickle up her backbone. She met his gaze head on and raised her chin. "I'll do whatever I must."

He tilted his head admiringly. "Have I ever told you how beautiful you are when you get riled up? You look just like your mother."

Brianna hid a frown. Previously he'd hinted at some kind of relationship with her mother but had never given any details. The string of compliments he lavished upon her made her uncomfortable, and that discomfort increased every time he became more forward in his advances. "You knew my mother, Mr. Ramseur?" she asked, trying to remain calm when all she cared about was learning more about Morgan.

"Call me Paul. I think we know each other well enough to dispose of the formalities."

I think not. She forced a stiff smile.

"I knew your mother, yes." His intense appraisal of her made her want to fidget, but then his lips curved downward. "We were engaged for a short time before she met your father." He must have caught the disbelief in her face, because he raised a brow. "Oh, it's quite true, I assure you." He smiled to himself at some distant memory.

Brianna swallowed the denial on her tongue. She couldn't imagine her mother ever being linked to this man. "I don't know what to say."

"Don't say anything, my dear. What's done is done. That was a long time ago, and since I am a practical man, I should like to focus on the present." He got up and sauntered to the sideboard, helping himself to a glass of sherry. "I might be able to help you learn more about Morgan. I do have some reliable connections in Richmond…" He left the sentence dangling, and she knew it was because he wanted something from her first. When she didn't answer, Ramseur gave her a wolfish smile and crossed the room to take her hands. "You must know how I feel about you by now. I had hoped you might regard me with the same…affection."

The instant the words were out, Brianna snatched

her hands away and stared up at him with mingled confusion and anger. "Meaning what, Mr. Ramseur? That you won't help me unless I agree to marry you?" She wouldn't subject herself to a life with him, not even for Morgan.

"Marriage is not necessary, my dear, if you would prefer a different arrangement."

Her shocked gasp made him stiffen. She backed away a step, too stunned by his forwardness to answer.

His brows lowered and his cheeks flushed as he glowered at her. "Good God, girl, I'm not going to force myself upon you. You needn't act as though I was about to throw you to the floor and have my way with you."

"I can't believe you suggested that I...that we..." She couldn't finish the vile sentence. At least he had the grace to flush.

He cleared his throat. "Well. I have my answer, don't I?" He tried for a polite smile. "Turned away by both mother and daughter," he muttered, setting his drink aside. "It seems I have no luck where the Douglas women are concerned."

Brianna didn't have the faintest idea of what to say in reply.

Ramseur tugged at the bottom of his waistcoat. "Let's just forget this unfortunate incident, shall we?"

Not likely.

At her reluctant nod, Ramseur retrieved his hat. "Give me a day or two to see what I can come up with about your brother. I'll be in touch." He left her frozen in place, staring after him.

Brianna had no intention of waiting for him to contact her again. Now that she knew where Morgan was, she was going to Richmond. But she needed money to get there and she'd spent most of her savings on the horses.

Rubbing the chill from her arms, Brianna ran to her bedchamber and packed a valise then threw on a shawl and raced outside. She stopped by the caretaker's house only long enough to tell Ray and Teela where she was going, then took Ray's old gelding from the stable and slipped a bridle over its head. Riding bareback, she clutched her bag to her chest and urged the horse into a gallop toward Gavin's father's house.

Leaping from the saddle when she reached the stately brick house, Brianna grabbed a handful of gravel from the driveway and started throwing the small pebbles at Gavin's bedroom window on the upper floor. She and Morgan had woken him this way dozens of time in the past when they wanted him to sneak out of the house at night.

Thwack! She hit the shutter.

Hefting her arm back, she wound up and launched another. *Thwack!*

Thwack...thwack... *Smash!*

The tinkling of glass made her cringe. She'd cracked the pane.

A second later, Gavin appeared at the window and shoved the sash up. He ducked his head out into the cool night air to glare down at her, dark hair all askew as he shoved on his spectacles. "Bree? What the *hell* are you doing out here at this time of night?"

"You've got to come down here right away," she said in a loud whisper, praying they hadn't woken Phillip. If Phillip found out about her plan, he'd do whatever he could to dissuade her.

"What's wrong?" Gavin demanded, his gaze on her packed bag.

"Just come down!"

Grumbling, he disappeared inside and shut the window. A minute later, she met him by the back door and launched into what had happened without giving him a chance to ask questions. "Paul Ramseur came by to tell me Morgan is in Libby prison and that if I would be so kind as to become his mistress, hinted that he would do what he could to help get Morgan paroled."

"What!" Gavin stopped shoving the tails of his nightshirt into his trousers and grabbed her by the shoulders. "My God, that pig of a bastard. I'll call him out for you. Let me get my gun." He whirled on his heel.

"Wait!" She snagged his arm. "Of course I refused, and would prefer never to lay eyes on him again, but that's neither here nor there. I need to get to Richmond as soon as possible and—"

"No more," Gavin interrupted, shaking his head. He yanked off his spectacles and scrubbed a hand tiredly over his face before placing them back on the bridge of his nose. "What sort of harebrained scheme are you plotting? Do you think you can just prance up to the prison authority and say, 'Please, sir, will you let my brother out?'"

"I don't know what I'm going to do once I get there, but I have to do *something*. You've heard how bad Libby is. What if he's wounded, or sick? He could be dying. I have to at least try to help."

"You're crazy for even contemplating such a thing. What good could you possibly do him? None. You'll get all the way there and find out you can't even see him, or that he's been transferred—"

"Don't bother trying to change my mind. I'm going, and I'm going tonight. I only came here to tell you what happened and to borrow some money for train fare. I'll pay you back as soon as I return."

Gavin gave an emphatic shake of his head. "Bree, I can't let you do this. If I do, Morgan will shoot me dead when he comes home."

She raised her chin. "I'm going."

After a long moment, he relented and sighed as if the weight of the world rested on his shoulders. "All right, fine. We'll get you on the first train out. You should be in Richmond within a few days at the latest."

She raised her eyebrows in surprise. "That's it? You're not going to try to stop me?"

"As if I have a choice? Heaven help the man who tries to stop you. I'll wire you some money once you arrive." He expelled a long-suffering sigh. "But if Morgan kills me for this later, my death'll be on your conscience."

CHAPTER FIFTEEN

September 23rd, 1864

This was going to be bad.

Justin's dark mood matched his men's grim expressions, though he tried to hide it.

Some of Mosby's men had attacked a wagon train and killed an unarmed Regular cavalry officer when he'd tried to surrender. Reinforcements rushing to the scene had captured six of Mosby's men and without trial or jury, Custer had sentenced them to death. In exchange for the murders of their eighteen comrades at Berryville, General Merritt selected the Fifth to carry out the executions of all six prisoners.

And that wasn't the worst of it.

Two troopers volunteered, one of whom had lost a brother to the guerillas at Berryville. It didn't matter if they had the stomach for such cold-blooded vengeance or not; the rest of the Fifth had no choice but to stay and watch the Rangers' executions.

Justin sat rigidly atop Boy-o, staring between the horse's ears at a point in the distance, trying to block out what was happening. This was not what he had signed up for. No matter how much he wanted vengeance for the dead Wolverines, this wasn't war. It was murder.

He prayed no one from his company would be ordered to participate in the grisly task. He cast a glance at Mitch and Williams, staring at the ground in front of their horses as though they couldn't bear to watch either. Mounted in parade formation, they waited.

The band struck up a death march. A cold shiver passed up Justin's spine. He shifted in the saddle and tried to appear unaffected for his men. If they had to witness this, he owed it to them to bear up, as was expected of his commission.

The execution detail dragged two prisoners forward and shoved them into the churchyard in plain view of any citizen who cared to view the spectacle. The Confederate prisoners stayed silent, glaring back at the massed Union soldiers with unabashed hatred.

Justin sat frozen, trying not to betray the sickness filling him. When the firing squad raised and aimed their weapons, he flinched at the crack of the pistols and stared past the victims, unable to watch them die like dogs in the street. One dropped instantly, but the other had to be shot several times before he died. Around him, Justin's men were deathly quiet.

When his company was dismissed, he raised his right hand and swept it downward in a curt motion. "Move out," he commanded, glad to leave the place. They fell into line with the others and headed northward out of town amidst shouts from the south and an additional pistol shot, signaling that another prisoner had died.

A few minutes later, two troopers rode past with the next victim tied between their saddles, dragging him through the dusty street toward an open field.

"Sir," Williams breathed in dismay beside him.

Justin got a better look at the prisoner, and horror twisted his belly.

He was no more than a teenager.

Surely they won't kill him. He watched in strained silence as they hauled the pitiable figure past the assembled column. Men all around him were staring at the ground, their heads hung low.

"Sir," Williams said again anxiously, as though expecting him to put a stop to it.

Justin gritted his teeth so hard his jaw ached. He was only a captain, for God's sake. What the hell could he do? The men in charge wanted vengeance and meant to have it.

A woman's scream ripped through the air, bringing every head up.

A figure in black raced out into the street, the hem of her dress brushing the dusty ground. "Don't kill him!" the middle-aged widow cried, sobbing while she flailed at the men who restrained her. "You must let him live! He's only seventeen!" Her voice cracked as she tried to reach her son. The doomed prisoner stared back at her with terrified eyes, his face pinched with panic. "He stole a horse to join them this morning. Oh, please, *please* give him back to me!"

Her weeping pleas made the hairs on Justin's nape stand on end. With every ounce of self-control he had left, he forced himself to sit still, unable to take his eyes off the boy.

When it was clear her son was going to die, the woman broke free of her captors, lunging for the boy with a scream that turned Justin's heart to ice. Nausea rolled in the pit of his stomach and threatened to bring up his lunch when one man volunteered to shoot the prisoner. With his mother again restrained, the guard ordered the boy to stand up. The prisoner rose on badly quivering legs, his face ashen. The trooper emptied his pistol into him right in front of his hysterical mother. He toppled over, twitched once then lay still.

"Henry, no! *Noooo!*"

His mother's sobs shattered the air while a pool of blood spread from her son's body. Only then did the men holding her think to turn her away from the sight. Her hysterical cries echoed across the road as they led her away.

Justin didn't dare look around him, sickened and ashamed. He led his men farther out of town, with Custer at the head of the column. When the shouts of a mob reached them, the regiment stopped again as a crowd of dismounted troopers shoved the last two prisoners forward toward the Shenandoah River.

The regimental band taunted them with the eerie strains of "Love Not, the One You Love May Die." One of them was a burly dark-haired man dressed in a tattered butternut uniform. He remained defiant when came abreast of them, his black eyes flashing fire as he met Justin's stare. The other prisoner was young, maybe in his twenties, and had lost all pretense of being brave. He wept openly, begging for a chaplain, but the commanding officer refused him even that small comfort.

Without pretense, the prisoners were led forward

with their hands tied behind them. The group stopped beneath a tree. No one uttered a sound as the executioners hoisted them atop two horses and slung ropes over the sturdy branches.

"Where's Mosby?" an officer demanded.

The big prisoner curled his lip. "You can go to hell."

The band continued playing its mournful dirge, the notes echoing through the autumn air.

The guard slipped the nooses over their necks. The smaller man prayed fervently, eyes closed, tears tracking down his cheeks. Neither struggled nor begged for mercy. The big one stared back at them with hatred, seemed to pick Justin out of the group and fixed him with cold, dark eyes. Justin's marrow chilled under the intensity of that gaze.

"Mosby'll hang ten of you for every one of us," he growled in a heavy Georgian accent.

Though Justin lowered his eyes, it didn't help. He would never forget the hatred in that dark stare or the horrors he'd witnessed today. He tried calling Brianna's face to memory to blot everything else out but couldn't hold the image. She would be horrified by this. Shame curled in his gut, so strong he couldn't push it away.

You're an officer. Act like one.

Someone cracked a whip. He covered a wince when the horses bolted and the men were hanged. They jerked in spasms, suffocating as they dangled from the tree. They stilled at last, bodies swaying, the ropes creaking in the sudden silence.

No one moved.

Custer finally ordered the regiment forward. Justin swallowed the bile in his throat and gave the order to move out. Riding past the hanged men, he saw that someone had pinned a note to the Georgian.

This will be the fate of Mosby and all his men.

With a heavy heart, he turned Boy-o's head and followed his regiment out of Front Royal.

****

Richmond, VA
September 28th, 1864

Brianna rose from her bed in the attic of her new employer's house and crossed to the washstand for her morning ablutions. She had moved into the cramped room next to Nan's, the Lancasters' housekeeper, after securing the position at the start of the week. She'd applied as Jenny Taylor, deciding it was safer to use her middle name in case her visits to her Yankee brother in the prison caused any suspicion. If anyone tried to follow up and investigate, he or she wouldn't be able to find out anything about her.

Since she wasn't sure how long she'd be in Richmond, Brianna had elected to take a job rather than live on the charity Gavin had so kindly offered her. During the interview, she had only told Mrs. Lancaster she was from Kentucky and had lost her husband and father to the war. Rosemary had clucked her tongue in sympathy and patted her hand, saying something about God rewarding the brave boys of the South for their sacrifice. Brianna had chosen not to correct the lady's assumption that both men had been Confederate soldiers.

The interview had been mercifully brief, and Rosemary had declared her a perfect addition to the household. Her duties included helping Nan with the household chores and being companion to Cassidy, the eighteen-year-old daughter.

As soon as her day's work was finished, Brianna left the house, pulling her shawl about her shoulders to stave off the cool bite in the air. The sun was setting over the James River when she reached Mayo's bridge and squinted across its span at the brown and white four-story buildings of Libby prison. Her heart quickened. Morgan was in there, just across the river. Excitement and nerves warred in her growling stomach. She'd wrapped her dinner in a cloth for Morgan, but would the guards even let her in? Would they harass her? They might insist on searching her, so she'd mentally prepared herself to withstand that. She'd endure whatever she must to see her brother.

Across the bridge, she turned onto Cary Street, her muscles coiling tighter with each step. Men's faces peered out the barred windows. Was Morgan one of them? Did he see her? She swallowed. So close now, just a few more yards.

At the main door, she approached the guard and waited until he met her eyes.

"Ma'am," he said, stepping forward. "May I help you?" He frowned at her as though convinced she was lost.

She straightened her spine. "I'm looking for my brother. I was told he's a prisoner here."

"Your brother?"

"Yes. Lieutenant Morgan Douglas, First Kentucky cavalry."

The guard's lips tightened beneath a sandy beard, his dark eyes full of disapproval. "This ain't the place for a lady like you."

She wasn't leaving until she got to speak with Morgan. "I've come a long way to see him."

He studied her then relented. "Come with me." He grasped her elbow and led her inside the dark building to another soldier behind a worn desk. She coughed at the reek of smoke and human waste in the air. "Lady's here to see her brother."

Brianna repeated the information to the clerk, her hand tightening on the bundle of food she'd brought. Her palms were damp against the linen.

"He's in the next building on the third floor," the clerk confirmed, and she let out a breath of relief.

"May I see him?"

He tapped his pencil against the register. "What's in there?" He gestured to her bundle.

She unwrapped it and showed him the food. "I brought it for him, if that's all right."

Maybe he was surprised by her politeness. Maybe few women came to visit here. At any rate, he examined the contents and nodded to the guard. "Go ahead, take her up." His eyes were surprisingly kind as he regarded her. "We only have officers here and they're generally well-behaved. But if you have any problems, just call out and a guard will assist you."

"Thank you." She followed her escort out to the next building and up the stairs, the stench of unwashed bodies strengthening. Her heart hammered in her ears. She could barely keep from running the rest of the way.

At the top of the second flight, the guard stepped aside, guiding her out of someone's way. "Miss Van Lew," he greeted, tipping his hat at the middle-aged woman. She spared a glance at Brianna, muttering a conversation to herself as she passed. Brianna stared after her.

"Miss Van Lew comes to visit the prisoners often," her guard said and dropped his voice to a whisper.

"She's a bit wrong in the head, but she's not dangerous. No need to be afraid of her." He turned down the upper corridor and guided her past the cells. Brianna caught her breath at all the men crammed into them, staring at her. She didn't see any beds or any other furniture. Where did they sleep, on the bare stone floors? Her outrage mounted at the appalling conditions. No privacy, no place for them to even relieve themselves without an audience.

"Visitor for Lieutenant Douglas," the guard announced. She craned her neck toward the next cell. Men shuffled out of the way, glancing at the back of the room. She swallowed, heart pounding. Where was he?

She stood in front of the bars, lifting on tiptoes to see over the crowd of men. It was awful to stand there and peer in at them like caged animals. A path formed in the sea of blue uniforms. Someone pushed through. When she saw his face, she gripped the bars of the cell as her knees buckled. "Morgan!"

He froze, his eyes widening. "Bree!" He squeezed through the opening his comrades made for him and rushed forward to grasp her hands through the bars. There were hollows beneath his now bearded cheeks and dark circles under his bright blue eyes. "Sweetheart, I can't believe it. What are you doing here?"

She laughed through her tears, wiping them with her shoulders so she wouldn't have to let go of him, and pressed against the bars to get as close as she could. "You're all right," she said in relief, scanning him for injury. The sight of him half starved twisted her heart.

"What the hell are you doing in Richmond?"

"I came to see you."

"What? Why would you—"

"I hadn't heard anything in months, and then Paul Ramseur came by and told me you were here, so…"

"So you packed a bag and caught the next train out," he finished, shaking his head. "I should probably tear a strip off you, but I'm so damn glad to see you I don't have the heart." He squeezed her hands again, frowning when he felt how cold they were. "Did Gavin come with you?"

"No, I'm alone. I found work over in Manchester."

The frown deepened in displeasure. "Doing what?"

"Cleaning, household chores. I get room and board and a small wage."

He stroked his thumbs over her knuckles, pausing when he noticed the wedding band missing from her left hand.

She flushed. "I've met someone."

A beat passed as he searched her face, realizing the significance of it. "He must be important to you."

"He is."

A smile brightened his handsome but thin features. "I'm happy for you, Bree. Who's the lucky man?"

She fidgeted, her gaze on their entwined hands. "He's a captain in the Wolverines. I met him at the hospital."

"I gather it's serious between you?"

Her eyes swung up to his. "I've promised to wait for him." It worried her that she hadn't heard from him since leaving Lexington. Gavin would absolutely have forwarded the letter she'd written to Justin, so maybe the return letters hadn't made it through the lines yet? She blew out a breath. "I barely know him, Morgan, but…I've fallen in love him."

"Hell, sweetheart, that's good enough for me. What's his name?"

"Justin Thompson."

"From Michigan."

"Yes, and that's enough on that subject for now." She tugged her hands free and bent to retrieve her bundle. "I brought you something to eat." She glanced at the others crowded around them. "I didn't know there would be so many of you. I'm sorry I didn't bring more."

A chorus of polite negations followed. Morgan took the cloth from her. "Thanks, Bree." He wolfed down part of the roll and one potato, then passed the rest to one of the men beside him.

Brianna bit her lip and Morgan caught her looking around at his living conditions.

"It's not so bad," he said with a shrug. "At least there are enough of us in here to share body warmth at night." She didn't laugh at his teasing tone. He reached for her hands again. "I hate that you're here. Please at least tell me you didn't walk here alone tonight."

She didn't bother lying.

"Dammit, you did! Is someone coming to get you?"

"No."

"For God's sake, Brianna," he muttered. "You can't be walking around this city alone at night."

"I bought some stock for the farm," she blurted to change the subject. "I went home for a while—"

"Why did you go home?"

"I'd been sick, and the surgeon at the hospital sent me home to recover."

He ran his gaze over her. "But you're better now?"

"Yes, fine. What about you? Have you been ill here?" The conditions seemed ripe for it.

He shrugged. "No more than anyone else." His cheeks were far too hollow. He'd certainly lost a lot of weight since she'd seen him last.

"Are you getting enough to eat?" Lord knew it was a struggle for everyone else in the city. The people of Richmond had trouble enough feeding themselves without a couple thousand Yankee prisoners to care for. At least Morgan was sheltered. Even if Libby was a miserable place, he and the others were better off than the NCOs and enlisted men kept in the open on Belle Isle in the middle of the James. Come winter, those men would freeze to death.

"We get by," he answered. "You?"

Before she could answer, her stomach let out an answering growl and his blue eyes narrowed in suspicion.

"Tell me you didn't just give me your dinner." When she didn't reply, his expression became outraged. "Jesus, Brianna—" He whipped around to see if there was anything left of the food she'd brought, but of course it had all been devoured. He fixed her with a hard stare. "Don't you ever go hungry for me, do you understand? I won't have you going without to feed me."

"Morgan, I'm fine. In my place you would have done the same thing for me."

"You are never to do that again, you hear me?"

She raised her chin. "I'm a grown woman and I won't die from missing a meal here and there." He opened his mouth to argue, but she held up a hand. "I can't stand the thought of you slowly starving," she whispered, her voice catching.

He sighed. "Ah, hell, come here." He pulled her by the back of the neck until he could press through the bars and kiss her forehead. It made her want to cry. She desperately wanted to free him from his awful cage.

"Where were you captured?" she asked quietly.

He tensed, and for a moment she thought he might not answer. "Outside Atlanta."

She raised her head to look at him.

The muscles in his jaw bunched and his eyes turned flinty as he continued. "It was my fault. My men were shipped off to Andersonville because of me."

She winced at the name of that iniquitous prison. Thousands of men had starved there until they were little more than skin-covered skeletons. "Why do you think it was your fault?"

"It's a long story involving a certain Southern belle I shouldn't have trusted."

Her eyes widened. "What?"

"No more about me. Now be quiet while I find you a ride home. You're a smart girl and I'm sure you realize someone might take you for a Union spy, slipping in and out of this place by yourself at this hour."

"But that woman I saw—"

"Miss Van Lew gets away with it because they think she's crazy, which you most definitely are not. I don't want you risking arrest." He ignored her protests and let out a sharp whistle. Moments later, the guard who'd brought her up appeared. "My sister is going back to Manchester now, and I don't like the thought of her walking alone. Is there any way someone could escort her?"

"I'll find someone." He glowered at Brianna. "You'd best not be traveling alone here, especially at night. Lord knows what might happen."

Morgan squeezed her hands. "Go home Greenbriar, Bree. Curl up under a warm blanket and think of all the money we'll make with our horses when the war is over."

"But—"

"Please, sweetheart. I'm worried enough about you as it is."

She didn't want to leave him here and he knew it, because he put on a bright smile. "Love you," he said.

Her eyes filled. He was the only family she had left.

"Don't cry." He leaned down so she could kiss his cheek.

As the guard led her away, she glanced back at Morgan over her shoulder and caught the haunted expression in his eyes.

CHAPTER SIXTEEN

Richmond, VA
October 18, 1864

Brianna had dreamed the terrible dream again, the same periodically recurring one she'd had since Caleb had died.

As always, she was trapped in a windowless room with no doors, a sense of impending dread closing in on her. The hair on her nape prickled, some sixth sense telling her she was no longer alone. Slowly turning around, she stopped dead when she saw the crude pine coffin lying in the middle of the room.

With a terrible sense of foreboding forcing her closer, she watched, almost detached from herself, as her hand moved toward the lid. The hinges groaned as she pried it open. Foul vapors escaped, the stench of decomposing flesh making her stomach roll. Pulled by the invisible force, she forced herself to peer inside.

A grief-stricken wail tore free of her throat.

Sometimes she saw Caleb inside. Or her father. Or Morgan.

This time, Justin's grotesquely swollen face met her gaze, his dark blue eyes blank in death. She stumbled back, skin crawling. His bloated body turned green and began to slowly rot before her horrified stare. Then his lifeless eyes suddenly cleared and focused on her, full of a terrible fear that sent shivers up her spine. "Brianna." She shrank back when his stiffened hands clawed at her. His panic was palpable, his decomposing flesh hideous to see. *"Help me."*

She screamed.

Gasping, Brianna lunged bolt upright in bed, trembling from head to toe. Tears spilled onto the twisted sheets around her and her skin was slick with sweat. Dear God, she hated that dream. She couldn't slow her pounding heart.

Shooting out a hand, she snatched Justin's watch from the nightstand. She felt better when she held it, so she clenched her fingers around it and forced herself to remember his words on the riverbank that night. About having a piece of him with her so she'd never be alone.

I'm not alone. I'm not alone.

She flipped open the cover, blinking back the tears to make out the time. Were her watery eyes making it seem as though the second hand wasn't moving? She shook it, held it up to her ear. No ticking. Only silence. Slowly, she lowered it to her lap. A sickening wave of dread washed over her.

It was just a coincidence, she told herself as panic crept up her spine with cold fingers. *It doesn't mean anything. He's fine. It was only a nightmare.*

Brianna closed her eyes and prayed for his safety, but the dread would not leave her. She hadn't heard one word from him since she'd left Lexington, and there was one obvious reason as to why that would be.

No. She refused to believe he was dead.

She hopped out of bed, wincing as her feet landed on the icy floorboards, and stumbled to the washstand to splash her face with cold water. She gasped as the cold spray hit her then braced her hands on the wooden top to collect herself. After a few moments, she dried her face and returned to bed. Though she burrowed deep under the covers for warmth, even the comforters couldn't erase the chill from her body. Holding Justin's eerily still watch in her shaking hand, she curled into a tight ball and stared out the window into the darkness, waiting for dawn to arrive.

Please, God, let him be safe. I need him to come back to me.

****

Cedar Creek, VA
October 19, 1864

As the sun sank behind the trees to the west in a blaze of crimson, Justin waited in formation for the order to attack. His right hand gripped his saber so hard his fingers ached. His left clenched the reins, every muscle in his body tensed as he sat poised in the saddle. Boy-o shifted under him restlessly, snorting and tossing his head as though he sensed what was coming. Justin stared down the line at the other two regiments massed to the right, then caught the first sign of movement as the right wing swung forward, their battle cry echoing through the autumn air.

The Wolverines peeled off the ridge from right to

left like a string pulling taut, and when the wave reached him at last, Justin dug his heels into Boy-o's flanks and exploded forward to lead his company. He charged across the open space toward the enemy at a full gallop, bellowing a war cry at the top of his lungs.

Cannons boomed and the earth trembled. The bitter burn of powder filled the air along with the blare of the bugles and the pounding of thousands of hooves. Saber raised, he charged with his men through a ravine and across a plateau to the waiting line of Confederate infantry. Rifle volleys cracked, sending up clouds of gray smoke. Men and horses fell behind him, beside him. Bullets zinged past, shells whistled and exploded in bursts of smoke and earth. Ahead in the distance, the rest of the regiment drew up short.

The enemy line had held under the force of the mounted charge.

Justin pulled Boy-o up sharply. His mount squealed and skidded to a stop amidst the flying lead. Justin assembled his men with a wave of his saber, breathing hard. "Fall back!" He led them back through heavy artillery fire to the ravine and up a hill with the others to prepare for another attempt at breaking the enemy line.

The Confederate gunners assailed them with solid shot and canister. The constant concussion pounded in his head, making his ears ring, hurting his lungs. Cruel metal fragments burst amongst the ranks, cutting some men and their horses to pieces.

Justin gritted his teeth and held his ground. If they didn't move soon, they'd all be blown to hell.

He waited in line with his men while the adrenaline rushed through his veins, sweat rolling down his temples. His hands were slippery with it inside his gauntlets, despite the chilly temperature. When the attack commenced, the line again peeled away, beginning at the far right.

Justin waited those few agonizing seconds for his company's turn with his heart thundering against his ribs. The wave reached him at last. *"Chaaarge!"* he bellowed, putting his spurs to Boy-o's flanks as the brigade surged forward with another terrible roar.

The cannon fire ripped at their ranks, the screaming and bursting of shells mixing with shouted orders and battle cries. Justin raced through it and galloped across the dewy grass into the maelstrom.

They crashed into the line of enemy infantry with the force of a tidal wave, and this time the Confederates wavered under the impact. Pistols fired. Sabers slashed. Bullets zipped past. Men screamed. Horses nickered and shrieked.

Steady. Almost there.

"Fire!" Justin yelled at last, and his men finally opened up with their Spencers. The enemy jolted under the shock of the volley, then seemed to melt. Hot lead whistled past him, over his head. Above the din, he heard the screams of the wounded and dying.

Gaps opened and closed in the enemy's ranks, swallowing and shifting, making elusive, swirling eddies in the sea of gray and butternut bodies. Sweat beaded his forehead and soaked his chest. The muscles in his arm strained, burning from fatigue as he slashed and fired, slashed and fired. The Michigan Brigade pushed forward, making steady progress until the enemy line at last broke. The Confederates moved back, then turned and ran.

A wild, triumphant roar went up from the Wolverines.

Elation tore through Justin. Sparing a glance behind him, searching for familiar faces, he moved his men to cover as the rebel artillery took aim at them once again. His gaze swept past his brother just as a shell exploded.

Mitch threw up his hands to shield his face as a blast of debris hit him. His body jerked, his hands grasping at the pommel of the saddle to keep his seat. But he missed and crashed to the ground, clutching his front. He lay there unmoving. Just like before, only...

Blood. So much blood.

"Mitch!" The scream tore from him.

Justin leaped out of the saddle and sprinted to his brother, his brain refusing to believe what he'd just seen. His legs felt like stone, his lungs burning. Mitch wasn't moving, and this was not like the last time.

He dropped beside him and grabbed his brother by the shoulders. Mitch lay in a fetal position in a spreading pool of blood. It streamed out of his mouth and nose, smelling warm and metallic. His stomach had a gaping hole in it where a shell fragment had ripped through his body, nearly disemboweling him. One trembling, white-knuckled hand clutched his intestines in a futile effort to hold them inside his body. He screamed and clenched Justin's uniform with the other.

Oh, Jesus, oh, Jesus...

"Get a surgeon!" Justin bellowed, ready to vomit. "Send him over, *now!*" He yanked Mitch against him, shielding him from another spray of debris. He was numb, couldn't breathe. Mitch was going to die. No one could survive that kind of wound. He cradled him, barely hearing the shaky gasps that rattled through his lungs.

"J-Justin," Mitch whimpered, tears sliding down his cheeks as he choked on his own blood. "Oh, God, *help* me..." He gasped for air and went rigid with a spasm of pain, his hand tightening on Justin's uniform. He growled low in his throat, shaking. "Don't let me die..."

Panic twisted in Justin's chest. "Look at me," he commanded, grasping his brother's jaw as he stared into those terrified eyes, forcing Mitch to hold his gaze. "Don't look at it," he barked when Mitch glanced down at his belly. "You look at me. Only at me."

Mitch focused on him, his face pale and waxy, smeared with blood. The blind terror in those eyes shredded Justin. "Help me..." he repeated.

Tears blurred Justin's vision. Mitch was bleeding to death, and there wasn't a goddamn thing he could do about it. "You hold on, do you hear me? Don't you let go." He shook him once for emphasis.

Mitch's eyes began to close and he fought to keep them open. "Don't want to...die... Oh, *God!*" His face twisted. His terrified gaze dropped to the terrible hole in his abdomen and the obscene amount of blood gushing out. They were both covered in it, their uniforms soaked through.

Justin forced his brother's head up. "Don't look at it, Mitch, look at me. And don't talk now," he ordered hoarsely. "I won't leave you, I swear I won't leave you. But you goddamn stay with me, do you hear?" Where in *hell* was the damned surgeon?

"God...h-help...m-me..." Mitch rasped the words, blood dripping from his mouth, down his chin in a hideous scarlet ribbon. "Can't see... There's nothing..." He choked again, spitting up mouthfuls of blood. When he focused once more, his eyes were so full of anguish it stabbed right through Justin's heart. "Dark. C-can't...s-see..."

"It's all right. I've got you. It's going to be all right."

His voice broke. The sounds of the battle seemed far away. All but blinded by the haze of tears stinging his own eyes, he shook with fear and shock. It took him a while to realize Mitch wasn't gasping for breath anymore. That the mangled body in his arms was still.

"Goddamn you, Mitchell," he roared, shaking the brother he loved beyond reason, refusing to let him give up. "Fight, you bastard! Do you hear me? Don't you *dare* die on me." He gave him another angry shake, stunned into stillness when the dark head lolled back, those eyes so like his own sliding half closed.

The bloody hand on Justin's coat loosened its grip. Fell away from his uniform.

Quaking, gulping lungfuls of air, he pulled back to gaze down at his brother. Mitch's face was almost serene, devoid of the paralyzing terror it had held only a minute before. He looked like he was asleep with his lashes swept against his cheeks like that, lips parted.

But he was not sleeping. And he would never wake again.

With shaking fingers, Justin felt for a pulse at the base of his throat, even though he knew he wouldn't find one. His tears splashed onto the pale face. The brave, impetuous heart in that shattered body had stopped beating.

Shells continued to explode around him, but he didn't hear them. He was only aware that his brother had just died in his arms. Justin let his head fall back and cried out in anguish.

Howling like a wounded animal, he hugged Mitch to him, certain he would die of the pain. For an eternity he remained like that, rocking him, face pressed close to that cooling cheek, sobbing like a child. Someone finally came and pried the lifeless body from his arms and dragged him to safety before leaving him to kneel alone on the cold ground, soaked with his brother's cooling blood.

CHAPTER SEVENTEEN

Waking up the next morning was the hardest thing Justin had ever done. He opened his eyes to find the unfamiliar scenery rolling like a green carpet outside the windows of the boxcar he occupied. In an instant, he remembered why he was there. Accompanying his brother's body back to Michigan for burial.

For a moment, time stood still as he struggled to breathe. He held Mitch's hat in his clenched hands, the pain more than he could bear. Fragmented images swept past him, of screaming shells, Mitch's agonized expression, the feel of him convulsing in his arms in the throes of death.

Angry tears pricked his eyes and he plunged shaking fingers into his hair. The pressure in his chest was suffocating, grief crashing over him in relentless, pounding waves. Mitch's pleading voice echoed in his head.

Justin...help me...

He couldn't bear knowing he would carry that

anguished sound of his brother's voice inside him forever. Sobs clawed at him. He fought them back, along with the urge to smash everything in that boxcar to vent his fury, his hopelessness. Mitch was gone. Never coming back.

Justin doubled over, covering his face with his hands as the tears came, scalding in their agony. *I can't take this.* The thought was loud in his head. Clear.

He gagged, choking on the bile that rose in his throat. He wanted to scream from the pain, his heart writhing in agony. The agony drained away all too soon, replaced by empty despair. With an exhausted sigh, he slumped against the seat and closed his eyes, hoping for the oblivion of sleep.

Maybe sleep would obliterate the smell of the blood and those hideous, gasping breaths.

It wasn't Mitch's face he saw burned on the inside of his eyelids, though. It was Brianna's. A different kind of grief blasted through him.

In desperate need of distraction, he conjured up memories of her at the hospital when she had changed his bandages. Her smile, the feel of her hands stroking his hair, the softness of her lips and the reassuring comfort of her embrace. He ached with the need to see her again, just to have her arms around him. She would understand the suffocating torment inside him and somehow help dull the pain.

But he hadn't heard a word from her in so long and had no idea where she was. If something had happened to her too—

No, he wouldn't even allow himself to think it. He closed his eyes as another wave of pain hit him. *Brianna, where are you?* He needed her more than ever.

****

Justin stepped off the train two days later into a world enveloped in gloomy, spiritless gray. Detroit welcomed him with a blast of cutting wind, his damp uniform chilling him to the bone. The leaden sky released torrents of rain on him, and a dense blanket of fog covered the ground. The air seemed dull and polluted; all the buildings and mills he passed were crumbling.

Hunching his shoulders, he drove the wagon through the muddy streets, while the horse's hooves sucked at the ooze with each step. No one looked at him, no one gave him a friendly smile or nod of acknowledgement. Not this time.

He kept hearing his mother's words on the day he and Mitch had left for the front the first time. *He's your responsibility now. Guard him well.* She'd said it in the study, with his father's eyes staring down at him from his oil portrait above the mantle. Christ, how was he going to tell her?

The wind slashed at him, shards of freezing rain stinging his face, but he barely felt it. Even the horse seemed mournful, its gait lethargic.

His mother might not survive this loss. Not after the way she'd been when his father died.

He was so tired, more exhausted than he'd ever been in his life. He felt removed from himself, mechanically going through the motions of living. If each day meant reliving the horrors of Cedar Creek— the wrenching, scalding agony, Mitch's panicked voice and this terrible emptiness—he didn't know how he'd go on.

All the misery honed into sharp focus when the

house finally came into view. The imposing brick mansion had always filled him with pride, but now it filled him with dread. He stopped the horse at the foot of the front steps. Like a condemned man, he swung down from the buckboard and dragged his feet up the stairs, forced his stiff fingers to curl into a fist and rapped on the front door.

Moments later, Aggie appeared in the open doorway, tall and thin in a brown calico dress, her lined face so dear to him that a lump formed high in his throat. Welcome rays of warm lamplight caught on her pinned-up salt-and-pepper hair and spilled out into the murk. Her pale green eyes widened at the sight of him, soaking wet and shivering, the rain pouring off his hat and down his back. "Justin!" She grabbed his arm and pulled. "Come in, lad."

She guided him inside without another word and removed his hat and poncho. Her eyes were worried, but she didn't say anything. God, he couldn't even bear to tell Aggie about Mitch. How the hell was he going to say it to his mother?

The familiar walls seemed to close in on him. For a moment he swayed on his feet. Being home was like sucking flames into his lungs, because Mitch's absence was even more acute. He cleared his throat. "I need to speak with my mother in private." His voice was raw, hoarse.

Wide-eyed, Aggie hurried off to find her and left him to stagger into the study.

Ignoring the depressing tableau across the room, he reached for a glass and the brandy decanter, fingers shaking so badly the liquor sloshed over the mahogany sideboard. He gulped it down and finally stared at the oil portrait of his father hanging above the mantle, the permanently empty chair beside it.

Now there would be another empty chair in the house.

Staring up at the portrait, he looked into his father's eyes. *I'm sorry, Father. I'm so damned sorry.*

His head throbbed and the room tilted. He steadied himself over the hearth, wishing he was anywhere but here.

"Justin?"

Flinching at his mother's anxious voice, he turned to face her. She stood in the doorway, a frail, diminutive woman in widow's weeds, with huge blue eyes and a graying head of once black hair, wringing her hands. "What…what are you doing here?" she asked, gaze scanning the room fearfully.

Looking for Mitch.

With a sinking heart, Justin closed his eyes. She knew. With a mother's instincts, she already knew.

He didn't move, didn't know what to say. He plunked the empty glass down and raised haunted eyes to hers. Finding no words, he nodded. "Gone," he whispered finally, his voice barely audible. "He's gone."

Her eyes went wild, her mouth opening and closing, hands flying to her throat. "No," she whispered, then started screaming. "No, no, no! Not my *son!*" She bolted into the hallway and ran for the front door, throwing it open before he could stop her. Her disbelieving gaze locked on the lone casket in the wagon bed. "Oh, dear Jesus—*Mitchell!*"

With that bloodcurdling shriek, she raced down the steps, stumbling and falling to her hands and knees in the mud before she clambered to her feet and plunged headlong for the wagon. Before she could reach it, Justin grabbed her around the waist and swung her off the ground. She fought like a wildcat, clawing and beating at his chest, screaming. Her hysteria pierced him to the core. Barely able to see through the tears in his eyes, he pressed his mother's face tight against his chest, ignoring the pain of her blows.

"Why, *why!*" she howled, hitting him with her clenched fists. The heart-wrenching sobs made his skin crawl.

He held her tighter, carried her beneath the shelter of the porch roof. "I don't know," he whispered, wishing he could trade places with his brother. It should be him lying there in that box, not Mitch. Never Mitch.

She took a long time to calm enough for him to release her. Trembling and weeping pitifully, she turned her eyes to the coffin. "Let me s-see him," she pleaded.

Justin blanched, his stomach knotting. Christ, he was going to throw up. "*No.*"

"Why n-not?"

Because he's lying in there with his guts torn out, and he's probably half rotted! he wanted to shout at her. "No, Mother, don't do this." He prepared to restrain her if she tried to climb in and pry the lid open.

"Come inside the house, loves," Aggie said gently from behind them. Tears tracked down her face as she took their arms and led them back inside. She seated them in the parlor and left.

The ensuing silence was suffocating.

"When?" his mother demanded, grief etched on her ashen face. Then she glanced away as though she couldn't bear the sight of him.

Because he looked so much like Mitch.

He swallowed the bile in his throat. "October nineteenth. At Cedar Creek, Virginia." Maybe he should have sent her a telegram first. Why had he thought telling her in person would be better?

She stared into the flames that snapped in the hearth, arms wrapped around her fragile body. "How did he die?"

He eyed her, teeth clenched. If she expected all the grisly details, she had another thing coming. "Shell fragment. I was with him."

Her lips quivered, eyes closing in despair. "Did he suffer long?"

Yes. He stared down at the carpet. "No, not long."

She started crying into her handkerchief, leaving him to wallow in his own grief. Aggie returned with the tea tray and poured his mother a cup. From past experience he already knew it was laced with something to help his mother sleep. Aggie forced it down her.

Justin thought he couldn't feel worse, but he'd been wrong. It was history repeating itself—the beginning of the same process his mother had undergone after his father had been killed. Sleeping drugs, followed by days of lying in bed, which stretched into weeks. Months of endless, heartbroken sobs coming from her bedroom. Night after night he'd lain awake, listening to her grieve. Thank God he would be gone in another few days. He couldn't stand watching it again.

When the drugged tea was gone, she spoke at last, her voice already taking on a slurred edge. "I shall send for Father Kirkpatrick this evening. We will have the funeral tomorrow afternoon."

"All right." He rose and walked out into the heavy rain, leading the horse behind him, and put the wagon in the stable. He hated to leave Mitch there, but he wasn't going to have the coffin moved inside in case his mother got it into her head to try and view his body.

The stableman took the horse, his eyes moist. Word had traveled fast. He patted Justin on the shoulder in sympathy.

When he came back into the house, the parlor was empty. His mother was probably already in bed, half knocked out by her medicine, and rather than going upstairs to subject himself to the torture of her tears, he stripped off his wet coat and shirt to stretch out on the chaise lounge to sleep. Aggie woke him sometime later when she covered him with a blanket, tucking it around his cold body. He hadn't realized he'd been shivering. She rubbed his tense shoulders and back and smoothed his hair, the gesture reminding him of Brianna. His throat closed up.

"I hurt for ye, lad," Aggie said, her pale eyes full of sorrow. "I know how much ye loved him. But don't give up on us now, boy-o. We all love ye very much. And we need ye."

Justin lay awake for a long time after she left, assaulted by more memories. Drifting off at last, he had one final thought. He wished Brianna was snuggled close against him and running her hands over him, helping him cope with this pain, helping him forget for just a little while. Shutting his eyes, he imagined pressing her down into his bed and making love to her, banishing death and sorrow as he lost himself inside her, forgetting everything but the warmth of her body and the healing balm of her love.

****

They buried Mitch the next afternoon while the rain poured down. A small crowd gathered around the grave that Justin had dug beneath an ancient oak in a far corner of the property. His mother wanted her boy to stay on their land, so Justin had chosen his brother's final resting place. He was exhausted and more than anything wanted this whole thing to be over.

Raised a Catholic, he had no doubt his devilish little brother had somehow charmed St. Peter into giving him a harp and a pair of wings up there at the Pearly Gates. He almost cracked a smile at the notion, but his brother being entombed in that coffin was enough to bring the numbness back.

Father Kirkpatrick droned on through the eulogy, while Justin's eyes remained on his mother as she cried into a handkerchief, her shuddering shoulders supported by Aggie. She would never recover from this blow. And he didn't blame her for not noticing he was in the same state. There was nothing he could do for her now. He had the feeling she blamed him for Mitch's death. Maybe that was why she wouldn't look at or speak to him. He only wished she wouldn't forget that he was still her son, and still alive.

Gradually his brain registered warmth and that his fingers weren't quite so cold anymore. He glanced beside him and found Laurel there, staring into the grave with damp eyes. She rubbed his fingers while water dripped from the umbrella she tried to shelter them both with. Through an odd sense of detachment, Justin realized he was soaked to the skin.

Something about the distress on Laurel's face and her concern for him was comforting. He imagined it was Brianna's hand holding his instead while he listened to the priest's words, bending down at the appropriate time to make a cross of earth on the casket. *Ashes to ashes, dust to dust.* His mother laid a rosary on Mitch's coffin and turned away. The rest of the mourners followed her back to the house.

He barely noticed the others leaving. The only thing he felt was the awful tightness in his chest. As the rain beat down on him, he stared down at the rough casket. How was he supposed to walk away and let them bury his brother under six feet of dirt, leaving him trapped in the cold ground? How could he abandon him there all alone when he had held that broken body in his arms and promised not to? Agony built in his chest until he thought he would scream.

He took a deep breath and let it out slowly, recruiting his courage.

That's not really Mitch in there. Just his shell.

Yeah, and maybe if he kept telling himself that, he'd believe it someday.

At the tug on his hand, he glanced down, having almost forgotten Laurel stood there with him. He closed his eyes.

I'm sorry, Mitch. I miss you like hell. If you're up there, say a prayer for us.

With a final look at the casket, he said his silent goodbyes to his brother and allowed Laurel to lead him away. Back at the house, the guests spoke in low tones, casting curious, sympathetic glances at him and his mother. Justin never let her out of his sight, standing close by in case she needed him. His presence seemed to comfort her, though she wouldn't look at or acknowledge him. When she rolled her head from one side to the other, he automatically reached out to rub the knotted muscles in her neck and shoulders. She froze at his touch then jerked away with a sob and fled the room. She might as well have kicked him in the gut.

Needing to escape for a while, he retreated to the

den, but it was even worse seeing his father's empty wing chair while he stared down at him from that damned canvas with acute disappointment. Justin wandered through the ground floor like a caged animal, the guests mostly giving him a wide berth. Their sympathetic stares made him want to throw something.

Aggie served pots of hot tea and cake along with other things she had prepared the night before. He didn't touch any of it. After the food was gone, the guests offered their individual condolences before taking their leave. Mr. Stevens and Laurel remained behind to help clean up.

Seated near the fire, Justin knew Laurel was somewhere nearby but didn't much care. He planned to get roaring drunk—he was already halfway there—and sleep the night and day away. Sleep was the only time he could escape the torture of reliving his brother's agonizing death.

Unless he dreamed about it again and woke up screaming like he had last night.

But when he woke tomorrow, he was leaving.

"Justin?"

Laurel's quiet voice scraped over his nerves and he didn't acknowledge her. Maybe if he ignored her she would go away.

The rustling of skirts told him he was wrong and a second later she kneeled in front of him on the rug. "Justin, I want to apologize for being so cold to you when you were last here."

His brows swooped upward. An apology from Laurel was a momentous occasion.

She chewed her lip. "I wasn't myself."

He didn't believe that for a second and told her so by turning back to the fire. Why was she still here? She had to smell the whiskey on him, and he'd made it abundantly clear he wanted to be alone.

She laid a hand on his forearm. "I'm so very sorry about your brother."

He nodded tightly. At least she was sincere about that.

"Will you be all right?"

No. "Yes."

She sighed and sat back on her heels. "You look so tired."

He faced her with tortured eyes. *Tired*? Tired could not begin to describe the bone-deep weariness, as heavy and drugging as the fever that had claimed him in the hospital after he'd been wounded. "I'm exhausted, yet I can't get his face out of my mind long enough to fall asleep." His words sounded so bitter. "But you wouldn't understand, because you've never seen a man die right before your eyes while you watch without being able to do anything."

Laurel was like a priceless antique, a beautiful ornament to adorn someone's parlor. She could never begin to imagine what horrors he'd seen. His eyes narrowed before he continued. "You wouldn't know what it's like to watch your brother's face turn white with pain and hear him scream and gasp for air. He clawed at me for help, he—" His voice caught and he turned his head away.

She was quiet for a time before she offered, "I'm sure you eased it for him by being there."

Cold comfort, he thought, clenching his jaw. He reached for his glass of whiskey, but she stopped him with a surprisingly firm grip on his arm.

"Getting yourself soused is not going to help. You need to rest. Come on, up you go. I'll help you to bed."

She must be crazy to think he would let her anywhere near his bedroom. "Where's your father?"

Laurel sighed impatiently. "He went home already. I meant to settle you on the sofa there." She indicated the one he'd slept on the night before. "Come on," she coaxed, tugging on his arm to urge him to stand, steadying him when he wobbled.

Once he was on the sofa, she bustled around, closing drapes and gathering pillows and quilts. He was staring at nothing when she returned to fluff the pillows and remove his coat. Already under the effects of the whiskey, he didn't help her undress him and she had to tug hard to remove the sleeves from his arms. She nearly fell when it came off with her last yank.

Justin closed his eyes, resenting her for making him yearn for Brianna even more. "You shouldn't be here, Laurel. I'm drunk."

She ignored the warning. "Yes, I can see that you are."

God, he needed Brianna so badly right now. His heart screamed for her. But he didn't know where she was. Might never find her again.

Jesus, don't let him cry in front of Laurel.

She stopped what she was doing and gave him a hard stare. "I'm not going to leave you alone like this, Justin, so you'd best get used to the notion. Now lie still and let me help you."

He wished she'd leave. But the thought of being alone suddenly filled him with panic. What if he couldn't stand it? What if he was tempted to go out into the stable, take his service revolver and blow the back of his out head just to stop the pain?

Christ, he could see it happening. Could almost feel the cold grip in his palm, almost hear the metallic click of the hammer as he cocked it.

Fear made him grab for her like a lifeline.

She jumped when he pulled her down beside him. Because she didn't say anything, he moved his head into her lap and closed his eyes. She ran a tentative hand over his hair.

Eyes closed tight, he concentrated on the feel of that hand and the memory it evoked, of another time and another woman. Then he thought of Mitch, lying trapped underground out there alone in the pitch-blackness, and the howling storm of grief came back. He turned his face into the warm body that held him. The pain would stop once he fell asleep, and with all the alcohol he had consumed it shouldn't be long now. He lay there, lulled by the fingers stroking his hair and the liquor warming his veins. Laurel was silent, he wasn't alone, and for the moment, that was all he cared about.

As she rose from the couch he woke and caught her arm. The liquor was doing its job, but he didn't want to be alone yet. He relaxed when she kneeled before him, her face level with his. In a wordless plea, he locked his arms around her. "Don't." He didn't know if he was begging her not to go, or warning her to keep her distance.

Through the haze of exhaustion and whiskey, he watched as she bent close. He twisted his face away to avoid the kiss. The pain inside him was agonizing enough without adding to it by betraying Brianna that way. Being held like this felt too good to push her away though. She was soft and warm. Her hands stroked his cheeks, his hair. Brianna had touched him like that. So gently. He moved closer, letting his hands find and grip her hips.

Oh, God, Brianna... He pulled her closer, lost in the

feel of her. Her hands moved over his face and throat, his chest, lower. He groaned and arched under her touch, shifting so she could reach more of him.

The hands left him. He mumbled her name and reached for her, desperate.

Oh, God, touch me. Love me. Don't let me go.

He was dimly aware of a door shutting somewhere in the distance. The pounding desire inside him was too strong to ignore. He rolled to his back and clumsily ripped the front of his trousers open, freeing his aching cock. When he couldn't stand the throb any longer, he fisted himself. He squeezed his eyes shut, lost in the raging fantasy. In his mind it was Brianna's hand stroking him, her touch a sweet agony on his aching flesh. Desperate for more, Justin envisioned burying his hands in her thick hair to keep her mouth on his, his body bursting, desperate. *Love me, angel.* He throbbed in her grip, each stroke taking him higher.

The fantasy raged on until he was poised on the brink of release. He covered her hand with his to hold her there, locked his fingers around hers. With a needful moan, he writhed beneath her touch and let go, his other hand fisting in her hair as he let oblivion claim him.

****

Justin stood at the Stevens's picket fence the next morning. He stared at the white house with the green shutters and drew a deep breath. He dreaded what was to come, and though he'd rather be shot again than face Laurel, he had to do this.

He'd awoken groggy and confused, a kink in his neck from his awkward position on the couch. His mouth was dry as cotton and his head pounded with every beat of his heart. As soon as he opened his gritty eyes, he remembered his brother lying in his lonely grave, and then bits and pieces of the previous evening came back to him. When at last he'd gathered the nerve to look down at himself, he found the evidence he'd been afraid of all over his belly. He'd been all but naked with his pants shoved past his hips, though he couldn't remember what had happened. He had a vague memory of Laurel stripping off his shirt and maybe kissing him, but that was all.

God, he was a perfect bastard.

He'd cleaned up and composed a short letter to Brianna before leaving the house. Even if her feelings for him had changed, she would want to know about Mitch.

He still didn't know why she'd stopped writing to him. Had she found someone else and forgotten him so soon?

He shook away the thought and stared at Laurel's bright red front door. No matter how awkward the situation, he had to deliver his weak and completely inadequate apology in person.

Truth was, he had no idea how far things had gone between them last night. Or how much she'd seen and heard. A surge of guilt and shame washed over him. He knew she thought herself in love with him, and last night would certainly have persuaded her he felt the same, even if she actually *hadn't* been with him at the end. Whatever she'd seen, she didn't realize that in his mind he'd been with Brianna the whole time.

Gathering his courage, Justin knocked on the front door. Mr. Stevens answered it with a warm smile, making him reasonably sure that Laurel hadn't said anything to her father. She appeared on the upstairs landing with a timid smile, a telltale blush highlighting her cheeks.

Mr. Stevens excused himself and retreated to his study, leaving them alone.

"Hello, Justin," Laurel said as she came down the stairs. "How are you feeling?" Something about the set of her shoulders made him think she was nervous. Her smile seemed forced.

"I'm fine," he replied, wishing he knew what the hell to say. Neither of them moved for a time, and he finally blurted, "I wanted to apol—"

"Let's go into the kitchen and have some tea," she suggested with forced cheeriness, rushing down the stairs and past him. He let her fuss over the teapot and bring a tray of baking to the table, proving how on edge she was. He'd done that to her.

"Do you take sugar?" she asked a little too brightly, her hand trembling as she offered him a teacup. He closed his fingers around hers, forcing her to look up at him.

"Laurel, I'm so sorry about last night." His guts twisted at the spasm of pain on her face. "My behavior was inexcusable."

She snatched her hand back and fiddled with the sugar bowl. "You did warn me you were drunk."

"That's no excuse."

"It's not an excuse, Justin. You tried to warn me, but I didn't listen. You didn't want to be alone, I didn't want to go, and I don't blame you for what happened." Spots of hectic color rode high on her cheekbones, and the gleam of tears in her eyes hit him like a blow.

"I never meant to hurt you." He wished he could take away the pain he'd caused. Jesus, everywhere he went he hurt people.

"I know." She lowered her eyes. "I don't suppose we can just forget it happened at all?"

"Can you?"

"Yes." Laurel looked back up at him. "This is all very simple. You needed someone last night, and she wasn't there. I was. You were thinking of your nurse."

He covered a flinch. "I don't remember much."

Her dark gaze held his, daring him to deny it. "Justin, you said her name when I kissed you. Twice. I couldn't stay, knowing you were pretending I was her."

The misery in her expression magnified before he closed his eyes and pressed his palms to his temples. "God," he said, aware of how inadequate the apology was, "I'm so sorry."

She bit her lip. "You must love her very much."

He owed her the truth. Pushing away from the table, he rubbed the back of his neck. "Laurel, don't make me hurt you any more than I already have."

"I don't think that's possible," she answered, raising her chin.

He took a deep breath, knowing he deserved her anger and disgust.

"I need to know. Please."

He regarded her for a moment, hoping his self-loathing didn't show. "Yes, I love her. More than anything."

Laurel leaped up with a sob and headed for the stairs, but he caught her and gathered her close. "I'm sorry," he murmured. "So damned sorry."

She only nodded, trying to hold back the sobs as they ripped through her. He held her until she calmed a little then allowed her to step away, putting distance between them.

He toyed with the brim of his hat. "I think it would be best for everyone if I didn't come home for a while." *Or at all.* "I don't want to make things any harder for my mother. Or you." When she didn't argue, he headed for the door.

"Wait," she cried, grabbing his arm. "Just...wait." Laurel gazed up at him, her heartbreak clear on her face. "I couldn't bear to lose you entirely. Please say I still have your friendship."

Justin gave her a sad smile. "You'll always have it."

"And don't say you're not coming back. Don't talk that way." She wiped at her eyes and saw him to the door, anxiety etched into her expression. "You *will* be careful, won't you?"

"Of course." He paused, feeling strangely hollow. "Take care, Laurel."

CHAPTER EIGHTEEN

Richmond, VA
December 25, 1864

Stepping into her bedchamber after delivering a small cake to Morgan—in spite of his continued protests about her visits to Libby—Brianna found a battered letter on her nightstand. She picked it up and studied the unfamiliar handwriting. Had Nan put it there? She poked her head into the hallway and saw the band of light coming from beneath the housekeeper's closed door. She knocked. "Nan?"

When it opened, the old housekeeper eyed her with concern, her gray curls tucked under a nightcap. "Jenny lamb. You all right?"

"Yes. Did you put this in my room?" She held up the letter.

"I did. A man came about an hour ago, said to give it to you."

Someone had delivered it to her? "Thank you, Nan.

Good night." She tiptoed back to her room. Had an operative in Elizabeth Van Lew's secret network brought it? She'd passed a few letters for Justin to her, hoping they would reach him faster than if she sent them back to Lexington for Gavin to forward. She had no idea if they'd gotten through the lines or if Justin had ever received them.

Brianna lit the lamp and curled up on her bed to open the envelope. Inside, she found another one. The familiar handwriting on it made her heart leap.

Justin.

He'd addressed it as Major Thompson. When had he been promoted? Eyes filling, she tore it open and held it up to the flame with trembling fingers. Was he all right?

My dearest Brianna,

I don't know if this letter will ever reach you, yet I have to write it. It is with deepest sorrow that I inform you my brother was killed at Cedar Creek on October 19th...

She sucked in a breath, a hand flying to her mouth. *Oh, Mitch.*

I was with him when he died.

She closed her eyes, a crushing ache in her chest. How Justin must be suffering. She hated not being there to comfort him.

I have returned home to see him buried and will then be rejoining my regiment. You may reach me there at the address given. I can only hope you are well, as I have not had word from you in weeks. I think of you often and pray for word from you soon.

Stay safe and warm.

Yours,

Justin

She read the letter a second time before setting it down and covering her face with her hands. The stark loneliness in his words cut her like a knife. He must not have received any of her letters, but how could that be? Either Miss Van Lew hadn't been able to get them through the lines, or someone had intercepted them. And he must not have received the letter she'd left with Gavin the night she'd departed for Richmond.

It didn't matter now. She had to go to him, even if it was risky to try and cross through the lines. If she half froze getting to him, it would be worth it just to hold him in her arms again. *Stay safe and warm.* The words were like an arrow in her heart. Was he out in the field, shivering from the cold right now? The thought brought a hot wash of tears to her eyes.

Resolved to find him no matter how long it took, she packed a bag, wrote a note to the others saying she had to leave due to a family emergency and would be back as soon as possible. She borrowed one of Cassidy's heavy winter coats and a muff then let herself out the back door and headed for the one place she knew she'd find help: Libby prison.

The night was bitterly cold, but Brianna moved with renewed purpose on her walk across the river. Sam, the guard she'd come to be on friendly terms with, saw her approach and rushed outside to meet her.

"What's wrong?" he demanded, looking her over as though concerned she might be hurt, sandy brows lowered over his dark eyes.

"I just received a disturbing letter and had to come speak to my brother again." She tucked her hands deeper into the muff to warm them. "May I see him?"

Sam took her elbow. "Get inside before you freeze to death. Lord, woman, you trying to catch your death walking back and forth in the snow like this?"

"It's urgent, Sam."

"I can see that." He took her to the stairs. "Mind telling me what's got you so upset?"

She hesitated then decided it couldn't do any harm to tell him. "My..." What was Justin? Not technically her fiancé. "A dear friend of mine sent word he lost his only brother at Cedar Creek. He needs me, and I intend to go to him."

Sam stopped, throwing her an incredulous look. "In this weather? By yourself?" Shaking his head, he helped her up the remaining steps. "Hey, Douglas! Got your sister here again, with some fool notion in her head to track someone down in..." He frowned. "Where did you say he was?"

"Actually I don't really know. That's why I wanted to talk to my brother."

Sam's lips pursed as though he'd just eaten something sour. "This friend of yours. He's a Yankee, isn't he."

"Yes."

"That's who you've been passing letters to Miss Van Lew for?"

Her mouth opened in shock. "How did you—"

"I notice things," he said with a shrug. "Why else would you need to give them to her? Only reason I know of is that you couldn't get 'em through the lines yourself."

And yet these past months he'd said nothing to anyone about it?

He shrugged. "Figured if you were a spy, you wouldn't have much to pass on from these boys anyhow."

She laughed in surprise.

"Bree?"

She heard Morgan before she saw him and, rounding the corner, found him already against the bars of his cell.

"What's the matter? Why are you back?"

"She wants to find some Yankee on the other end of the state," Sam informed him.

Morgan grabbed her hands, rubbing to warm them. "Who? Your Wolverine?"

"Yes. He's a major now. They promoted him. I don't know where he is though. Will he have gone into winter quarters yet?"

"Possibly. Somewhere in the Shenandoah, I'd imagine. Shouldn't be too hard to find out where. They've ruffled a lot of folks' feathers around those parts. Someone's got to know where they are."

Sam crossed his arms and gave her a flat look. "When you say a dear 'friend', what do you mean exactly?"

"Her fiancé," Morgan said.

She fidgeted. "We're not engaged yet. Not officially."

Sam's eyebrows went up. "Then why are you so dead set on finding him?"

"He needs me. I'm going. That's the end of it."

Morgan rubbed her hands between his some more, though his fingers were every bit as cold as hers. She'd never get used to seeing him locked up like this. "Be tough going, getting through the lines," he warned her. "And even if you found out where the winter quarters were, he might be out on campaign somewhere."

She realized all of that. "I have to try. Will you help me?"

He expelled a weary sigh. "Sweetheart, you know I

would, but what the hell can I do from in here?"

She swung hopeful eyes on Sam, who scowled harder. "Please, Sam? Consider it the best Christmas gift you've ever given anyone."

He grunted, paced and grumbled a bit before stopping in front of Morgan and rubbed a hand over his beard. "You're really gonna allow this?"

Her brother chuckled. "How am I going to stop her? And trust me, sergeant. You don't *allow* my sister to do anything. I'd feel a whole lot better knowing you were taking care of her, though."

Sam pondered it for a moment, holding Morgan's gaze. Then he huffed out an irritated breath. "Fine, I'll take her. I got leave starting in the morning anyhow and I'd planned to surprise my mama with a short visit."

Brianna threw her arms around his wiry shoulders. Oh thank God, she was going to find Justin.

Sam gave her back an awkward pat. "Don't know if we'll get far, but I'm not gonna let you do this on your own. Wouldn't sleep a wink until I saw you again." He set her firmly away from him, pinned her with his dark stare. "Even with the right papers, they might not let us through, and it's gonna be a damn cold trip as it is."

"I understand." Her heart knocked against her ribs. "When can we leave?"

"Best I can do is tomorrow afternoon. I'll come by with a wagon and pick you up on my way outta town."

****

Near Winchester, VA
December 29, 1864

"Just another few miles, ma'am, on the other side

215

of yonder ridge." Sam pointed to the row of trees outlined in moonlight on the slope before them, where he would hand her over to the Yankee pickets. From there she would have to find another escort for the remainder of the journey.

Brianna pulled the blanket tighter around herself, huddling into its woolen folds to ward off the bite of the wind. The wagon rocked and creaked its way down the winding road, jarring her stiff joints and sore muscles.

"Can't say I'll miss this wagon, Sam. I'll be bruised for a whole week after this trip."

He grunted. "Well, the army ain't exactly much for fancy travelin', ma'am."

"We should have ridden those thoroughbreds I saw back in Fredericksburg instead."

"Yes, ma'am. You surely do have an eye for horseflesh, I'll say that for you."

"Why, Sam, a compliment? I'm flattered."

He grunted, didn't look at her. His jaw flexed beneath his sandy beard, his bushy brows lowered over his eyes in disapproval. "Do you have somewhere to stay when you get there?"

"I'm sure I'll find something."

"Mm-hm. And what if he's not even there?"

She cast an annoyed glance at her reluctant companion. "Then I'll find out where he went and ride out in the morning."

"All by your lonesome, I suppose," he grumbled, disdain dripping from the words.

"If I have to."

"Lord save me, woman—"

"Halt!"

Sam jerked the horse to a stop at the harsh command. Two rebel pickets emerged from the woods at the sides of the road, rifles in hand. Sam handed them their papers and tapped his boot on the wagon floor impatiently while he waited to be waved through. The younger of the pickets handed the documents up to him and stared at Brianna, doffing his hat quickly as an afterthought.

Sam snatched the papers back and glared at him. "Quit your gawkin', boy. What's the matter with you? Ain't you ever seen a woman before?"

"Yessir." He stepped back, tipping his kepi at her again. "Just not one so pretty."

Sam glared, picked up the reins and set the wagon in motion once more. "You'd best blink, boy, before your eyeballs freeze up," he barked over his shoulder, then shot her an irritated glance. "And *that* is why females like you have no business being in an army camp at all, let alone without a chaperone."

"Because he looked at me?" She rolled her eyes. "Sam, I'm a widow, and I nursed for a long time. I know how to take care of myself around soldiers."

"That's not the issue," he spluttered, hands twitching on the reins. "Damn fool woman."

"If I need chaperoning so badly, then why don't you stay with me?"

His eyebrows shot up and disappeared under the lank hair falling over his forehead. He stared between the horse's ears, mouth set in a grim line. "I got things to do," he muttered.

"That's too bad," she teased, resting her head against his lean shoulder with a yawn. "You would have been an excellent chaperone. Why, no man in his right mind would dare come within a hundred yards of me when you have that look on your face."

****

HQ Fifth Michigan Cavalry, Winchester, VA
December 30, 1864

Justin's pen halted in the middle of a sentence when someone knocked on the door. "Come in," he called without looking up from the latest dispatch.

"You have a visitor, sir."

Justin frowned and checked the clock on the wall. It was after midnight. He looked back at the lieutenant, standing half-asleep in the doorway.

"Yessir, I know it's late, but…"

"But what, Lieutenant? You know I'm busy." He gestured to the piles of papers spread out on the desk. "Couldn't this wait until morning?"

"No sir, it's a lady."

"A lady? At this hour?" A terrible suspicion formed. "Tell me it's not Mrs. Blythe." She was the latest to seek out his attentions and was somewhat…tenacious in her efforts.

"No, not her. Not any other woman from the area. She seems to know you, sir. Damn, I've forgotten her name. She must have traveled all week, because she came in on a wagon that left Fredericksburg on Tuesday."

A woman had come all the way from Fredericksburg by wagon to see him? In this weather? Justin couldn't fathom who she might be. Surely God wouldn't be so cruel as to place Laurel on his doorstep, would he? "Is she downstairs right now?"

"Yessir. Did you want me to send her away until tomorrow?"

He sighed, rubbed his tired, burning eyes and

shook his head. "No, I'll see her." He stood and reached for his frock coat. What kind of woman came calling at this hour?

The lieutenant snapped his fingers, his face suddenly brightening. "Taylor," he said. "That's her last name."

Justin whipped around, frozen in the act of shrugging into his jacket. His pulse jumped, fingers tightening on the wool. For a moment he couldn't breathe. "Are you sure?"

"Yessir, I'm quite sure. Is everything all right?"

Justin ignored him. *Brianna? Here?* He yanked on the jacket, tore out of the room and all but ran down the hallway.

Brianna barely heard the footsteps descending the stairs over the pounding of her heart. Gleaming black knee-high boots appeared, then a pair of long muscular legs, followed by a spotless blue tunic over wide shoulders. And then Justin's face came into view. He froze when he saw her, staring like she was an apparition. The sight of him took her breath away.

"Brianna," he said hoarsely.

Tears welled up. Her heart beat so hard it made her dizzy. "Hello, Major." Her voice was a near whisper, but it seemed to unfreeze him. In three strides he was down the stairs and hauling her in his arms, holding tight. Pressing her face into his throat with a soft cry, she clung to him, aware of the thudding of his pulse beneath her cold cheek and the strength of his arms around her. He felt amazing, better than she'd dreamed. That he seemed so happy to see her made more tears blur her eyes. His grip was almost bruising but she didn't care, absorbing the feel of him, real and whole as she let out a soggy laugh against the dark blue wool of his frock coat.

Justin breathed in deep and murmured her name, pulling back to study her with glistening eyes. He touched her cheeks, wiped her tears away and kissed her, his lips hungry and warm. With an inarticulate sound of need she stood on tiptoe to slide her fingers into his thick hair and opened for the hungry glide of his tongue. He tasted of coffee laced with sugar. A shockwave of sensation rushed through her body, hitting her low in the belly like a fist.

He pulled away far too soon and crushed her to him once more, his face pressed into her hair. Smiling, she leaned up to kiss his temple and closed her eyes as she cradled him, reveling in the moment. She'd dreamed of this for so long, she could hardly believe it was actually happening. When he finally straightened, his hands came up to frame her face, warm against her skin.

"You're really here," he murmured. "I feel like I'm dreaming."

"I would have come sooner, but I only got your letter about your brother a few days ago."

His eyes clouded. "You just received it? I sent it in October."

That didn't matter now. "I'm so sorry about Mitch."

"Thank you." He kissed the bridge of her nose, his voice turning rough. "It's been...difficult for me."

"I came as soon as I could. If you hadn't already gone into winter quarters, I may never have found you." She didn't want to ever let go of him.

He shook his head. "You came all the way from Fredericksburg in this weather just to see me?"

"Richmond."

"Richmond! That's where you've been all this time? Oh, angel, you're freezing. Come here." He curved around her, rubbing his hands over her back to warm her. Though she was already warm to her toes from seeing him, a shiver rippled through her. He cursed. "Come on. Let's get you in front of a fire with something hot to drink."

"Not yet," she whispered.

His hands stilled on her back. "No?"

"I don't want you to let go."

He chuckled and buried his face in her hair. "Damn, I've missed you, Bree."

"Missed you too," she mumbled against his shoulder. As his breath warmed the top of her head, the spicy scent of his soap reached her nose. She sighed and burrowed closer, could have stayed that way forever and died happy.

Justin continued stroking the length of her spine, at once soothing and arousing. "How about some tea?" he finally asked.

She glanced around the room, noted how quiet it was. She didn't want to wake anyone up just to make her a drink.

He wrapped his fingers around hers and brought them to his mouth to blow on them. A tremor of need snaked up her spine at the intimate act. He smiled. "You don't have anywhere to stay, do you." It wasn't a question.

"Not yet."

"I'll take care of it." He led her into a dining room and sat her in one of the high-backed chairs at the long table. "Be right back."

She felt badly for disturbing anyone, though she

supposed it wouldn't be proper to sleep on the sofa in the parlor.

He returned a few minutes later and gave her that slow smile that did funny things to her insides. "You can stay in my room. I'll bunk with Williams tonight. He's not half as beautiful as you, but it's a sacrifice I'm willing to make to know you're safe and warm in my bed." He gave her a wicked grin. "Even if I'm not in it with you."

His words sent another shaft of longing through her. She would love to have him beside her throughout the night, preferably naked. "Are you sure?"

"Absolutely. You hungry?"

"No, I ate earlier."

He ignored her and rummaged through one of the cupboards, filled a plate with bread and butter. "If you want something else, I can find the cook."

"This is plenty. Thank you." Her eyes drank him in. He was even more handsome than she remembered. He looked bigger, too. He'd regained the weight and muscle he'd lost after being wounded. It seemed so long ago now. Years instead of months. Her voice was rough when she spoke. "I've missed you so much."

He dropped into the chair next to hers and rubbed a thumb across her lips. "Me, too. More than you could ever imagine."

"Not possible. I wrote you dozens of letters. I guess they never made it to Lexington for my friend to pass on."

"No, and I was sure something had happened to you." Justin cupped her cheek in his broad palm. "What were you doing in Richmond?"

"My brother's there. In Libby."

He winced. "I'm sorry."

"He's all right. Hungry and crowded and dispirited,

but otherwise healthy." At least he was alive. Unlike Mitch. She wanted to ask Justin about it but decided to wait until he brought it up.

He tilted his head and eyed her. "You've lost weight. Your face is thinner. Have you been getting enough to eat? I understand times are hard there."

Brianna picked at her bread and butter. Did she look that bad? "Yes, times are very hard right now."

His eyes were guilt-stricken. "Jesus, the whole time we were stripping the Shenandoah, I never dreamed I was affecting you."

"I get by. I'm staying with a fairly well-off family, so we have more than most." She didn't want him blaming himself for her going hungry. And she didn't dare tell him she'd lost some of the weight because she skipped meals to make sure Morgan was fed.

His expression was so absorbed as he watched her eat, she laughed and demanded, "What?"

"I hate the thought of you going hungry. I hate even more that I had a hand in it."

She swallowed the mouthful of bread. "It's war, Justin. What you did in the valley weakened the Confederate army, too." In addition to leaving many citizens starving and homeless. How awful for him to have had to do that kind of work.

The simple meal filled the grinding void in her stomach. Warm, happy, replete, she smiled up at him. Neither of them had declared their love this time. They'd been apart for too long, yet she had no doubt of his love for her now. She saw it glowing in his eyes.

"Want more?" he asked.

She shook her head, not wanting to keep him up any longer because he had to be tired. It was almost one in the morning.

He rose. "You must be exhausted, angel." The endearment slid through her, wrapped around her heart. "If you're done here, I'll show you to your room."

She stood. "Will I see you tomorrow?" He had duties to fulfill. She didn't expect him to drop everything simply because she'd shown up on his doorstep. She'd been so focused on getting to him, she hadn't put much thought into what would happen when she arrived. She hoped she wouldn't be in the way.

His cheek creased as he smiled. "I'll go up and rearrange my schedule right now."

"Oh, no, don't—"

He stopped her by taking her face between his hands. "You think I wouldn't move heaven and earth to spend every possible minute with you? When we've been apart for six months and you've traveled halfway across the state in the middle of winter to find me?"

The longing behind the words hit her like a blow. She slid her arms around his waist and leaned up on tiptoe to kiss him, not caring who saw them. His arms felt like steel around her, his kiss almost desperate as he took her mouth and swept his tongue inside to taste her. Her heart squeezed at his unspoken need, the lingering grief she longed to soothe.

"I've missed you so goddamn much," he whispered unsteadily.

The vulnerability in him rocked her. She trailed her fingers through his hair. "I'm here. We're together now."

The clock chimed one, and he raised his head. "I'd better get you to your room." Taking her hand, he led her up the carved staircase to the second floor hallway, lined with doors on both sides. He stopped at the fourth one on the left, opened it and stepped back. A fire blazed in the hearth, no doubt courtesy of his lieutenant. The bed was neatly made against one wall, covered with a red and blue patchwork quilt. Justin's clothes lay folded in a pile on the bureau in the corner next to the washstand and dressing screen. Her carpetbag sat next to it. She glanced at him in question.

"I'll be across the hall, two doors to the right," he said. "Need anything before I go?"

You. I need you. "This is perfect." She only wished she could pull him down on the bed with her and not let him go until morning. But maybe that might still happen someday.

Justin kissed her again, this time slow and sweet enough to drag a moan from her when he pulled away. "Goodnight, then." She could see in his eyes how much he hated to leave her.

"Sleep well," she whispered.

His smile made her tingle all over. "You too."

She closed the door behind him, leaned against it, and sighed to relieve the disappointment inside her. After undressing and changing into her nightgown, she crawled into the large bed. Justin's scent was everywhere, imprinted on the pillows and sheets. With the cozy fire crackling beside her and a bright new day to look forward to, Brianna hugged a pillow to her chest and breathed in its smell deeply, wishing she were cradling him in her arms instead.

CHAPTER NINETEEN

Outside her bedroom window next morning the snow fell in thick flakes, forming drifts along the streets and sidewalks. Shortly after she'd risen, Lieutenant Williams had shown up with a breakfast tray and told her Justin would come for her around noon.

She remembered him instantly. "You came to see him when he was in the hospital, didn't you? And you were with him the day our wagon broke down on the road to White House Landing."

"Yes, ma'am. I'm flattered that you remember me."

She liked Williams. His brown eyes were kind. "Thank you for sharing your room with him. I hope I'm not too much of an inconvenience."

"Not at all, ma'am. Lucky for me he doesn't snore, though I wouldn't have complained. There's not much I wouldn't do for Major Thompson." His smile made his eyes warm as a mug of chocolate, and just as sweet. "He's real glad to have you here, ma'am."

"I'm glad to be here, lieutenant."

"It's been a long time since I've seen him smile. Really smile, I mean."

The words made her ache. "I would have come sooner if I could have."

Williams held up a hand. "At least you're here now. That's about the best late Christmas present I could think of for him."

She waited a beat before speaking. "Is he… How is he? Really."

"He's a trooper, ma'am, gets the job done no matter what. Doesn't talk much about what happened to his brother."

No, he wouldn't.

"The men and officers hold him in the highest regard. You'll see what I mean if you spend a bit of time here. He's one of the most respected officers in the Michigan Brigade."

"That doesn't surprise me in the least. I only hope I can earn half that much respect while I'm here."

"Already done, ma'am." Pausing in the doorway, he grinned. "After all, you came all this way to be with him, didn't you?"

Bolstered by the comment, she passed a few hours reading in her room so as not to get in anyone's way. When the knock came at her door, she sprang to her feet and opened it, and her heart skipped at the sight of Justin filling the jambs.

He gave her a knee-melting smile and bowed at the waist. "Good afternoon. Did you sleep well?"

"Yes." She tucked her hand into his.

"Dream about me?" His eyes smoldered.

"I did." She smothered a pang at the yearning on his face. "Are you sure you want to take me out? I don't mind waiting until later."

He laid a finger on her lips. "I've got a sleigh all rigged up outside."

A sleigh ride? How wonderful! "I'll get my coat. Should I bring a blanket?"

"No." His eyes glowed with a sensual light. "I'll make sure I keep you warm."

Her body tightened at the prospect. Brianna took the arm he offered, aware of all the men staring at her as they walked passed, those beneath him in rank saluting.

Outside, two bay horses stood harnessed at the front of the sleigh, the ground covered in a blanket of pristine white. Crisp air filled her lungs, tingled her cheeks. She had butterflies in her stomach when Justin helped her into the seat and climbed in beside her to tuck a heavy blanket around her before setting her feet on some warming bricks. For some reason, those simple gestures made tears prick her eyes. It had been so, so long since anyone had taken care of her, even in such small ways. She cherished his thoughtfulness.

"Warm enough?" he asked her.

So happy her heart was about to burst, she laughed. "What if I said no?"

His eyes heated. "I'd think of something."

"Then the truth is, I'm freezing."

He laughed and set an arm around her to pull her into his side.

The flirting felt so good. She hadn't done anything like it years.

Justin tugged his hat lower on his forehead. "All right, before you distract me enough to make me drive us into a snow bank, let me show you some of Winchester."

With a snap of the reins, he urged the horses

forward. Brianna snuggled into him, reveling in his nearness as he named the buildings and churches they passed. The icy breeze felt exhilarating. She closed her eyes and tilted her head back to let snowflakes drift down and land on her wind-kissed skin. A smile curved her lips.

"You're so beautiful," Justin murmured. "Even more beautiful than I remembered."

"Thank you." She tucked her hand into the crook of his arm. "I wouldn't have thought it possible for you to be more handsome than you were, but seeing you with that healthy glow in your cheeks proves me wrong. You look even better with your weight and muscle back on."

"Speaking of weight, I'm taking you someplace where I can feed you something to stick to your ribs."

She raised her brows. "You want to fatten me up?"

"I want to make sure you're not hungry," he corrected.

His voice had an edge to it. Was he still blaming himself? She touched his forearm, the muscles hard beneath her gloved fingers. "I really am fine."

"You'll be even better after your stomach's full."

Sensing it was pointless to argue, she leaned against him and enjoyed the ride. The runners made a quiet hissing sound as they glided over the snow, and the horses' hooves punching through the frozen crust on top with a crunch. At a building a few blocks off the main road, they stopped and Justin swung her down, his hands lingering on her waist. Right there in the street in front of anyone who cared to witness it, he kissed her slow and deep, making her toes curl in her boots. Then he led her inside the cozy restaurant, decorated with garlands and a Christmas tree set in the corner by a roaring fire. More men smiled and saluted him while he ushered her to a table near the hearth.

Charmed, she studied him as he ordered them glasses of mulled wine and beef stew with a crusty loaf of bread. His profile was bathed in the firelight, the golden flicker caressing his face. When he asked about her family's business, she told him about the stock she'd acquired and her plans with Morgan to turn it into the best property in Lexington.

His brows lowered. "Is that something you want? Or is it more to help your brother?"

"For him, mostly. It would pay the taxes and other expenses, anyhow."

"So what do *you* want?"

A husband and children of her own, but... She toyed with her wineglass, wondering how he would react to her answer. Only one way to find out, wasn't there? "Part of me misses treating patients. To be honest, I sometimes dream of being able to study medicine at a university one day." When he didn't say anything, she shifted in her chair. "To become a doctor."

He waited to respond until she glanced up at him. "I think you'd be an amazing doctor."

He did? He wasn't scandalized by the idea? "Thank you."

"You probably know more about medicine than half the practicing physicians out there right now. Dr. Healey seemed to think highly of your knowledge and skill, and I know I certainly benefitted from it."

Brianna bit back a smile, warmed by the compliment. "At the risk of sounding arrogant, I think I do too."

He laughed into his glass before setting it down. "What about the family you told me you wanted?"

She raised her eyebrows.

"Do you still want children?"

Was he offering? She stared at him, her lower abdomen tightening in reflex. She would love to marry him and have a family. And the making of them—she could hardly wait for that with Justin. "Yes, I've always wanted to have children of my own. You?"

One side of his mouth tipped up, his eyes lit with an intimate glow. "I'm warming to the idea, especially if I had them with you."

His answer surprised and delighted her. "Oh."

"I own part—well, now *most* of a lumber mill back home, so I have the means to support a family, but..."

He owned most of it now because Mitch had died. She waited for him to go on, worried if she mentioned his brother he would close down. "But what?"

His gaze dropped to his fingers, which toyed with the silverware. "I'm not sure I want to go back there. Not to stay, anyhow."

Why, she wanted to ask. *Because your brother is buried there?* Or was it something more than that?

He seemed relieved when the waiter arrived with their food. They tucked into their meals, sharing occasional smiles. She loved the simple intimacy of being with him like this.

Over a dessert of spice cake with lemon sauce, she told him about her position in the Lancaster household and her visits with Morgan at Libby, the conditions there. He seemed like he was about to say something when a voice spoke up behind them.

"Major Thompson."

Justin glanced over his shoulder, and Brianna's eyes went wide. The man coming toward them was dressed for snow but even with his uniform hidden, his curly gold locks and moustache were instantly recognizable. General Custer stood at their table.

Justin rose. "Sir," he said, shaking the hand offered to him.

The general smiled at her. "I wanted to meet this mysterious woman the whole Brigade is talking about."

She flushed. They were already talking about her?

"Sir, this is Mrs. Brianna Taylor."

"Your fiancée. I heard."

She tried not to gape. His fiancée? Is that what he'd told everyone?

"I can't recommend marriage highly enough," Custer said. "Better put your furlough to good use, Major, and marry the girl right here in Winchester."

Justin was spared a reply when someone across the room called out to the general. With a warm smile and a polite goodbye, Custer took his leave.

When Justin sat again, Brianna laughed in awe. "I just met General Custer."

He grinned. "You did. Now that's something to tell the grandchildren."

She hoped he meant theirs. When he'd paid the bill he took her outside, where a young sergeant waited with the sleigh. Justin handed her up again. "Want more warming bricks for the ride back?"

"No. You do a better job than they do."

He grinned and kissed her, then carried on with the tour. The snow had stopped and the wind had ceased. The naked trees lining the streets and squares were frosted white. The city looked like something out of a painting under its wintry veil. She could only imagine how pretty it would be in the spring when all the buds and flowers came out. Would the war finally be over by then? She didn't want to be separated from him again.

"When does your furlough start?" she asked.

"In a few days. I've got a month before I have to report back for duty."

And head back to the front. *No, don't think about that.* "Are you going home then?" If he was, she would return to Richmond. Morgan would be hungry without her visits.

"I haven't decided yet."

She understood. Going home had been scary for her, too.

He stopped the horses in a park, took her hands and tucked them in the crook of his arm. "I'm so glad you came."

"I am, too." Being with him was worth every cold, bone-jarring mile she'd traveled.

"So, apparently the whole town already thinks of you as my fiancée."

Her heart tripped. "Yes, I heard that." *Don't get your hopes up. Don't you dare.*

Justin glanced away. When he met her eyes again she saw the longing there, the love. "Want to make it official?"

"Do you?" she countered.

"More than anything." He framed her face with his hands. "I love you, Brianna. Will you be my wife?"

"Yes," she whispered, and wrapped her arms around his shoulders. Was she dreaming? If she was, she didn't ever want to wake up.

Justin hugged her tight and let out a ragged breath.

She pushed back until she could meet his gaze. "When?"

His deep blue eyes twinkled at her eagerness. "Is tomorrow too soon?"

"I'll see if I can find time in my busy schedule, but

yes, that sounds perfect."

Surprise flashed across his face. "You would marry me tomorrow?"

"Yes." She'd marry him right now if they could find someone to preside and a couple of witnesses. Right here in the snowy park in front of their sleigh. "I love you and I can't wait to be your wife."

His arms closed hard around her and he pulled her into his lap to cradle her against his body. "Angel, I love you too." His soft laugh ruffled her hair. "I don't know if I can wait until tomorrow."

She rained kisses across his face, down to his lips where she lingered. "You can spend tonight thinking about all the ways to keep me warm after the ceremony."

"God," he whispered, tensing beneath her hands. He set a gloved palm around her nape and sought her mouth, making her gasp and tremble as his tongue slid into her mouth. She leaned closer and pushed her breasts against his chest, moaned at the immediate tightening in her body. As his mouth burned a path down her throat, she tipped her head back on a sigh.

It was snowing again. She savored Justin's heat and strength, the dizzying trail of his tongue against her neck making her shiver in delight. He sucked at a sensitive spot and she jerked, but his strong hands held her steady, making her melt as fast as the snowflakes on her burning skin. Her eyes drifted closed. She loved him so much it hurt.

Held tight in her future husband's arms, Brianna held her face up to the sky as the snow drifted down, brushing her smiling face like the caress of an angel's wings.

CHAPTER TWENTY

He was a married man.

It still seemed surreal. Mere hours ago, Justin had stood at the altar beside Brianna and taken his vows. She'd been so beautiful in the lavender gown someone had loaned her for the occasion, her happy smile so full of love it humbled him. He'd placed the sapphire ring he'd bought that morning on her finger and taken her as his wife, then kissed her in front of the pastor, Williams, and the landlady of the boardinghouse. Coming out of the church, he'd stopped dead at the sight of his entire regiment mounted and waiting in formation. They'd given a raucous cheer and paraded past to salute them. The gesture had touched him deeply.

Afterward, the officers threw them a dinner, and the Brigade band was there to play. All night, while he'd fed Brianna tidbits from the banquet and twirled her in his arms across the dance floor, all he could think about was pulling off that lavender gown and pressing her deep into the nearest bed while he made love to her until she came apart beneath him.

But now that he was here outside their hotel room, he was stalling.

He wanted to throw the door open, stalk across the room and kiss her until she couldn't breathe or think, strip her naked and have her panting underneath him while he pleasured her with his hands and mouth.

A niggling doubt kept him from opening the door.

She might not be ready. They'd only just reunited yesterday after spending months apart, and part of him was still surprised that she'd agreed to marry him so soon. He paused, hand tightening on the doorknob. His heart pounded as though he was about to face a firing squad.

She'd already had a wedding night with a man she'd loved.

This first time set the tone for everything. She was a woman; she'd have certain expectations for their wedding night. He needed to get it right. The last thing he wanted to do was walk in there and fall on her like a ravenous animal, but that was exactly what he was afraid might happen. She was a sensual woman already aware of the pleasures of the marriage bed, and they'd been apart for too long. He wasn't sure he could control the need driving him.

But he was sure as hell going to try.

He twisted the knob. Entering the room and closing the door behind him, Justin took one look at his beautiful wife and his mind went blank.

Crouched in front of the fireplace wearing nothing but a filmy white nightgown, Brianna smiled at him over her shoulder. His mouth went dry. Her thick mahogany hair spilled to her waist in waves as she stood, the flickering flames turning the material transparent enough for him to see every line of her delectable body. Oh yeah, she was definitely naked under there. He went rock hard in his dress trousers and had to shift his stance.

"Hello." She rose and walked toward him with a pronounced sway of her hips.

"Hello," he echoed, fighting the urge to take her down to the rug and pin her beneath him. Jesus, she was gorgeous. His heart thudded in his ears as he tried to gauge her mood. She didn't seem nervous. In fact, she looked rather...hungry. He suddenly couldn't get enough air.

She stopped inches away from him, close enough for him to breathe in the spicy sweet scent of her, her exquisite silhouette exposed through the thin gown. He dragged his gaze from the hard points of her rose-tinted nipples that pressed against the fabric. Her hair looked so shiny and soft. He reached up to skim his fingers through a lock of it.

"You all right?" she asked.

"Yes." Damn it, he was botching this whole thing. He should have opened the door and swept her up in his arms—

"You seem a little...unsettled."

Maybe because he wanted to take her so badly he was shaking.

A soft smile curved her mouth. "You're not having second thoughts about marrying me, are you? We've only been man and wife for a few hours, so I couldn't have done anything too awful yet, could I?"

The teasing light in her eyes made him feel like an idiot. He didn't have the faintest idea what to say. Plus his tongue felt like it was glued to the roof of his mouth.

Brianna smothered a laugh and closed the space between them, twining her arms around his shoulders. He slid his around her waist, his hands flexing on her firm flesh. He wanted to lay her on the bed and hold her to it while he kissed and licked every part of her. Until she writhed and sobbed with the need for release.

"Not at all." He forced the raging hunger down, fighting the primitive need inside him.

Her eyes laughed up at him. "Justin, are you nervous?"

"No." Just because he was standing there with his boots nailed to the floor didn't mean he was nervous.

Her lips quirked in amusement. She lowered her voice to an intimate whisper. "You realize I've already seen you naked, right?"

"I'm extremely aware of it."

Her eyes twinkled as she took his hand and tugged him toward the bed. "You don't need to worry. I'll be gentle."

He laughed at that, and the band around his chest loosened. Judging by the seductive glow in her eyes, coaxing her was the last thing he needed to worry about tonight. Damn, she was breathtaking. He stopped her next to the bed to drag her against him, savoring the pressure of her unrestrained breasts pressed to his chest. The warmth of her skin radiated through the thin fabric of her nightgown as he slid his hands up her spine to hold the back of her head. "I love you," he whispered.

She smiled in answer. "Show me."

With pleasure.

He bent his head and took her mouth, absorbing the heady sigh she gave. She leaned into him, her body wrapped in that flimsy layer of material, making him half-crazy with the need to get her naked. He held her still and kissed her deeply, exploring her mouth with his tongue. Brianna was just as eager as him. She undid the buttons of his dress coat and helped him shrug out of it, then his waistcoat. When she opened his shirt beneath it and laid her hands on his bare chest, he let out a ragged groan, his cock hard and pulsing.

The kiss turned hungry, almost frantic. He let one hand trail down to lock on the curve of her hip. She felt incredible, firm yet lushly feminine. His breath was unsteady when he lifted his head to gaze at her. Her eyes were dilated with desire, black swallowing gray. Her lips were swollen and glistening from his kisses.

Impatient, she pushed the shirt off his shoulders and hummed in approval as she nuzzled his skin with the tip of her nose. His hands tunneled into her hair when her lips trailed across his chest, following her fingers when they moved down over his ribs to the healed wound she'd sewn up. She pressed hot kisses to the length of the scar, ran her tongue over it. The gesture turned his heart over and enflamed him at the same time. He growled low in his throat and tugged her upward to meet his kiss.

Her hands closed over the waistband of his trousers, undid the buttons and slid them down his thighs with his drawers. Making a soft sound of need into his mouth, she moved one silken palm over the naked length of his erection.

God. His whole body jolted as he sucked in a breath. "Bree…" He was a heartbeat away from ripping the gown off her and throwing her onto the bed. His hands contracted on her hip and hair as he battled the fog of lust engulfing him.

"I've dreamed of this for so long." Her grip

tightened around his aching flesh and she flicked her tongue over the pulse point in his throat. His eyes closed in ecstasy. "Lie down so I can enjoy you," she whispered.

Kicking off his boots and trousers, he grabbed her and laid her on the bed on her back. Her eyes glowed up at him in invitation. He set one knee on the mattress and reached for the buttons at her neck but she evaded him and pushed his hands away before hiking up the hem of her nightgown to kneel before him. She ran her hands over his shoulders and chest and drank him in with her gaze, which settled on his engorged cock, making the relentless throb worse. He let her look her fill and reveled in the feel of her hands roving over his heated skin. She made him writhe and arch as she petted him everywhere but the aching erection throbbing against his belly.

"I imagined doing this to you while you were at the hospital," she whispered, her focus on the way her fingers trailed over the twitching muscles in his abdomen.

Damn, was she trying to kill him? He ached so badly it was all he could do not to wrench the gown up to her waist and roll her beneath him. Somehow he held back and let her explore his body. He could barely breathe for the sensual hunger on her face. "Take off your gown."

Instead she angled her head and kissed him deeper, her tongue twining around his, and at last closed her hand over his aching length. He gasped and grabbed her waist. His muscles trembled as he battled back the tide of dark need demanding he take control. She stroked him experimentally, her palm smooth and cool against his raging hot skin. Justin moaned and lifted into her touch, thrilled that she was so uninhibited. Sweet God, it was so good... He'd dreamed of this so many times—

She pulled her hand away.

Breathless, he watched as she lifted the hem of her gown over her head and let it drop to the floor. "Brianna," he rasped, forcing it out of his tight throat. She was even more stunning than he'd imagined. Unbelievably beautiful. Her smooth, creamy skin and high, round breasts topped by deep pink nipples. Her stomach was flat, the dark curls between her thighs already glistening with her arousal. His erection pounded in agony.

Helpless to stop himself, he reached out and cupped her breasts in his hands, fascinated at the way her hard nipples responded to his slightest touch. She made a purring sound and arched her back, letting her eyes close. He feathered his thumb across one tight peak, and was rewarded by her quick intake of breath as the sensitive flesh drew taut. Spots of color rode high on her cheeks, her lips parting in pleasure.

Justin set his hands at her waist and lifted her to straddle him, then cradled her breasts in both hands and bent to take one rigid tip into his mouth. Brianna moaned and whispered his name, her hands sliding into his hair to hold him closer as he sucked her. Her skin was so warm, smelled of spices and soap. God, he could do this forever, pleasuring her while she writhed in his lap. He flicked his tongue over her captive flesh and sucked harder, rolling the other between his thumb and forefinger. Her soft cries filled the room, testing his restraint.

Brianna shifted restlessly and wriggled closer until the dampness of her sex pressed against his throbbing erection. The contact wrenched a groan out of him. Needing to watch her climax for him, he slid one hand down between them to caress her belly and the inside of her thighs until she arched into his touch. Between her thighs he brushed his fingertips against her tender pink folds in a teasing caress, finding her soft and slick. She whimpered and clutched his head tighter to her breast, rocking her hips against his searching fingers.

He could feel the need in her, the same desperation that tormented him. Justin switched to her other breast. He sucked as he stroked the slick petals of her sex, rubbing around the swollen nub of her clitoris. She opened her thighs wider for him, the muscles in her legs trembling. Justin curled his tongue around her nipple, pressed a finger against her opening and eased it inside. Her body clenched around him, so hot and wet he almost growled. He held his finger there for a few seconds then slowly thrust in and out, placing his thumb over her swollen bud to give her the contact she sought.

Crying out, Brianna rocked against his hand and held his face against her breasts. He was frantic to be inside her. Her body quivered in his grip, her head tipped back, gorgeous hair flowing to her waist. *"Justin."* Her voice was raw, his name a hoarse plea for more. For release.

The primal side of him took over. He rolled her beneath him and covered her with his weight, settling between her splayed thighs. Immediately she wrapped them around him, digging her heels into his flanks. Justin braced his weight on one forearm and bent to torment her stiff nipples with his mouth while he continued to stroke between her legs. Brianna sighed and opened her eyes, heavy lidded and dark with pleasure.

Unable to help himself, Justin rubbed his erection against the smooth skin on her thigh. She was wet and willing, more than ready for him.

Slow down. Make it good for her.

He raised his head from her breast to flick his tongue across her lower lip, and stole inside a moment before retreating. She murmured against his mouth and lifted up for more, legs tightening around him, trying to pull him inside. Justin couldn't wait another moment. He pulled his hand from her body, grasped his swollen cock and positioned himself at her entrance.

His free hand tunneled into her hair. He kissed her hard, deep, and slid the head of his erection against her, making her slick and desperate for him. Her spine arched in a silent plea, but he merely slid his mouth over her jaw and down her throat, nibbled and nuzzled his way to her breasts. She gave a breathless cry and gripped him tighter, urging him to enter her.

"Justin..."

The stark plea in her voice made his heart pound. He was dying to push into her. But he wanted to hold her like this, stroke and kiss her all over, stare down into her face as he made her climax first without the distraction of his own pleasure.

He shifted his weight and trailed his hand over her stomach to her hip, down one silky smooth thigh. Back up the inside of it. "You're so soft," he whispered reverently against her breast. His fingers stroked with a feather-light touch over her slick heat.

"Ohhh," she gasped, lifting. Her hands clutched at his hair, demanding more.

His head swam as the sweet scent of her arousal reached him. Holding her still with his weight, he worked two fingers into her and pressed upward, searching for the spot that would give her the most pleasure. He knew he'd found it when her hips jerked and a broken moan spilled from the back of her throat. She was so responsive to his every touch, so uninhibited. His muscles trembled with the effort of holding back.

Justin withdrew his fingers and swirled them in slow circles across her glistening nub. She let out a choked cry and buried her face against his shoulder. All his protective instincts lit up.

"Shhh," he crooned in reassurance, leaning more of his weight on her. Anchoring her with his body as he drove her higher. "Don't hold back. Give me all of you." He kept circling that fragile bud and made note of her every subtle movement that told him what felt best for her.

Brianna panted against his throat and dug her fingers into his back. She trembled beneath him, face flushed, eyes squeezed shut. Exactly as he'd imagined her in his fantasies, only a thousand times better. Her erotic cries sliced through him.

"I know, love," he murmured against her breast, slowing his touch a little. Caressing the sensitive bundle of nerves. "So sweet."

She turned her head away with a gasp. "Please."

"Shhh." He stretched out over her to drop fervent kisses over her chin and nose, across her cheeks and eyelids. With an inarticulate sound of need, she grabbed his shoulders and twisted her head to find his mouth and stroke her tongue against his. Breathing hard, Justin rose up on his forearm. Brianna held his gaze and raised her hips, bit her lower lip as the head of his erection lodged against her. He stopped, held himself still though his body screamed at him to plunge inside her.

His beautiful wife lay panting beneath him, offering her body and heart to him. This was his chance to show her what she'd meant to him all these long, lonely months. He would give her unspeakable pleasure in return for every soothing touch she'd given him in the hospital, for every time he'd dreamed of her when he'd laid his head down at night, shivering out in the field. He wanted to love her with all the longing he'd carried in his heart, through the hell of war and his brother's horrific death.

Staring down into her luminous eyes, Justin flexed his hips and buried himself inside her. With a throttled groan he dropped his head to her shoulder, struggling to hang on. Brianna squeezed him so tightly every ripple of her internal muscles threatened to send him over the edge. His hands fisted in the sheets beside her head. Sweat broke out across his skin at the sweet friction of being inside her. He shuddered, tried to breathe.

"More," she whispered, arching up.

Justin lifted his head, shifted his weight and reached a hand down to where their bodies joined. He stroked the swollen bud that throbbed under his fingers, caressing it in lazy circles as he watched her face. The sounds she made turned sharp, plaintive.

Giving rein to the savage need inside him, he thrust into her with a hard, deep rhythm as the pleasure intensified. A ragged sound escaped him. So damn close...

"Yes," she urged.

He slid his tongue into her mouth and gave her what she wanted, swallowing her frantic cries as he took her hard and fast. The incredible friction intensified, and the feel of her hands digging into his shoulders sent a dark thrill through him. Her breathing changed, turned shallow. She threw her head back, and the muscles deep inside her body clenched around him.

Justin rode her hard and fast, the ropes under the mattress creaking as he watched her ignite. Her pink lips parted in a throaty cry, her body pulsing in the throes of release. His cock swelled, caressed by every intimate flutter. Sensation rocketed down his spine as he held her there, release racing toward him. Helpless to stop it, he let out a guttural cry and exploded, the pleasure so intense he couldn't breathe. When the spasms finally faded, he dropped his head next to hers on the pillow and breathed in her scent, limp and satiated. He couldn't have moved if his life depended on it.

A long time later, Brianna began raining gentle kisses on his face. He raised his head to find her eyes were damp with a sheen of tears. His beautiful, amazingly erotic wife. "Bree," he whispered in awe. He had no words. None at all.

"Hmmm." Her sigh was dreamy. "That was definitely worth the wait."

With a laugh, Justin kissed her smiling mouth. "Glad you think so." And to think this intimacy would only get better between them with time. He turned them so she was sprawled against his chest and soothed her with sweeps of his palm over her back, tender kisses across her face.

She pushed his hair away from his temples and gazed up at him with languorous silver eyes. "I love you."

He grinned. "Love you too." Wrapping her up in his arms, he pulled the blankets over them and ran one hand over her curves, savoring the velvet of her skin against his palm. So far, marriage was even better than he'd imagined.

CHAPTER TWENTY ONE

Detroit, MI
January 9, 1865

"Let's go, Bree."

She didn't want to.

"Come on." Chuckling, Justin took the hand she'd wrapped around the carriage door latch and pried her stiff fingers loose.

She wasn't ready to do this yet. The two-story brick manor loomed outside the coach window, shadowy and imposing. She wished they'd stayed in Winchester for the rest of their honeymoon instead of coming to Detroit to stay with his mother.

Justin sighed at her reluctance. "Angel, we've been stuck in here long enough. Stop worrying. There's no reason to be nervous."

That was the second time he'd said that, and she still didn't believe him.

Because *he* was the reason she was so nervous. In

the three days since they'd left Winchester, he'd become increasingly remote and withdrawn, so unlike the attentive, affectionate husband she'd come to know. And his posture had changed the moment the Detroit rail station had come into view outside their frosted train car window. The whole carriage ride to the house he'd been distracted. He wasn't looking forward to coming home. Was it because Mitch was buried here? Or was it because he dreaded seeing his mother? He'd already warned Brianna that she wouldn't be herself, still grief stricken over Mitch.

Whatever was bothering him, Brianna was about to find out what it was.

He tugged again. "Let's get inside where it's warm."

She allowed him to help her climb out, then gripped his arm and followed him to the front door, mentally preparing herself for meeting her mother-in-law. *What if she doesn't like me?*

She didn't know why the thought came to her. She hadn't even met the woman yet, so what could she have possibly done to earn her dislike? It was just that she'd known Caleb's parents for years before he had asked for her hand.

Justin glanced down at her and caught her chewing her lip. He gave her a reassuring smile. "It'll be fine. I love you, and so will my mother."

Heart racing, she smoothed her hair. What a sight she must be, with her traveling outfit all wrinkled and her hair mussed. She wanted to make a favorable impression.

The door opened, and she almost retreated a step when a tall, gray-haired tornado roared out and grabbed Justin in a bone-crushing hug, crowing in a thick Scottish accent. "There's my lad!"

Justin removed himself from the woman's arms to introduce her. "Aggie," he announced proudly, "this is my beautiful wife, Brianna."

"Brianna!" Aggie crowed, holding out her arms to envelop her. "Praise be! I'm the housekeeper and mistress of the kitchen, among other things."

Brianna gasped at the strength of the woman's grip and darted an uncertain look at Justin, who eyed them in obvious enjoyment. She patted Aggie's back, her cheek smothered against the ample bosom. What would Mrs. Thompson's welcome be like if this was the housekeeper? "Hello, Aggie," she managed, pulling her face from its apron-covered cushion. "I'm pleased to meet you."

Aggie grinned at her. "Och, saints! Did ye hear the lass? She's *pleased to meet me,* she is. Such a polite little miss. My, my, I never did meet anyone with such nice manners." She released Brianna long enough to let her straighten and then grasped her upper arms to hold her still. "Oh! Isn't she a picture." She gave Justin a wink. "She's a keeper, she is."

"Glad you think so, Aggie. I agree."

Aggie took each of them by the arm and ushered them inside. Brianna caught the smug look Justin gave her that said, *I told you so.*

The house was enormous, filled with dark wood and the lemony scent of furniture polish. Everything gleamed with a rich luster, from the parquet floor where she could almost see her reflection to the walnut banister that led up a curving stairway. The place smelled clean and fresh, and the rooms she could see from the foyer were inviting and cozy, despite their grandeur.

Shuffling footsteps from above made her look to the upper landing. Someone hovered there, hidden in shadow. Justin came up behind her, and Brianna sensed his sudden tension as he laid a hand on her shoulder.

"Hello, Mother."

The figure stepped into the light, and Brianna swallowed a gasp. This was Justin's mother? She was diminutive, almost shrunken in her shroud of black. Her grayed hair was pinned back into a severe chignon that pulled at the skin of her eyes. As she made her way down the stairs, her gait was stiff and awkward, making her look much older than she was. Her white fingers clutched the edges of her black shawl together at her throat. No smile of greeting showed on her pale, pinched face, or on the thinned, bloodless lips. Her dark eyes were sunken, her cheekbones sharp blades beneath her skin. The shadows beneath her eyes looked like bruises.

Justin's hand tightened a fraction on her shoulder. Unease settled in Brianna's stomach. She waited in breathless silence to see how this would go, but she already feared the worst. Just as she'd dreaded, this was not a happy homecoming. Her heart bled for Justin.

His mother paused on the lowest step and curled skeletal fingers around the newel post as if she needed the support to hold her upright. She cleared her throat and managed a hoarse, "Hello."

That was all. No cry of gladness at seeing her only son. No hug. Not even a smile.

Brianna's gut knotted. This was awful. Obviously the woman was unwell, but still she would have expected his mother to show some sign of warmth or gladness. The silence stretched taut as a wire between them. Brianna stepped into the breach, desperate to make things right.

"I'm Brianna," she said, stepping away from Justin. As she approached to shake the woman's hand, her steps faltered. Mrs. Thompson stared at her out of sunken eyes, but her expression remained curiously blank. Brianna cast a furtive glance over her shoulder and caught the grim set of Justin's jaw. She gathered her nerve, put on a smile to face her once more. "I'm…your new daughter-in-law." Had she not received Justin's telegram informing her of the marriage?

The woman might have been a statue for all the reaction she gave.

Keep talking. Smooth it over. "I've heard so much about you, and I'm pleased to finally meet you." She could feel the blood rushing to her cheeks. Even if the wedding news came as a shock, didn't she remember the letters Brianna had sent to her when Justin was in the hospital, and afterward, when he and Mitch had come home to recover?

Those thin lips pursed into a harsh line then smoothed back out. A flicker of movement, nothing more.

Utter silence filled the room. Brianna swallowed the lump in her throat, not knowing what else to say. Justin came to her rescue, saving her from more embarrassment by pushing past and going up to his mother. He bent to draw her into his arms, but the tiny woman remained stiff, her eyes glassy, almost vacant. After a second he stepped back, and Brianna caught the flash of pain on his face. It almost broke her heart.

"Perhaps Aggie could make us some tea," he said in a rough voice.

He returned to take Brianna's elbow but wouldn't meet her eyes. She wanted to draw him into her arms and comfort him, and refrained only because it would hurt his pride. Wanting to be anywhere but it this dark, depressing house, she nonetheless let him escort her to the parlor and seat her before returning for his mother.

Aggie bustled in with a hopeful expression. "How did it go?"

Brianna swallowed. "I...I think it might be best if we stayed somewhere else."

Aggie made a scoffing sound. "Nonsense. This is his home, and yours now too. The both of you are welcome anytime. The mistress...she isn't herself these days."

Ever since Mitch had been killed, she meant. "Has she been like this since it happened?"

"Aye. Though she's improved somewhat."

This was *improvement?*

"Tonight's the first time she's been downstairs." Aggie's eyes darted to the doorway, a pucker forming on her brow. "How's my dearest lad taking it?"

Brianna wrapped her arms about her waist. "He's..." *Devastated. Guilt-stricken.* "He's bearing up."

Aggie shook her head. "Poor lad. I was so hoping seeing him would snap her out of it, but I suppose I was bein' fanciful."

Brianna sensed great kindness in the woman. Judging from how warmly she'd greeted Justin, she loved him to pieces, and Brianna knew she had an ally where her husband's welfare was concerned. "What should I do?"

The other woman's eyes filled with sympathy. She set a motherly hand on Brianna's arm. "Just love him, lass. Love him with all ye've got. Lord knows the missus won't be able to. Not for a few months, maybe years. Maybe never. She was bad the first time, but this..." She shook her head. "This about killed her, it did."

Brianna frowned. "The first time?"

"Och, aye. After the master died in the last war, she didn't come out of her room for months, and that's when she had both the wee lads to cheer her. Took almost two years to get her off the laudanum."

Laudanum. Of course. Why hadn't she recognized the signs and symptoms right in front of her? The unnatural pallor, the gauntness, the glazed expression. The grief was part of it, but the drug explained the total lack of emotion. Well, Brianna could definitely do something about that, couldn't she? She'd wait a while, see if things improved, and if they didn't, with Justin's permission she could intervene and wean her off the medication.

His booted footsteps hit the parquet floor, and a moment later he appeared in the doorway. His expression was set, shoulders stiff. "My mother won't be joining us tonight. She's retired to her room with a headache."

An excuse? More likely another symptom that she was addicted to the laudanum and became ill when she went too long between doses. Brianna held her tongue, in truth relieved that they wouldn't be forced to suffer more of what they'd endured in the foyer. She hated to see him hurting like this, though.

She rose and slid her hand into his, twining their fingers together, and gave him a loving smile. "Why don't we go into the kitchen? I can help Aggie, and you two can catch up." She tugged on his arm, and he leaned down to kiss the top of her head.

"Thank you," he whispered, eyes full of gratitude.

"I love you," she told him simply. Mitch would have wanted him to find love and happiness, she was certain of it. When she glanced back at Aggie, she saw tears in the woman's eyes.

"You know, lad," she said to Justin, "you definitely picked a keeper with this one."

He smiled a little and stroked his hand over Brianna's spine. "I sure did, Aggie."

****

The next few days passed with no improvement between Justin and his mother. Mrs. Thompson spent most of the time in her room, taking meals only if someone brought her a tray. Brianna and Aggie made a valiant effort to lift Justin's spirits, but the tension was already taking an emotional and physical toll on him. She'd noticed it the first night there.

Brianna woke every morning alone in their bed, and at night when Justin came up—if he didn't wander the house all night or sleep elsewhere—he crawled in beside her long after she was asleep and didn't reach for her. During the day, he'd been at the lumber mill to meet with his foreman, to the bank to discuss his finances, and to his lawyer to amend his will, making her a beneficiary. On the second night he'd had a bad nightmare, and when she tried to talk to him about it he'd shut her out and left the room.

Brianna attempted to ignore how lonely and isolated she felt, telling herself he was grieving all over again, for both Mitch and his mother. As much as she could, she gave him his space. But the last time she'd tried to initiate physical intimacy, Justin had instead turned her onto her side and pulled her back against his chest and pretended to sleep. Not like him at all.

His withdrawal from her might not have worried her so much if she hadn't noticed the smell of the whiskey on him last night when he finally came to bed. That, coupled with the shadows beneath his eyes and the buried pain in his expression, made her feel as if a giant fist squeezed her chest. Being here was the last thing any of them needed. They should leave well enough alone and go back to Winchester, enjoy what little time remained of Justin's leave.

On the fourth day of their visit, she was in the kitchen with Aggie when her eyes strayed to the door off the main hall that was always closed. No one ever went in there but Justin's mother, Aggie had said, except to clean. "Aggie, what's so special about that room?" she finally asked.

Aggie paused in the midst of mashing potatoes, lips flattening into a hard line. "That's the den, lass. Mr. Brandon's portrait and chair are in there."

Justin's father. Justin avoided the room, too, she'd noticed.

Looking around to ensure they were alone, Aggie lowered her voice to a whisper. "Nothing's been changed since the day he died. Not one thing. His pipe and tobacco pouch are still on the side table where he left them, and his empty tea cup is still beside his chair."

A shrine. To a dead husband.

At her shocked expression, Aggie sighed. "Might as well see it now. You'll understand better what I'm sayin' to ye."

She went to the den door, waited for Aggie to push it open and light a lamp. Heart heavy, Brianna moved inside, taking in the single brown leather armchair with its matching ottoman beside the fireplace. The seat and armrests were worn from use, and the pipe, tobacco and teacup were placed just as she'd been told. It looked like Mr. Thompson had just left the room and was expected back at any moment.

Her gaze lifted to the oil portrait suspended over the mantel. Justin's father had been a handsome man, and his sons strongly resembled him except for their deep blue eyes. A dress sword she assumed was his lay displayed across the mantel. The dark green wallpaper might have made the room feel cozy if it hadn't all seemed so dark and depressing. The room was a frozen tableau, as if he might walk back in and pick up his pipe, then sink into that chair next to the fire. Like he'd never been gone.

The Vacant Chair, she thought with a hard swallow, remembering the song's lyrics.

We shall meet but we shall miss him.
There will be one vacant chair.
We shall linger to caress him
When we breathe our evening prayer.

Now another chair sat vacant, this one next to the head of the table that everyone avoided. Mitch's place, still set for him.

Her throat tightened. "Oh, Aggie."

"Aye, almost breaks your heart, it does."

"Bree?"

She whipped around at Justin's voice and put a hand to her chest. He stood in the hall, his gaze troubled as he looked into the room. His shirt was rumpled, his eyes bloodshot, and if she stepped closer she knew she'd smell more whiskey on him. "Sorry. I didn't hear you."

He merely stared at her, and she was afraid she'd intruded on something he would rather have kept private. "That's my father," he said finally, nodding at the portrait.

"Yes. You look like him. He was a handsome man."

A frown drew his brows together. "I don't remember much about him." He sounded perplexed. "I was ten when he died."

Being in here was making him even sadder. She stepped out with Aggie, closed the door behind her and took his hand. She felt guilty for intruding on his family's privacy, even though she'd done nothing wrong.

"It's all right," he said. "I don't mind you looking around. My mother's behavior might make more sense now." He pulled from her grasp and rubbed his hand over the back of his neck. As though ashamed of it, or maybe the way he'd been avoiding her. She hoped it was the latter.

Yes, the room explained a lot. And now, more than ever, she knew that being here was toxic for her husband. The guilt and grief within these walls were slowly suffocating him. "Are you hungry? Aggie and I made a roast with gravy and—"

"No. Not hungry."

She closed the gap between them and gripped his hand to re-establish the connection they'd been missing since their first night here. "You've hardly eaten anything since we've arrived."

He averted his eyes and fidgeted as though he wanted to shake off her touch and leave. And maybe he did. "I have some things to take care of in town," he said, glancing at her. "Will you be all right with Aggie?"

Why shouldn't I be? I've spent nearly all my time here with her because you've been avoiding me like some kind of contagious disease. No, she couldn't say that to him. The last thing she wanted was to drive him further away. "I'll be fine. When will you be back?"

Again he withdrew his hand from hers. "Not sure. Few hours, maybe."

He couldn't stand to be in the house. That was why he was gone so often, and she couldn't blame him for wanting to escape. But where did he go? Besides out to drink. Riding aimlessly? Or to his brother's grave tucked beneath the oak tree? She hated that he shut her out. She wanted to ease his suffering, prove to him how much she loved him.

Brianna forced her frustration down. They'd be leaving here soon enough. For now, she couldn't do anything but let him work through this on his own and pray he'd revert back to the man she'd fallen in love with once they left. But given his imminent return to the war and hers to Richmond, his neglect of her was all the more hurtful.

"Just be careful," she said, because it was all she had left to say.

He gave her a half smile and bent to kiss her. A slow, lingering kiss that made her heart beat faster and filled her with hope. "Don't worry. I'll see you later."

No, you won't, she thought, watching him walk away. As the front door closed with a thud behind him, she knew she'd be spending yet another night alone in his bed.

CHAPTER TWENTY TWO

At breakfast the next morning, Brianna found Justin already at the table. He offered a tentative smile and rose to kiss her before pulling out a chair for her beside him.

"Good morning," she said, trying to keep things on an even footing. "Sleep well?"

"Fine," he answered, not meeting her eyes as he poured them both coffee from the steaming pot Aggie must have set out. His eyes seemed redder, the shadows below them darker, his whiskers dark on his unshaven face.

Let it go, she warned herself, resisting the surge of her temper. It wasn't as if she was suspicious that he'd gone to find comfort in another woman's arms. Blasting him was only going to alienate him more, but it wasn't easy to hold her tongue. She hadn't married him to be alone, and she hated that he was hurting.

Someone knocked on the front door. He excused himself, no doubt eager to escape her scrutiny, and reappeared a minute later with the last person on earth she wanted to see.

Laurel Stevens swept into the room and greeted her with a brittle smile. Brianna set down her cup and stood to face her, a hard knot forming in her stomach. "Good morning." She did her best to keep her tone civil. Was it her imagination, or did Justin seem even more uncomfortable? He wouldn't look at either of them.

Laurel held her stiff smile. "Good morning. You look lovely."

Do I. Gritting her teeth, Brianna indicated a chair across from her. "Please, join us."

Laurel hesitated, tilting her head questioningly at Justin as if there was some doubt whether she would join them. Whatever she'd come to say, Brianna would find out soon enough.

When Justin pulled out Laurel's chair, she sat and accepted the basket of rolls Brianna passed her. The silence was already grating on her nerves.

"I heard Justin had married and brought you home, and I wanted to congratulate you in person," Laurel began in a pleasant tone Brianna knew was as forced as her smile.

"I'm so glad you came," she answered sweetly, shooting her husband a sharp look out of the corner of her eye.

Laurel took a piece of ham from the platter. "Justin swears you saved his life at the hospital. I wanted to thank you for that."

She avoided the other woman's assessing gaze. "I did what I could for him. He's lucky he's as strong as he is, or he might not have pulled through."

"By strong, do you mean stubborn?"

"My, you do know him well, don't you?"

She shrugged, a secretive smile playing about her lips as she cast a sideways glance at him. "Fairly well, yes."

Brianna's hand tightened around her fork at the innuendo. She'd already been in a bad mood, and now her temper was at a simmer.

Rather than respond to the loaded comment, Justin focused on his breakfast before at last addressing Laurel. "You look well." His polite words did little to dispel the lingering awkwardness. It was obvious he was less than thrilled to see her here.

Laurel beamed. "Thank you." Her eyes strayed to the doorway before she asked in a hushed tone, "How is your mother?"

His hand froze around his cutlery. "She's...the same."

"Oh." Her brown eyes softened. "She seemed to perk up somewhat when I stopped by last week."

Brianna fought not to narrow her eyes at the other woman, uncertain whether it was a verbal barb or not.

"I'd hoped you and your new wife being here would have helped," Laurel finished.

Brianna wouldn't bet on that.

"It hasn't so far," Justin said.

Laurel looked at her with what seemed like genuine sympathy in her eyes. "I'm sorry you had to see her like this. She usually is a likeable woman."

Grief could make people become unrecognizable. Brianna knew that better than anyone. "She's been through a difficult time."

"Yes, it's been very hard on her. I've stopped by a few times to visit, and she's always kept to her bed. My father has tried also, but..."

But she always refused their company.

Laurel suddenly stiffened in her chair. Justin's head snapped up.

Brianna swiveled in her chair and found a ghost standing in the doorway. Mrs. Thompson raked her deep-set eyes over each of them, looking frail enough that a puff of wind would have knocked her off her feet. Shrouded by her black clothing, her skin was so pale she might have been a specter. A collective tension took over the room as everyone held their breath and waited for some sign of greeting from her.

Justin rose and went to her. "Good morning, Mother." He took her bony arm and brought her to the table. "Come sit down and eat with us. Laurel came by to congratulate us, and to inquire after your health."

Mrs. Thompson blinked and swallowed, the convulsive movement exaggerated by the thinness of her throat. Her condition appalled Brianna. What physician would allow her to consume such quantities of laudanum as to turn her into a walking corpse? Brianna slid her chair over to make room for her husband, assuming he would place his mother at the head of the table.

Mrs. Thompson dug her heels in, and Justin shot her a questioning look.

She swayed on her feet, and Brianna instinctively jumped up to help catch her in case she toppled.

Raising a fragile white hand to her mouth, her mother-in-law's gaunt eyes fixed on the empty chair next to the one Justin had pulled out for her.

Mitch's chair.

Brianna's heart sank, aching for her husband even as she braced for his mother's reaction.

"That..." Mrs. Thompson's voice was raspy, hoarse from lack of use and unshed tears. "That was my baby's place."

Brianna bit down on the inside of her cheek, sharing a worried glance with Justin.

"Come sit and eat something," he urged again, making a noticeable effort to curb his usual air of command into something gentler.

His mother wrenched her arm away and hit him with a glare so hostile it made Brianna's skin prickle. "He should be here. With us." Venom spewed from her eyes. "It's *your* fault he's gone. Why didn't you look after him?" She fired the awful words like bullets. "You should have protected him."

Brianna and Laurel gasped, but Justin only stared at his mother and tightened his jaw, fighting back a response. It would have been kinder if she'd used a weapon instead of those bitter words, thrown like daggers into his heart. Brianna's hands clenched around her napkin as she waited for Justin to put her in her place, to say something in his defense. He didn't. He simply watched his mother with anger simmering in his eyes, nostrils flaring.

Mrs. Thompson shook her head and wrung her bony hands. "Why did you come back here? To remind me of what I lost every time I look at you? Parade your Rebel wife in front of me to gloat of your happiness when I suffer every minute with the knowledge that my baby is lying frozen in his *grave?*"

Brianna held her breath, appalled.

Justin's eyes turned wintry. "That's enough." His voice was hard, icy.

His mother wasn't done. "This is still *my* house. I never asked you to come back!" Her tone rose to a shrill pitch, her eyes glistening, lips trembling. "Just *go.* I don't want you here. I don't want to see you ever again."

"Siobhan!"

Brianna's gaze snapped to Aggie, who barreled through from the kitchen with murder in her eyes. She marched up and grabbed her mistress's arm, dragging her out of the room and up the stairs as her voice carried back to them. "How dare ye speak to him like that? Have ye gone daft? That boy's all you've got left, and I'll not stand by and let ye abuse him to vent your bile." A door slammed upstairs.

In the yawning silence that followed, Justin stood there as if he'd been shot. And he had been. In the heart.

Brianna reached for his hand in an offer of comfort.

"Don't." He yanked away from her grasp like she'd burned him, his face flushed with anger and embarrassment. And beneath it all, a stark grief that made her want to cry. "If you'll both excuse me," he muttered. He stormed out the front door and slammed it shut behind him. The sound reverberated off the vaulted ceiling.

Brianna exhaled and rubbed a hand over her face. This was a nightmare.

Laurel shifted uneasily next to the table, her eyes wide, the animosity between her and Brianna evaporating in the face of Mrs. Thompson's tirade. "I didn't know it was this bad. I can't believe she said that."

But she had. Brianna's chest felt too tight, like an iron band squeezed it. Justin had already been suffering, and this would wound him deeply. As long as she lived, she'd never forget his gut-wrenching expression when his mother had lit into him. Her temper went from a simmer to a rolling boil. Rather than squelch it, Brianna let it burn. And it felt *good.*

Justin wasn't going to stand up to his mother. He felt too guilty, too responsible for her emotional state and wouldn't risk upsetting her further, lest she do something desperate and attempt to take her own life. But things had gone too far and Brianna refused to stand idly by any longer. Should she interfere with her mother-in-law? She wanted to. Would he forgive her for it, or would she only make things worse? Either way, she refused to watch that woman destroy Justin, no matter how terrible her grief was.

The slamming of her heart against her ribs answered for her. Her blood was up. There was no stopping the inevitable now.

Ignoring Laurel, she stormed past her up the stairs and threw open the master bedroom door to find the cavernous space illuminated by a single candle. Aggie was already settling her mistress beneath the covers of the massive four-post bed. Brianna paused a moment in the doorway, grasping at the reins of her control.

Catching sight of her, Aggie and her mother-in-law both started.

Mrs. Thompson's eyes rounded, then narrowed to slits. "You were not invited—"

"There's something I need to discuss with you," Brianna said flatly.

The woman raised her chin in a haughty manner. "This is my private chamber. I have nothing to say to you."

Brianna set her jaw and counted to ten, all the while holding that sunken gaze. "Well *I* have something to say to *you.*" Her chest rose and fell with her rapid breaths. Her heart was pounding out of control, her hands were shaking, her breath sticking in her throat. It took all her restraint not to yell her next words. "Justin may remind you of Mitchell every time you look at him, but he's all you have left." His mother opened her mouth to snap something, but Brianna cut her off. "I know about the laudanum. You might think it's helping, but I promise you it's making things worse."

The bony fingers clutched at the blanket pulled up to her waist. "How *dare* you."

Brianna edged closer to the bed, fought to keep from shouting. Aggie was backing away, staring at her with a mixture of apprehension and interest. "How dare *you* accuse Justin of not protecting his brother? It was battle! He was there when Mitchell died. For that alone, do you not think he's suffered enough? Do you not think he blames himself anyway, even though there was nothing he could have done to prevent it?"

"You know nothing—*nothing*—about a mother's grief for her child." Bright red flags stained the prominent cheekbones, garish against her unnatural pallor.

"You're right, I don't. What I do know is that you're venting your bitterness on your only surviving child."

Those eyes filled with raw grief and rage. "You've never grown your babies inside you, suffered the agony of their birth and raised them alone because your husband is killed in a war, only to see both your children off to the next one and then only one of them comes home."

No, Brianna didn't know how that felt. But she knew exactly what loss felt like, and she didn't want to feel it again by losing Justin. She leaned closer to her. "Exactly. Did it ever occur to you that next time *he* might not come home either?"

Deep-set sapphire eyes glared up at her, and

Brianna noted the trembling in the woman's lower lip.

Sensing her point was being made, Brianna continued. "The war isn't over. Justin's going back to his regiment in one week, and *he might not come back* this time. As it is, it might be too late to fix what you've done. Is that what you want?"

The graying head snapped aside, but Brianna caught the worried frown on the woman's face. "Don't be ridiculous."

Brianna choked down the tears clogging her throat. The worst of her anger had passed, and now the grief was taking over. She could barely get the words out, but she'd be damned if she'd give this callous, selfish woman the satisfaction of seeing her cry. "Can't you see you're killing him? And I will not permit it to continue another moment. I love him too much. Aggie? Give me the medicine." She held out her palm in silent demand. Aggie gaped at her, then, after a frozen moment walked over to gingerly place the bottle of laudanum into Brianna's hand.

Her mother-in-law's gaze fixed on it with greedy attention, an addict's panic gleaming in her eyes as she realized Brianna meant to take it away.

Brianna didn't let the fear in the other woman's gaze dissuade her. "Your grief is poisoning everyone in this house. How do you think Justin will suffer when your addiction to this kills you too?"

Mrs. Thompson slapped the hand holding the bottle away, her eyes spitting flames. "*Get out.*"

With pleasure. Brianna drew a steadying breath. "Very well. But starting now, you will be weaned off the laudanum."

Her skeletal fingers twitched, her distress obvious as she stared at the bottle in Brianna's hand as though she couldn't live without it. A sheen of perspiration dampened her forehead. "You wouldn't dare."

"Oh yes, I would. Aggie knows where all the bottles are hidden, and if there are others, be assured we'll find them all. I intend to visit your physician to discuss it with him today." With that, she whirled and left the room, still riding the wave of righteous anger.

At the foot of the stairs, she heard a strangled sound and looked back. On the upper landing, Aggie stood smothering a laugh, grinning at her. "Glory be, lass, never in my life have I seen the missus so cowed by anyone, not even Mr. Brandon, bless his soul."

Her temper was fading, leaving her feeling tired and drained. "Well, her suffering's far from over. Withdrawal from laudanum is going to be an ugly process."

Laurel came out of the dining room then, an almost wistful expression on her face. She gave Brianna a sad smile, seemed to struggle to speak for a moment. When she found her voice at last, it was hoarse with unshed tears. "That was so brave of you. We should have had that confrontation with her long ago." She faltered for a moment before continuing. "I can see why he loves you so much. I didn't think any woman would be worthy of him." She swallowed. "But I see now that I was wrong."

Brianna didn't reply, too stunned to answer.

Laurel drew in a shaky breath, her smile poignant. "I'm glad he's got you to stand by him."

More of her anger dissipated as she realized what the younger woman *wasn't* saying. Laurel had, at least in her mind, loved him. Deeply. Maybe she still did. Brianna's heart went out to her. Losing a man like Justin would be a bitter pill indeed. "I will always take care of him," she said, both her words and tone making it clear that she wouldn't tolerate any further attention from Laurel toward her husband. "I love him."

A mist of tears filled those pretty brown eyes. "Yes. I can see that you do."

Brianna knew they'd reached an understanding. "Thank you." Turning on her heel, she left Laurel in the dining room and went to find her coat. What Justin would say about all this was anyone's guess, but Brianna was betting it wouldn't be pleasant.

CHAPTER TWENTY THREE

Staring down at the white marble headstone while the cold wind whipped at his clothing, Justin felt the bleakness overtake him. Coming here had been a huge mistake, and one he bitterly regretted. Now Brianna had seen the madness inside his mother, and he'd been moody and withdrawn since they'd arrived. He wished Mitch were here so he could talk to him, but instead he lay six feet beneath Justin's feet, his grave covered in a pristine blanket of snow.

A horse snorted off to the right.

Justin jerked his head around to find Brianna riding toward him. The wind tugged at her hair and coat. "What are you doing out here?" She had to be freezing. He rushed up as she dismounted and closed his hands about her waist to lower her to the ground. "It's too cold to be riding, and the horse could have tripped and thrown you—"

"I suppose you've forgotten I was born and raised on a horse farm? Kentucky gets plenty of snow, so I'm familiar with winter riding." Her cheeks and nose were pink from the cold, her thin gloves inadequate protection from it.

"I haven't forgotten," he said with a smile. He raised her hands to his mouth and blew on them, rubbed them together to warm them. She shivered, and he pulled her to his chest, enfolding her in his arms. It felt good to hold her. As though she'd been craving that closeness, she pressed nearer, her cheek resting over his heart. He kissed her temple and eased his head away slightly. "You came out here to find me?"

She nodded, her hair brushing his chin. "Thought you might be here."

He glanced toward the snow-covered grave. "I needed some air. Some time to think." Before he would have said or done something he couldn't take back.

Brianna folded her arms across her chest and stepped back, regarding him with a guilty expression. She let out a heavy sigh. "You should know that I confronted your mother."

She hadn't. Yet he could tell by the look on her face that she had. He groaned and let her go, raking his fingers through his windblown hair. "For God's sake, Bree." The whole thing was an unmitigated disaster, and now Brianna was involved in it.

"I'm not sorry. If you're not willing to defend yourself, then someone has to."

"You don't understand," he said tiredly.

"I understand perfectly." She drew a deep breath, paused as though gathering her mettle. "And I've just come from seeing her physician." He raised a brow in surprise but she continued. "He's agreed to wean her off the laudanum completely, beginning today."

He ran a hand over his face before answering.

"Christ, that's going to make her even worse." Hard to believe, but true.

"Initially, yes. But if she doesn't stop the addiction, she'll die." She cocked her head. "And, in light of the way things stand, I think perhaps we should leave and wait until things have calmed down a bit before coming back to visit her."

He turned away, hands on hips as he stared at Mitch's grave. A full minute passed before he replied. "You're right." He tipped his head towards the dull gray sky. "I should never have brought you here." What the hell had he been *thinking*? This was their honeymoon, for God's sake. "I should have known better when I suspected she'd be like this."

"She's your mother. It's only natural for you to be worried about her and want to take care of her. But you can't help her the way she is right now. She's too wrapped up in her own pain and drowning herself with the laudanum so she doesn't have to face reality. I'm sorry if you're angry with me, but I—"

"Bree." His voice was quiet as he reached out a hand and caught hers. Her breath snagged. Would his touch always affect her so much? He hoped so. He stroked his thumb over the back of her hand. "I'm not angry. I'm touched that you would go to such lengths to defend me, but I can take care of myself. You don't need to defend me. Not from my mother or anything else." He would have confronted his mother this morning had he not been so taken aback by her attack.

Brianna's cheeks flushed a deeper pink. Her gaze dropped to her boots, buried ankle-deep in the snow. She had to be freezing. "She was cruel to you. I didn't like it."

His lips quirked. "I could tell." The grin faded as he

looked back at the grave. "She's worse this time, much worse than she was with my father, but in a way she's right. I can only hurt her by being here. Mitch looked so much like me." He strode over to take her horse's bridle and brought the animal to her. "Come on. Let's get you back to the house before you catch your death out here."

Justin helped her into the saddle and swung onto own his horse beside her. He'd never seen her on horseback before. She cut a fine figure, straight and confident as she handled the horse with effortless skill.

His watched her appreciatively, noted the sensual heat in her eyes as she smiled up at him. "You have a fine seat," he remarked.

She laughed. "I should, since I learned to ride before I could walk." With a challenging look at him, she set her heels to her mount's sides and tore off through the snow.

Behind her, Justin gave a bark of laughter and joined the chase. It felt good to be out galloping across the snow with her. Freeing. Bending low over his horse's neck, he savored the powerful surge of the animal beneath him, the frigid wind blowing over his face and through his hair. Brianna's hair came loose of its pins and trailed behind her in a dark auburn banner. Justin was right behind her, the drumming of hoof beats loud over the hush of the wintry landscape.

When the stable at last came into view, she slowed to a walk, let Justin come abreast of her and gave him a saucy smile. They'd be so good together at Greenbriar, where they could have a fresh start. He wanted to help her make the most of the legacy her father had left her.

She beamed up at him. "Ever think of running a horse farm?"

He tousled her hair, grinning. "You know, I might like to try that." He wrapped his gloved fingers around her hand and squeezed. "I've never been to Kentucky."

"I think you'd love it."

He flashed her an adoring smile. "With you there, how could I not?"

Her face lit up at those simple words, and it seemed like the tension of the past few days fell away. They led their horses into the stable, passed them to the stableman and started for the house, arm in arm.

Justin stopped at the walkway leading to the house and took her face in his hands. "I'll handle my mother from now on, all right? I never meant to put you in a position where you would have to do that for me."

"I know."

He turned his head to stare at the front door, that now-familiar knot forming in his stomach. "What do you think? Do we risk going in?" he asked in a joking tone, though he knew he couldn't avoid what was coming. This altercation with his mother was long overdue.

"Better than freezing out here," Brianna answered with a supportive smile. "And besides, you're a cavalry major. I'm sure you know how to execute a tactical withdrawal when you need to."

Oh, but he wouldn't withdraw from this battlefield. Not when it involved Brianna's future as well. Justin set an arm about her shoulders and started up the steps. She cringed at the shrieks coming from inside and glanced uncertainly up at him. He bent and pressed a firm kiss to her mouth. "Stay downstairs while I handle this. There's no reason for you to be in the line of fire this time." He climbed the rest of the steps with her, determination radiating from every line of his body.

****

When the grandfather clock chimed two in the morning, Brianna opened her eyes. Sitting up, she found herself in the same state as when she'd gone to bed four hours prior. Alone.

The other side of the bed didn't show a single wrinkle, and there was no indentation in the pillow. Justin had once again chosen to sleep elsewhere, no matter how things had improved between them earlier. Well, there would be no more of this sleeping alone nonsense.

She sat up and threw back the covers, her bare feet hitting the cold floorboards.

She marched to the guestroom in her nightgown and wrapper, but found it empty. Maybe Justin was getting himself drunk again. Her jaw flexed. She was sick to death of the way he avoided her and insisted on working out his misery alone. Worse, she hated her helplessness, despised being unable to soothe him.

She hadn't seen him since his confrontation with his mother that afternoon. From the volume of their voices coming from the end of the hall, it had been ugly, but she'd resisted the urge to lend a hand, instead staying in their room as he'd asked. Whatever his mother had said to him, it must have been awful, because he'd slammed out of the house and ridden away into town.

Rushing downstairs, she almost missed the hushed creak of a floorboard. She stilled, waiting, then crept toward the library and saw his silhouette outlined against the window. His hands were braced on the sill as he stared out into the night. She stayed where she was, hurt even more because he must have heard her coming down the stairs and hadn't said a word. She felt the chill of it all the way to her heart.

She swallowed. "Justin, why are you avoiding me?"

He glanced over his shoulder at her and she bit her lip. The raw suffering in his face made her throat clench. She hugged herself for warmth, standing there in the shadows in her nightgown. He turned his head away.

Her stomach dropped at his dismissal. Perhaps he blamed her for the argument between him and his mother. She squared her shoulders. "You won't even speak to me?"

He didn't answer, only bent his head as if it was too heavy to lift under the burden of his misery. Did he regret marrying her? Was he feeling trapped? His silence was answer enough.

"Fine," she said, pivoting on her heel.

"Wait."

She stopped at his weary command, fearful of what he would say.

"It's not you."

She half turned. "Then talk to me."

When he spoke again, his voice vibrated with suppressed emotion. "I can still hear him screaming." The muscles in his back and shoulders tensed under his rumpled shirt.

Her heart turned over. She didn't know what to say to ease his pain and was afraid to push, but she needed him to talk to her. "What happened to him?"

Justin ran a hand over his chin, looking so weary.

She took a hesitant step forward. "Please tell me."

His bloodshot eyes cut over to her, the pain in their depths hitting her like a fist. "He died in my arms. Did I tell you that?"

She shook her head, praying he'd open up. He

looked so haunted she almost gave in and stopped pushing. But then he would never heal, and if this wall stayed between them, their marriage would never last. "You never said anything about what happened."

He swallowed and stared out the window, seemed to collect himself. "Shell fragment. Ripped him right open." His hand motioned across his own belly. "He was terrified. In agony. I couldn't do anything. Not a damn thing."

Brianna stayed where she was, fighting the urge to hold him. She knew exactly what that kind of helplessness felt like, but to be holding your own brother when he died that way... "I'm so sorry."

"He screamed, Brianna. God, his screams." A shaky hand raked through his hair. "I could see his intestines coming out."

Brianna forced herself not to flinch. *Sweet God.*

"At the end he said he couldn't see. That it was dark. I thought it was because his eyes were failing already, but now I wonder if he meant he didn't see the light people are supposed to see when they die. The light that's supposed to take them to heaven." His eyes were tortured as he looked over his shoulder at her. "What if there isn't anything more, Bree? What if he knew there wasn't a heaven?"

She struggled to think of something comforting. "None of us can know for sure. That's why it's called faith."

"Faith," he scoffed, anger glinting in his eyes. "You really think God's up there? You've seen what war does to men. With hundreds of thousands of us butchering and killing each other in this war, both sides praying to the same God, you still believe He exists?"

"Yes." And she believed in heaven as well, because

of Caleb and her parents.

"My brother bled to death on that field at Cedar Creek, screaming and choking on his own blood. He didn't want to die—he was goddamn terrified. He begged me to help him—" His voice cracked and he bent over to grab the windowsill with white-knuckled hands. "Jesus!" A strangled sob escaped him.

She couldn't watch him suffer like this. Brianna crossed the room and laid a hand on his trembling back. He flinched and pulled away, fighting for control, but not for another second would she let him bear this alone. Her fingers wrapped around his hand. It was freezing.

He twisted away as though he couldn't bear her touch. "Don't. I can't... I don't..."

She needed to hold him. Bracing herself in case he shoved her away, she pressed against his back and slid both arms around his waist. He went rigid, sucking in a deep breath. She held on harder. A tremor rippled through him. Then another, and she realized what it meant. He was crying, and doing everything possible not to.

His devastation broke her heart. Still unsure of her welcome, she laid her cheek against his back and gave him the wordless comfort of her embrace, afraid to say anything. She curved her body around his and stayed like that until the tremors subsided. Though breathing evened out, the tension in his muscles remained. Was he angry? She lifted her head. "Justin?"

She gasped when he whirled on her, breaking her hold and confronting her with blazing, tear-filled eyes. So much anger in his face. So much pain and guilt and grief. Hating that she'd seen him so vulnerable.

Hurting for him, Brianna raised her hand to his

rough cheek, startled by the heat against her chilled fingers. He yanked it away, his grip on her fingers almost bruising. She flinched, heart pounding as she inwardly shrank from the buried rage in his eyes.

He didn't release her. Merely stared down at her with that tortured expression that made her bleed inside.

"You should go back to bed." His voice was hoarse, all that volatility roiling beneath the calm facade.

"I don't want to sleep without you." Risking more rejection, she placed her free hand over his racing heart. His skin was so hot beneath the soft cotton lawn, the muscles under it knotted with tension. Aching to comfort him, she pressed close and swallowed a gasp of surprise when her belly made contact with the unmistakable ridge of his erection. She blinked up at him, an answering wave of heat sweeping through her.

He closed his eyes. "I'm not in control of myself."

"I can see that." *I'm here. Let me help you heal.*

His lids flipped open. The heat in his sapphire gaze made the breath catch in her throat. His eyes scorched her face. She didn't pull away.

His hands were unsteady as they burrowed into her hair, holding tight. "You should go." It was a warning. One she had no intention of heeding.

She shivered in his grasp. "You won't hurt me." The words came out as a breathless whisper.

"No." His thumb brushed over her cheek, a muscle jumping in his jaw. "But if you stay, I'm not going to be gentle."

She swallowed at the warning, didn't move. Backing down was not in her nature.

Justin searched her eyes, challenging her, his arousal wedged between them. "Last chance."

She raised her chin. "I'm not leaving." Without her permission, a fine quivering took hold of her legs.

Despite her brave stance, she cried out when he grabbed her around the waist and drove her back against the wall, pinning her there with his body. He dragged her head back by her hair and devoured her mouth, ignoring her squeak of alarm. The air slammed out of her lungs; her fingers gripped his shoulders. The desperate urgency in his kiss jolted her out of her shock. This wasn't about anger. He *needed* her. Needed to find solace inside her. His body screamed it.

Softening, she kissed him back and wound her arms around his neck as she slid her tongue against his.

Justin let out a tortured moan and she pulled her head back to put some distance between them. His eyes blazed down at her, the pupils swallowing the blue of his irises. His cheeks were flushed, chest heaving as he panted. On the edge of control. As he'd warned her. "Justin—"

He smothered her protest with another ravenous kiss and shoved a hand into the neckline of her nightgown to squeeze her breast as he rubbed his hard erection between her legs. She whimpered at the sudden spike of pleasure, the twinge of fear heightening sensation.

"I want you," he muttered raggedly against her throat, teeth nipping at the tender skin. "Now. Right here."

Wrapping him up in her arms, Brianna gathered her courage. Though she'd never seen this rougher side of him, she knew he wouldn't hurt her. "Yes."

He yanked up her nightgown and tumbled her to her back on the rug below the window. Before she could move, he covered her with his weight and shoved her into the floor. The heat and solid weight of him sent another shockwave through her, tore a gasp from her. She wrapped her legs around him. He growled and pressed his erection against the damp throb between her thighs. Brianna hitched in a breath and lifted her hips, her hands tearing at the shirt covering his back. She wanted his skin against hers. This instant.

He rose up on his knees and wrenched the shirt over his head. Kissing her deep and hard, he ran his hands over her naked skin with proprietary boldness. His mouth slid down her throat to her breasts, sucking hard at their tender tips while he held her still in an implacable grip. Brianna could only lift up and dig her fingers into his scalp, offering herself to him.

Justin undid his pants and peeled them off, kicking them aside as he laved and sucked her nipples. He did it until he had her writhing, dying for him to touch the aching place between her legs. With a low growl, he surged up to grab her hand from his back and wrap it around his thick, aroused flesh. She tightened her grip on him and wrung a groan from his throat, but he didn't enter her. His other hand slid over her quivering stomach to the damp place between her legs and slipped two fingers inside, stroking hard and fast. Her lips parted on a breathless gasp, the pleasure sharp and bright, fuelled by the wildness in him.

He swallowed her strangled cry and urged her hand to move faster on his erection. She squeezed tighter as his mouth moved back to her breasts, loving the feel of him swelling against her palm, and knew he would enter her soon. Already shaking, her body was gearing up for the coming explosion. She couldn't breathe. Couldn't see. Couldn't think. Could only feel those long fingers sliding over that spot inside where she ached and throbbed, while he took her higher with the pull of his mouth on her aching nipples.

When he at last settled between her thighs, she nearly wept with relief.

"Hold onto me," he rasped above her.

Her hands flew to his shoulders. He pressed against her opening, the heat of his thick flesh wringing a gasp from her before he drove inside with one thrust, igniting every nerve ending in her body. Brianna groaned his name and held on, twisting in his grip. Lightning sizzled through her veins. One hand went to his hip, urging him to move faster. Harder. She wanted all of him, everything he had to give.

Levering up on his hands, Justin rose above her and watched her face as he drove into her, moving with so much more force than he ever had before. Brianna closed her eyes in helpless pleasure, delighting in the way his muscles bunched under her grasping fingers.

"No, *look* at me."

Her eyes snapped open at the forceful command. She whimpered and trembled beneath him, holding his gaze as she lifted into his thrusts. The hunger still flamed in his eyes but the anger was gone, replaced by naked longing. The compulsion to hold him close and comfort him almost made her weep.

Justin cradled her head between his hands, refusing to let her look away. He took her with hard, selfish strokes, his skin glazed with perspiration. When he kissed her this time, the gesture was so full of need and love it made her eyes sting. She surged beneath him, moaning her pleasure as he moved within her, his big, muscular body pumping in the silver light spilling through the window. *He is so beautiful like this.* She was close now, her body gripping the hard length that stroked inside her, her engorged clitoris rubbing against his lower belly at the end of each thrust. Release hovered there, tantalizingly close yet maddeningly out of reach. She held on harder and moved with him, crying out into his mouth. *Almost there...*

Above her, Justin suddenly drove deep and froze. His head fell back amid a throttled roar, his teeth bared in feral pleasure. His whole body shuddered as he pulsed deep inside her, over and over before he stilled. When he collapsed against her with a groan, Brianna quivered beneath his weight. Biting her lip, she closed her eyes and withheld the frustrated whimper locked in her throat.

The quiet tick of the clock on the mantle seemed loud in the silence.

After a few minutes, he raised his head and slid an unsteady hand over her hair. "Bree?"

She opened her eyes. Tried to stop trembling.

With an uncertain expression, he began to pull out. The friction as he withdrew made her suck in a breath. He froze. "Did I hurt you?"

Still biting her lip, she shook her head.

The alarm faded from his eyes, replaced with dawning realization. "Angel." He slid his hand up the inside of her thigh, making her grab his shoulders and pray for more. She jerked when his fingers grazed her painfully aroused flesh. "Were you close?"

She squeezed her eyes shut and nodded. *Please, please, please...*

But then he stopped. Her eyes snapped open in disbelief as he stood and pulled his pants up. He gathered her wrapper and set it about her shoulders, then scooped her up in his arms. "Justin, what—"

"I'm going to finish this in our bed."

CHAPTER TWENTY FOUR

Justin carried her upstairs to his bedroom and put her under the thick covers to wait for him, cursing himself for his behavior. For him the sex had been incredible, the pleasure all-consuming. He'd been rough and selfish, focused solely on losing himself in her body, taking the solace she offered. And still she wanted him enough that she'd almost reached climax. He intended to make sure she enjoyed one now, and revel in every moment of taking her there.

Brianna snuggled under the covers and watched him light a fire in the hearth beside the bed. When the kindling caught and burst into flames he gathered the basin and washcloth on the washstand and took it to the fireplace. He wet the cloth and wrung it out, holding it to the flames until it was hot to the touch. Returning to the bed, he eased the counterpane and sheets away from her body and drank her in with his gaze. Firelight danced over her pale skin, caressing it with flickering light and shadow.

The cloth was warm and soft beneath his palm as he moved it over the delicate skin of her abdomen. Brianna stared up at him with heavy-lidded eyes. He slid the cloth lower, gently sliding it over her mound and between her thighs until he had cleaned every trace of himself from her flesh. Her teeth were sunk into her lower lip, her pink nipples standing erect, hands twitching on the sheets. The musky-sweet scent of her arousal hit him, making his mouth water. Setting the cloth aside in the wash basin, Justin leaned down to trail kisses across her face, then lay beside her to pull her into his arms. She locked hers around him and held on tight.

With a groan of contentment, Brianna burrowed closer to his warmth and he kissed her. She opened her mouth under his and met the slow glide of his tongue, her fingers clenching on his shoulders at the seductive languor in him. When he finally pulled back, her eyes were glowing, the irises all but swallowed by her pupils.

He layered leisurely kisses down her throat to her breasts. He lapped at her nipples until she dragged his head closer, then pulled the sensitive flesh into his mouth and sucked. Slow and easy, driving her higher with each languorous tug of his lips and tongue. Not enough to make her climax, though. He wanted her to drown in sensation first, to lavish all his attention upon her and make up for the selfish way he'd just taken her. She deserved far better than that.

"Now," she breathed tugging on his shoulders, opening her legs to wind them around his thighs.

He ignored her, instead taking his time blazing a damp path to her belly with his mouth, down over the rise of her hip. He could feel her trembling now, the anticipation rising higher as he came close to where she throbbed for his touch, then passed by it to kiss the tops of her thighs. She dropped her head back to the pillow with a soft groan, earning a chuckle from him.

With reverent hands he stroked the length of her legs, taking one chilled foot and placing it on his shoulder. Her sole was icy against his burning skin. She stiffened at the change in position and tried to squirm away, but he firmed his grip on her ankle and gazed up at her with a set expression. "Don't move."

She seemed to hold her breath and a slight tremor rolled through her. Feeling vulnerable?

He smiled against her soft skin, charmed by the sudden shyness in her. He planned to make her crave this. "Open."

Still watching him, she slowly parted her thighs and allowed him a glimpse of her sex. Dark curls shielded plump folds that shone with the evidence of her arousal. He swallowed a groan, dying to taste her.

He nuzzled her calf with his cheek, caressed the back of her knee and up to her thigh as he wedged his shoulders between her legs and moved in close. The muscles in her thighs shook slightly and her breathing was unsteady. She sucked in a breath when his fingers brushed over her damp core, squeezing her eyes shut. The raw need on her face was the most beautiful thing he'd ever seen. He sank a finger inside while his thumb stroked in circles across the swollen nub at the top of her sex. She twisted up with a sob, but he merely pinned her with one arm across her tense belly. "Shhh," he soothed. "Relax and let me love you." And then he lowered his head and put his mouth to her.

She gasped, the sound like tearing silk in the quiet room. Her hands flew to his shoulders. "No—"

Justin pressed his free hand against her right thigh

to open her wider, exerting enough force to overcome her slight resistance. When he had her open enough, he held her still and used his mouth to torment her exquisitely sensitive flesh.

She was so soft and warm, tangy sweet against his tongue. The sounds she made were incredible. Though he sensed her desperation, his movements were slow and patient, making her strain beneath him. He flicked his tongue repeatedly across her sweetest spot, tearing a ragged cry out of her. Tipping his head to watch her face, he held her gaze and licked at her reverently, loving every moment of it. She whispered his name and squirmed beneath his loving onslaught. Melting against his mouth.

Justin pushed her toward release, sure and relentless, adding another finger inside her to magnify the pleasure. Helpless to control her response, she squeezed her eyes shut and gripped his hair in desperation, moving restlessly against his tongue. At last he took the swollen bud into his mouth and sucked, watching her reaction. A glaze of perspiration covered her skin, shimmering in the dancing firelight. She made a high, choked sound and clutched his head to her. Her muscles gripped his fingers tightly. So close now. With a final flick of his tongue he flung her over the edge, reveling in her wild cry as the climax tore through her.

When she opened her eyes, he was kneeling between her open thighs, staring down at her. He brushed a lock of hair from her damp forehead with a gentle hand. "You're so beautiful. Did you enjoy that?"

"Yes." Blushing, she held out her arms to him. He grinned and kissed her lips, sharing her intoxicating taste with her, then nuzzled her jaw. Her arms locked around his shoulders when he began to shift away.

"Stay with me?"

The vulnerability in her voice hit him straight in the heart. *Angel...*

Justin stretched out alongside her and buried his face in the curve of her throat, feeling possessive and protective all at once. Pulling her into his body, he pulled the covers up and wrapped his arms tight around her, surrounding her in his warmth and strength. "Love you so much." She was the greatest treasure he'd ever been given.

Brianna snuggled closer with a contented sigh and laid her head on his chest, and soon her breathing turned deep and even. Justin fell asleep with her soft weight blanketing him, grateful for the gift of having her by his side for the rest of their lives.

Brianna woke early next morning expecting to find Justin beside her, but the bed was empty again. She jerked upright, searching around the room for him. Their bags were set by the door. Were they leaving? She threw back the blankets, washed, dressed and pinned up her hair. His footsteps sounded in the hall. She braced herself, not knowing what kind of mood he'd be in this morning. He'd been so caring and attentive last night, giving her hope that they'd re-established that intimate connection they'd lost since arriving here.

Justin opened the door, his expression weary but resolved, and put on a smile when he saw her dressed and ready to go. "Morning. Sleep well?"

She blushed at the memory of how wild and uninhibited they'd been together last night. "Yes. You?"

He nodded, his gaze moving to their bags. "Train leaves in about two hours. I thought we'd get an early start."

She crossed to him and slid her arms about his waist, relieved when he hugged her in return rather than stiffen and endure the embrace. "I've been thinking," she said against his uniform. "I love you and I don't want you to have to choose sides between your mother and me. That's not what I intended when I interfered. Having the laudanum taken away was the only thing I could do to help, even though she won't see it that way. I'll understand if you want to stay with her. I can go back to—"

"No." The word was low, impassioned, and his arms tightened. "I've only got a few days' leave left, and most of it's going to be eaten up traveling. Once my furlough is up, there's no telling when we'll see each other next." He kissed her temple, her cheek, his lips warm and tender on her skin, his arms fierce about her. "I don't want to lose another minute of my time with you."

She loved this man so much. "If that's what you want."

He buried his face in her hair. "Yes."

Brianna clung to him, aware that all too soon she'd have to send him back to the war.

In the study, Siobhan sat huddled beneath the folds of her favorite afghan on a settee across from her husband's leather armchair. A fire blazed in the hearth, but she didn't feel any of its warmth. She was cold all the way to her bones, had hardly slept in two days. Her skin hurt. Her head throbbed. Every time she moved too quickly, she feared she might be sick to her stomach. This was Brianna's fault. All of it. Each agonizing second she had to endure without her medicine had been forced upon her by that high-and-mighty Southern witch her son had married. Hatred rose, sharp and powerful.

Out in the foyer, Aggie and Laurel were saying goodbye to Justin and his harridan of a wife. A pang shot through her at the thought of not seeing her son off, but she was grateful his wife was leaving. Good riddance. She hoped they never came back, so she never had to look into those cold gray eyes again. How could they do this to her? She was suffering unbearably without her medicine, and no one cared. Not even Aggie.

Heavy footsteps in the hallway grew louder as they approached. They stopped outside the den door.

She held her breath.

The door creaked open. Hushed footfalls fell on the carpet.

Without looking up, she knew Justin stood behind her. The scent of his cologne reached her, so familiar it brought the burn of tears and she had to bite her lip to keep from crying. He stood there a moment longer in silence and when she didn't speak, laid a solid hand on her shoulder.

She shuddered at the contact, pain racing over her skin and into the muscle. His touch lightened but his hand stayed where it was, warm and strong. Like him. She thought of the pain he was causing her, couldn't bear to look up into the face that was so like his brother's.

What was he waiting for? After their altercation yesterday, she had nothing left to say.

He leaned down and kissed her cheek without a word.

No! He's dead to me too.

A silent sob ripped through her, shaking her

shoulders. She refused to make a sound, refused to look at him.

"Goodbye, Mother."

When she made no response, he withdrew his hand and walked out of the room. His retreating footsteps echoed in the hall. Her heart began to pound out of control, a sense of panic taking hold until she was panting for breath.

A few moments later, the front door shut with a thud.

So. They were gone.

A curious tightening took hold of her lungs. As though a hand was squeezing all the air from her body. Her pulse raced. Sweat bloomed on her forehead and across her upper lip. A bolt of terror shot through her. What if Justin never came back? What if the last words she ever spoke to him were the ones she'd screamed at him yesterday afternoon?

It should have been you who died on that field!

Terror seized her. Had she really said that terrible thing? She fought for breath, hands digging into the arms of Brandon's chair. *Breathe! Steady*. She sucked in a shaky breath. Then another. Kept inhaling until the room stopped swimming. The attack passed, the taut band about her chest releasing inch by slow inch. Exhausted, she laid her head back and closed her eyes. When she opened them, she gazed up into her husband's face, frozen forever in his portrait.

This time his eyes seemed to stare down at her with reproach.

Siobhan shut her lids to block out the sight and hunched deeper into her blanket. Justin was already gone, even if she had wanted to make amends, and she didn't have the energy or the will to pour out her heart on paper. *Too late. Too late to do anything about it now.*

No one understood her suffering. No one cared about her pain.

Drowning in the tide of her misery, she curled up in her chair and let her bitter tears fall.

****

Winchester, VA
February 8, 1865

"For the love of God, don't do this, Bree."

Standing on the freezing platform next to the train waiting to take her on the first leg of her journey back to Richmond, Brianna shivered. Justin's tormented expression pulled at her, but her mind was made up. They'd gone over this so many times and always came back to the same thing. He was heading out with his regiment in the morning, and if she stayed here there was nothing for her.

"You don't have to go," he said again, holding her upper arms tightly. The icy air turned his words into vapor, rising like a silver mist into the air. "Stay here with the other wives, or go home to Lexington. At least then I know you'll be safe and have support."

He'd begged her all week to change her mind. They'd moved back into the boardinghouse in Winchester and spent the rest of Justin's furlough together. Last night General Custer and his wife, Libbie, had held a ball for the brigade. While the Brigade Band played, Brianna had twirled in Justin's arms as snow drifted down outside the candle-lit windows. The whole time, her heart had been heavy as lead because she dreaded this new separation.

"I can't," she said, voice catching. "I can't stay here going out of my mind with worry every time an officer comes up the steps and I think they're bringing me a telegram to say you've been wounded or killed. Besides, my brother is still locked up in Libby, and the conditions there..." She shook her head, wanting him to understand. "I need to go back to him. If things are worse now, he could be starving. I can't let that happen. I'm all he has left in this world."

His jaw tightened, eyes burning with frustration. "And what if someone turns you in as a spy because they've seen you coming in and out of the prison? I don't want you anywhere near Richmond when the end comes. The way things stand it won't be much longer. We're closing in on it, and when it falls it won't be pretty." He shook his head, his eyes pleading with her. "It's too dangerous, Brianna. Please don't go back there."

She knew how hard it must have been for him to beg her, especially out here in view of anyone who cared to eavesdrop. He was a prideful man, respected amongst his peers and by his men. But she couldn't wait here while he was off on campaign again. She'd go mad. At least in Richmond she had plenty to keep her busy and people who needed her. There, she wouldn't have the constant reminder of the possibility of Justin's death each time one of the Brigade's wives received news that her husband had been killed in the field. And her brother *did* need her, even if he'd never admit it.

She swallowed the lump in her throat, hating to cause him worry. "I have to go back. Please understand."

He let out a defeated sigh, then hauled her close

and crushed her to him. The desperate embrace conveyed his distress, his fear. He buried his face in her hair. "Damn, you're a stubborn little thing."

She gave a watery laugh and gripped the back of his coat in her gloved fingers. "Can't help it. I'm half Irish."

"Swear to me you'll be careful."

"I swear."

He cursed, wouldn't let her go. "I feel so damn helpless."

She squeezed him harder. "I'll be fine, and it's only for a while." She hoped. This terrible war had to end sometime, and with the Union victories last year, it seemed the tide had finally turned in their favor. "It's you I'm worried about. You're the one going back to the front." Her throat closed up.

He titled her face up to his, his thumbs brushing at the tears brimming her lashes. "Don't cry." A plea, not an order.

It was impossible not to. If she lost him, she would never survive it.

"I'm safer now than I've ever been," he told her. "I won't be in the thick of things like I was as a captain."

She sniffed. "Liar." A rush of fear shot through her. If anything happened to him, she'd—

The train's whistle blasted.

His eyes were troubled as he stroked her cheek. "Take care of yourself."

The conductor called out to her. "Ma'am? Train's leavin'."

Oh God, this was it. Yet another goodbye, one of so many in her life. "I will." Her eyes drank him in, memorizing every detail of his face. She framed his cheeks between her hands. "Come back to me. I don't care what you have to do, just come back to me."

"I swear it." He hugged her and pressed a hard kiss against her trembling lips. "I'll come back, angel. I *love* you."

"I know. I love you too."

When the whistle shrilled again, she forced herself to tear away from him. Chest tight as a vise, she boarded and rushed to her seat to press her palm against the window. On the platform, Justin put his hat on, tugged at the brim and waved. With a lurch and a shudder, the train began moving. The tears flowed faster now, coursing down her cheeks.

Forcing a wobbly smile, she watched him blow a kiss from the platform. She grabbed it in one fist and placed it to her lips, then over her heart, as he'd done aboard the steamer at White House Landing. He stood there in the cold and watched as she moved away from him, the cape of his light blue greatcoat blowing in the wind.

CHAPTER TWENTY FIVE

Outside Richmond, VA
March 28, 1865

From their camp on the opposite bank, Justin gazed across the river at the spires of Richmond that rose above the budding treetops, while distant bells echoed across the water. It was strange to stand in the same place as McClellan's boys had nearly two years earlier, but the end was close now. Through the constant flurry of battles and skirmishes, the Michigan Brigade and the rest of the cavalry corps continued to tighten the noose around the Confederate army.

The far bank was dotted with pink cherry blossoms. Brianna was there. Just there, across the James River. And she was going hungry again, partly because of him and his men stripping the Shenandoah of its food supply.

He hadn't seen her for more than a month, since the day he'd put her on that southbound train at Winchester. Only a few letters had arrived since. All these weeks later, he feared even more for her safety when the city fell. Did the citizens of Richmond realize how close they were to defeat? Along with their armies, the people were starving, the situation so desperate that old men and young boys were left to defend the dying cause. The Rebel lines at Petersburg were in peril, and once they collapsed the enemy would have to evacuate Richmond. That day couldn't be more than a week or two away. He had to find a way to get Brianna the hell out of there before then.

He couldn't stop thinking about her. It killed him to know she must be half-starved and working herself to the point of exhaustion, struggling to keep her visits to Libby prison a secret from everyone. Stationed so close without being able to help her tore him up inside.

"Major!" Williams waved at him from the top of the hill. "Colonel wants to see you, sir."

Justin strode up the grassy slope and waited for admittance into the tent. Bent over writing at his desk, Colonel Hastings looked up as he entered. He was only twenty-two, even younger than Justin, but still an imposing man with broad shoulders and keen, dark eyes. His brown hair was impeccably combed, his face clean shaven. Though the lack of a beard gave him a boyish appearance, no man who'd fought either with or against him would ever make the mistake of questioning his prowess as a commander.

"Ah, Major Thompson," Hastings said. "I have a special assignment for you."

"Sir." Justin stepped up beside him and leaned over the desktop, covered with a map of Richmond. Were they going in? His heart quickened. If they did, there was a chance he might be able to find Brianna.

Hastings leaned back in his camp chair with a

speculative smile. "Sheridan wants more information about the enemy's strength in the region. I want you to take a small scouting party to do some reconnaissance and report back to me. Troop numbers, defenses, ammunition and any other surprises the Rebs are hiding."

"Of course, sir."

Hastings rubbed a hand over his jaw, the wheels turning in his sly head, and fixed Justin with a pointed stare. "So that leaves just one question, Major, and I want your honest opinion on the matter." He leaned back farther and crossed his arms over his chest, a speculative glint in his dark eyes. "How do you feel about a tour of Richmond?"

Justin felt like he couldn't get there fast enough. He smiled in anticipation. "I'm looking forward to it sir."

He exited the tent and went to find Williams. "Did you get the uniforms the colonel asked for?" Justin asked him.

Williams's lips twitched beneath the trimmed moustache of his tidy goatee. "I did, sir, but the Rebs were mighty put out."

"Yes, I imagine they would be." Being taken prisoner and forced to strip down to your underwear would put anyone in a bad mood.

Williams fell in step beside him, heading back to Justin's tent. "So, we finally get to see Richmond. I hear the ladies are beautiful there, sir."

Justin smiled and called Brianna's face to mind. "Now that's a fact, lieutenant. That is indeed a fact." And if their luck held, they'd be meeting the most beautiful one of all tonight.

He pushed aside his tent flap and stepped inside to find the pile of confiscated uniforms on his camp bed.

The prospect of a covert operation behind enemy lines fired his blood. He held up two different pairs of ragged trousers and faced his lieutenant. "Well, what will it be, Williams? Gray or butternut?"

****

Six hours later, Justin's good mood had long since vanished.

"She's my *wife*." He couldn't keep the frustration out of his voice. After taking care of their reconnaissance duties, it had taken him half the night to find Brianna's brother in the infirmary at Libby and learn where she was staying, and now her employer was being impossible.

"I can't believe she would lie to us about something as important as that," Mrs. Lancaster insisted to him in her front parlor. "She's been here for months and works very hard indeed, without complaint. Why would she subject herself to such work if she were a gently bred belle? She must know that I would have helped her any way I could, had your story been true. Why, I am simply sick at the thought of forcing a young lady such as that to work as a house servant." She set down her teacup and sat taller on the sofa, her formidable breasts heaving with outrage. "She and my daughter have become the best of friends, yet she has never mentioned anything of a husband to Cassidy, has she, dear?"

The young woman seated next to her mother shook her head, pale blue eyes wide.

Justin leaned forward, his body language conveying his urgency. His time in Richmond was running out. "I believe you, Mrs. Lancaster. I don't for a moment doubt your sincerity." He fought for patience. "But I'm telling you, the woman you know as Jenny is in truth my wife, Brianna."

Mrs. Lancaster's lips thinned in consternation, graying brows forming an angry slash above her eyes. "Nan!" she barked, making Cassidy jump and shoot her mother a sidelong glance.

The maid appeared in the doorway, peeking her capped head into the room. "Yes, ma'am?"

"Nan, these two gentlemen have been asking questions about our dear Jenny. Do you have any reason to believe she is not who she claims to be?"

"No, ma'am."

Mrs. Lancaster nodded in satisfaction. "And she has never told you anything about any secrets she might have?"

"No, ma'am."

Her mistress nodded in satisfaction. "Thank you, Nan. That will be all—except for another pot of chicory coffee for our guests. We haven't any sugar left, though I'm sure you won't mind," she said to Justin.

Justin stared after the aging housekeeper, ready to gnash his teeth. She was lying; he could read it in the tension in her stance, the unease in her eyes. Was she doing it to protect Brianna? He glanced over at Williams, who stared at the spot Nan had just vacated.

About to open his mouth to try again, Williams beat him to it. He shifted to face the daughter and said, "Miss Lancaster, it is imperative that you tell us anything you know, for Jenny's safety. We have reason to believe she may be in trouble."

Her eyes widened. "I assure you, sir, if I knew anything I would tell y—"

"What sort of trouble?" her mother demanded in a

suspicious tone.

The spying kind, where she could land in prison, Justin thought.

Or worse.

In his peripheral vision, Justin caught a shadow near the doorway. The housekeeper was eavesdropping. She knew something, he was certain of it.

"Well, I am sorry I couldn't be of more help, and I certainly do hope you find your wife before any harm comes to her," said Mrs. Lancaster. "When I see Jenny next, you may be assured I will get to the bottom of this."

Withholding a growl of frustration, he got to his feet. Bowed. "Thank you for your hospitality, ladies."

Their hostess inclined her head. "Not at all."

Williams followed him to the front door, where Nan hovered with her hand on the knob. As he came closer, she backed up a step and averted her eyes. He stopped in front of her. "When you see her," he began in a low voice, and the woman's eyes darted up to his, "tell her to stay close to the house. Richmond will fall soon, and then I'll get word to her as soon as I can."

Nan swallowed and didn't answer.

"And tell her I love her." He pulled his hat on and started down the front steps, his chest aching.

"Wait."

He pivoted.

Nan came out on the stoop and shut the door behind her, glancing around to make sure no one could overhear her. "She went to Libby. She goes there every other day."

"Yes, I know, I spoke to her brother, who's very ill. Apparently she was there earlier today and left hours ago to see if she could find him some medicine." The man was so ill that Justin wasn't sure he'd live to see the end of the war. It had to be killing Brianna. "When the city falls, all of you stay here with the doors locked tight. Her brother will make sure you're all safe until he can get you out of Richmond." The city had a pitiful number of home guard and supplies left to defend itself with. Justin hated that he wouldn't be here to protect Brianna when the end came, but there was nothing more he could do.

"Thanks be to God," the woman whispered, crossing herself.

"Things are going to turn ugly," Justin warned. "Don't leave the house, do you understand?"

"Yes. I'll watch out for her."

It was better than nothing. "Thank you." He took his horse's reins from Williams and swung into the saddle to trot away from the brick house, swamped in disappointment. Damn. He'd been so close to finding her. His eyes scanned the streets in the hopes he might still spot her. It was late, and she shouldn't be walking out here alone. Anything could happen to her.

Brianna walked at a fast pace on her shortcut home, plagued by a sense of unease. Maybe she should have taken the longer, safer route back home after her fruitless search for a tonic that might help Morgan. Food was hard enough to come by in the city, let alone medicine. With nothing to show for her efforts, she'd just wanted to get home quickly after seeing her brother so sick in the prison hospital.

Up ahead in the distance, she saw two men on horseback and instinctively ducked out of sight. The one in front seemed to be searching for someone, now and then slowing his horse, his head turning back and forth. Her heart thumped in her ears. People recognized her in town now. They knew she went to Libby to see her brother, knew she spoke to Elizabeth Van Lew. Justin, Morgan and Sam had all warned her someone might think she was a spy, and she was wary enough to pause for a few minutes in her hiding spot, waiting for the mounted men to leave. When they moved on at a trot, she let out a relieved breath and hurried onward.

Still no sign of her. And Justin was out of time. They'd already risked everything by crossing the lines with the borrowed enemy uniforms. He and Williams had to get back to their own lines before they drew any more suspicion from the home guard.

"Sir," Williams began.

"What?"

Williams jerked his chin to the right. "We're about to be intercepted."

Oh, hell. He'd been so focused on searching for Brianna he'd let his guard down. Now three Confederates came toward them from the opposite end of the street, hands on the butts of their pistols.

"Halt," one of them called.

Justin stopped his horse and faced the group, his muscles tensed. He put the hint of a drawl into his voice. "Evenin'."

The man in the lead drew near, face shadowed by the brim of his hat. "Evenin'. May I see your passes?"

He fished in his breast pocket for the forged document and handed it over. The tension spread inside him until his hands grew damp inside his gloves.

The Confederate scratched his salt-and-pepper beard as he studied the pieces of paper. He frowned, and Justin's heart sank. Sensing his nervousness, his horse shied a little. "Easy," he murmured, trying to appear calm. Williams shot him an uneasy glance.

The man raised his head, and Justin stilled at the shock of recognition he saw on the other man's face. The man knew him? From where? He fought to remain motionless.

The soldier shook his head in wonder and stared at him. "You were at the Wilderness. You carried me to the hospital."

Justin stared back in shock. The man from the fire. The one he and Mitch had rescued.

Justin couldn't believe the Reb had survived being gut shot, let alone that he'd run into him in Richmond tonight. He held the man's astonished gaze, waiting for him to give the order for his arrest. Instead, the man grabbed Justin's horse's bridle and walked him away from the group.

Justin eyed the man's pistol. If he spurred the horse he might have a chance to escape, but he'd probably wind up shot in the back, and he would never leave Williams behind to face their punishment alone.

When they were out of earshot, the Reb fixed him with a hard stare. "What in Sam hell are you doing in Richmond?" he demanded in a near whisper, eyes narrowed. "You a spy? Because last I saw, you were wearing a different color uniform. Which side you fightin' for?"

The man already knew the truth. It wouldn't do any more damage to tell him about Brianna. "My wife is here."

The graying eyebrows shot up to disappear beneath the brim his hat. "Your wife?"

Justin fought the urge to bolt, wishing he knew

305

what the hell the man planned to do with him. "Her brother is in Libby. She's here to be near him."

The man digested that for a moment. "And you came here through the lines dressed in *those* so you could see her?" He looked skeptical.

Justin knew how crazy it sounded. "Yes." Among other things, like observing the number of remaining Confederate troops in the city. Christ, could they just get this over with? If he was lucky he'd wind up in Libby, too. If not, they'd shoot him dead on the spot or hang him in the morning for spying.

The Confederate shook his head in wonder. "And did you see her?"

"No. I couldn't find her." What did the Reb care about it?

"What's your wife's name, and where does she live?"

Justin's spine went rigid. No way would he give up Brianna so she could be imprisoned as well. They'd arrest her on trumped-up charges of spying or conspiracy.

"I'm not going to arrest her," the man said in disgust. "Here." He dug in a pocket for a stub of a pencil. He offered it and the back of Justin's pass to write on. "Jot down a note, if you want, and I'll see that she gets it."

What the... Justin stared at him as resentment bubbled up. "So she can visit both me and her brother in prison?"

The Reb sighed and pushed the paper and pencil at him. "Just write it."

"I want your word that you won't arrest her."

"And you've got it."

At this point, what choice did he have? Justin

wrote a short note, gave the man her name and address and handed it over, prepared for his arrest.

Keeping her eyes downcast so she wouldn't draw unwanted attention, Brianna hurried through the dark, deserted alleyways with her woolen cloak wrapped snugly about her shoulders. The prospect of her cozy bed and a full night's sleep propelled her aching feet down the road in an unsavory area of town. She passed another bar, this time drawing whistles and lewd remarks from some soldiers on the front steps. Ignoring them, she hastened along, driven by footsteps and drunken voices behind her.

She shouldn't be here. She knew better. The men continued to shout things to her, more obscene by the second. Streamers of alarm slid through her. In danger of robbery, rape or worse, she headed for the next building, where she'd turn right and change her route. A jolt of panic hit her as a glance over her shoulder showed one of them coming after her.

Stifling a cry, Brianna took up her skirts and ran. She'd almost made it to the end of the alley when rough hands yanked her backward and threw her to the ground. She shrank from the filthy hands gripping her throat.

"Whatcha got on you, beautiful? Jewelry? Money?" He pawed through her clothing for valuables.

She slapped at his hands and scuttled backward. Caleb's ring was on her right hand, Justin's on her left, and his watch was in her pocket. She would never give up any of them.

Undeterred by her blows, the man searched her roughly. Her hands dug into his arms to hold him away and she screamed for all she was worth. The onlookers hooted and shouted encouragement, while their comrade fought to restrain her.

"Yer mighty strong, arncha?" he slurred. "And loud, too!"

No one helped her. Men stood by not fifty feet from where she lay, and even though she thought she screamed loud enough to wake President Lincoln in Washington, no one came to her aid. Anger lashed through her, giving her added strength as she fought back. If he had rape on his mind, he would have to kill her before she gave into him. She kicked and struggled, managed to land blows about his face with clenched fists. He swore and released her. Panting, she shot to her feet and took off in a burst of speed.

But he was too quick for her. A heartbeat later, he slammed into her from behind and took her to the ground. Bright lights exploded as pain coursed through her chest. "Stay still!" he snarled, his sour breath making her long to retch.

He was *not* going to take what little she had left of Caleb or Justin. If he intended to kill her for it, she wasn't going to make it easy for him.

Curling her fingers like claws, Brianna raked them down his face. He howled then reared up and swung an arm back to hit her in the face. She tasted blood, warm and metallic. Hard hands locked around her throat. She gasped and thrashed, panic taking hold when she couldn't get a breath.

More lights burst in front of her eyes.

No air. She tore at his hands. The pressure didn't loosen.

"Let her go," a hard voice said from the shadows. *"Now."*

The grip on her throat disappeared, and past her

heaving gasps she heard the click of a hammer cocking. Her attacker squinted into the darkness and stood. She wrenched upwards and crawled to her knees, coughing and gasping in painful gulps.

"Get away from her, you filthy son of a bitch." Her rescuer held his weapon leveled at the man. "On your knees. Now."

Brianna scrambled to her feet, cradling her tender throat. Her attacker darted rat-like eyes down the alley, as if he might try to flee.

"I said, *on your knees*."

He stayed frozen another moment, then leaped up and made a run for it.

A shot rang out. Bits of brain and blood sprayed over the alley. She stifled a scream and lurched away until her back pressed flat against the cold brick wall behind her. Breathless, she watched her protector bend down beside the lifeless gray-clad body, and two more soldiers materialized behind him.

"Get rid of him. Go to the courthouse and file a report telling Major Cahill what happened," the shadowy figure said to his waiting troops. "I'll see to the lady."

The Confederate from the Wilderness tucked the note and pencil into a pocket then released the bridle and stepped back. Holstered his pistol.

Justin held his breath, not daring to move.

"Major Cahill!"

The man's head swiveled at his comrade's shout.

A young soldier ran up. "Trouble a few blocks from here, sir. Troops shot a man accosting a lady."

"Be right there." Cahill glanced back at Justin and smiled, then held out a hand. "Good luck to you, sir."

Justin couldn't believe it. He was letting him go? Still wary, he hesitated a moment, then shook the offered hand. Williams rode his mount over to them, face pale.

Cahill's grin widened as he stepped back. "I told you I'd never forget you. And I like to repay my debts. So you two go on now, and be careful of them pickets. They get mighty twitchy this time of night. And don't worry, I'll make sure your wife gets this." He patted his coat pocket.

For the first time since they'd been stopped, Justin's lungs took in a full breath. "Thank you."

"My pleasure." Cahill slapped Justin's horse on the rump, sending him trotting off toward their own lines.

CHAPTER TWENTY SIX

When the major arrived, Brianna was huddled under her shawl. Her legs shook, but she was still on her feet. The middle-aged newcomer approached her with a bowlegged gait. "Ma'am. Are you all right?"

She barely managed a nod.

The graying officer unbuttoned his tattered greatcoat and placed it around her shivering shoulders. "I'm Major Cahill, ma'am." His dark gaze swept over her face. "I'm so terribly sorry about this. Can't imagine what's gotten into these animals. Do you think you can walk, or shall I find us a wagon?"

"I can w-walk," she replied hoarsely. Her throat was sore and her teeth chattered, but otherwise she was okay.

He grasped her elbow and led her away, and she stumbled. He offered to carry her but she refused, so he set a sturdy arm around her shoulders and guided her down the street.

"Where do you live?" he asked her.

She recited her address.

He hissed in a breath and stopped so suddenly she stumbled again. "What's your name?"

She blinked at the sharp edge to his tone. "Jen— Brianna," she corrected quickly, cursing herself for not being more careful. No one here would know her by her real name. "Thompson."

He gaped at her. "Mother of God."

She stared up at him. No one here knew that name except for Morgan. Not even Nan. "What?" Fear edged up her spine. Had someone issued an arrest warrant for her?

He dragged a hand over his face. "I just saw your husband."

She must have heard him wrong. "You... What?"

"He was here, looking for you."

She shook her head. "No, you must be mistaken. My husband is—"

"Riding back to his lines wearing butternut," Cahill muttered under his breath.

A loud roar filled her ears. "P-pardon?"

"He gave me this for you. I was going to drop it off personally tomorrow." He fished in his pocket and pulled out a piece of paper.

Her fingers quivered as she took it. The familiar handwriting made her heart twist.

Dearest Brianna,

Stay safe and warm. I will come for you as soon as I can.

All my love,

Justin.

She clapped a hand over her mouth to hold back a cry as the pain hit her. Justin had been here? Had risked his life to sneak into Richmond to see her, and she'd *missed* him? She wanted his arms around her so badly right now. Knowing she'd lost her chance hurt so much she couldn't breathe.

Cahill set his arm around her again and started walking, despite her stiffness. "He saved my life, you know. At the Wilderness. Dragged me out of the fire and carried me to the hospital on his horse."

She started to cry. How could she have missed him? How could God be that cruel? And if the major knew him, he would have known Justin was a Yankee. "What line was he riding to?"

Cahill waved her concern away. "I know you won't tell anyone I let him go. Figured it was the least I could do to repay him. Though I'm mighty glad to know he was telling the truth about you." He squeezed her shoulder. "Cheer up, now. He looked right as rain, and the war won't last much longer."

She shot him a doubtful look through her tears.

"Most of us, we know it's all but over now. We're just too darned proud to give up yet." There was a wry twist to his mouth. "How is it you married a Yank, anyhow?"

She drew in a breath. "He was wounded and became a patient of mine at a hospital."

"That right? Lucky fellow. I was only in the hospital once, back after the Wilderness. Awful place."

Sniffing, she fought to control her voice. "We had a lot of wounded from that fight."

He studied her as they strolled down the street. "It's been a hell of a war."

Yes, it had. She prayed every night for it to end, and it seemed so close now. But oh, Justin... She cast a longing glance over her shoulder.

"He's long gone by now," Cahill said. "Halfway back

to his regiment, I would imagine. What's his rank and outfit?"

"He's a major. Fifth Michigan Cavalry."

He winced. "Lord, when I decide to do a good deed, I really do it well, don't I?"

Brianna didn't answer, looking over her shoulder into the shadows and straining to hear faint hoof beats that might mean he wasn't gone yet.

Major Cahill stopped and studied her for a moment. Finally, he relented with a sigh. "Sergeant, bring me a horse."

"Sir," Williams whispered anxiously beside him.

"I know," Justin snapped. The galloping hoof beats were coming closer.

Ah damn, Cahill had reported them. The muscles in his stomach drew taut.

He drew his revolver and turned in the saddle to confront the new threat. Dammit, they were almost to the Rebel lines. His heart rate doubled in the tense silence. Too late to run for it now. All he could do was stand and fight his way out of this and pray he made it out alive.

A horse appeared at the end of the road, running flat-out toward them. Justin squinted in the darkness. It looked like it carried two riders on its back. He raised his revolver. "Get ready."

"Justin!"

He jerked at the sound of the female shout. His hand froze around the revolver.

One of the riders waved their arm in a frantic motion. "Justin!" The familiar voice made his lungs seize.

Brianna? He yanked his horse's head around and

kicked the animal into a canter.

"Sir?" Williams asked from behind him.

"Go ahead. I'll catch up." He didn't wait for a reply, wouldn't have heard it anyway over the pounding of his heart.

Another frantic wave. "Justin!"

Oh God, it *was* her. "Brianna!" He drove his heels into the horse's sides and tore out to meet her. Cahill brought the other horse to a plunging stop, and Justin leaped from his saddle to reach up for his wife.

She jumped straight into his arms.

He caught her and held her fiercely against him. "*Bree.*"

She was shaking and crying, little sobs jerking through her as he tried to surround her with his body. Christ, he felt a little unsteady himself.

"She's a bit shaken up," Cahill said.

Justin spared a glance at the man, who was scanning their surroundings. "Thank you," was all he could manage.

Cahill nodded. "Glad my men got there in time."

In time for what?

The man's words penetrated through his elation, and Justin remembered overhearing that a woman had been assaulted earlier. Without thinking, he took Brianna's face between his hands and tilted her head up. The faint moonlight gave him just enough light to make out the smear of blood on her lower lip and the faint bruise starting across one high cheekbone. "Jesus," he breathed, anger rising swift and brutal inside him. "What happened?"

"I'm fine," she whispered, digging her fingers into his shoulders. "Really, I am."

He smoothed a thumb over her damaged lip,

battling the lethal rage sweeping over him. He would kill whoever had done this to her.

"The man's paying for it in hell right now," Cahill said, turning his back to give them privacy.

Justin gently wiped away a tear that had slipped over her lower lashes. Her beautiful eyes were silver with them. "Sweetheart, what happened?"

"Just a thief," she managed, still quivering all over. "He tried to take your watch."

She'd been assaulted because of his damn *watch*? "Dammit, please tell me you handed it over."

"No." She shook her head emphatically. "Never."

It scared the holy hell out of him that she would stand and fight to protect a stupid piece of jewelry. But she was clearly upset, and he wasn't going to lecture her on it now. "Angel, look at you," he whispered and kissed her gently, mindful of her cut lip. She made a choked sound and wrapped her arms around his neck, lifting into the kiss. He soothed her with nibbles and the slow sweep of his tongue before placing tiny kisses all over every mark on her face.

Her quivers lessened and the taut muscles in her back seemed to relax. "I can't believe you're here, in this." She ran her fingers over the shoulder of his worn butternut uniform.

"I know," he said against her cheek. "It's a long story."

Cahill coughed discreetly to get their attention. "Hate to break up the reunion, but you'd best get movin'."

Brianna slid her fingers into his hair and gazed deep into his eyes for a moment before she buried her face in his neck. "Be safe."

He was so torn. The thought of leaving her when

she was hurt and frightened made him feel like an anvil sat on his chest. "Bree, look at me."

She raised her head, blinking away tears.

He ignored the prickle of warning crawling over his nape that he had to go, now, and cupped her face between his hands. "Come with me. Right now."

"I can't." Her face twisted in anguish. "I want to, but I can't. My brother's ill, really ill. They don't have a full-time doctor available at Libby, so they let me in to nurse him once a day. I can't leave him. He'll die without me and the little food I bring him."

Hell. The thought of her coming and going from that dank prison made his skin crawl. The urge to grab her and gallop away was almost overpowering, but there was no point arguing with her. She'd never forgive him if he forcibly took her away from the brother she'd come to Richmond to be near. He ran a hand over the length of her spine. "Do you know what's going to happen here?"

Eyes solemn, she nodded. And much as she tried to hide it, he saw the fear buried there. It made him want to shake her. "It won't be much longer now, but when the city falls it's going to fall hard. Do you understand what I'm telling you?"

She clutched his upper arms. "Yes."

God, he couldn't believe he was going to have to leave her behind in harm's way. "Stay in the house when it does. Keep everything locked up tight, and if you do have to go out, stay on your side of the river. And never, *ever* leave the house alone."

"I won't." Her throat moved when she swallowed, drawing his attention to the purple marks staining her creamy skin.

"Jesus, what—"

"I'm all right." One slender hand went to her throat. "No real damage."

He met her eyes as he caressed her satiny cheek. He shook his head.

"I know. But you have to go, now." With a deep breath she stepped back, as though making the decision for him.

He didn't even have any money with him to give her. Pursing his lips, he grabbed her chilled hands. "I'll take you back to the house."

"No." Fear crept into her eyes, eclipsing the sadness. "No, you can't. It's too dangerous and you need to get back to your lines."

Who was she to talk after what she'd been through tonight and what she'd face if she stayed in Richmond? The hell it was too dangerous for him. "I'm taking you back."

"I'll see her home safely," Cahill offered, stepping closer. "And she's right, you need to be riding outta here right quick."

Glancing behind him, he found Williams waiting a short distance away, still mounted. They had yet to clear the Rebel pickets and line and make it back to their own in their butternut uniforms without being shot. With a frustrated sigh, he turned back to Brianna. "Come here." When he opened his arms, she pressed full length against him and wrapped her arms tightly around his back. Justin squeezed his eyes shut and hugged her one last time. Hard. To tell her without words how much he didn't want to let her go. It wasn't enough. Not even close. Never would be.

"Love you."

The whispered words punched him right in the heart. "God, I love you too." Forcing himself to release her, he took a step back and reached for his horse's bridle. He looked over at Cahill. "You'll take care of her?"

"You have my word."

He read the steely resolve in the other man's eyes and felt satisfied he would protect Brianna. It was all he could ask for.

Settling into the saddle, Justin stared down at his wife. Her hair was mussed and sliding from its pins, her lips swollen. Liquid with unshed tears, her wide gray eyes gazed back at him. She was the most precious thing in the world to him.

His voice was rough. "You stay safe, you hear me?"

She nodded, eyes haunted by the knowledge that they might not see each other again. "You too."

The muscles in his jaw bunched. "I'll come for you as soon as I can."

"Yes, please do."

He couldn't get anything else out past the lump in his throat. All he could manage was a tight nod.

Feeling like he was tearing off his own skin, he wheeled his horse around and galloped toward the Confederate line with Williams right behind him.

CHAPTER TWENTY SEVEN

Richmond, VA
Sunday April 2nd, 1865

Sitting near the front of St. Paul's Episcopal Church, Mrs. Lancaster pointed out President Davis's solitary figure several rows in front of them. Brianna watched him while she fanned her neck during the minister's sermon.

He was concluding his speech when a man hurried down the aisle and bent to speak with the President, whose face took on an unhealthy gray pallor. He rose quickly and left the church. The service ended in unease, the parishioners pouring out into the street.

A light breeze swept off the James, the daffodils and budding branches swaying along the streets. The sun shone brightly over Richmond, despite the war and the Yankees lying entrenched on three sides of the city.

Whatever message Davis had received had not been good news for the citizens of Richmond.

Hope made Brianna's heart knock in her chest, but Mrs. Lancaster was near to swooning with fear. Brianna felt even more protective of the woman since Justin's visit. That night Mrs. Lancaster had told her how desperate Justin was to find her, scolded her for keeping such a secret from her, then hugged Brianna to her formidable bosom and sworn to be like her family until Justin came back for her. Brianna still hadn't told her that Justin was really a Union officer.

"Mark my word, the Yankees are coming. Maybe this minute." Mrs. Lancaster's rash words alarmed several people, who rushed away with wide eyes.

Brianna and Nan hurried her and her daughter into the carriage and bade the driver to take them home. When they arrived, Mrs. Lancaster insisted on going to a friend's house to await any news. Brianna escorted Cassidy into the house.

Hours later, when she was busy in the kitchen with Nan preparing the evening meal, a commotion broke out in the foyer. Hurrying to the front hall, they both stopped short at the dreadful expression on Mrs. Lancaster's face. She was white as flour, pressing a handkerchief to her trembling lips as she stared at them with swimming eyes.

The woman's shaking hands rose to her throat. "They've left us!" she cried in a voice edged with hysteria.

"Who?" Brianna asked.

She started pacing across the polished floor. "Nan, get me my smelling salts before I faint!" She paused, glancing wildly about the room. Her theatrical wail bounced unchecked through the vaulted archways.

"Who's leaving?" Brianna pressed.

Terrified light blue eyes swung back to her. "The

government! They're leaving us and the army's going with them. Oh, lord, the Yankees will come and destroy us!"

A curious numbness flooded Brianna. Davis and his government were leaving Richmond with the army? Her mind raced, trying to make sense of it all. They must have abandoned Petersburg. That meant the lines were broken! She'd known the end was near, but it had happened so much faster than she had dared hope.

A new wave of panic seized Mrs. Lancaster, and her eyes grew frenzied. "They will rape us and burn this house! Oh, my grandmother's silver, my china…" She reached out and dug her fingers into Nan's arm, who had retrieved the vial of smelling salts. "Quick! Fetch my valuables while I get a shovel. We'll bury everything in the rose garden. Those blue devils won't get a thing from me, by God!"

Heart about to burst, Brianna ushered her distraught employer to an overstuffed chair in the parlor and brought her a steaming cup of tea.

Mrs. Lancaster peered up at her. "Thank you, Jen— I mean, Brianna dear." The delicate cup rattled against its saucer. "I'm sorry. I should not be so selfish in my distress. You must be worried as well with the Yankees so near. After all, you are a Southerner."

Yes, whose Yankee husband and brother would, with any luck, be paying a visit soon.

Brianna laid a soothing hand on the woman's wrist, belying the joy racing through her. The war was all but over. Justin would come for her. Morgan was on the mend and would be free. She struggled to mask her elation. "It will be all right, ma'am, the Yankees will not harm us. They are soldiers, not animals." Even as she said the words, she recalled how the *Richmond*

Examiner had painted them to be vicious, heartless barbarians, burning and pillaging as they went. War was a desperate endeavor. Even men like Morgan and Justin sometimes did the unthinkable to bring the suffering to an end.

Mrs. Lancaster stared at her in disbelief. "You can't be serious! The Yankees are dreadful beasts! Why, only last week I received a letter from my cousin in Charleston about the horrible behavior of those animals. Oh, we will surely be robbed and raped or worse." Her eyes squeezed shut.

Brianna was never more aware of the bitter divide that had torn the country apart. "No, ma'am. We'll be safe. I've been through much worse than an occupation, and if I can live through that, we can surely make it through this together." *Besides, Justin and my brother will not let anything happen to us.* She gave Mrs. Lancaster's damp hand a quick squeeze. "I think a short nap would do you a world of good."

Brianna took her up to her bedroom and helped her under the covers, pausing at the window to peer outside for any signs of the Union troops. Seeing none, she pulled the drapes closed and enveloped the room in darkness.

Not here yet, she thought. But very soon.

****

At four o'clock that afternoon, the official announcement came and the clamor of terrified citizens grew outside in the streets. Men were sent out to destroy the liquor supplies to prevent alcohol from adding to the problems once the officials left the city. People began fighting for the rationed commodity, some going so far as to scoop it up in shoes and hats.

The crowd threw the warehouses open, revealing mountains of food that had lain undetected by the citizens through these lean times, hoarded away for purposes known only to the government. The outraged mob stormed the buildings, grabbing anything they could carry. The rabble grew violent and riots broke out, looters capitalizing on the destruction.

Brianna kept her mistress upstairs and away from the windows to shield her from the sights and sounds. The level of panic gripping the city frightened her. Everywhere she looked, families were packing wagons and fleeing down the pedestrian-choked roads. Richmond had become a frenzied animal, turning on itself, even aiding in its own destruction. Behind locked doors, she waited tensely for the rabble to reach their door. A loaded Springfield rifle was positioned there. If she had to, she would use it.

She pulled a curtain aside and gazed out across the river toward Libby. Had they released the prisoners yet? Morgan might be caught up in the mob somewhere.

She and Nan kept a watchful eye on the chaos for the rest of the day. The rioters and looters never came, and that evening she helped Mrs. Lancaster soothe a blinding headache before turning in for the night. Brianna was sound asleep in her attic room hours later when a huge explosion rocked the house.

She shot up in bed with a smothered gasp, her heart galloping. Her window had shattered. The walls shook and the entire house seemed to wobble on its foundation for a few moments. Things fell off walls and clattered amongst the cupboards, tables and mantelpieces. When everything stilled, she heard Mrs. Lancaster screaming.

Oh, God, was she hurt? Had something fallen on her? Brianna leaped out of bed and tore down the hall, nearly got run over by Cassidy as she raced to her mother's bedroom, a nightcap clinging to the blond curls streaming behind her. When Brianna reached the bedchamber, Mrs. Lancaster was on the carpet huddled in a ball, still screaming as if the end of the world had come. She latched onto Brianna's legs and dragged her down to the floor by her nightgown. Crouched on the carpet with Mrs. Lancaster and Cassidy, she tried to determine what had happened.

"They've come to kill us!" her hysterical mistress sobbed, fingernails digging into Brianna's arms.

She freed herself and went to the shattered window, taking a cautious look outside. On the other side of town, flames rose in an angry maelstrom. Fiery tongues licked high into the black sky, smoke soaring so high it blotted out the moonlight. Several small explosions followed. She felt the concussion of them in her chest.

The ammunition stores. The retreating army must have destroyed them to keep the supplies out of Union hands.

A thrill raced through her. The Union troops had to be close.

Please God, let this mean it's over.

She returned to her almost catatonic employer and helped her to bed. "I think they blew up the armory, to keep the weapons from going to the Yankees," she said, blotting the tears that coursed down Rosemary's cheeks. "I daresay they might have given us some sort of warning first." A relieved laugh escaped her.

Her employer stared at her as though she'd lost her mind.

325

On the street below, someone went from door to door yelling, "Fire!"

Brianna shivered, thanking God they were across the city from the doomed arsenal. She didn't need to be told that the inferno would spread fast with no soldiers around to staunch it, and the looting would only get worse.

Mrs. Lancaster opened her mouth to say something, but Cassidy leaped up into her bed, sobbing. Patting her daughter's hand, she shifted her gaze back to Brianna. "There, there, my darling," she soothed, as much to herself as to her daughter. "Brianna says they have blown up the armory, that's all." Her eyes lost some of their wildness, then narrowed on her in annoyance. "Although she should be under these covers with us, worrying about her own neck. I cannot understand why she hasn't the sense God gave a goose!"

Flushing, Brianna bobbed a curtsy and left the frightened women to console themselves. She hurried downstairs to find Nan already standing guard by the door in her nightgown, weapon in hand. Without a word, her friend handed her the loaded Springfield. As the minutes passed the rifle got heavier, but Brianna held it tight. If anyone dared to break in, they would be sorry.

Together they kept silent vigil until the sun appeared on the smoke-smudged horizon, waiting for the approaching Union army they knew was coming.

****

The morning of April 4th, Brianna watched from the window as the first columns of blue-clad soldiers entered the city and hoisted a U.S. flag from the state building. It didn't even look like Richmond anymore. Retreating Confederate troops, rioters and the arsenal fires had burned much of the once-beautiful city, and the skyline was a charcoal smudge against the horizon.

As soon the Union troops arrived, however, that all changed. An eerie calm spread through the streets, but Brianna kept the doors locked and covered the broken windows. Though she and Nan were exhausted after their guard duty, they set out to clean up the mess. Fallen bricks and broken glass littered the streets. Several nearby homes and buildings were reduced to charred rubble. Everyone waited anxiously to learn how the occupying army would treat Richmond's citizens.

A guard detail came to the house and informed them a soldier would be posted there to ensure no harm came to the women. The news consoled Mrs. Lancaster somewhat, but when the lady gathered her courage and peered out to see a colored soldier on her front steps, she made such a scene that Cassidy lapsed into another crying fit. Brianna would have laughed if she hadn't been so worn with worry. It was over, and it looked as though their Northern guests would be staying for some time.

After supper, Brianna went back to her post at the front door. Things remained quiet outside, but amid the conquering army, people were on edge and she worried more fighting might break out. Across the river, her eyes swept over the smoldering devastation toward Libby prison. Her brother's health had been improving before the city fell, but she hadn't risked visiting him because of the fires and mobs in the streets. The Union troops must have liberated all the prisoners by now. Had Morgan been too sick to leave? Was he in a hospital somewhere? For all she knew, they might have sent him to the Union base at City Point for treatment.

She wasn't sure where Justin was. His brigade had been active all around Richmond these past weeks. From what the papers said, he was probably chasing what remained of Lee's army of Northern Virginia, moving away to the west.

Withholding a sigh, she shifted her gaze to the end of the street. A man's silhouette came into view. Tall, dressed in a Federal uniform, his gait was somewhat slow and awkward. Her fingers tightened on the rifle as she watched him approach. Something about him seemed familiar. The tilt of his head, maybe.

She sucked in a breath, her heart leaping in her chest.

Morgan. Morgan is here.

She dropped her weapon and tore down the steps, her feet flying over the debris-strewn sidewalk until she launched herself into his waiting arms with a glad cry. He hugged her so tight her ribs ached.

"Morgan," she whispered, burying her face into his ragged coat, feeling like a lost little girl instead of a grown woman who'd survived the devastation of war.

"I'm all right, Bree." His voice was rough.

"You're so pale," she whispered, looking up into his dear face. "And you've lost more weight." She laid her hand on his brow, found it hot. "How bad are you?"

He wove on his feet. "Better than I was."

She seized his arm. "Come inside this instant. You need to lie down and then I'll get you some broth."

He stopped her, shook his head. "It's my turn to take care of you now."

She read the protective glitter in his feverish eyes and knew he was torn up about not being with her when the city fell. From where she stood, he looked like he might topple at any second. "You can take care of me once you're better," she promised, and towed him up the stairs into the house.

****

Appomattox Court House
April 9th 1865

Justin darted a furtive glance over his shoulder at the empty road behind their position and shifted to keep his seat when Boy-o jerked as a shell burst nearby. Still no sign of any reinforcements. Where the hell was the infantry? They couldn't hold this junction on their own, and God only knew how long they'd last under this kind of pressure. The Confederate infantry swelled in front of them with superior numbers, threatening to spread past their flanks and surround them.

Bugles blared commands through the din of artillery and rifle fire.

"Fall back!" Justin commanded, and guided his troopers to the rear while the enemy kept advancing with their shrill yell. Had he actually thought it might end today? That they would finally cut off and surround what was left of Lee's army and force surrender?

"Fall back and keep moving!" Bullets whizzed past, peppering the ground around him. He'd already lost two men that morning. He didn't want to lose anyone else, especially when the end was so agonizingly close. But they couldn't yield all this ground. Couldn't let Lee get past them, out into the open where he could run free to regroup and refortify. Neither could they withstand this new attack.

He urged Boy-o further up the road. The horse tossed its head as if he protested the decision. Justin fired his revolver at the enemy until it was empty, and rummaged in his cartridge box for more ammo.

When he looked up, the Confederates were closing in on them from both sides, like a horseshoe. His men kept to their methodical withdrawal, shooting at the enemy ranks with their Spencers. Sweat filmed his skin. So goddamn close, and they were pulling back. If they could just hang on, buy even a few more minutes, maybe their reinforcements would arrive. The end was right in front of them—they could all see it, taste it.

He ground his teeth in aggravation. Careful to keep their formation orderly, he drew his men back from the front lines. The Fifth and the rest of the cavalry withdrew beyond Appomattox station, bending and melting under the onslaught of the advancing foe. Frustration and helplessness seethed inside him. Dammit, the end was right *here*!

A sudden cheer went up from the advance guard. Justin whipped about, heart thudding. The Union infantry suddenly appeared down the road. His men howled in victory. The hair on his arms stood on end. Now it would happen—Lee could never hold against such overwhelming numbers. Elation pulsed through his body.

He drove his heels into Boy-o's sides and rushed to bolster their flank, charging into an open field to form ranks and wait in position. The enemy spread out to mirror their line, squaring off for another attack, even though they must have known how futile the effort was. The Confederacy was on its deathbed and down to its last painful gasp. It was Palm Sunday, a fitting day for the end.

Justin peered down the mounted line beside him. The men's eyes were alight with the knowledge of certain victory, every hand clenched purposefully around the hilt of their saber. Four years of hell and it all came down to this. One more battle, just one more charge to repel, and it would be finished. They could all go home.

Goose bumps erupted over his body. He would make this charge for Mitch. For every one of his fallen comrades. For his father, who'd died defending this country. For Brianna and their future together.

Chills raced over his skin as he gazed out over that vast green space. More bugle calls split the air, the men preparing for the attack. He raised his saber and awaited the signal to charge. The swallow-tailed points of the regiment's guidon whipped in the breeze against the clear blue morning sky. Horses stamped and swished their tails. The jingle of bridles mixed with the shouted commands. Justin tensed, leaned forward in his stirrups. Any moment now...

"Sir!"

Justin jerked his gaze to Williams, whose eyes were wide. "What?"

"Take a look for yourself." He thrust a pair of field glasses at him.

Justin looked through them and felt a jolt of shock reverberate up his spine. A messenger galloped from the Confederate line carrying a white flag. *My God, a truce.*

Was this it? Was it over? Heart in his throat, he followed the soldier's progress, fingers clenching around the glasses when the rider passed it to someone from the Seventh Michigan. The officer who received it rode back to their lines and presented it to Custer.

A moment later, Custer tore off to deliver the Confederate's message, presumably to General Grant. As word spread down the line, cheer after cheer rose up from the jubilant men.

Justin held his breath and stole a glance at the Confederate force across the field. "They're breaking ranks," he said breathlessly. "And stacking their weapons!" In shock, he lowered the glasses and met Williams's tear-glazed eyes.

"Glory be to God, sir, it's over. It's *over!*"

Justin couldn't summon the energy to cheer. He couldn't speak past the sudden lump in his throat, had to look away before he started crying. An odd stillness overcame him. Was it really done? He'd known for weeks the end was near, but now that it seemed to be happening, he felt numb.

Williams grabbed him by the shoulders. "We did it, sir. We won the damned war!"

Some of the ice that had settled around his heart melted, and a smile trembled on his lips. "We won."

Williams leaned over to throw an arm around him, laughing tearfully. Justin returned the embrace, eyes squeezed shut as he sent up a prayer of thanks, the first prayer he'd said since his brother died. God, how he wished Mitch could have seen this. And Brianna—she'd been in Richmond this whole time, had been there when it fell. He'd tried like hell to find a way to get to her, but the constant fighting had made seeing her impossible.

"We'll be sent home," Williams said against his shoulder, squeezing hard. "I'll get to see my baby when it's born."

Returning his friend's embrace, Justin didn't have the heart to tell him their job wasn't over yet. Lee might be surrendering, but Johnston's army was still out there somewhere. Once *they* gave up, the war would be over. And not until.

CHAPTER TWENTY EIGHT

Washington, D.C.
May 23, 1865

When they arrived in the nation's capital from City Point, Morgan took Brianna directly to the hotel where Justin had reserved rooms for them. He pressed a kiss to her brow. He looked much better now, having regained some of the weight he'd lost. "I'm going to find my regiment. Leave a note for me at the front desk so I know what your plans are."

She didn't know where Justin wanted to go after he was discharged. A single letter was all she'd received from him since Lee's surrender at Appomattox. "I will." She loved her brother so much and was proud of him. "We won," she whispered to him, still in awe it was over.

"We sure did." He hugged her goodbye, holding on for a moment. "Maybe I'll see you in Lexington."

"Maybe." She didn't want to let him go. She'd missed too much time with him already. But she had a new life to lead and a new husband to share it with. And Morgan had his own future to determine.

"Be happy, Bree."

"I will be." She held her smile as he left, tall and proud, despite the size he'd yet to put back on from his illness. Standing by the window overlooking the street, she watched him exit the hotel and stroll out of sight. The tick of the mantle clock made her realize how quiet it was. Her stomach was full, she was safe and warm, and in a few hours Justin would walk through the door. For good. She hugged herself and glanced at the wide bed, hardly able to believe she would be holding him in it later.

He was already here, somewhere in the city with the rest of the Michigan Brigade. Eager to get to the parade site, she took her parasol and headed out with the throngs going to watch the Grand Review. Band music reached her long before she got there. The streets along the parade route were crowded with onlookers waving flags and banners. Women and children clutched flowers to throw at the victorious troops. She found a spot close to the Presidential box where President Johnson sat and felt a pang of regret that Lincoln wasn't here to see this. He'd been a great man and a strong leader, and he'd been taken from the country much too soon.

She waited in place as people squeezed in around her on all sides. Brass bands played and vendors hawked their wares, selling food and trinkets for the war weary crowds to commemorate the occasion. She had to stand on tiptoe to see over the feathered hat of the woman in front of her.

A loud cheer rose up from down the block, and excitement buzzed in her stomach. She didn't have any idea when Justin's division was scheduled to ride past, but she would happily stand there all day just for the chance to see him in the review with his regiment. She stood on her toes as a precise formation of soldiers marched up in their blue uniforms, rifles held against their shoulders. Their bayonets gleamed in the sun, each step in precise cadence, their perfectly timed paces hitting the pavement like drum beats. Their smiles and obvious pride brought tears to her eyes. How much they'd all suffered to reach this day.

Almost an hour passed before the first division of cavalry advanced. Her heart pounded as she again strained to see over the people in front of her. The spectators roared, their applause and cheers seeming much louder than before. Then she saw why. General Custer rode at the head of the Third Division, resplendent in his famous blue velvet uniform and red neckerchief.

He had almost reached the place where she stood when something spooked his horse. The General twisted in the saddle as his mount reared and tore down the street. Everyone gasped, the woman in front of her crying out in alarm. Custer held his seat superbly and brought the animal under control in short order, his golden curls bouncing as his horse came plunging down on its front hooves. As the crowd roared in appreciation of Custer's skill, she smirked. Had he done it on purpose? From what Justin had told her about him, she wouldn't put it past the flamboyant general, and he certainly hadn't seemed short on confidence when she met him.

Turning her attention to the end of the column, she waited breathlessly to find out which division was next. When she spotted another body of mounted troopers wearing red neckerchiefs coming toward her, her throat tightened. The Wolverines were there at last. Her husband was *there.* She recognized General Merritt in the lead and could hardly breathe. Where was the Fifth? Were the regiments proceeding in numerical order? The Michigan Brigade began to file past, and her eyes fell on a man riding near the head of the next regiment.

Her heart skipped a beat. Her hands flew to her mouth.

Justin. She smiled so wide her cheeks ached. Oh, dear God, he was magnificent.

Her heart pounded against her ribs as he rode by at the front of his regiment, tall and handsome atop Boy-o. He held a glinting saber raised in salute in his gauntleted right hand, and his red neckerchief fluttered in the breeze along with the flags and swallowtail guidon. Larger than life, mounted upon his favorite horse. Boy-o's coal black coat gleamed in the sunlight. Goose bumps raced over her skin. Brianna thought her chest would burst with pride. When Justin came abreast of her, she jumped up and down and yelled out as loud as she could to him, but her voice was lost in the roar of the crowd and he didn't see her waving her arms.

Through teary eyes she watched him lead his men along the route until they turned the corner and he became a speck in the distance. Exhaling, she pressed a hand to her heart and blew out a breath. If she lived to be a hundred, she'd never forget the sight of him today.

She made her way through the melee back to the hotel, smiling the whole time. She couldn't wait for him to burst into their room and take her into his arms, to hold him again. The future stretched out before her with limitless potential, the rest of their lives ripe with possibility. Dizzy with joy, she tossed her bonnet on the bed where she'd be making love with her husband in a matter of hours.

She should pinch herself, just to make sure she wasn't dreaming.

To kill time, she ordered a light supper and the staff brought up hot water for a bath in a hip tub. After a good soak, she toweled off and dressed in a fresh gown of deep blue sprigged cotton. She kept glancing out the window in the hope of spying her husband coming along the sidewalk but gave up after a couple of hours. The sun dipped below the buildings, bathing them and the trees lining the street in shades of gold and rust. Several times she heard footsteps in the hallway and her heart started to race, but they always passed by her door. She'd dozed off in a chair next to the low burning fire when a brisk knock finally came.

Brianna bolted upright, blinking, and the knob turned. She jumped out of her chair and lunged for the door, heart hammering. *He's finally here*. When she was halfway to it the door swung open to reveal her husband. A funny sound escaped her throat, almost a cry, and she clapped her hands over her nose and mouth.

Justin wore a huge smile, his sapphire eyes shining as he reached for her. "Hi, angel."

Brianna threw her arms around his neck and he lifted her off the floor to sweep her around in a jubilant circle. She laughed, kissing him wherever her lips landed, squeezing him so hard her arms trembled. He chuckled against her mouth and crushed her against his chest. "Justin," she croaked, hardly able to believe he was there. "Justin, Justin."

"I missed you so much." His voice was rough. After

a moment, he set her away from him and took her hands in his. "Let me look at you."

She wiped her hands over her cheeks to erase her tears as his eyes swept over her. "I promised myself I wouldn't cry."

He grinned and kissed her again. "It's all right."

"I saw you in the parade today. You were the most incredible sight I have ever seen, and I'm so proud to be your wife." She hugged him again, absorbing the laugh that rumbled through his chest. "I've dreamed about this for so long. I can't believe it's happening."

"I know. And once we're mustered out back in Michigan, I'll be home with you for good. Then you'll be sorry." He eased a lock of hair away from her face and bent his head, finding her mouth with his.

Brianna swayed in his embrace and opened to him like a flower in the sun. Hunger roared through her veins. He growled at her eagerness and took her deeper, sliding his tongue against hers in a slow, erotic assault that had her gasping and fighting to be closer. One of his hands slid up to cup her breast.

Her back arched. "I want you." She was starved for him. Couldn't wait a moment longer.

He dropped his mouth to the side of her neck and stroked his tongue over her skin. "You've got me," he muttered, taking her hand and sliding it down to cover the hard length that pushed against the front of his trousers. "Every last inch of me."

Someone coughed from the hallway, the door still wide open.

Neither of them cared enough to stop.

A discreet clearing of a throat followed. "I'll just, uh...close the door for you." It clicked shut.

Laughing, Brianna started in on the buttons of

Justin's coat. He dragged her nearer, tugged on the ties that held up her skirts and shoved the mass of cotton to the floor. They struggled with each other's clothing, throwing garments aside in a heap until he was naked and she wore only her chemise and stockings. She could hardly breathe. If she didn't have him inside her in the next few seconds, she would die from the pressure building in her. Impatient, she grabbed hold of his shoulders and pulled him toward the bed.

They fell in a tangle of limbs on the clean sheets she'd turned down. Justin rose on his knees to peel the rest of her clothes off and lowered his weight onto her, kissing her with an urgency that bordered on desperation. After a while, he raised his head and gazed at her with blazing eyes. "I can't wait this time."

"Then don't," she urged, wrapping her legs around his hips to pull him inside. He settled against her, his solid, hungry weight pressing her into the bed, surrounding her with his warmth and strength. She was so wet already, aching for him. "I want you inside me. Right now."

He pushed forward and drove himself inside her with one thrust. They both cried out at the feel of it. Brianna locked her body around him, holding him as tight and as close as she could. He braced himself on his hands and rode her hard, stroking the thick, hard length of him inside her.

She gave herself up to his wild, plunging rhythm, stunned by the intense pleasure coursing through her with so little effort. Each time he rubbed against the knot of sensation inside her, the mindlessness increased until she strained up beneath him and dug her nails into his back. Finally he groaned and shuddered once as he neared the peak, and it triggered her own release. She cried out with him in fulfillment, let herself sink deep into the velvet oblivion. Relaxed and breathless, she tucked him in close to her body and nuzzled the damp raven hair at his temple, marveling that she had him in her arms again.

Justin levered up on his elbows, eyes sparkling. "I love the way you welcome me home."

She laughed. "I love it, too." Her hands traveled the long length of his back, tracing the smooth bands of muscle beneath his hot skin. "Want me to do it again?"

He smiled against her mouth, kissing her slow and sweet, his tongue caressing her lips.

She turned her head aside. "Is that a yes? Because to do it properly, I'm going to need a few more days in bed with you."

He eased up to meet her gaze, a wicked gleam in his deep blue eyes. "Careful what you wish for, angel."

****

Justin returned from a meeting the next morning and hesitated in the doorway of their hotel room, staring down at his hat clenched in his hands. With one look at his face, Brianna's stomach dropped. He shut the door quietly behind him, jaw set, his troubled expression putting her on edge.

"What is it?" she demanded, instantly on her feet and willing her pulse to slow down.

Rather than answer, he sat her on the edge of the bed and sank down beside her, his gaze on the floor. He wouldn't look at her. After a moment of taut silence he dropped his head into his hands and dragged them through his hair.

His obvious distress frightened her. "Justin?"

When he finally glanced up at her, the haunted look in his eyes made her certain someone had died. She laid a hand on his arm, finding the muscles beneath her palm rock hard.

He studied her for a long moment, searching her eyes. "I don't know how to tell you." He closed his mouth, shook his head.

The blood pounded in her ears. "Tell me what?" Dear God, what could be so bad that he couldn't even say it?

"We've been ordered to the frontier," he said dully.

She shook her head. "I don't understand. *Who*?"

"The brigade." He rubbed a hand over the back of his neck. "They're sending us out to fight the Indians."

Her heart went into free-fall. *No.* There had to be some mistake. The war was over. He had served his time, done his duty, suffered enough. This couldn't be real. "But they can't do this. Can they?" The question came out as a plea.

He closed his eyes and tipped his head back, still rubbing the back of his neck. "There was a misunderstanding about our papers. Our terms of enlistment were for three years, unless we were discharged before then."

"Yes, but the war's over." She fought a wave of panic. Denial screamed in her head.

Justin shook his head and looked at her. "They're making us serve the whole enlistment." His eyes were weary, sad. "Grant's sending us out tonight."

Tonight? She shot off the bed and paced, rubbed her hands up and down her chilled arms because she didn't know what else to do besides start screaming. *Oh God, oh God, oh God...*

"Bree," he said softly.

She shook her head, kept moving. She didn't want to hear any more. Couldn't look at him for fear she'd crumple into a ball and howl like a madwoman. This war had cost them both so much. She'd lost a husband she'd loved with everything she had, her father, her home. She'd endured the horrors of the hospitals to lend comfort where she could, and finally met Justin. For almost an entire year she'd prayed for him to return safely to her. She'd agonized about his safety, worn herself out worrying about him. Half starved herself to be close to her brother. Traveled hundreds of miles through snow and rain and mud for the chance to see Justin.

And what of his sacrifices? He'd held his dying brother in his arms, lost friends, and in all ways that mattered, had lost his mother as well.

They'd borne all of that. And now he was being sent to a different front? One he hadn't signed on for?

"Angel, look at me."

She stopped with her back to him and closed her eyes. Counted to ten, forced her choppy breathing under control. He was disheartened enough. She could hear it in the husky timbre of his voice. He didn't need her adding to his misery with her own. As soon as she trusted herself not to break down, she faced him. The torment in his eyes almost did her in. *Don't cry. Don't cry.*

Justin came to her, took hold of her shoulders. "I'm so sorry."

Despite her vow, her eyes filled. *He* was sorry? None of this was his fault. She was devastated for him. Terrified for him. Fighting Indians in the middle of nowhere? The Union cavalry couldn't possibly be prepared for that. So why would the army send them? She wrapped her arms around his back and absorbed his heavy sigh. Her tears dripped onto his uniform coat. A sob shuddered through her. "No. *No.*"

"God." His arms tightened protectively. "Bree..."

She forced herself to calm down, took another shaky breath. "H-how long?"

"Until the three years are up."

She lost it. Completely lost control. To have him home safe and sound after everything they'd endured, only to have him torn away for *this,* was an unspeakable cruelty. *Why?* she wanted to scream. It wasn't fair. Why him? How could she bear this?

"Ah, damn. I know," he said against the top of her head. "I'm so sorry, sweetheart."

She couldn't speak, only cried harder. He held her through the torrent, murmuring soft things, stroking her back until she lifted her head with a soggy sniff. A few more hours together. That's all they had left. She wiped her face. "S-sorry. Didn't mean to do that."

"Don't apologize. You're entitled." He let out a ragged sigh and steered her over to the bed, where they sat next to each other again and stared into the flames burning low in the fireplace. "This is going to kill the boys," he said finally.

"They don't know yet?"

"No. They still think they're going home."

Oh, God, this was so awful.

"You can imagine what this is going to do to the brigade's morale."

It would destroy it. "Isn't there something that can be done?"

"I wish there were. I've already tried everything I know of."

Brianna didn't know what to say. She didn't want to make it worse for him—she'd already broken down and added to his burden. She hated feeling so helpless. "Is there anything I can do?"

His smile was so sad it almost broke her heart. "No, but damn, I hate having to leave you again."

Of course he would be thinking of her instead of himself, even though he was being sent to the frontier to fight an unknown, savage enemy. She slid her arms around him and urged him to lie down beside her. Curled up against his side, she searched for words of comfort. He needed to see her strong right now, and she needed to prove he didn't have to worry about her while he was away. Her fingers smoothed his silky hair. "We've weathered the storm this far. We can make it through anything now."

A wry smile touched his lips. "Spoken like a brave cavalry wife."

"Well, that's what I am. And I can take care of myself. You concentrate on coming home safely, and that's all."

He kissed her temple. "Yes, ma'am."

She'd run out of words now. Had nothing left to say that might help or comfort either of them, and his introspective silence said the same for him. They probably had less than eight hours together.

She wasn't going to waste another moment of it.

Coming up on one elbow, she cupped the side of his face. He met her gaze, his eyes delving into hers. His warm scent reached out to her, a mix of soap and spices. Leaning down, she pressed him onto his back and kissed him. He allowed her to take the lead, though she could feel the coiled tension in his body, ready to unleash his need on her.

345

Her tongue touched his, gliding over it in a silky caress. She drew it out, keeping control until she had him breathing hard, his hands buried in her hair. Satisfied that he was now thinking of nothing but burying himself inside her, she undressed them both and kissed his naked chest, the rigid muscles in his belly, lower to rub her cheek against the scalding-hot length of his erection.

"Bree." His voice was low, almost a growl.

She looked up at him, parting her lips to let the tip of her tongue flick at the tender underside of his cock. Justin stared down at her with smoldering eyes, his jaw clenched. She knew how much he loved this. Tasting him lightly, she hummed in enjoyment before opening her lips to take him deep into her mouth. He hissed and grabbed her hair with a choked moan, arching in ecstasy. She swirled her tongue leisurely around the swollen head, savoring the bursting heat and salty flavor of him.

"Right there," he murmured. His long fingers tightened in her hair with a delicious tug, holding her in place. "So good, angel."

In answer, Brianna sucked him deeper until he was helpless beneath her. His muscles drew rigid with strain, and an agonized moan tore from him. Knowing he was close, she reluctantly released him with one last luxurious pull of her mouth, a lascivious swirl of her tongue. She crawled back up his body to take his mouth, and straddled him. His hands cupped her breasts and teased her aching nipples while his tongue slid against hers. Breaking the kiss to stare into his eyes, she finally eased down and took him inside her body. Her head tipped back at the feel of him stretching and filling her. Justin's deep groan reverberated in the air around them.

He held her hips while she rode him slow and sweet, and stared up at her with desperate longing. His throat moved as he swallowed, and when he spoke, his voice was rough. "Love me, Bree."

Bittersweet pain filled her chest. "Always and forever," she whispered and leaned down to seal their mouths together, riding him a little faster.

His tormented growl echoed inside her heart. Loving him this way was so much stronger than words. The melding of breath and flesh, experiencing each gasp and sigh, each muted sound of pleasure as she gave herself to him, body and soul. He reached a hand between them to stroke over her slick flesh where their bodies joined, and in seconds the first wave of her orgasm rolled through her. Justin peaked moments later with a massive shudder and a harsh shout. The whole time she stared into his eyes, their love shining bright as the sun through the gloom of their sadness.

Held in the protection of his arms afterward, she searched for something that would lighten his burden. Forcing a smile, she passed a hand over his stubbled cheek. "Well, there's one good thing about this."

One coal-black brow arched upward. "What's that?"

"Just imagine the homecoming you'll get next time."

He gave a gruff chuckle against her temple and held her tight against his heart.

CHAPTER TWENTY NINE

Fort Leavenworth, KS
June 5th, 1865

In light of their unexpected orders, Justin had known keeping morale up would be hard, but even he would never have guessed how miserable the men were out here. They'd lost some of them to desertion after stopping at St. Louis, and taking the precaution of mooring away from the dock hadn't done a damned thing to stave off would-be deserters. Several troopers were so incensed by their forced service that they'd actually attacked the officers put in charge of keeping them on board the transport steamers and thrown them into the river. Most of those who'd jumped in and swam to shore were never seen again, and the remainder of the wretched men had steamed onward when the ship pulled out.

Making landfall, they rode to Fort Leavenworth, a speck of civilization in a dusty sea of prairie. Everyone was thoroughly demoralized, knowing that beyond the perimeter of the fort, postings on an endless plain awaited them, along with the threat of attacks from hostile natives. Several of the high-ranking officers had given speeches to try and boost the mood of the command.

A wasted effort. Any headway they'd gained had been crushed when the powers in Washington announced the regiments would be split up from one another to serve in different commands. To Justin, it was the final insult in this whole debacle. Truly it was a wonder they hadn't had a full-out armed mutiny on their hands yet.

He pulled off his hat to wipe his sleeve across his sweaty forehead. It came away coated with grime. It was as dusty out here as it had been that day at Cold Harbor, he reflected, glancing behind him to where Williams sulked in his saddle. His wife was expecting their first child any day, and he wasn't going to be there. Justin wasn't happy either. Brianna had chosen to go home to Lexington. Morgan's regiment had been mustered out at the end of the war, so at least she had her brother there while she was again forced to endure this long separation. Justin had sent Boy-o to Greenbriar as a surprise to her, because the loyal horse had done his duty and shouldn't have to serve this latest term of service just because Justin wasn't as fortunate. He hoped the gesture would make Brianna smile.

His new mount was a flighty thing, but for now he had no choice but to work with it. If it didn't shape up in a week or two though, he'd have to find another one. He couldn't fight anything with a horse that wouldn't stay put, let alone a tribe of incensed Indians. He got the feeling the horse hated this duty as much as he did. The gelding always had its ears back when anyone came close. He wasn't sure if the crop marks scarring its rump had come before the bad attitude, or after.

They traveled a mile or two farther, and when a ribbon of blue stream appeared in the distance, he rode for it and called a halt. The men dismounted with weary groans and stretched their legs. Some pulled off their boots to dangle their feet in the water while the horses drank, others stripping down and wading in to find relief from the broiling sun. Justin squatted down on the bank and held the reins as his horse drank the cool water between its teeth with a loud sucking noise.

Williams sat next to him with a heavy sigh. "When do you figure they'll send us out there?" He indicated the prairie with a jerk of his chin.

"In a few days, probably."

The lieutenant shook his head. "I keep hoping this has all been a mistake." He raised his brown gaze to Justin. "That someone will come to their senses and send us home."

"You think the brass in Washington have senses?"

He laughed. "I suppose you're right—"

Justin's horse jerked its head and let out a shrill cry, its ears pressed back and the whites of its eyes showing.

Justin grabbed the reins tighter and leaped to his feet with Williams. "Easy," he said in a low voice, searching the ground for whatever had frightened the knot-headed animal.

"Snake," Williams blurted, backing away and pointing to a spot in the grass beside the horse.

The animal shrieked and reared up on its hind hooves. Justin dropped the reins in case it bolted and dragged him along with it. He hadn't survived the damned war to be killed by a terrified horse.

The snake raised its head and a distinctive rattle sounded, coiled and ready to strike. Justin froze. One wrong move and he'd either get bitten or trampled by his horse.

He stared at the ugly diamond-shaped head and beady black eyes. His hand went to his sidearm. The snake's black forked tongue darted out, a menacing hissing sound blending with the rattle. *Shit*. His horse was going to have a fit. Even as he thought it, a shrill whinny split the air.

"Don't move, Major," one of the men down the bank called, leveling his pistol at it.

"Christ, don't shoot it," he growled, knowing his horse would go berserk. "Just get the damn horse—"

His mount let out a scream and bucked wildly, its hooves scrabbling for purchase on the edge of the bank when its forelegs landed. Justin lunged backward to get the hell out of the way of the thrashing hooves. He wasn't fast enough.

"Look out, sir!"

A hoof caught him in the shoulder and sent him flying. Pain fractured through him at the impact. He hit the ground hard and brought his arms up in a futile effort to shield himself from more blows.

Hands grabbed at the back of his uniform, trying to pull him clear. He looked over in time to see the snake strike. He jerked back in reflex, falling away from the friendly hands just as a shot rang out.

A blaze of pain exploded as the bullet struck and threw him headlong into the water.

****

Lexington, VA

June 9, 1865

The trip home to Kentucky passed in a gloomy blur. No matter how hard Brianna tried to keep a lid on her emotions, the sadness overwhelmed her in a black tide and sucked her under, far out into that dark sea.

Standing on the platform with a forced, bright smile as Justin's train pulled away was somehow harder than seeing him off during the war. The thought of him out on the barren plains fighting against an enemy they had no experience with scared her to death. Her mind kept recalling each gruesome detail of every Indian attack she'd read about in the papers. Arrows. Scalpings. Mutilated bodies. How on earth was a cavalry brigade that had been trained to engage an enemy with conventional weapons and tactics supposed to fight such an unpredictable foe?

Justin hadn't spoken to her about his feelings on the matter. He knew how upset she was and had carefully steered the conversation away when she'd tried to discuss it. He had to be afraid on some level though, for his men and for himself. Even without that further worry, he was going to have his hands full keeping the men's spirits up. Every one of them had expected to go home and be discharged after the Grand Review.

At the train station, Morgan and Gavin were waiting for her. The instant she set foot on the platform, her brother pulled her into his arms. He murmured something about how Justin would be fine, that the time would pass quickly, but she couldn't manage more than a forced half-smile in response. While he drove them home in a buggy, he and Gavin updated her on the state of affairs at Greenbriar. During everyone's absence, Teela and Ray had once again kept the place running smoothly. Morgan had made steady progress in replenishing the breeding stock, and most of the taxes had been paid.

She listened halfheartedly as he detailed the finances, but her heart wasn't in it. What did she care about ledgers and breeding stock when her husband was out there fighting for his life on the frontier?

Morgan stopped when he noticed her lack of interest.

She felt badly. "I'm sorry. I'm not in a very good frame of mind right now."

Gavin squeezed her shoulder. "He knows. He's babbling away to try and keep you from thinking about it."

"Thanks, but it's not going to help."

Morgan glanced at her then back at the road as he drove the buggy through the town traffic, out to where the lush meadows dipped and swelled as far as the eye could see. "Got something at home that might cheer you up."

She sighed. Unless it was Justin, she didn't want to know.

For the rest of the trip, the two men kept the conversation light, but she paid only passing attention. When Greenbriar's white rail fence came into view, snaking along the pastures until the house appeared, she should have been elated to be home with the war behind them. At best, the sight of the white two-story house filled her with wistful longing.

"Come on," Morgan said, handing her down. "Let's get you settled."

As soon as they hit the front steps, the glossy black door swung open and Teela and her husband came rushing out to greet her. She hugged them both and went inside, hit by a jolt of unreality. This didn't feel like home now. Not without Justin by her side.

Teela beamed at her. "My baby girl. I hear ya got yourself a good man. I can't wait to meet him."

Morgan gave the housekeeper a quelling look before turning back to Brianna. "Why don't you go upstairs and change, honey. Then I'll take you out to the stables for a tour."

Although she'd rather have rested, she agreed. What else did she have to do to pass the time? She followed Teela upstairs and entered her old bedroom, struck by how surreal it felt to be standing there again. Even though her room had stayed the same, everything in her life had changed.

At Teela's gentle urging, she changed clothes and pulled on a pair of boots before meeting Morgan and Gavin downstairs. They led her across the back lawn and through the garden filled with deep pink foxgloves and lemon yellow roses about to burst open. Clearing the black wrought-iron gate at the end of the garden path, they stepped through an arbor dripping with sweet-scented honeysuckle that led to the main paddock.

The white federal-style building that served as the stable sat under a canopy of two-hundred-year old oaks. New horses filled the closest three corrals. They raised their heads and pricked their ears up as the three of them approached. She stopped to pet one, a quarter horse with wide-spaced, gentle eyes. She ran a hand over its velvet muzzle, the earthy scent of horse taking her back to her earliest memories of being in the stable. It also made her think of the snowy day she'd ridden out to find Justin at his mother's house.

"I'll go find our new foreman so I can introduce you," Morgan said.

"You hired a foreman?"

"Yeah. Knows his stuff. Came by here a couple weeks ago looking for a job."

Probably a soldier returned from war needing work. She kept petting the horse. A minute later, she heard Morgan speaking with another man at the stable door, along with the clop of hooves. They were in shadow, but she could tell the foreman was a little shorter than her brother. He walked with a slight sway in his step, as though he were bowlegged.

"—be mighty glad to see her," the man said, his accent pure Virginia and somehow familiar.

Morgan emerged into the sunlight. The foreman was a step or two behind him, the brim of his hat obscuring his face as he led the horse.

"I believe you know my sister, Brianna," Morgan said.

What? She turned around. And then she stared, mouth falling open when the other man raised his head and a salt-and-pepper beard came into view. "Major Cahill?" The Confederate who'd assisted her and let Justin return to his command. And he was leading Boy-o.

The man grinned, tipped his hat. "Not a major anymore, Mrs. Thompson. Just plain Isaiah will do, or Cahill, whichever you prefer. How are you?"

She rushed over and threw her arms about him. "I don't believe it—how did you end up here? With him?" She nodded toward Boy-o.

Isaiah patted her back and laughed. "A few weeks ago I promised a certain Yankee officer I'd see you home safely, and I since got a letter from him saying that meant here, in Lexington. Bein' as there's nothing left for me in Richmond and I needed a job, your brother was kind enough to offer me one. Seems your husband thought highly enough of my actions in Richmond that night to provide a glowing reference." His dark eyes twinkled.

"I'm so glad." She turned her attention to Boy-o and hugged his thick neck, laughing as the horse lipped at her hair. "And what about this shameless fellow? My husband and you came up with this surprise?"

"Yes, ma'am. We thought it would cheer you up some."

She leaned her forehead against the horse's glossy black coat, swallowing back tears. Was Justin all right out there? He had to be. She wouldn't accept any other alternative. With effort, she put on a smile and faced Isaiah again. "What about your family?"

"We all live in town now." Isaiah scratched the side of his face. "Not sure if I'll ever be able to repay y'all for this, but I'm damn sure I know a thing or two about horses. I'll do a good job for you."

She smiled and looked at her brother. Morgan wore a satisfied grin, his arms folded across his chest.

Isaiah cleared his throat. "Well now. I'd best be gettin' back to work, afore the boss-man sends me packing for bein' lazy."

Morgan slapped the man's shoulder. "You'll have to do worse than this, I'm afraid."

With a two-fingered salute, Isaiah ambled back into the stable with Boy-o in tow.

Morgan slid an arm around her shoulders. "That help?"

"Yes." Justin's thoughtfulness put a lump in her throat.

Morgan showed her the new mares and studs he'd bought, outlined the chores he wanted done, then took her out for a ride on Boy-o to inspect the property lines, noting the sections of fencing that needed to be repaired or replaced. It felt good to be on horseback again with the breeze flowing over her skin, and being on Justin's favorite horse made her feel connected to him somehow. The familiar sweet scent of the emerald green grass soothed and refreshed her.

Once the horses were put away, she went with Morgan back into the house and found Gavin in the kitchen with a glass of lemonade. He poured them each one and started to sit, then hopped up like he'd sat on a nail.

"Almost forgot to give you this," he said, digging in his back pocket for an envelope. "Ray went into town and came back with it."

She sat her glass down with a thud. Her heart rattled in her chest as she stared at the telegram. If it was about Justin… It had to be about him, and the only reason to send word now would be if something had happened to him. The room tilted.

"Whoa," Morgan exclaimed, grabbing her waist with a steadying hand. "It's all right, honey, just breathe."

She did, sucking in gulps of air, but it didn't help. Her blood was like ice water in her veins, so cold it burned.

Gavin glanced at Morgan, then back at her. "Want me to open it?"

She shook her head. "No. I'll do it." She reached out a trembling hand, took the envelope from him, and forced herself to tear it open. Pulling the telegram free, her heart slammed against her ribs as her eyes skipped over the message.

Justin had been wounded.

The words blurred. "*No.*"

Morgan cursed and wrapped his arms around her, holding on hard. "Oh, Jesus, Bree, I'm so sorry."

She barely heard him, clinging to his strong frame for a moment with the telegram still clutched in her hand. It didn't say anything about how severe the wound was.

"I'm so damned sorry," Morgan was saying.

She shook her head. *Think, Brianna. Most of the wounded men you saw were sent home.* Pulling herself together, she read the remainder of the telegram. She hardly dared hope what it said was true. Was it possible?

"Bree? Honey, say something."

"It's over," she said hoarsely.

"What's over?"

She squeezed her eyes shut, laughed even though she must appear crazy. "He's been wounded and they're sending him home. He and the rest of the regiment. They're being mustered out. He's coming *home*!"

Morgan huffed out a breath and rested his chin on the top of her head. "We thought he'd died."

"No." She scrubbed a hand over her face, overjoyed he was coming home yet worried about his condition. She grabbed Morgan by the shirt front and shook him once in elation. "He's coming *home*."

Gavin reached out to pat her back. "We're glad for you, honey."

Brianna stood abruptly, breaking free of her brother's embrace. "They're sending them back to Detroit. I need to get there before he does."

She needed to make sure he received a proper homecoming. And that meant she had an important task to complete before he got there.

CHAPTER THIRTY

Detroit, MI
June 29, 1865

Siobhan huddled deeper into the crocheted blanket she'd wrapped around herself and reached for the cold teacup at her elbow. The fire burned low, its flames flickering in a hypnotic pattern in the hearth beneath her husband's portrait. His pipe and other things had been removed a few months ago, and she and Aggie had rearranged the furniture. It no longer looked like a shrine, but a comfortable room to sit by the fire and read in.

Though her health had improved and she no longer took any laudanum, it might have been the middle of January instead of the height of summer for all she cared. She rarely sat out on the verandah to enjoy the carefully tended grounds. Barely went outside at all, except to visit Mitchell's grave. Even those trips had decreased in frequency over the past months. Instead of going every day, she went only twice a week now.

The gardens were bursting with color and life, but she didn't care to spend any time looking at them. Somehow it was worse knowing that flowers thrived in prolific abundance while her baby lay in the ground.

Her shaky sigh seemed loud in the empty room. To her lonely ears, it echoed off the vaulted wooden panels on the ceiling, further reminding her how still and empty the house was.

Except for Aggie, she was all alone.

And whose fault is that?

The grief came unbidden. War had cost her everything. Her husband. Both her sons. Oh, Justin was alive, but he was as good as dead to her now. He'd left her too. Shoved aside by her icy disdain.

Because of your bitterness.

She clutched the blanket tighter, trying to block out the way her conscience needled her. It was always there, reminding her that she'd pushed him away and it left a greasy queasiness in the pit of her stomach. Because of her harsh words, she would never see her eldest son again, or the children he and his wife would have someday. Her own grandchildren would never know her because of her hateful behavior. Sometimes she wanted to close her eyes and never wake up again.

Siobhan wiped the tears from her cheeks with her palms and pressed her lips together. For all her misery, she didn't have the courage to take her own life. She was too afraid of botching the job, and the prospect of an eternity of suffering for her sins on the other side terrified her. Staring into the hearth, she wondered what Justin would do if she tried to re-establish contact. He'd be polite, most likely. She'd raised him to be that way. Would he even want to re-establish their relationship after they way she'd treated him?

Cowardice had caused all this damage in the first place. She wouldn't allow it to control her life any longer. She rose to gather her writing desk from the shelf.

For a long time now she'd known she had no one to blame but herself for the rift between them. He'd been devastated about his brother. On some level, she'd known it, and yet still wanted to hurt him for letting Mitchell die.

As if he could have stopped it. You don't think he would have done anything to prevent it if he could have?

Yes. Of course he would have. The guilt rose up to press against her aching lungs, making it hard to breathe.

Oh, how she wished she could take back what she'd done. She prayed every day for forgiveness. And now that she'd seen the error of her ways, it was too late to make amends with the only family she had left.

The shuffling of Aggie's slippered feet came from the hallway, and Siobhan glanced over at the doorway as the housekeeper appeared. "Someone's come ta see ye, mum."

A visitor? She hadn't heard anyone at the door, too engrossed in her dark thoughts. She sighed tiredly, a headache throbbing behind her eyes. "Who is it, Aggie?"

"Miss Brianna, mum."

Her heart leaped in her chest, knocking a painful tattoo against her ribs. Why was she here? Had Justin been killed? *Please no, please no...* Weaving like a drunk, she steadied herself against her husband's chair and rushed out into the hall.

As she emerged from the study, Brianna turned,

362

beautiful and radiant in a gown of soft green. A cool, polite smile curved her lips. It was more than Siobhan deserved from her.

She stopped, hand over her chest in relief. That smile meant her son had to be alive. Still, her knees shook. "Justin," she croaked. "Is he all right?"

Surprise showed in those wide gray eyes. "You heard?"

"Heard what?"

"That he'd been wounded."

Siobhan sagged, had to reach out a hand to steady herself against the wall.

"No, he's all right." Brianna stepped forward as though to catch her, but Siobhan shrank back.

The words slowly penetrated the fog of terror in her brain. "He's...all right?"

"I wasn't sure at first either, but when I started demanding answers they assured me it wasn't serious."

"Praise God, I thought—" She shook her head to clear it. Why was Brianna here, then? They hadn't parted on good terms, and Lord knew she'd been awful to the girl.

"I didn't mean to make you worry. I only thought it would be best if I came in person, rather than send a telegram. I asked Aggie not to tell you of my plans, in case you would have been upset."

"Then you've...you've come to see *me*?" Even to her own ears she sounded bewildered.

"That's right." Brianna's smile was kind, and Siobhan suddenly understood why her son had fallen so deeply in love with this girl. "I have." Instead of explaining her presence, her daughter-in-law closed the gap between them until the hems of their skirts touched and took Siobhan's cold hands in her warm ones.

Surprised and humbled by the affectionate gesture, she blinked up at Brianna and an odd sort of calm overtook her. "I'm glad you came," she whispered, overwhelmed by her thoughtfulness. Perhaps it wasn't too late for them. Perhaps she could make it right between her and Justin and his wife.

Brianna's smile widened, revealing pretty white teeth. "I'm very happy you feel that way. I lost my family a long time ago. I would love to be part of one again." With that she leaned down and enveloped her in a hug.

Siobhan went stiff, her throat tightening at the embrace. Slowly, she slid her own arms around Brianna's back. Before, she'd been too caught up in her own pain to notice anyone else's. Now she recognized the pain her daughter-in-law felt. Loss. Siobhan understood it better than most.

Tears burned behind her closed lids. A new beginning, she thought in reverence. Another chance.

Praise God.

Brianna stepped back, eyes dancing. "As for Justin, he's coming home."

Her breath snagged. "When?"

"Any day now. They've sent the entire regiment home to be mustered out on the first of July."

Siobhan cried out in joyous disbelief, brought her hands to her mouth. "So it's over? He's done with the cavalry?"

"All done. He'll never have to fight again."

"Oh, praise God!" Without thinking, she grabbed Brianna about the waist and squeezed.

Aggie came over, crowing in her Scots brogue, and engulfed them both in her stranglehold. They all laughed together, their eyes wet with relief and elation.

Once Aggie released them, Siobhan patted Brianna's smooth cheek. "Go get settled upstairs in your room, my dear. Then we'll celebrate."

"A fine feast this calls for," Aggie cried, taking Brianna's arm to lead her upstairs.

Alone in the foyer, Siobhan's heart overflowed with gratitude. Justin was coming back to her. Even after all she'd put him through, he was coming back.

Overcome with excitement, she returned to the study and dropped onto her knees in front of her husband's portrait, her hand automatically finding the gold crucifix hanging around her neck. Though she smiled, her lips trembled as she looked up into Brandon's eyes, captured forever on the canvas. "Our son is coming home," she told him, hoping he already knew somehow. "He's coming *home*."

****

June 1865

The last few miles to Detroit seemed the longest Justin had ever traveled. All around him the men of the Fifth Michigan crowded against the train's windows, hoping to catch a glimpse of their loved ones as they approached the station.

Brianna would be out there somewhere, waiting for him. He knew without a doubt she'd traveled here to be standing on the platform when he disembarked. The thought of walking into her arms made his heart hammer. They'd been through so much, both together and apart. Sacrificed so much. And a week after his happiness had been dealt the mortal blow of being sent to the frontier, a miracle had made someone in Washington see the light and send them all home. He was almost there.

"Think your lovely wife is out there, sir?"

He glanced over at Williams with a smile. "She's there."

"Try and take care not to trample the men getting to her, sir. Would be a shame to come all this way and lose some of the boys the day before we muster out."

He laughed. Brianna had better prepare herself. She'd be lucky if he let her out of their bed at all for the next week. His blood pounded in his veins at the thought of having her naked body beneath him. Above him. In front of him. Any way he could get her.

The train slowed. Its wheels hissed and the car ceased the swaying motion he'd grown so used to. He couldn't help but smile at the men's cheers as the assembled crowd came into view. A brass band blared away at the end of the platform, banners and flags flying high to greet the regiment. His heart swelled and he immediately scanned the crowd for Brianna's mahogany hair.

But a sudden pain spiked his chest because Mitch wasn't beside him, and because his mother wouldn't be here to greet him. He'd already made arrangements to stay in a hotel rather than go home, since it seemed wiser to stop in for a visit rather than put himself and Brianna in the miserable position of having to endure his mother's bitter disdain again.

"There's my Charlotte!" Williams cried, pressing his hand to the window.

Justin searched the sea of faces but couldn't find Brianna. She would be here, wouldn't she? For the first time he began to doubt she'd made the long trip from

Lexington.

Someone threw the door open, and the men poured out amidst cheers and applause. He glimpsed the back of Williams's head through the crowd as his wife descended upon his tall frame with a tiny newborn infant cradled in her arms. Smiling, Justin looked past him for Brianna, his reconnaissance made easier thanks to his height. Keeping out of the way as best he could, he glanced right and left but still didn't see her. The smile faded away. His heart sank. Maybe she hadn't come. Maybe she was waiting for him in Lexington instead.

The crowd started to thin. Then from the corner of his eye, he caught sight of someone waving frantically. He followed the arm in its pale green sleeve and caught a glimpse of mahogany hair.

Brianna. His feet started moving without him being conscious of it.

"Justin!"

Finally he saw her ecstatic face as she pushed her way toward him through the crowd. Dressed in an apple green gown, she looked as fresh and lovely as a summer morning. The sunlight made her hair gleam with red highlights, and her gray eyes sparkled with joy. She was the most beautiful thing he'd ever seen. His eyes filled up, pressure building in his chest until his heart knocked against his ribs.

Two steps from him, she launched herself into his waiting arms and wound hers around him, hugging him so hard he grunted and had to laugh. She laughed too, lifting her hands to his cheeks and gazing into his eyes before covering his face with ecstatic kisses. He caught the back of her head in one hand to kiss her as hard and as deep as he could. In return, she gave as good as she got until he had to set her away just to breathe.

"Hi again, angel."

She ran her gaze over him, her eyes shadowed with concern. "You're really all right?"

He frowned. "Of course, why wouldn't I be?"

Her eyes kept darting over him. "I got a telegram saying you'd been wounded."

Oh, hell... He pulled his collar aside to show her the short row of stitches on the top of his shoulder. "It was nothing, just a graze from a stupid accident. Damned horse knocked me into a bullet." He laughed at the relief on her face. "I'm sorry you were worried."

Her smile was so brilliant it almost hurt his eyes. "Welcome home, sweetheart."

Justin would never leave her again. "Thank you. I'm happier to be here than you'll ever know." He buried his face in her hair and breathed her in, cinnamon, cloves and sunshine.

All too soon she pulled away and took his hand. "Come on." She looked determined.

He laughed. "Are you dragging me off somewhere private to have your way with me for the rest of the night?"

Her eyes gleamed up at him. "Sorry. You're going to have to wait a little while longer for that."

Couldn't be soon enough for him, but he followed her, humbled by the love shining in her eyes. How had he been so lucky to find her?

When she towed him around the corner into the comparatively dim interior of the station and stopped, he glanced at her questioningly. "What?"

She nodded over her shoulder. "Someone else came to welcome you home."

Aggie, he thought. *Has to be Aggie.* But when he

turned his head, he came to a stop so sudden that he jerked in his boots.

It couldn't be. Just couldn't be.

He gaped for a moment while his heart thudded in his ears.

His mother was there, rushing toward him with a wide smile and eyes that glimmered with tears. He wasn't imagining this. The pressure in his chest was too real to be a dream. She rushed right up and clasped him in a hard embrace, and he almost went to his knees.

"My son," she whispered against his cheek when he bent to return the hug. "My beautiful, splendid son, I'm so proud of you. Welcome home."

Her words tore a choked gasp out of him and he pulled her closer, the remaining shred of the boy in him painfully grateful for her love and acceptance. For just a moment he allowed himself to close his eyes and hold on, shocked at how healed he felt because of her thin arms around him. As he straightened, hiding his wet eyes, he was completely undone by the two women beaming up at him.

Brianna had done this. She had somehow done the impossible and mended the rift before he'd arrived. He hadn't realized it fully at the time, but Brianna had pulled his mother out of the depths of her grief and brought her amongst the living the day she'd intervened and taken the laudanum away. And in the process, made it possible for them to be a family again.

First she'd saved his life, and now she'd saved his soul as well.

He owed her everything for that.

Unable to think of a single thing to say to her, all he could manage was a hoarse, "Thank you."

Brianna's smile was soft with love and

understanding. "You're welcome." She curled an arm around his waist, while his mother tugged on his hand. "Aggie's cooked enough food to feed an entire company. Let's go home."

Home. Until a few minutes ago he'd thought he could never go back, and now Brianna had changed everything. She'd healed them all.

Whether they spent their lives in Detroit, Lexington or anywhere else, home was wherever she was. Heart full to bursting, Justin bent to whisper against his wife's ear. "I'm going to spend the rest of my life showing you how much I love you."

Her answering smile lit him up inside. "I look forward to that."

So did he.

Flanked by the two people he loved most in the world, he stepped out of the station's shadows and into the summer sunshine a free man.

-End-

Complete Booklist

Suspense Series (romantic suspense)
Out of Her League
Cover of Darkness
No Turning Back
Relentless
Absolution

Bagram Special Ops Series (military romantic suspense)
Deadly Descent
Tactical Strike
Lethal Pursuit

Empowered Series (paranormal romance)
Darkest Caress

Historical Romance
The Vacant Chair

ABOUT THE AUTHOR

Kaylea Cross writes edge-of-your-seat military romantic suspense. Her work has won many awards and has been nominated for both the Daphne du Maurier and the National Readers' Choice Awards. A Registered Massage Therapist by trade, Kaylea is also an avid gardener, artist, Civil War buff, Special Ops aficionado, belly dance enthusiast and former nationally-carded softball pitcher. She and lives in Vancouver, BC with her husband and sons. You can visit Kaylea at www.kayleacross.com